D0110861

BY MONICA MURPHY

Stealing Rose

Stealing Rose

A Novel

Monica Murphy

BANTAM BOOKS

NEW YORK

Stealing Rose is a work of fiction. Names, characters, places, and incidents either are the products of the author's imagination or are used fictitiously. Any resemblance to actual persons, living or dead, events, or locales is entirely coincidental.

A Bantam Books Trade Paperback Original

Copyright © 2015 by Monica Murphy
Excerpt from *Taming Lily* by Monica Murphy copyright © 2015 by Monica Murphy

All rights reserved.

Published in the United States by Bantam Books, an imprint of Random House, a division of Random House LLC, a Penguin Random House Company, New York.

BANTAM BOOKS and the HOUSE colophon are registered trademarks of Random House LLC.

This book contains an excerpt from the forthcoming book *Taming Lily* by Monica Murphy. This excerpt has been set for this edition only and may not reflect the final content of the forthcoming edition.

Library of Congress Cataloging-in-Publication Data
Murphy, Monica.
Stealing rose : a novel / Monica Murphy.
pages cm. — (The Fowler sisters ; 2)
ISBN 978-0-553-39328-6 (softcover)—
ISBN 978-0-553-39329-3 (eBook)
1. Upper class—Fiction. 2. Jewel thieves—Fiction. 3. Man-woman relationships—Fiction. I. Title.
PS3613.U7525S74 2015
813'.6—dc23   2014038447

Printed in the United States of America on acid-free paper

www.bantamdell.com

987654321

Book design by Karin Batten

Stolen kisses are always the sweetest.

—LEIGH HUNT

Stealing
Rose

Chapter One

Rose

WHAT DO YOU DO WHEN YOU DISCOVER SOMETHING ABOUT your family that you never wanted to know?

You pretend it doesn't exist. That your perfect little family is precisely that—untouched. Pristine. No amount of tragedy has ever put its fingers upon us. At least, that's what we want you to believe. There are books out there, unauthorized biographies about my grandmother and her legacy, Fleur Cosmetics. About how my father and my sisters and I have continued on with that legacy as best we can, referencing us as if we're somehow insufficient. Daddy is the one who made the company flourish, though he gives all credit to Grandma and she takes it, the greedy old lady that she is.

I love that greedy old lady to bits. I really do.

My oldest sister, Lily, has done a piss-poor job of carrying on the legacy, and she'd be the first to admit it. Her brutal honesty is one of the things I love best about her, though most of the time I resent her actions and the attention they receive. She is all about the spotlight and when it doesn't shine on her, she will do whatever it takes to snatch back that light so she can revel in it.

Then there's Violet, the middle sister. The quiet one. The secretly strong one. Oh my God, is she strong. She's been through so much. Tragedy has placed its hands all over her, yet somehow she's always risen above it. Now she's so happy with her man, Ryder, and I can't begrudge her that. He's so intense sometimes it's almost scary, but then he sees Violet and his eyes get this dreamy sort of haze to them . . . he's a total goner for her.

It's sweet. *Too* sweet. My jealous side can hardly take it.

Me? I'm the Fowler sister everyone believes is normal, with a bit of a fighter streak in me. Grandma says I'm closest to her personality-wise and I want to believe her, but I don't know. Do I really want to be like her? Like any of them? My disillusion with the Fowler image is firmly secure on the worst night possible.

I don't know what to believe anymore, after what I just found out about our mother. The tragedy that no one ever, ever talks about—even those unauthorized, horribly scandalous family biographies gloss over the death of Victoria Fowler. I don't remember much about her, and what I do recall is fuzzy at best. Those memories are fueled by my sisters, though, since they actually do remember Mom, especially Lily. The loss was especially hard on her. Hence Lily's outrageous behavior from the age of about fourteen until now.

At least, that's what we all blame it on, including Lily. I'd like for once to see her take full responsibility for her actions, but I doubt that will ever happen.

There is more to our mother's death than I ever knew. I wonder if Lily or Violet knows. It's such a touchy subject, one I don't broach with them . . . ever. As for Daddy, I never talk about Mom with him. He swept our mother's death under the rug, something he's so good at doing. Threw himself into his work instead of focusing on his daughters, though he wasn't a bad father per se. A tad neglectful sometimes?

Yes. Most definitely.

We strive for perfection, yet every last one of us is far from perfect. When I was little, I was protected in this silvery, pillow-soft cocoon where nothing ever touched me, or the people I loved. Not even my mother's tragic death brought by her own doing could bother me. How could it, when no one ever talked about it?

But I want to talk about her now, after reading her last diary. The one I discovered when I was given a box of her old things by Daddy. He finally cleaned out our mother's rooms and closet. He'd kept them preserved for so long, but now that his new . . . girlfriend is in the picture, he's banished all reminders of our mother from his home.

Forever.

I couldn't even look at the contents of that box without nerves eating me up and feeling nauseated. I kept what was in there a secret from myself for months. Until a few nights ago, when I finally opened the box and found her diary filled with passages she wrote up until she took her own life.

Fascinating reading. And sad.

So incredibly sad.

What's happening tonight . . . things could be revealed. Moments from our family history are going on blatant display. All of it controlled by my grandmother, which means . . .

It will all be glossed over—become glossy perfection. Isn't that the term Violet used for her collection when they discussed packaging? That could be the Fowler family theme.

I watch as Grandma approaches me, a fond smile on her face, her eyes misty with memories.

"I want you to wear this tonight." Grandma Dahlia presents the large, square box to me, her frail hands shaking the slightest bit, causing light to glint off the diamond rings on her fingers. "It hasn't been worn by anyone in ages."

We're in my hotel room, my grandmother having knocked on the door only minutes before as I was getting ready. We were all supposed to meet later but here she is, resplendent in her gorgeous black lace dress, a sweet smile on her face as she studies me.

I have no idea why she's doing this and I don't like the uneasiness that settles over me as I take the box from her, my fingers smoothing over the black velvet. It's old, the color slightly faded, and it's heavy. Slowly I open the box, anticipation and fear curling through me, and I gasp at what I see lying inside.

A necklace. But not just any necklace—the stones alternate between a brilliant white and a soft, blush pink, and each one is perfectly cut, perfectly matched. "It's beautiful," I murmur, surprised at the size of the stones. I've never seen this necklace before in my life, and I thought my sisters and I had all played with or worn every piece of fine jewelry there is in the family. "What are the pink stones?" I ask as I drift my fingers across the necklace almost reverently.

"Why, they're diamonds of course, some of the rarest in existence. Your grandfather gave this necklace to me long, long ago." Grandma sounds at once both proud and sad. "A present for when your aunt Poppy was born." A wistful sigh escapes her and she looks away, her mouth turned down, her eyes shining with unshed tears. "You remind me of her. So much."

"I do?" I purposely keep my voice soft, not wanting to upset her. I didn't know my aunt Poppy, though I wish I had. She died in a horrible car accident before I was born. I've seen photos and yes, there's a resemblance, but I never thought I looked much like her.

More tragedy. More death. Another family member we lost that we rarely mention. It's frustrating, how easily we forget what happened to those who are gone. If I disappeared, would everyone eventually forget me, too?

I don't want to forget anyone. Not my mother. Not my aunt Poppy. I want to know more. But tonight is supposed to be special, so I should let it go. This night is for my grandma, for the family, for Fleur.

I will myself to let it all go.

"Oh, yes." Grandma turns to face me once more, the tears gone, the familiar determined look back in place. She rarely shows any signs of weakness and I love that about her. She's such a strong influence on all of us, and right now I'm in need of some of that strength. "There's some similarity in your looks, but really it's your attitude. The way you speak, the way you behave, how you think. It's just like my Poppy. She was so vibrant, so full of life, and she was never afraid to back down from something she believed in. Just like you." She reaches out and clasps my face in her wrinkled hands, her fingers cold against my skin. I smile at her but it feels fake, and I let it fade. The velvet box is clutched in my hands, my fingers digging into the stones. "Wear this tonight and think of Poppy. Think of Fleur."

"But Grandma, tonight is all about *you*." We're in Cannes for the movie festival, here to watch the premiere of a documentary about Grandmother and how she started Fleur. She monitored every step of this documentary and claims it is a collaboration of love between her and the director and producers of the piece.

More like my grandmother dictated to them exactly what she wanted mentioned. Again, no one crosses Dahlia Fowler. To do so would be taking an extreme risk. The woman has no problem making claims of ruining people.

She *has* ruined people. Time and again.

"*You* should wear this necklace. Not me," I say when she still hasn't said anything. She's staring at me as if she can look right through me and I blink, hard. Blocking my thoughts, my anger, my frustration. But she can probably see it.

Grandma just chooses not to talk about it.

"No." She shakes her head and drops her hands from my face. "You should wear it. It's yours for tonight. Violet has her young man and Lily has . . . whatever it is she thinks she wants. Such a disappointment that she's not here." Her mouth screws up into this bitter line and I want to smack my sister for yet again letting everyone down. "You . . . you deserve this. Wear it proudly. It's your legacy, too, my love. Never forget it."

My legacy. Most of the time, I don't feel like it's mine. It's Daddy's and Violet's. It's slowly becoming Ryder's. Lily's? Not so much. She loves to wear Fleur cosmetics and spend the Fleur money, but that's about it. She has no desire to be a part of the family business. She's allergic to work.

Lucky bitch gets away with it, too.

I work like crazy and no one notices. I'm tired of putting the time in. I'm tired of dealing with Daddy and his horrific relationship with that slut Pilar Vasquez. The woman is scheming to become a permanent part of Fleur Cosmetics—by nabbing the last name Fowler—pure and simple. Does she really care for him? Doubtful. But my father is so blinded by lust he can't see beyond her big tits and her supposed great ideas.

"My legacy," I murmur as I withdraw the necklace from the velvet casing and hold it up to the light. It sparkles, the blush-colored stones even more dazzling when they shine. I vaguely remember hearing of the Poppy Necklace and I'm pretty sure I'm holding it in my hands at this very moment.

The necklace will look amazing with the white dress I'm wearing tonight. White may signify virginity and purity and all that other nonsense, but wait until everyone sees *this* dress. It'll blow their minds.

And I'm in the mood to shock this evening. This is my last hurrah before I give notice to my father next week. Yes, I'm quitting Fleur. I can't imagine staying there now. I made my escape for a short period of time after it came out that Daddy was dating one of the most conniving employees Fleur Cosmetics has ever had under its roof. Pilar rubs it in our faces as much as possible that she has our father wrapped around her little finger.

I hate her. I refuse to work with her, especially now that I've heard rumors that Daddy is promoting her. Not that he'd ever come to me and tell me about it. No one tells me anything. I'm ignored at Fleur. So much so that I don't think it's even worth continuing to work there . . .

Considering this evening will most likely be the last I'm representing the Fowler family for a long time—I know Daddy is going to be furious over my giving notice—I'm going all out. Besides, I've never been to the Festival de Cannes before. The necklace will only add to the effect.

Our family has been on public display our entire lives, and most of the time I don't mind, though I prefer to be in the background, much like Violet. Leave it to Lily to be our public representative. Not that Lily makes Daddy happy with her antics. Or Grandma, considering how scandalous my oldest sister is. She's tamed down somewhat, but she still has a flair for the outrageous.

I'm stealing that flair for the outrageous from her tonight, though. Since arriving in France, the energy surrounding the festivities has renewed me. Inspired me to take a chance and do something daring. Wild.

Like wearing a dress that might cause a scandal. Like mentally preparing the speech I'm going to give my father when I turn in my two weeks' notice once we're back home.

"Yes," Grandma says firmly. "Your legacy. And Violet's. Even Lily's. I'm proud of what I've accomplished, but I'm even more excited to see what you and Violet do with Fleur. Perhaps even Lily, if she ever gets her head out of her ass."

"Grandma!" I shouldn't be shocked at what she says, but every once in a while she does surprise me.

"What? It's true." Grandma shrugs. "Besides, someday I'll be gone, you know."

"But . . ." I start to protest and she shushes me in an instant.

"Hush, you know it's true. I'm eighty-three years old. I can't live forever, as much as I'd like to." She waves a hand at the necklace I'm still clutching in one hand, the velvet box in the other. "Turn around, my child, and let me put that on you. Why are you still in your robe? Shouldn't you be dressed already? The premiere is going to start soon."

"I'm almost done." Nerves suddenly eat at my stomach and I turn around at Grandma's direction, setting the box on the dresser beside me and handing the necklace to her so she can help put it around my neck. I'm taller than her, so I bend at the knees, making it easier for her to slip the necklace on. "Hair and makeup is finished. I just need to put on my dress and shoes."

"You'd best hurry, then." She slips the necklace around my neck and hooks the clasp before stepping away from me. "There. Let's see how it looks."

I turn to face her once more, my chin lifted, the weight of the diamonds heavy against my chest. I can't believe she's letting me wear it. From the few stories I've heard about it, the necklace rarely if ever makes public appearances. "What do you think?" I ask.

She contemplates me, her expression serious, eyes narrowed. "It's beautiful. Originally I thought I wanted Lily to wear it since she's the oldest, but she's not here. And the more I thought about it, the more I realized you're a better fit since you're so much like Poppy."

Guilt assaults me and I fight it down. I refuse to feel bad for what I'm about to do. I can't help it if Daddy chooses his conniving girlfriend over me. And I won't let him run right over me without a care. I need to stand up for what I believe in.

And what I believe in means never letting Pilar Vasquez have any sort of authority over me. That bitch can die before I ever let her tell me what to do.

"You didn't want Violet to wear it, hmm?" I touch the necklace, turning toward the mirror to my right. The necklace is stunning, even against the white silk robe I have on, and I stare at my reflection, overwhelmed at what the necklace represents.

Grandma's right. Fleur is my legacy, too. I need to remember that. Not get caught up in the mess that's been created by Violet and Ryder against Daddy and . . . Pilar.

Ew. Just thinking about that bitch makes me want to puke.

But I can't stand by and let everything happen *to* me. I need to make a stand. I need to let Father know that I don't approve of his tactics. Something needs to be done. Someone needs to say something.

If that has to be me, then so be it.

"Please. Violet has that lovely diamond on her finger. She doesn't need any other piece of jewelry right now." Grandma waves a dismissive hand at my suggestion. She's right. Ryder asked Violet to marry him only a few days ago and my sister is positively giddy over it.

For so long I'd been afraid she'd saddle herself to that idiot Zachary Lawrence, but thankfully she saw the light and found a man who cherishes her. Understands her. Respects her. That he's gorgeous and sexy as hell doesn't hurt matters.

I'm a little envious of my sister's happiness, but I can't begrudge her finally finding joy. She's had so many challenges and she's fought every single one of them. I'm proud of her. Happy for her.

Truly.

"Enjoy that necklace. There's a segment in the documentary about it." Grandma winks and starts toward the door. "We'll meet in your father's suite in twenty minutes. Don't be late, you hear me?"

"I hear you," I call to her, shaking my head as she exits my room with a loud slam of the door.

I turn to face the mirror once again, my hands going to the belt of my robe and untying it, letting the white silk part before I shrug it from my shoulders. The fabric falls to the floor in a crumpled heap around my feet and I kick it away, then stand tall.

The necklace looks good against my skin and I take a deep

breath, watching my naked breasts rise and fall. I might need to have a drink or two before I don the dress. I'll need the liquid courage to face my family later.

Daddy will probably hate the dress. Violet will be scandalized. Grandma will laugh and silently cheer me on. And Pilar? She's accompanying us tonight, which I hate. I don't give two shits what she thinks about the dress. Or me. Or any of us.

Sighing, I go to the closet and pull the dress out, smoothing my hands over the layers of white, frothy chiffon that make up the skirt. Considering it's strapless, the necklace will be showcased perfectly. I wonder what sort of story surrounds the piece of jewelry?

I'll find out soon enough.

"NICE DRESS."

A shiver moves down my spine at the sound of the warm, inviting tone. I glance over my shoulder to find a very handsome man standing there, an arrogant smirk on his face as he blatantly scans me from head to toe.

My smile falls and I straighten my spine. I was tricked by his voice. He sounded flirty and fun, but really he's just a creeper. Not bothering to say anything, I turn my back to him but he halts my progress, his hand going around the crook of my elbow.

I glance down at his offending hand on my arm before I lift my head and send him a withering stare. He doesn't even flinch. He doesn't let me go, either. "Aren't you Rose Fowler?"

He has an accent, but I can't tell from where. The room is filled with a variety of accents and languages; people from all over the world are at this party tonight. "I am," I say, trying to discreetly pull out of his hold. But his fingers tighten not so discreetly on my flesh and I feel like I'm trapped.

"I thought so." He flashes me a smile, but it doesn't quite meet his dark eyes. Everything about him is dark. His hair, his swarthy complexion, the way he's looking at me. A ripple of unease washes over me and I glance around, looking for my father, my sister, or preferably Ryder, who'd tell this asshole where to go if I asked him to. "Interesting documentary on your family."

"Thank you." I'm trying to be polite but he's making it so hard. He pulls me a little closer to him and I'm assaulted by the scent of his strong cologne, put off by the way his fingers smooth over my skin in a seeming caress. "If you could let me go, please. I have someone waiting for me."

"Who?" He smiles, his teeth overly white, especially against his dark skin.

He's making me angry. "Um, that's none of your business."

"You're here alone tonight, aren't you? I saw you on the red carpet." He tugs so hard on my arm my footsteps falter and I nearly fall into him. "Let's go have a drink."

Politeness flies out the window as I rest my hand against his chest and give him a push. But he doesn't budge. His fingers are so tight they're pinching my flesh, and he'll probably leave a mark. "Let. Me. Go," I say through clenched teeth, fighting the panic flaring deep within me.

"You heard the lady," another man practically growls from behind me, his deep, very pissed-off voice setting every hair on my body on end. "Get your fucking hands off her. Now."

The man's fingers spring away from my arm like someone turned a key and unlocked his hold on me. Backing away with his hands in front of him as if he's pleading for mercy, he laughs nervously. "Didn't know she was with you," he says shakily just before he turns and practically sprints away from us.

Rubbing my arm, I turn to thank my savior, but the words die on my lips. Dark brown eyes watch me, the man's demeanor still and silent, his full mouth pulled into a straight line. He's wearing a black suit, not a tuxedo, and it appears a little frayed around the edges. As if he's had it for a while and it's been to the dry cleaner one too many times. Despite the aged suit, he has an elegant yet rough air about him. As if he doesn't quite belong among this glittering, powerful, and extremely rich crowd.

"Thank you," I croak, clearing my throat and feeling like an idiot.

"Are you all right?" He steps closer, but his presence doesn't feel threatening. More like protective, what with the look of concern marring his handsome features. His brows are drawn downward and a lock of golden-brown hair hangs over his forehead.

That I have the sudden urge to push the hair away from his face and test its softness is . . . crazy.

"I'm fine." I offer him a shaky smile, which only makes him frown deeper. "Did you know him?"

"Never seen him before in my life. But a lot of assholes come to these parties. Cannes is full of them," he says, sounding disgusted.

I want to laugh. My savior has no problem being crude and I can appreciate it. At least what he says is real. Most of the people I encounter speak carefully, as if they're afraid they'll somehow offend me.

"Thank you for scaring him away." I absently rub at my arm, glancing down to see the imprint of the man's fingers glaring red on my skin.

"He marked you." He grabs hold of me, his large hand engulfing mine as he holds my arm out to inspect it. His jaw goes tight and he lifts his head, scanning the room with ruthless efficiency. "I should kick the shit out of him."

"It's no big deal." My heart is all fluttery at the protective streak this man is displaying and I tell myself to get over it. "It's already starting to fade. See?"

Slowly he tilts his head down, his lips parting as he examines my arm. He releases my hand, his thumb smoothing lightly over the imprints, causing gooseflesh to follow in the wake of his touch. "Does it hurt?"

"No." I shake my head, watching in fascination as he continues to touch me. His hand is so large, his skin tanned and the pad of his thumb rough. I can't help but wonder at the difference between the two men. Both of them strangers, yet my reaction to each is so completely different.

"Good," he says gruffly, though I can tell he's not satisfied with my answer. His hand drops away from my arm and I wonder for a moment if he's going to take off after my so-called assailant, but he remains rooted in place, standing next to me as if he were put on this earth to be my protector for the evening. "Want a drink?"

"Oh, please." Before I can tell him what I want, he walks away without another word, his broad-shouldered body cutting a swath through the crowd, and they all part for him obediently. He's a head taller than the majority of the people in the room, so it's not difficult to keep tabs on him as he strides toward the bar across the way.

He doesn't smile at a soul, doesn't stop to make pleasant conversation with anyone, either.

I'm completely fascinated.

"Who's the guy?" Violet magically appears at my side, her gaze dropping to my dress, pointedly taking in the slits in my skirt, my thighs playing peek-a-boo whenever I move. "Did you draw him in with the dress or what?"

"Not everyone is as scandalized with the dress as you are," I mutter, irritated that she's ruining my mood. Violet and I are usually on the same side about everything, but the moment I made my appearance at Daddy's suite before we all went to the premiere together, I knew she wasn't happy with my choice of attire.

And that hurt, despite my brave face and carefree attitude. I blame it on the fact that she's always had a motherly, almost protective attitude toward me. Daddy didn't like the dress, either, but that's no surprise. Ryder gave me a high-five with a wicked grin on his face before we left the suite, and I appreciated that. Clung to his approval like some sort of anchor that was saving me from drowning. I needed any show of support to get through tonight.

You did this to yourself. The only one you have to blame is . . . you.

That naggy little voice inside my head needs to shut up.

"Can I be honest with you?" Violet turns to face me, her expression somber, warning me I'm not going to want to hear what she has to say.

I barely withhold the sigh that wants to escape when I answer, "Go for it."

"You're reminding me of Lily." She wrinkles her nose, looking both cute and disgusted. That's the ultimate low blow, saying I remind her of *Lily*. I feel like she stabbed me right in the heart. "The flashy outfit, the necklace. Did you know Grandma was going to let you wear it tonight?"

Ah, is that what this is about? That Grandma let me wear the necklace and not her? Maybe it was stupid, wearing such a dress. The press had shouted at me continuously as we posed on the red carpet. Asking me who designed it, where was Lily, since when did I get so bold. Hardly any of them asked about the necklace.

I wonder if that made Grandma mad.

"No, I didn't," I answer. "She brought it to me about a half hour before we all met. I had no idea she had it with her."

"She mentioned to me she was going to bring it to Cannes a while ago. But I figured she would want Lily to wear it. Since she's not here . . ." Violet's voice trails off.

"You're right, she did want Lily to wear it. She also said I reminded her most of Poppy." I absently drift my fingers across the stones, my thumb smoothing over the largest one set in the center. "So she let me wear it tonight. Said you didn't need to because you already have your big diamond on your finger."

Violet immediately holds her hand out, the diamond catching the light just right and making it sparkle. A little smile curls her lips as she stares at it. "She's probably right."

"I know," I say dryly, my gaze snagging on my savior, who's still waiting in line at the bar. His shoulders are terribly broad and he's so tall. His hair is longish in the back, in dire need of a trim, and he reaches back at the exact moment the thought passes through my mind, scratching at his nape absently before he turns, his gaze meeting mine all the way across the room.

The look in his eyes renders me completely still. Even my breath stalls in my lungs. I part my lips, the low roar in my ears growing louder, drowning out what Violet's saying to me, blocking out every little sound until all I can focus on is him.

He doesn't look away. Doesn't smile or lift a brow or wave a hand, no acknowledgment that we're watching each other. Slowly, the movement so subtle I almost don't notice it, he works his square jaw, his lips pressing together, his chest rising with his deep inhale. Squinting his eyes, one side of his mouth goes up slightly, the lopsided ghost of a smile appearing before it's gone.

In a snap.

The man turns, his back facing me once more, and I wonder if I imagined it all. Blinking, I tear my gaze from him and turn to my sister, who hasn't stopped talking. I have no idea what she just said. None.

All I can think about is the man who saved me.

And I don't even know his name.

Chapter Two

Caden

THE MOMENT I SEE THE NECKLACE AROUND THE WRONG SISTER'S neck, I'm infuriated.

Pissed.

Mad as hell.

Yeah. All that.

I had a plan and I hate deviating from the plan. I thought Lily Fowler was coming to this premiere. This is one of the biggest moments for the Fowler family and their business. And their oldest daughter isn't even here with them at the freaking Cannes Film Festival, so what the fuck?

Not that I thought Lily would be wearing the necklace. I figured it would be Violet. The quiet sister who's the true force to reckon with at Fleur, the driven one who's taking the cosmetics company and pushing it forward. I hadn't considered the new boyfriend, though. That guy never leaves her side and glowers at whoever looks at her with even halfhearted interest.

It's freaking Rose Fowler wearing the damn necklace instead. The baby sister, who's barely old enough to drink legally. The gorgeous-as-hell and completely untouchable sister is wearing a necklace that I heard from inside sources would be featured in the documentary. I have connections. Hell, I have someone who would pay me top dollar if I bring the necklace to him. I'm here in Cannes at his insistence and he sent me here to grab it. We both had a hunch it might be seen tonight, and that's why I'm here.

Considering I'd known Lily Fowler in my previous life, I figured I might have an in. Though saying I "know" Lily is a slight exaggeration. We went to school together but I'm younger than her; I was a sophomore when she was a junior. It was my final year there, before the last of the money ran out and I had to finish high school in the public school system, much to my mother's horror and disgust.

We never talked, but back then I had a small crush on Lily. I wanted to get close to her for more reasons than one and we hooked up at a party. She was drunk and we clicked instantly, but that wasn't hard since I'd been in full hustle mode. We talked, we flirted, and next thing I knew, we were making out in a dark corner at the party.

I would've gotten into her panties, too, if she hadn't passed out in my arms. My crush died a quick death when I realized what a mess she was.

So I plucked the giant diamond earrings from her lobes instead. Earned a fat amount of money for those stones, too.

Not that she ever knew. And if she did, she certainly didn't say anything. There were no news reports, no gossip sites talking about Lily Fowler's missing diamonds, no police report filed that I know of.

It was as if the entire matter . . . never happened. We even spoke a few times after that incident and she acted like she didn't have a clue what really went down. Confirmation I got away with it.

Wild.

That was the first time I'd stolen anything of real value and the high I got from it, how easy it had been, knowing I could give Mom money to help put toward the overdue bills . . .

I was hooked.

And I had an in. I'd grown up with the rich kids. Hell, I used to be one of them. A rich kid, a spoiled-rotten only child who got whatever he wanted from his daddy, with time to kill and money to burn. Until everything was taken away from us, bit by bit, dollar by dollar. Until we were left with nothing.

So I had to go out and fend for us by helping Mom, because fuck all if my father stuck around and took care of the one woman who stood by his side through everything. All the scandal. All the heartbreak. All the devastation. She never walked away from him—and she had good reason to do so. Instead, she told him everything was going to be all right, as long as they had each other. Yet he still left her.

Deserted her.

Abandoned us both.

Not having Lily here tonight might have thrown me a little, but I ran with it. That's what I do. If I let every little hitch hold me back, then I would have stopped long ago. Or I would have ended up in prison.

But nothing keeps me down. I'd come all the way to Cannes to pick up a few items. Came on my friend's private jet, this asshole I've known since we were ten and in private school. I gave him his first joint and that was it. We were bonded for life.

The guy has so much money he probably shits hundred-dollar bills. But I won't take from him. I have standards. I don't steal from my friends.

People I don't know? They're fair fucking game.

Tonight is open game. The security is loose. The jewels are large and everywhere. The owners of said jewels are careless. More intent on showing off than protecting them, which is fine by me. I'm like a kid in a candy store—I don't know which way to turn, what to check out next. I want to sample it all, take it all, too, but I need to be discreet. Particular. I need to make the most of this visit and choose the pieces that'll take us the furthest.

Like the Poppy Necklace curled around Rose Fowler's beautiful neck. I want it. So does my contact, an old client I haven't worked for since forever. I've been warned off this guy, but the payout is too large to resist. My fingers literally itch to snatch the necklace off Rose's neck. But how? It's not a subtle piece and this won't be easy.

But I love a good challenge. I've kept my eye on her from the moment I spotted her at the party. Always staying in the background, calculating every which way I could get the necklace from her.

Then I go and make the biggest mistake of all—becoming heroic and telling that piece of Eurotrash to get his paws off her. I'd been tempted to kick his ass but Rose had stopped me, thank Christ. I don't know what the hell got into me.

Fine. I know. Seeing the marks on her skin from his slimy fingers pissed me off. I don't know her, don't care to know her, but I get all caveman and ready to defend her honor? Makes no sense. She's pretty, yeah. Sexy as hell in that damn dress, her long, hot-as-fuck legs on blatant display and fueling my imagination.

Which I have no business fueling. I'm here for one purpose—and sex isn't it.

So I ignored the look we shared when I caught her staring at me from across the room. I broke eye contact first, turning away from her and stepping up to the bar so I could order us two glasses of Champagne. I then made my way across the room, ignoring everyone, not making eye contact. I don't want a single person to remember me tonight.

Yet here I am approaching Rose once more, drink in hand, extended out toward her so she can take it. Her delicate fingers slide against mine when she accepts the glass and the shock I feel at first contact shoots through me like a bolt of lightning.

White hot and electrifying.

Her eyes widen the slightest bit and her hand trembles as she lifts the glass to her lips, taking a long swallow. "Thank you for the Champagne," she murmurs.

"You're welcome." I tip my head toward her and lift my glass, my gaze scanning the room. I see a woman I recognize as being the young plaything to a wealthy film investor wearing a bracelet lined with some of the biggest diamonds and sapphires I've ever seen—and I've seen some pretty damn big stones in my time. She's waving her arm around, the gems catching the light, mesmerizing me.

That would be a nice catch. I have a solid inside track with my usual guy who can get me decent cash for high-end stolen goods, no questions asked. It's amazing what you can make happen when you go looking for it.

"Do you know her?"

Rose's voice breaks through my thoughts and I flick my gaze to her, schooling my expression. "Who?"

"The woman you're looking at."

Fucking hell. I need to get away from Rose Fowler quick. She's just too perceptive and during a night when I want no one to notice me, I'm with a woman who's seeing every little thing I do. *Stupid.* "No. She just . . ." I'm grasping for an explanation. ". . . She reminds me of someone I used to know." *Lies.* I need to change the subject quick. "Great movie."

"Ah." She nods and smiles, her gaze wistful. "Thank you. I'm so proud of my grandmother tonight. So you enjoyed the documentary?"

And now she's engaging me in conversation. I study her face, the clarity of her light brown eyes as she studies me, her creamy skin, the way her lips move when she talks.

"I did. Your family has accomplished much in a short amount of time." My gaze zeroes in on those pretty lips. They're full, the bottom lip bigger than the top, and the shape reminds me of a sexy pout. Her lips are slicked in this perfect red shade, stark against her otherwise natural appearance.

"My grandma is a very determined woman." She smiles, her teeth white against the deep red of her lips. "No one messes with Dahlia."

I have the distinct feeling no one messes with Rose either, but I keep my mouth shut. Instead, I let my gaze drop to her throat, the necklace that hangs from her neck and rests against her chest. Her skin is impossibly smooth, her bare shoulders, the hint of cleavage the neckline of her dress offers me . . .

Hell. She's unbelievably gorgeous. Prettier than Lily. Prettier than any other woman I've ever seen. She has the face of an angel. Innocent and sweet, yet with a body that makes me think of all the sinful things we can do together . . .

It's a sexy contradiction. One I can't even consider.

I'd like to consider taking the necklace, but how the hell can I get my hands on it without her noticing?

"Does anyone mess with *you*?"

She smiles blithely. "Only sleazy Europeans who don't know how to keep their hands to themselves."

A chuckle escapes me and I shake my head. I shouldn't react to what this woman is saying to me. I need to get away from her.

Tilting her head back, she polishes her Champagne off in a couple of swallows, her eyes sliding closed as she drinks. I watch her, fascinated with the slim column of her neck, the light golden-brown hair pulled into a knot at the back of her head. I wonder what she might look like with her hair down. Wavy and falling about her bare shoulders, a sultry gleam in her eye as she approaches me . . .

"Let's get out of here," she says, her throaty invitation sending a shot of longing coursing through my body.

Say no. "Where would you like to go?"

She inclines her head toward a set of double doors not far from where we're standing. "Outside. I hear there's a pool out there." Without another word she walks away from me, her skirt billowing around her legs, the scandalous dress causing enough of a stir that others watch her. I don't follow her, turning to the side so I face the wall, my back to the curious onlookers, and when I glance in her direction, I find that she's stopped. Waving her hand at me to follow her like an impatient mother dealing with a bratty child.

I hold up my still full Champagne glass, indicating I want to finish it first, and she rolls her eyes, shaking her head as she turns away to push through the doors, the black night sky appearing for a fleeting moment before the doors swing shut, swallowing Rose whole.

She's gone. I should be relieved. I sip my Champagne, the alcohol crisp and cool as it slides down my throat, yet all I can feel is the crashing disappointment that she left me.

Ridiculous.

Downing the rest of my Champagne, I set the glass on a nearby table and descend into the crowd, staying close to the woman with the flashy bracelet. She's oblivious to my presence. She's also the perfect mark.

Absolutely perfect.

My gaze tracks her movements, the careless way she moves her arms about as she talks animatedly to the person standing next to her. She's loud, speaking fast and furious French I can barely understand—and I took three years of French in high school. Of course, all I can remember are the most basic sentences and the occasional curse word.

Lot of good that will do me.

The bracelet loosens around her wrist and she clamps her other hand over it, laughing as she says something about the clasp being old.

My heart rate kicks up. Here's my chance. She fixes the clasp with a quick flick of her fingers and continues talking, her movements more subdued, but I know that's temporary. She'll revert to her old habits quick.

And she doesn't disappoint.

I adjust my position so my back is mostly to her and I engage in conversation with a beautiful woman standing a little off to the side of the circle that has formed around my mark. She's older; there's a wedding ring around her finger and I wonder how long she's been married. Clearly her husband neglects her, because she is fully attuned to my flirtatious attempts at conversation. Her body language screams interest as she turns more fully toward me and I turn just a hair toward my mark.

The woman is gesturing wildly again, speaking of Dahlia Fowler—*interesting*. Her wrists are flying this way and that and I swear I can hear the jangle of the bracelet's clasp the moment it comes undone. She doesn't falter in her conversation, as her complaints against Dahlia are long and numerous and there is much nodding in agreement from her audience.

Even more interesting.

I turn my head as discreetly as possible, catching out of the corner of my eye her wrist and the bracelet I covet. It's so close.

It's so loose.

I plan the moment of attack. On three, it'll happen.

One . . .

I laugh at something the woman I'm flirting with says, throwing back my head and putting every bit of acting skill I have into the movement, as if I'm overcome.

Two . . .

Stepping backward, my entire body grazes my gesturing mark, and I bump into her. She gasps, as does the other woman, and they both lean forward, reaching for me at the exact same time.

Three . . .

I reach for the bracelet and slip it off the woman's wrist.

I slice my other hand into the air, knocking the glass of wine from my companion's hand, creating the distraction I need. The glass falls to the ground with a tinkling crash, the glass scattering everywhere, remnants of alcohol spattering across our feet. I step back, the bracelet going into my coat pocket with a flick of my wrist, and the woman with the now missing bracelet reaches toward the other one as I step back, the both of them gasping over the spilled liquor and their ruined shoes.

"*Chéri,* did you . . ." The film financer's mistress makes a motion across the top of her hand. ". . . cut yourself? *Oui?*" She nods toward my left hand.

I hold my hand out to inspect it. There's a small slice across the tip of my index finger, which probably happened when I made contact with my companion's drink. "I did. I'll go look for a first aid kit."

I duck out and leave them chattering among themselves, my heart racing like a kettledrum inside my chest the entire time. I don't look back, keeping my strides even, my gaze directed straight ahead. I push open the very double doors Rose Fowler just made her escape through, the humid night air clasping me in its sticky embrace, and I make my way across the terrace, then down the stairs, before I head toward the lit rectangular pool. The water glimmers a bright turquoise and the fountain in the center flows with a gentle rhythm, the sound soothing in the otherwise quiet of the night.

In a few minutes, the woman will notice her bracelet is gone, if she hasn't already. Just beyond the pool is the beach, and I'll walk among the shadows close to the line of palm trees before I cut through one of the hotels down the way, where I can make my escape. Hopefully no one will notice me.

But I barely make it past the pool when I hear a familiar voice.

"Well, well, if it isn't my savior."

Slowing my pace, I turn to find Rose sitting on the edge of a lounge chair near the pool, her shoulders hunched and those long, sexy-as-fuck legs spread wide so they're both bare, the long slits in her skirt revealing them. An empty glass dangles from one hand and a bottle of Champagne hangs from the other.

She offers a smirk of a smile, her delicate brows rising in some sort of challenge. Someone already looks a little drunk. We haven't been apart longer than fifteen minutes. Twenty, tops.

Slowly I approach her, telling myself I'm an idiot for even stopping. "Drinking alone?"

The smile grows and it lights up her entire face. "Something I rarely do, but yes. I am. Unless you'd care to join me."

I don't. I do. I'm torn.

"And if you don't, I understand." She waves me away, then brings the bottle to her lips and takes a swig. She sets the bottle on the ground beside her and then reaches forward, slipping her strappy little sandals off one foot, then the other. "They were killing me," she mutters, rubbing the bottom of her foot.

I watch in fascination as she bends over her feet, offering me a spectacular view of her cleavage. Her breasts are full and if the front of her dress slips down any farther, I'll catch a glimpse of nipple. "Maybe you should slow down . . ." I start to say, but she pops up to her feet, throwing her arms above her head as she starts to spin in a circle, her frothy skirt flowing around her.

"I don't want to slow down. I *always* slow down and that's so incredibly boring." She drops her arms and looks up at me, her eyes sparkling, an almost manic expression on her face. "I think I want to swim."

Without another word she walks over to the pool and stares at the water, her bare toes curling around the edge of the pavers that surround the pool. A warm breeze washes over us and she tilts her head back, her eyes sliding closed as she throws her arms out to her sides and holds them palms up.

"Have you ever done something reckless?" she asks, her voice soft.

All the fucking time. "Have you?"

She opens her eyes and looks over at me. "I asked first," she says before she resumes her position.

"Yeah. Haven't we all?"

"No. Not me, not really. I may act all tough, like I take no crap, but that's all it is. An act. I prefer things to be safe. I don't like to take risks. And I am definitely not reckless." She drops her arms to her sides for the briefest moment before she's reaching under her arm and unzipping the dress. The top gaps, revealing nothing but bare skin and that she's not wearing a bra.

Christ.

As the dress falls away from her body and lands in a heap at her feet, I realize she's not wearing any panties, either. She's standing in front of me completely naked—the Poppy Necklace like a glittering, expensive collar around her neck—and my mouth goes dry as I drink her in. My entire body stirs, including my cock, and I lick my lips, fighting the hunger that threatens to take over.

It's been a long time since I've been with a woman. Longer still since I felt so attracted to one. And I am definitely, without a fucking doubt, attracted to Rose Fowler.

A tiny, sly smile curls her lush lips as I stare at her, as if she can read my thoughts and approves of their direction. And then without a word, she dives into the pool, hardly making a splash.

I watch in fascination when moments later she pops her head up, treading water. "You should join me."

The absolute last thing I can do. "I don't think so."

"Aw, why not?" She mock pouts. "Scared of the water?"

"No."

"Scared of me?" She laughs.

"Not at all."

"Then join me." She smiles and swims closer to the edge, standing in the water where it reaches her waist. Her skin is covered with little droplets of water; her pale pink nipples are hard, and my cock is, too.

Rubbing a hand over my face, I grit my teeth together and slip my other hand in the pocket of my suit jacket, fingering the cool stones stashed away inside. "I can't."

Her expression turns solemn and she lifts her arms, smoothing back her hair. The movement lifts her breasts, showing off the dip in her waist, the sleekness of her belly. *Jesus,* her body will be the fucking death of me. "Are you gay or what?"

I laugh and shake my head. "No."

She drops her arms so they splash in the water, frustration written all over her features. "Then why won't you join me?"

A burst of sound comes from the building behind us and I turn to see a group of partygoers spill out onto the terrace, led by the woman whose bracelet is currently resting in my pocket. *Shit.* "Come here," I urge her, reaching out for her hands with both of mine.

Rose frowns. "You can't lift me out of the pool."

"Watch me." I wave my fingers at her, then scan the area, my gaze returning to the terrace. The group of people is still there, milling about, though they haven't come down the stairs yet. But it's only a matter of time before they'll be looking for me, and I swear I can hear the woman commanding everyone about in her very loud, very shrill French. "Come on." I return my attention to Rose, who's still contemplating me as if I've lost my mind, which I probably have. "Hurry."

She takes my hands and I pull her out of the pool since she doesn't weigh a damn thing, setting her on her feet directly in front of me. She's dripping wet and I let my gaze roam all over her perfect body, memorizing her every feature so I can commit her to memory and pull this moment out for later. "What are you doing?"

Before I can overthink it I grab her, my arm clamping tight around her slender waist, my hand sprawled across one perfect ass cheek. Her skin is damp and soft and chilled from the water and I give her plump flesh a firm squeeze, savoring the gasp that escapes her when I touch her like that.

"Kiss me for luck," I whisper as my head descends toward hers. She's frowning, her gaze landing on my lips, watching as I make my descent until her lids flutter closed and I press my mouth to hers in a lingering, chaste kiss.

She steps closer and rests her hands on my chest and I break the kiss first. Opening my eyes to drink in this naked, wet nymph pressed against me, her skin pale and gleaming in the moonlight. I touch the necklace, tracing the stones, wishing like crazy I could snatch it from her neck. The necklace is perfection. It's a rare piece, expensive and exquisitely made, and it's killing me to have it so close and knowing I can't have it.

Yet.

Her chest lifts on a deep inhale, making my gaze drop to her breasts, and my finger falls as if I have no control, circling around her left pink nipple once. Only once. It's the single indulgence I'll allow myself and it's fucking torture, touching her like this, feeling the little nub of flesh tighten, hearing her sharp inhale, scenting her arousal. I'd much rather take it further and draw that perfect little nipple into my mouth and suck. Hard. Run my hands and lips and tongue all over her body until she's begging me to fuck her.

But I don't do any of that. Instead, I tell her solemnly, "Thank you," and I kiss her again, deeper this time, my tongue sliding against hers for the briefest, most mind-numbing moment before I pull away, releasing my hold on her. I start to back away, regret taking hold and making me feel like an asshole.

I *am* an asshole. There's no denying that fact.

"Thank you for what?" she asks when she opens her eyes. She brings her arms up, covering her breasts, looking incredibly vulnerable standing by the edge of the glowing turquoise pool, naked and wet and trembling. The lights from the city are bright as they surround us; I can hear the sounds of the sea, the clank of the boats that are docked nearby.

All the while, the necklace sparkles around her neck like a beacon, mocking me. Driving me to distraction. I stare at it.

Stare at her. That's what I want. Her. And the necklace. But I can't have either.

I can't have both.

"For giving me a night I'll never forget," I tell her before I turn.

And leave her behind. Never once looking back.

No matter how much it kills me.

Chapter Three

Rose

"AND THEN HE JUST . . . LEFT ME." I THROW MY HANDS UP INTO the air, my mind circling back to the craziness of last night yet again. How I got a little drunk and swam in a pool naked before my sexy stranger pulled me out of the water and kissed me. Groped my butt. Touched my nipple. And then sauntered away without a care in the world.

Never to return. Leaving me a shaky, aroused mess.

I threw my dress on over my wet body and made my way back to the hotel, alone. Stupid, but I was in this weird, mind-numbing daze. At one point I even wondered if it had really happened, my encounter with the man by the pool.

Violet squints at me, frowning. "Are you serious?"

I nod and don't say anything else, just letting my story sink in for a while. We're in London; I'm here for the next few days at Fleur's UK headquarters before I head back home and face Daddy.

He's so upset and I don't want to deal with his anger. He's already mad at me about the dress and that I ditched everyone at the after-party. Like they missed me. I tried to return the neck-lace to Grandma earlier this morning before we checked out of the hotel but she wouldn't hear of it, demanding that I keep it, that I'm the rightful owner now. I didn't want the responsibility of traveling with the necklace, especially after I heard about that one woman's piece of jewelry being lost or stolen at the after-party.

So I wore the necklace on the plane, tucked under my sweater, feeling stupid but knowing it was the only way I could ensure the jewelry was safe. I'm wearing it now—still under the sweater because I just know Violet would give me grief if she knew I had it on.

"So he left you? After he kissed you? And you don't know who he is." Violet shakes her head. "That's just odd."

"I know. I never did catch his name." I tap the edge of my pen against my pursed lips, hating that I know nothing about this man beyond what he tastes like . . . what it feels like to be touched by him. His hands, his finger seared my skin, he imprinted himself on me with the slightest touch, and just thinking about him and what he made me feel leaves me heady with desire.

So ridiculous.

"*Hmm.* Have you ever considered that maybe he's the one who stole that bracelet from the woman at the party?" Violet asks, her expression one of genuine concern.

I adore my sister. I really do. She was more like a mother to me since I never knew ours, and Lily couldn't be bothered with me. But too often, Violet is like an overprotective nanny who won't let me play on the swing set at the playground. I can't even appreciate it anymore. It feels too cloying.

I hate it.

"Why would he spend time with me like that if he'd just stolen a valuable piece of jewelry?" I roll my eyes and drop my pen on top of Violet's desk so that it rolls back toward me. I snatch it up, tapping it against the edge of her desk so that she sends me an annoyed glare. "Come on, you're reaching."

"You never know. There were all sorts of unsavory people in Cannes." Violet mock shudders. "One man tried to hit on me. I had to hold back Ryder for fear he would beat his face in if I let him go."

I love it. Ryder is so possessive of Violet. Not in a creepy, controlling way but in a he-loves-her-so-much-he-can't-live-without-her way. "Wish I could've seen that."

"No. Really you don't," Violet says drolly, just as she reaches out and snatches the pen from my fingers. "You're driving me crazy. Why don't you go see what Ryder's up to?" His office is only a few doors down from hers.

"Are you trying to get rid of me?" I'm slightly offended, not that I should blame Violet. I'm not in the mood to work. Knowing that I'm walking away from Fleur for a while—I hope temporarily, but maybe Daddy will be so furious he'll make it permanent—isn't helping my attitude.

"You don't seem like you're much in the mood to work." Violet tilts her head toward me, reaching up to play with the diamond stud in her ear. A nervous little habit she has; I recognize it immediately. "What's going on with you, Rose? You've been acting . . . *odd* ever since Cannes."

Sighing, I lean back in my chair, wondering if I can confide in Violet and know that she won't run off and tell our father. "I don't know. It's just . . . it's been hard, not having you around at Fleur."

Violet's expression is one of immediate guilt and her hand drops from her ear, landing with a thud on top of her desk. "I probably should've never left."

"No, no. I'm not saying that." Reaching out, I set my hand over hers. "You definitely should've come here. Look at how great you and Ryder are doing. It's amazing, our gains within the UK market. Daddy's so proud of you."

Violet grimaces. She hates when I call him Daddy. Their relationship is strained at best. Funny, considering how much praise he heaps on her. "So why is it so difficult without me there?"

"Pilar." I practically spit her name out. The way Violet's eyes darken, the sudden scowl on her face, I know I've touched a nerve. Doesn't help that the love of her life used to sleep with Pilar. *Ick*. "Daddy's going to promote her."

"Promote her into what position?" Violet appears outraged, which I love. That's exactly the reaction I'm looking for. I want a partner in my anger. I've felt too alone for far too long.

I shrug. Does it really matter? She's getting exactly what she wants because our father is so twisted up over her. "Not sure yet. Rumors are circulating and I'm fairly certain she's behind them. Daddy's not denying it, either."

"So you don't know for sure yet—"

"Come on," I interrupt her. "You know he'll promote her. He's completely enamored of her. She can do no wrong."

"Well, she's always been good at her job," Violet points out.

"Don't defend her!" I slap my hand against the edge of the desk, startling Violet so much she practically jumps in her seat. "She doesn't deserve it. She's a snake in the grass and you know it. She tried to *destroy* your relationship with Ryder—more than once, I might add. She helped break you and Zachary up, not that that was a bad thing, but you know what I mean. She's . . . hell-bent on getting whatever she wants and she doesn't care who gets hurt in the process."

Violet leans back in her chair, her lips a thin line, her fingers nervously turning her diamond earring again and again. "You don't have to yell at me," she murmurs.

"And you don't have to say such nice things about her, either." I make a face, my tone going snotty. " 'Oh, she's so wonderful at her job. She's perfect.' *Barf*." I roll my eyes. Only with Violet can I be so real, so open with my feelings. No way could I act like this with anyone else.

At least my sister has Ryder. He sees the real Violet, just like I do. He probably sees even more of her true self and no matter how much I try to tell myself it's ridiculous, that little fact makes me jealous.

Stupid but true.

"Tell me how you really feel about her," Violet says dryly.

"No, *you* tell me how you really feel about her," I retort, wanting to know. *Needing* to know. "And be honest, Violet."

Sighing, Violet closes her eyes briefly, dropping both of her hands into her lap. "Fine. You're right. She's awful. She'll be sweet to your face and connive behind your back. She'll do whatever it takes to get what she wants. I hate the connection Ryder has to her, but there's nothing I can do about it."

"You don't think . . ." My voice trails off and I can hardly get out my next words. My sister has dealt with enough crap in her life. All I want is for her to be happy. "He's not still interested in her, is he?"

"Oh my God, *no*. He's not interested in anyone else but me," Violet says firmly, that dreamy glow back in her eyes, the one she always gets when she talks about Ryder. "He's in love with me. I know she can't stand that, but there's nothing she can do to change it. We're engaged. We're getting married."

A smile curls my lips despite the unpleasant source of this conversation. "I'm so happy for you, Violet. Seriously. You're going to get *married*."

"I know. To Ryder." Her smile is dreamy too. It matches the look in her eyes. "I still can't believe he's mine. I don't think Pilar can believe it either, though why she's worried about him when she's involved with our father, I'll never get."

I wave my hand. "Let's stop talking about her. I can't stand it anymore." My mind races to change the subject, but Violet beats me.

"So what's going on with you?" she asks quietly. "I feel like there's more you're not saying."

Dipping my head, I stare at my hands as I grip my knees. I don't know what to tell her. I'm torn. "I'm unhappy at Fleur."

"Because of Pilar."

"Because of a lot of things, not just Pilar." Things I can't even really name, but my unhappiness is there. A living, breathing thing I can't avoid. Seeing Pilar's smug face every day as she walks by my office, hanging on Daddy's arm, just fuels my misery. I swear she knows it, too, which sucks. She makes me feel young. Stupid. Impotent in my authority at Fleur, if I even have any. My position there is superfluous at best. The only reason I have it is because my last name is Fowler, and Pilar never lets me forget it. I thought after Violet left that could be my moment to break out and shine, but Pilar took over the spotlight instead. "I need a break."

"Oh, Rose." I jerk my head up to meet her gaze, seeing the disappointment etched all over her face. "Don't let her drive you away. Fleur is yours, not hers. It's ours. Pilar is just jealous that she's not a Fowler."

Spot-on as usual. "It would be really easy for her to become a Fowler by marrying Daddy," I say.

Violet's eyes widen and she rests her fluttering hand over her chest. "You don't think he would . . . he would do that, do you?"

"I don't know what to think about him anymore." Or our mother. I still haven't told Violet what I discovered in the diary. Her last entries were vague, but I read enough to figure out what she was thinking just before she took her own life.

And it's not good.

"They haven't been dating long."

"Long enough for her to be staying the night most of the week at his place."

Violet scowls. "He won't marry her."

"You don't know that for sure." I cross my arms in front of my chest, feeling like a spoiled little girl. I swear sometimes I revert back to my childish ways when I'm with Violet. Really it's just the both of us falling back into our respective roles.

"You know what you need? A change of scenery." She points her index finger at me, her gaze narrowed. "Come work with us for a few weeks."

I'm incredulous at her suggestion. "Here? In London?"

"Yes, I know . . . I know it's sort of last minute, but I would love to have you here. For two weeks, a month, what do you think? I'll call Father and let him know you want to stay here for a while. I'm sure he'll be on board."

Hope rises within me and I try to squash it down. "Do you really think he will be? And are you sure you want me here with you?"

"I miss you too, you know," she admits softly. "Ryder and I don't plan on leaving London anytime soon, so it would be great to have you here. I could show you around the city, we could go shopping."

I start to laugh. "I thought you wanted me here to work."

"Well, we can call it that." Violet shrugs. "And you'll come into the office and work when you want, no pressure. We can also go visit the Paris office if you want. Oh, Rose. You should stay here. I know Father will approve. He wanted this for me, to spread my wings and work at other Fleur locations. I know he'll want the same for you."

I'm not so sure about that, but I don't want to argue with Violet. Besides, I love her idea. I want to take her up on her offer. "But what about Ryder?"

She frowns. "What about him?"

"Will he want me around, staying at your place? I'm sure he'd prefer privacy."

Violet actually blushes. I'm sure their sex life is off the charts, not that I want to think about it. But with a handsome man like Ryder, who fairly vibrates with all that pent-up sexual edginess, I can only imagine what he must do for Violet. *To* Violet.

Jealous again.

"Am I right?" I prod.

Violet shrugs. "It's only for a month. And he adores you."

Even if that's true, they'll want their privacy. "I should go back to New York." I sigh and shake my head, my gaze going to the window to my right. All of London is spread out before us, an endless view of nothing but buildings and British flags, the sky a brilliant blue scattered with fluffy white clouds. It's a perfect late spring day in the city and I have the sudden urge to go outside. Run around and pretend I have zero responsibilities, at least for a little while.

"No," Violet says vehemently. "Stay here with me. Back in New York, you're restless. Unhappy. And that'll only lead you into trouble."

I frown. "What in the world are you talking about?"

"The way you behaved at the premiere, it was so unlike you. First there's the dress. Have you seen the papers, by the way? Talk about a scandal."

My stomach sinks. I haven't seen the papers. I've avoided them. "Is it that bad?"

"Probably worse." She rolls her eyes and reaches into her desk drawer, pulling out one of the tabloids that are so popular here. She tosses it across the desk so that it lands in front of me with a plop. "They're saying you're giving Lily a run for her money."

I barely glance at the photo on the front of the paper. That I actually made the very front of the *Daily Mail*'s gossip page is both thrilling and horrifying. Finally I'm recognized for being me, though they have to mention Lily too, of course. And huh. It's not the most flattering article either, showcasing the fashion faux pas at Cannes yesterday. *Great.* "I can't believe you waited this long to bring it up."

"I didn't want to upset you. I'm upset enough already."

My gaze drops to the photo of me on the red carpet, both of my legs on blatant display what with the slits up to my hip bones. I look . . . amazing, and completely exposed. The necklace glitters around my throat, the pink stones vibrant against my skin. "Did Grandma see this?"

"I don't know. She's probably only just landed in New York since her flight was after ours." Violet snatches the paper away from me and shoves it back into her desk drawer. "You're lucky no one found out about your mysterious man who felt you up after you skinny-dipped in the pool," she retorts.

Leaping to my feet, I glare at her, anger coursing through my veins. "I thought you wouldn't judge." I should never have told her what happened. I didn't give her all the details, but I did let it slip that I stripped off my dress and jumped into the pool.

Her words ring in my head and I feel foolish. I don't measure up. I'm in Lily's and Violet's shadows and I hate it. The biggest obstacle I've ever had to overcome is being their baby sister. They'll always be ahead of me, no matter what I do or what I say.

Being the youngest sucks.

"I worry about you, Rose," Violet says, her voice steady, her demeanor calm. She folds her hands together on top of the desk, looking every inch the successful businesswoman. While I'm the floundering, trying-to-find-my-place Fowler sister. Clearly I'm the only one worked up here. "I was afraid something like this would happen, what with the flashy dress and wearing that necklace."

"You're jealous of the necklace, aren't you? You hate that Grandma gave it to me and not you," I throw out, trying to hurt her the way she's hurting me.

And it works. Somewhat. She flinches at my accusation but otherwise, no reaction. "I don't care about the necklace."

"You so do."

"I'm concerned about your behavior and how you're acting, not the stupid necklace," she says, her voice rising the slightest bit. She's angry now.

Good. I'm angry too.

"Did you ever think I'm just acting like . . . me?"

Leaning back in her chair, she frowns. "Rose . . ."

"I'm serious. Maybe I'm just being myself, you know? I've always been in your shadow or Lily's shadow, and I've never done anything on my own. Just for me." I grab my purse from where I set it on the floor by my chair and start to exit her office.

"Rose, don't go," she calls, and I pause in front of the closed door, my hand resting on the handle. "Stay and talk to me."

With a sigh, I glance at her over my shoulder, offering her a pitiful smile. "There's nothing left to discuss. I just . . . I need to be alone for a little bit, okay?"

"Okay." She nods, looking contrite. She doesn't like to fight and neither do I. "You'll come over for dinner tonight?"

I'm staying at a hotel for the next few nights but if I do decide to prolong my stay in London, do I really want to move in with my sister and her boyfriend? "Are you cooking?" I ask cautiously. Violet can't cook. None of us can.

"No, we're getting takeout. From this great little Indian restaurant that's not too far from our flat. Ryder would eat there seven days a week if I let him," Violet explains, amusement tingeing her voice.

"Fine. Yes. I'll come to dinner. See you later." I hurry out of her office before she says something else and convinces me to stay with her.

I want to be alone right now. So I can try to process my turbulent thoughts.

Not that I have much faith in myself at the moment.

Chapter Four

Caden

"SO HOW LONG DO YOU PLAN ON STAYING WITH ME?" WHITNEY purrs, wrapping her arms around my neck, her fingers diving into my hair. I've barely shut the door and she's already pressed her body against me, her hips nudging mine.

I disentangle myself from her grip. The woman is like an octopus, hands everywhere, all at once. "I don't know," I tell her, dropping my bag on the floor right by the front door. "A few weeks? Maybe a month?"

The smile on her face is nothing short of pleased. I've been friends with Whitney Banks for what feels like forever. More like since we were little kids and we went to the same private school together. Her banker father—always loved that their last name is Banks, so fitting—got a job transfer just before junior high ended and she moved with her family to London. We would see each other on occasion when she came back to the States and one night, while she was in New York the summer after we graduated high school, we were at a party together and got drunk.

And we had sex.

Ever since then, whenever we see each other—which is rare—we usually end up fucking. I'm never with anyone and neither is she. We both have zero interest in relationships, but our friendship with a little fucking on the side works quite nicely.

Though right now I'm exhausted. The last thing I want to do is fuck. I need a shower first. And then a nap.

Whitney, on the other hand, appears raring to go.

"Put your bag in my room." She comes for me once more, her arms going around my waist this time as she tips her head back, waiting for my kiss. I dutifully deliver it, dropping a quick kiss on her lips.

"You don't want me in your room," I murmur against her perfectly glossed pink lips.

Whitney smiles, her hands slipping down to grip my ass. "Oh, I definitely want you in my room. Easy access." She is beautiful and she knows it. Perfect blond hair cut into a fashionable bob, plump lips, sparkling blue eyes, and a willowy body that can wear just about anything. She's usually clad in as little clothing as possible and can get away with it, since she's more on the slender than the curvy side.

I think immediately of Rose Fowler's curves. She has a woman's body. Full breasts, nipped-in waist, and rounded hips, and her ass is a perfect handful. Hard to believe I walked away from her like I did.

Not that I had a choice. I needed to get out of there. The lynch mob didn't find me, thank God, and while I heard rumblings about the bracelet being stolen, there was no public notice made.

The rich do not like to talk about their goods being stolen—I discovered this early on in my so-called career. They'd rather sweep the embarrassing loss under the rug, collect their insurance payout, and move on. Dire stories on the local news about a jewel thief aren't becoming, which is fine by me.

Their lack of talking to the authorities made my endeavors easier to carry out. Though I'm disappointed I didn't get ahold of the Poppy Necklace. I've already heard from Dexter, my old contact who wants to add the piece to his collection. He's displeased and has been urging me to go after it, but I put him off.

I stayed on in Cannes for a few days, cashing in the bracelet and collecting a hefty payment. Found out Rose Fowler left Cannes the day after I saw her, so that was a lost cause. I hung out on the beaches and flirted with various women, snagging a few gold pieces that were worth a decent amount. I garnered enough to pay for Mom's expenses for the next five months at least, maybe six.

The relief of that is tremendous. I can finally relax and do something for myself for a little while.

"What brings you here?" Whitney hasn't removed her arms from my waist or her hands from my ass, and I again have to pull myself out of her grip. I walk over to the couch and sit down, leaning my head back so I can stare up at the ceiling.

"I needed a vacation." Not too far from the truth. Considering the bills are taken care of, I'm allowed a pit stop in London before I head home. My friend Mitchell, owner of the private jet, already planned to go to London and I decided to hitch a ride. Though I might end up staying longer, depending on what I find around here.

I need a change of pace, new scenery. Not only to get away from New York but also to lie low. I'd worked like a motherfucker the last few months, getting more daring with every job. To the point where I was probably starting to look suspect, so I reined it in. Went to parties and actually didn't steal a damn thing before I up and disappeared for good.

A new place means new people. New valuables. New jewels. Considering London is fucking full of old money, this should be a field day. A summer in London sounded rather profitable. Don't know why I never thought of it before.

"Well, yay for vacations. You're always so busy. You never come to my side of the pond." Whitney smiles and plops on the couch beside me, snuggling close, her head against my chest. She has no idea what I actually "do" and I'd like to keep it that way. I'm pretty sure she thinks all I do is fuck around all day, which is fine. That's all she does too. She lives off her daddy's money. "I'm excited that you're here."

"Yeah, me too," I say, my words sounding hollow. I'm glad to be here, thankful for Whitney's hospitality and friendship. She doesn't normally put conditions on it, but I hope she doesn't think I'm going to fuck her for a bed to sleep in.

When she rests her hand on my cock and starts rubbing, I *know* she expects me to fuck her for a bed to sleep in.

"Whit." I grab her hand and clasp it tight in mine. "I'm tired. I need to sleep before I can even think of doing . . . that."

She smiles, flashing me her brilliant white teeth. "Exhaustion never stopped you before. I remember nights of getting high, getting drunk, and fucking for hours." Her throaty laugh is telling me she enjoys those memories.

I remember them too. Fondly. "I'm not high and I'm not drunk. I'm just worn out."

"Too much alcohol usually deflates a cock," she says, like she's making some major observation.

"Not mine." I let go of her hand and trail my finger across her cheek but she jerks away from my touch, her lips pushed into a pout that usually works on me.

But not this time. Instead of sucking up to her and letting her get her way, I rise from the couch and stretch my arms above my head with an exaggerated yawn before I settle my hands on my hips. "Where's your bathroom?"

She waves her hand toward the short hall to my left, her gaze not meeting mine. She's mad, but she'll get over it. "Down there, first door on the right."

"Got extra towels?" I go to the front door and grab my duffel bag. I always pack light so it's easier to make my escape if necessary.

"Of course," she retorts with a huff. "What sort of hostess do you think I am?"

Going to the couch, I place a quick kiss to her forehead and cup her chin with my hand, forcing her to look at me. "A great one," I murmur with a gentle smile. I don't want her on my bad side, but damn it, I'm not interested in a summer full of screwing Whitney, either. We're rarely together for a long period of time, so having a quick one-off is normal for us.

Spending weeks on end together? Not so normal.

Her mouth twists into a wry little smile. "Go take your shower. I'll be waiting for you."

Hell. She's not going to let this go until I get her off at least once.

Locking myself in her bathroom, I flick on the light and take in the room. It's white, with chrome towel bars and handles, a three-tiered chrome-and-glass shelf right next to the white pedestal sink, the shelves overflowing with fluffy white towels. I go to the tub and turn on the water, shedding my clothes with quick efficiency before I slip into the shower, pulling the curtain shut and letting the water pour over me in a steady stream.

It's warm and the pressure is high, the water beating against my skin in pulsating jets. I wash my hair and then lather up, scrubbing my body clean, smoothing my hand over my cock. Closing my eyes, the image of a naked Rose Fowler pops into my brain. How wet her skin was, her hair slicked back from her angel face, the taste of her, warm and wet and with a hint of Champagne.

My cock lengthens, hardens. She's been my beat-off material for the last few days. I have Whitney with her hands all over my dick and I barely react. I merely think of Rose and I'm hard as steel.

Leaning against the smooth white-tiled wall, I wrap my soap-slicked fingers around my cock and start stroking. My eyes are closed, imagining wet and sexy Rose kneeling before me, that pretty, innocent face staring up at me just before she lowers her thick lashes and leans forward, her perfect, lush mouth wrapping tight around my cock.

Jesus. I jerk hard, the orgasm coming at me fast. I can feel it forming at the base of my spine, like billowy clouds that grow dark and turbulent, heavy and swollen, eager to release the buildup of stormy rain.

This is me. My cock. Ready to fucking explode at any minute.

It slams into me, hard and fast, a little groan escaping me as my semen spurts out in long, ropey streams, hitting the wall before it's washed away. I slump against the wall, my exhaustion taking over. Combined with the brief satisfaction I gave myself, I'm ready to collapse into bed.

I get out of the shower and dry off quick, changing into a T-shirt and sweats before I exit the bathroom, glancing into an open door to find Whitney lying on top of her bed. Completely naked.

Shit.

"Whit." I stay in the doorway, my already spent cock half-heartedly rousing when she rolls over onto her back and spreads her legs, offering me a special view. "What the hell are you doing?"

"What does it look like I'm doing?" She smiles, her hand trailing down to play between her legs. "I've missed you, Caden. I don't know what else I can do to get that through your head."

"Jesus, woman." I drop my duffel just inside her bedroom by the door. I don't want to stay in her bed. I don't want her to get any ideas. "Let me get some sleep first."

"No." She sits up, scrambling to her knees, her expression fierce. "I thought by you staying with me, this was the sort of arrangement we would have. Am I wrong?" *Hell.* I didn't think this through. I should've known Whitney would have expectations. Women are a pleasant distraction, one I haven't indulged in for a long time. But I hadn't planned on playing boyfriend/girlfriend with Whitney for the next few weeks.

I wish had a male friend who lived in London.

Deciding to hell with it, slowly I approach the bed, tearing off my shirt before I join her. "You're not wrong," I tell her, lying through my teeth. "But you want me at my best, right?"

She runs her hands over my chest before sliding one beneath the waistband of my sweats. "I want you any way I can get you. I'm horny. I've missed your dick."

"What's up with you? You're not usually so—needy." I choke the last word out when she wraps her fingers tight around my cock and starts to stroke.

"It's been a while. Had a bad breakup a few months ago and no one has interested me since." She's pushing my sweatpants off, her fingers never leaving my cock as she continues to stroke.

"You had a boyfriend?" I'm surprised. We were always on the same page when it came to relationships. As in, we didn't believe in them.

Shrugging, she removes her hands from my body and leans back against the headboard, suddenly looking vulnerable. "I thought we were in a relationship. Clearly I was wrong."

"That's where you made your first mistake." The moment the words are said, I know I definitely made a mistake. She sends me a deathly glare, curling her arms in front of her chest as if she can ward me off.

"Maybe you *should* sleep in the guest room," she says sullenly, kicking out her foot so she's nudging my knee. Hard. "For now."

Ha. Well, that worked and I didn't even mean it to. "I'm sorry, Whit." I grab my shirt and pull it back on. Whitney Banks is a spoiled little princess who always gets what she wants. So when she's denied something, she lashes out. Sometimes physically. She slapped my face one time years ago and we got into a drunken shouting match.

"Ugh. Whatever. Don't apologize. You're probably right." She pokes me in the thigh with her big toe, then scoots her leg away from me. She's not inviting me back to her bed and I'm okay with that.

I get off the bed and go to grab my bag. She doesn't say a word and neither do I, though I see her watching me, the scowl on her face unmistakable. Just as I'm about to make my way to the guest room, Whitney speaks up. "I'm going to dinner tonight with a group of friends. Care to join me?"

"That sounds good." I glance at her from over my shoulder. "You don't mind if I go?"

"Of course not. I'm sure my friends will love you. We're going to a pub. I hope you like fish and chips?" She makes a little face.

"Do *you* like fish and chips?" I chuckle, thankful her anger seems to have evaporated quickly. Her rapid-fire moods can make my head spin and I want things easy between us, not a twisted-up, uncomfortable mess.

"Not really. The food here isn't that great. I eat my way through Manhattan every time I go back to visit."

The conversation goes on like this until I yawn and she shoos me away to take a nap. She's still naked, not embarrassed in the least. I would never describe Whitney as modest. The girl had a wild streak when we were younger and she was always tearing off her clothes back in the day.

I open the guest room door and glance around in horror. There are shopping bags and shoe boxes everywhere. All from expensive stores or top designers, most of them are empty. It looks like this room has become Whitney's closet—or more like her post-shopping dumping ground.

Pushing the empty bags off the bed and onto the floor, I leave my duffel bag on a nearby chair and then pull the comforter back, sliding in between the cool sheets with a contented sigh.

I've been on the go for months. Constantly tense, working

every angle I have, and it finally paid off. Mom is financially secure for the rest of the year. I have cash in my pocket. I'm in London, where I can probably gain more pickups and possibly pay for a solid year of Mom's bills. I wonder if she has a clue where I'm getting my money.

Probably not, I think as I drift off. And that's for the best.

"WE'RE REALLY GOING TO TAKE THE TUBE?" I SOUND LIKE A whiner, but I'd rather take a fucking taxi than deal with London's subway system in the early evening. I know it'll be crowded with nine-to-fivers going home after a long, miserable day stuck behind their desks.

"Oh, stop being such a stuck-up asshole and deal with it." Whitney races down the stairs that lead into the station and I follow her, not surprised at all by the amount of bustling, harried people crowding the place. The stench of sweat combined with too much perfume and a hint of burning rubber fills my nostrils and I wrinkle my nose.

Welcome to London.

I grab hold of the back of Whitney's sweater as she leads me through the crowds, going through the turnstile after her when she scans her Oyster transportation card and pays for the both of us. A beautiful woman in a blue dress smiles at me as I pass by her and I smile back.

"Stop flirting," Whitney chastises me.

"Do you have eyes in the back of your head?" I ask her. I'm amused that she even caught me.

"No, more like every woman you walk by is staring at you."

"Now, now, don't be jealous," I tease, and she swats my hand off of her sweater.

We find our route and get on the packed train a few minutes later. When the doors shut and the train goes into motion, I rock back into the woman standing behind me. I offer her an apology and she shakes her head, murmuring an apology as well.

Hmm. This would be the perfect place to pickpocket the shit out of people.

The thought comes to me unbidden as I glance around. Not that I do that sort of thing, not anymore. I used to, when I was first starting out and feeling my way through my newfound so-called career. But what started me on the path of high-end jewelry was none other than the girl whose diamond earrings I stole one night at a party.

Thanks, Lily Fowler, for the inspiration.

"When's our stop?" I ask Whitney when I hear the auto-mated voice make an announcement.

"Covent Garden. Don't worry about it—I'll let you know when it's coming up."

The trip is quick, our stop announced less than ten minutes after I asked Whitney about it. I follow her out of the train and through the under-construction station, up the endless stairs until we pop up onto the street, miles away from Whitney's flat.

"Who are we meeting tonight anyway?" I ask as we walk down the sidewalk, passing all sorts of shops and restaurants. The area is crowded, filled with the young and old, families and couples and a group of teens that go running past us, yelling at each other and laughing.

I remember when I was young like that, without a fucking care in the world. Wasn't that long ago, either. Until everything went to hell and I was left having to pick up the pieces.

"A small group of people, mostly transplanted Americans. It's so weird, how we all seem drawn to each other," Whitney explains. "I can spot an American a mile away, I swear."

"Like seeks like, I guess, right?" When she nods, I continue. "So where are we going?"

"Oh, it's a really cool pub—you'll like it. The White Swan.

They have amazing beer and a great dinner menu. One of the better places to eat in this city," she says with a cheeky smile.

Ha. I hope she's not shitting me. I'm starving. "Will I know any of your friends?"

"Maybe? I'm not sure. Two of them—they're a couple—I just recently met. They're here in London temporarily and we were introduced through a mutual friend. But normally they live in New York."

It may be a huge city but I swear Manhattan feels like a small town, especially with our exclusive circle. That I'm still allowed to be a part of it is some sort of miracle. Though I've worked damn hard to seem like I still belong. "What are their names?"

"Violet Fowler and her fiancé, Ryder McKay. You've heard of the Fowler sisters, right? She's an heiress to Fleur Cosmetics. Anyway, she and her boyfriend are here working at the London office." Whitney stops when she realizes I'm frozen on the sidewalk. "Caden?" She frowns as she turns to face me. "What's wrong? We need to hurry so we can grab a good table."

Fucking fuck. We're meeting Violet Fowler and her boyfriend? Fiancé? Whatever the hell he is? I saw Violet when we were in Cannes, but I never spoke to her. I don't know her, our paths have never crossed, and I sure as hell don't know Ryder McKay.

I know her sisters, though. Lily is back in the States. Rose . . . I'm not sure where she is. Did she go back to New York? Or is she still in Europe somewhere, traveling? She can do whatever she wants. She definitely doesn't need to work.

"*Caden.*" I glance up when I hear Whitney's impatient voice. She's already resumed walking toward the pub, waving her hand at me, the universal sign of "hurry up." I go into motion, my stride easy, my smile firmly in place. No reaction, no anything. I'm my usual smooth self.

"Sorry, thought I saw someone I knew," I lie when I reach her, curling my arm around hers. "Let's hurry so we can go grab that table."

Chapter Five

Rose

"COME WITH US," VIOLET PLEADS. "YOU'LL LOVE WHITNEY. I met her a few months ago and we became instant friends."

I shake my head, clutching my cell tight to my ear. I'm not about to be the third wheel at some couples-only dinner at a quaint pub. No, thank you. "I think I'll stay in tonight." I've already been in London a week, doing a fabulous job of avoiding my dad, Pilar, and even Violet, to an extent. We told our father I was staying on to work at the London office, which he'd reluctantly agreed was a good thing to do. I was off the hook for most of the summer, he said. Not that I'm needed at the moment. He made sure and added that last little bit during our conference call.

Thanks for the vote of confidence, Daddy.

"Oh, come on. It's a big group of us. Not a bunch of couples or anything. And it's not too far from where you're staying," Violet says pointedly. She's still unhappy that I'm not staying with her at her place. Instead, I'm at an exclusive little boutique hotel for at least the next few weeks.

"The pub is in Covent Garden?" I ask as I settle on the edge of the bed. The hushed silence of the room is starting to get to me. Being on my own too much is making me realize that I'm lonely.

"Yes, the White Swan. I think it's like a five-minute walk from your hotel. Please, just . . . just stop by and see if you want to stay. If not, you can bail. But at least give us a chance." Violet pauses. "You've been cooped up in that hotel room too much. Have I mentioned I've lied to Father about you when he's called?"

"What do you mean, you've lied about me?" I sit up straighter, waiting for Violet's answer.

"I told him you've been in the office all *week*," she stresses. "Instead of telling him the truth. That you're moping around feeling sorry for yourself."

"I am not."

"You are too," she returns, her voice harsh. "You won't come into the office, you won't leave your hotel room. You act like you're depressed."

"Maybe I *am* depressed," I mutter, glancing out the window. I stare at the building across from me, the open windows full of happy people in their sunny flats. I see a couple enter their living room, holding hands as they turn toward each other and kiss.

Ugh. Romance. I look away.

"What happened to my tough, feisty little sister? The one who always had a smart comment and loved to give me endless crap?" Violet asks, sounding incredulous. "Because I know I'm not talking to that girl right now. It's like she's disappeared."

"She sort of has," I admit with a sigh, flopping backward so I lie sprawled across the bed. "I don't know what's wrong with me."

"You know what I think? You need to do something different. After you graduated college, you immediately threw yourself into Fleur, and there's been no looking back. It's all work, work, work. It's not healthy. You need to take some time for you."

Really? The nerve of Violet. She's no different. "You did the same exact thing," I point out to her, and she laughs nervously.

"Yes, well . . . then I met Ryder. And he's turned my world completely upside down in the best possible way." I swear to God I can feel her blushing over the phone. My silly, embarrassed older sister.

"Are you saying he taught you how to take some time just for you?" I'm digging and I don't really care if she gets mad or not. She's the one who started this conversation.

"He's taught me a lot of things," she says softly. Vaguely. "More than anything, he taught me it's okay to give up some—control."

I don't believe it. "Really? You, the ultimate control freak, learned how to give up control?"

"I'm not talking about business. I mean more like with my personal life," Violet admits.

Hmmm. I think I know where she's going with this conversation. And I'm delightfully shocked. "Are you talking about your sex life?"

"Rose!" She laughs nervously.

This conversation is hilarious. And enlightening. I didn't know Violet had it in her, talking about sex. She's always so straitlaced. She leaves the wild stuff to Lily. And lately, to me. "Give me a break. You're the one who started this."

"Fine, fine. You're right. Yes. I'm talking about my sex life. There's something rather . . . freeing in letting a man take over," she admits, her voice low.

"Why, I never imagined you saying anything like this to me. *Ever,*" I say, stressing the last word. "Though I knew the minute I first saw him that Ryder McKay had a sexy streak in him a mile long."

"I don't even want to talk about this with you," she says.

Now it's my turn to laugh. "What? You're not going to tell me Ryder's penis size? Because I'm sure he's got a monster in his trousers." I'm trying to irritate her, like the old days.

It feels good.

"You're disgusting," she says good-naturedly. And that tells me all I need to know.

Ryder McKay's penis is most likely ginormous. *Lucky bitch*.

"Whatever. Your protesting is way too happy." I pause with a little sigh. "Okay, I'll go."

"Wait. What?"

She's going to make me say it again on purpose. *Fine*. I'll play along. "I'll stop by the pub and have a drink. If it's not my scene, I'm out. Are you happy now?"

"Yes, I'm happy." And she really does sound happy, too, which makes me feel bad. I've let my sister down. I've worried her, and I hate that. "It'll totally be your scene, I swear. Very low key. You know me. I don't like to party and get drunk."

No. She really doesn't. We've both seen what happens when someone loses all control and parties nonstop, thanks to our big sister.

"Just stop by, have a drink, maybe eat dinner with us if you're feeling comfortable," Violet continues. "And if you're not, you can leave after one beer."

"I don't even drink beer. Neither do you," I say as I stare at the ceiling.

"I do now. Ryder's taught me how to appreciate a good beer," she says, sounding haughty, all while talking about freaking beer.

"I'm sure," I say dryly, making her laugh. "Tell me what time and I'll be there."

We hang up after she gives me the details and I realize I have maybe two hours to get ready. I hop into the shower—first one I've taken in two days; yes, maybe Violet is right, I am disgustingly pitiful—and I soak under the hot spray of water for far too long, finally shutting it off before I turn into a complete prune.

I slather on lotion and do my hair. Apply makeup—the latest from Fleur, of course—and thumb through the clothes I brought

with me that are hanging in the closet. I haven't even gone shopping since I arrived in London, so it's all old stuff. Boring.

With the exception of a sweet little summer dress I brought
with me. Late spring in London has been warm and I know I can
get away with the thin cotton dress, especially if I bring a sweater
with me.

But I don't want to bring a sweater. I slip the dress on, not
bothering with a bra or even panties. It fits loose, the top a
blue-and-white stripe with a button-up bodice, and the floral
print skirt falls just above my knees, swinging about my legs in
an almost flirtatious way. The mix of patterns shouldn't work
but somehow it does, and when I stop in front of the mirror on
the back of the bathroom door I stare at myself.

I look young. Carefree. I'd curled my hair after drying it, just
the ends, and it falls past my shoulders in free-flowing waves.
The makeup is subtle since I always apply it with a light hand,
and I have pearl studs in my ears. My mom's earrings—we were
all given a different pair from her jewelry collection when we
turned sixteen.

Life has been so harried lately that I haven't done much re-
laxing. Maybe my down-in-the-dumps wallowing in my hotel
room has done me wonders.

I know I definitely feel good. The perk in my step as I make
my way down the sidewalk toward the pub is a good sign too.
The sun shines upon my skin, warming me, and I smile at a cute
guy in a crisp suit as we pass each other by, thrilled by the light
of awareness I see in his gaze.

When was the last time I was with a guy? I've been on a few
dates since I broke up with my last boyfriend. That breakup
messed with my head, but I'm over him now. I fooled around
with a few of those dates, but nothing serious. I've been far more
intimate with my vibrator lately—a gift I received at a bridal
shower when I won one of those stupid games we're always re-

quired to play. It had been a bit of a gag when they handed it over, much giggling and tossing around of innuendo-filled comments when I pulled the silver bullet out of the gift bag.

But that little silver bullet has come in handy over the last few months. It's almost embarrassing to admit. I'm a girl in my early twenties. The world is my oyster and all that crap. I should be having the sexual time of my life with a hot guy, not a discreet vibrator I hide in my bedside drawer.

I immediately think of the guy I met in Cannes and I slow my steps, allow myself to daydream a little bit. He'd been hot. Tall and broad, with that gorgeous face and the sun-kissed hair. The perfect lips and that long, slightly rough index finger circling around my nipple . . .

"Watch it!"

The man's voice startles me and I leap out of the way of the bicyclist riding past, who sends me a menacing glare. I return the glower, pissed that I almost ran into him, pissed even more that he had to yell at me like that.

Jerk.

I guess that's what I get for daydreaming about sexy strangers who kiss me and abandon me, all in a matter of five minutes. Was the entirely too brief incident in Cannes a sign of things to come? Is that what I have to look forward to? Becoming consumed with work, having missed opportunities, and going home alone every night?

How depressing.

Stopping short, I realize I'm in front of the White Swan. It's a beautiful pub, the exterior painted black with white-framed windows, the name painted in gold. Flowers spill out of boxes set just above the pub, and a giant lantern flickers as it swings gently to and fro with the breeze.

Nerves assail me out of nowhere and I bite my lower lip, unsure if I should enter or not. Why am I cautious now? It's no big deal. If I hate hanging out with Violet's friends, I can leave.

"Rose."

I glance up to see Violet standing in the doorway of the pub, looking adorable in a flippy black skirt and a plain white T-shirt, a bold, chunky silver necklace dressing up the outfit. Slowly I approach her, pleased at the smile on her face, the way she glances down at her left hand and twists the diamond ring Ryder just gave her into place.

My sister looks so happy. And I'm filled with the sudden need to keep on making her happy, too.

"I'm so glad you're here," Violet says as she pulls me into a hug.

I cling to her for probably a little too long, but she doesn't protest. "I'm glad I came too," I admit as I pull away from her.

She sends me a look, one I recognize and that I've received many times. It's the stern, I'm-going-into-mother-mode look she's so fond of giving me. I step back and she holds out my arms, examining me before she nods her approval. "Cute dress."

"Love your outfit too," I return.

Violet takes my hand and pulls me into the pub. "It's casual Friday at the office. You'd know this if you came in once in a while."

"Give me a break," I murmur, hoping she won't keep badgering me for not going to the Fleur offices. I want a guilt-free night, not one where my sister is trying to make me feel bad.

"All the single guys in here are going to give you the eye, what with the short skirt," she continues as she pulls me through the pub. It's already crowded, filled with plenty of the work types who are just off for the weekend, many of the men clad in fashionable suits and with equally fashionable haircuts. The place practically breathes *GQ*.

"Maybe I'm trying to attract a few guys. Looks like there are plenty to choose from," I observe.

Violet flashes me a smile from over her shoulder. "Well, you're a breath of fresh air compared to the corporate working girls who usually fill this place up. You're all cute and flirty to-night."

I *feel* cute and flirty tonight. And I like it.

A lot.

"Okay, here we are. This is my sister Rose, everyone. Rose, this is . . . everyone," Violet announces as she stops at a round table filled with people. I stand at her side, releasing her hand as Ryder gets up from where he's sitting and approaches me, giving me a brief hug and a kiss on the cheek.

"Rose," he says with a cheeky smile before he releases me and kisses Violet full on the lips, making her wobble a little on her feet.

I'm so caught up in my sister and her future husband that when I finally check out the friendly faces sitting at the table, my gaze snags on one in particular. A rather familiar face. One I had just been thinking about, believing I'd never see him again.

My mysterious stranger. The man who kissed me senseless, squeezed my ass, and then walked away from me as if I were a brief pit stop.

"Rose." Ryder slings his arm around my shoulders, the grin on his face infectious despite my shock. I think he's had a few beers already. "I'd like you to meet our friends." He starts the introductions and I nod and smile at them, murmuring a hello as I try to avoid my stranger. Because really, this is incredibly em-barrassing and weird considering the last time I saw him I was naked.

In his arms.

His hands on my ass and his tongue in my mouth.

"And this is Whitney," Violet pipes up, going to stand beside a beautiful, very blond and very icy woman who's wearing a brittle smile that could shatter at any moment. Her eyes are big and blue, her hair shaped into a stylish bob that frames her heart-shaped face perfectly. I think I hate her. "She's my dearest friend since arriving in London. I know you'll adore her."

Considering the proprietary way she's snugly pressed against my mysterious stranger, I'm sure I'll just adore her too.

Not really.

"So nice to meet you," I say weakly at Whitney, and she nods and murmurs much the same. Not that I really hear her.

My gaze is stuck on my stranger, who's staring at me with the same sort of bewilderment that I'm feeling. He looks completely different tonight compared to the last time I saw him. Wearing jeans and a faded red T-shirt, his light brown hair mussed, stubble covering his cheeks, those intense brown eyes locked on mine. He looks like . . . a regular guy.

A gorgeous regular guy, though, most definitely.

"And this is Whitney's friend Caden. He just came into town," Violet says, patting Caden—hearing his name just made me shiver, *oh my God*—on the shoulder.

"Caden." I repeat his name, liking the way it feels on my tongue, how it sounds when I say it. It's a good name, strong and sexy, and it fits him. "Nice to meet you."

"Likewise." He smiles but it doesn't quite reach his eyes, and the disappointment that hits me as I watch Whitney put her arm around his shoulders and nuzzle his cheek with her nose almost makes me sag in defeat.

Almost.

Instead, I stand a little straighter and glance over at my sister, giving her a look that says plenty without having to utter a word. She rushes over to my side, asking Ryder to order me a beer, and I let her take over, finding me a seat, offering me a menu as she settles beside me and leans in close, her gaze imploring.

I tilt my head, my lips at her ear. "I know him."

"Who?" She scrunches her brows, confused.

Dipping closer, I practically eat her ear as I whisper, "Caden."

"How?"

Pressing my lips together, I move away from her, shaking my head. Can I tell her who he is? She'll be shocked and heaven forbid, she might go to Whitney and ask about Caden. The last thing I want to happen.

He doesn't deserve my attention and least of all, my interest. I am absolutely, 100 percent not interested in him. Not at all.

Nope.

So it means nothing that I polish off my beer in about five minutes after receiving it. And that I order a steak dinner—make that rare—and eat it with relish, drinking another beer . . . and then another. I'm laughing and joking with Ryder and one of his friends—his name is Nigel and he's cute as can be, but I'm afraid he might play for the other team. Or maybe he doesn't; I don't know. But they help me forget, Ryder and Nigel. And Violet.

Yes, I've forgotten all about my mysterious, handsome not-a-stranger. How every time I glance in his direction he's watching me. At first he looked away, as if he didn't want to be caught.

But after about the tenth meeting of gazes, he doesn't even blink. He's blatantly staring at me and I can't look away. Violet is engaged in some deep conversation with Whitney—*God,* I hate her and I don't even know her, what is wrong with me?—and Ryder is listening to some work story Nigel is telling.

I'm staring. Caught. Trapped by his gaze, and I want to be. My head is spinning. My body is . . . aching. Caden's gaze drops to my mouth, lingering there for what feels like forever, and my lips tingle. As if he's just kissed them. And then his gaze drops lower, to my chest, and my nipples harden. Like I have no control over them, which I really don't since I'm not wearing a bra and *whoops,* I'm not wearing panties, either, because I wanted to feel young and flirty tonight.

It's as if my body knew and prepared itself. The restlessness has hit me full force and I squirm in my chair, my heavy breasts brushing against the thin fabric of my dress almost painful.

I can't take it.

Touching Ryder's arm, he turns to look at me questioningly and I murmur, "I'll be right back."

He frowns. "You okay?"

"Just going to the ladies'," I reassure him as I get up and leave the table.

I can feel Caden's eyes on me as I walk away, and I'm tempted to look back so I can gauge his reaction.

But I don't look back. I won't give him the satisfaction. I stare straight ahead, making my way through the crowded pub, toward the hall on the opposite end of the room where the bathrooms are located.

Once I make it inside, I brace my hands on the edge of the counter and stare at myself in the mirror. Again. Just like earlier, before I left my hotel room. Though now I look different. My cheeks are flushed, as is the skin on my chest, and my nipples are still poking against the fabric of my dress. My hair has lost some of its curl and my eyes sparkle with an almost unnatural glow.

I look drunk.

I look aroused.

I am definitely both.

The door swings open and my gaze darts to the doorway in the mirror's reflection, my mouth dropping open in shock before I whirl around. "What are you doing?"

Caden closes the door and leans against it, his arm sneaking out behind him to turn the lock. He doesn't answer my question. He doesn't say a word as he pushes away from the door and stalks toward me. His stride is predatory, his expression full of dark intent.

I grip the counter, my fingers tight around the tiled edge, my knees weakening as he draws closer. The scent of him—citrusy and clean—washes over me and I part my lips, the protest dying when he reaches out and touches my cheek. His touch is gentle, his fingertips rough as they slide across my skin, into my hair.

My eyelids waver and my vision grows fuzzy when he presses his body to mine and dips his head, his mouth hovering above mine. His breath wafts over my lips and pleasure swamps me, settling between my legs, making me damp.

Making me weak.

Chapter Six

Caden

THE MOMENT WE ARRIVED AT THE PUB AND WHITNEY INTRO-
duced me to Violet and Ryder, Violet mentioned her sister would
be joining us later.

And I knew she wasn't referring to Lily.

It was still a shock, seeing Rose approach the table. I thought
her stunning the night of the movie premiere but seeing her now,
in her pretty little dress that exposes a lot of leg, her hair down
and her entire appearance so natural . . .

Seeing her in those first few stunned minutes, I felt . . . entranced. Intoxicated, and I hadn't even had a drink yet. She was
just so pretty, her skin damn near glowed. Everything about her
was perfection, at least in my eyes, and I physically yearned to
be close to her.

I should be focusing on my newfound opportunity to snag
the Poppy Necklace. Not thinking about how I can possibly kiss
her again. Seeing her, though, having her close enough to
touch . . . I forget all about the necklace. All I can think about is
her.

She hadn't expected to see me and my being at the table
threw her off, I could tell. She tried her best to ignore me. I think
she was mad that I came with Whitney, who acted like a possessive girlfriend. Made me wonder if Whitney could sense the

sparks flying between me and Rose and was doing her best to play interference.

That didn't stop me. Whitney started talking with Violet, and that freed me to watch Rose unabashedly. The way she laughed and joked with Ryder and his friend. I liked the sound of her laughter. Full-bodied and unrestrained. She drank at least three beers, maybe four, and she consumed the bloodiest steak I've seen in a long-ass time, like she was one of the guys.

It was sexy as fuck.

I couldn't take my eyes off her. And eventually, she couldn't take her eyes off me. I wanted her. Just like before, that night in Cannes with her naked and in the pool, her beautiful body on display just for me. I had my hands on her, my mouth on hers, and then I walked away.

Now, at this moment, in a small bathroom in a pub in the middle of Covent Garden on a Friday night, I'm not walking away. *Hell no.*

I cradle her head between my hands, my fingers buried in her silky, soft hair, my thumbs caressing her cheeks. Her eyelids are heavy, her lips damp and parted, and I want to kiss her as much as I want to take my next breath.

"Tell me you feel this," I demand, needing the confirmation before I go any further.

"Feel what?" She's playing dumb. Her breath quickens as I continue to touch her, and the shiver that steals over her skin is a sure sign she's just as affected as I am.

"This . . . connection between us." I touch the corner of her mouth. "I feel it." I earn an eye roll for my words but I'm not deterred. She's putting on an act.

"What about your girlfriend?" She meets my gaze steadily, those honey-gold eyes doing things to me. Like making my dick hard.

My girlfriend? Oh . . . Whitney. "She's not my girlfriend."

One perfectly arched brow lifts. "Does *she* know that?"

I smile. I like this girl. She has a smart mouth and it's sorta hot. "Probably not."

She releases her death grip on the counter and settles her hands on my chest, giving me a shove. But I don't budge and she doesn't like it. "That presents a problem."

"What does?" Christ, I wish she'd stop talking so I can kiss her. I want to know if she tastes as good as I remember.

"Your not-a-girlfriend girlfriend." She pushes at my chest again but I brace myself, which just frustrates her further. "You're taken."

"No, I'm not," I say truthfully. "It's not my fault she thinks we're a couple."

"You're staying with her, right? Here in London?"

I don't answer her. If I tell her the truth she'll reject me. Instead, I press my mouth to hers, silencing whatever argument she might have offered. She makes a strangled noise deep in her throat but I'm persistent, deepening the kiss, sliding my tongue between her lips and touching hers.

She tastes as good as I remember, maybe even better. And she feels amazing in my arms, all warm and soft curves, her breasts pressed snug against my chest. She's not wearing a bra and I can feel her hard nipples. I want to touch them. Lick them. Suck them.

I drift my hand down along her neck, across her collarbone, my fingers teasing along the neckline of her dress. She shivers beneath my touch, a little whimper falling from her lips when I tangle my tongue with hers at the same time I dip my hand beneath the bodice.

And encounter nothing but warm, plump skin.

"You shouldn't do this," she murmurs when I break the kiss to trail my lips along the length of her neck, my fingers going to the tiny buttons that run down the front of her bodice. I undo them one by one, exposing her, my gaze dropping as I spread the fabric wide and take in her perfect breasts topped with rosy nipples.

"Do what?" I ask as I rain kisses along the tops of her breasts. She puts her hands on either side of my head, her fingers going into my hair, much like I held her only a moment ago, but she's not pushing me away.

She's guiding me toward her nipple and I circle it with my tongue, draw it into my mouth and suck. Hard.

"Touch me like this. Kiss me like this," Rose says breathlessly as she tosses her head back, her eyes sliding closed as she moans. I smile against her skin as I move to her other nipple, giving it the same treatment.

"You want it," I tell her. Her skin is sweet and warm and she smells fucking amazing. I'm feeling her up in the middle of a bathroom and I don't really give a damn. I have to have her.

"I don't even know you," she whispers when I lift away from her breasts, her eyes hazy with lust as she watches me. "We need to get back out there."

I kiss her, my tongue teasing hers before I break away. "Not yet."

"They'll get suspicious."

"Who?" I keep my gaze on hers as I slip my hand from her breast and touch her thigh, slipping beneath the skirt of her dress.

"Your girlfriend."

I chuckle and shake my head. "I told you. She's not my girlfriend." My fingers rise farther, farther still, and I encounter nothing but bare skin. "Are you wearing panties?"

Rose slowly shakes her head, sinking her teeth into her plump lower lip.

"Consistent, aren't you," I murmur as I slip my hand to her trembling belly, sliding it lower until I'm cupping her between her legs. I can feel the heat emanating from her pussy and my cock stiffens, strangled beneath the fly of my jeans. "Spread your legs."

She does as I ask without hesitation, her thighs opening enough to let me in, and I run my fingers over her slit, back and forth, searching her folds. "You're fucking soaked."

Another whimper escapes her and she closes her eyes, tilting her head back, lost to the pleasure. "Look at me," I command and she lifts her head, meeting my gaze, hers full of anticipation and fear and arousal. "Feels good?"

Rose nods but otherwise doesn't say a word and for whatever reason, that pisses me off. I want her to be as into this as I am and I can't tell if she really is or not.

I stroke her, trace her folds, circle her clit, slip a finger inside her welcoming body, and she moans. Moans louder when I remove my fingers from her pussy and rest them against her mouth. "Open up."

Her eyes go wide and slowly she parts her lips, allowing me to slip my fingers inside her mouth. "Taste how much you want me," I whisper, smiling when I see the spark of anger in her gaze.

She probably thinks I'm an arrogant asshole. I don't really care. This is hot as fuck, making her taste herself, watching her squirm. She sucks my fingers into her mouth, all four of them, and I can only imagine her giving me a blow job.

"Get 'em nice and wet," I whisper, and she sucks harder before I pull them from her mouth and return them to her pussy, teasing her swollen clit. "Fuck, you feel amazing."

Her eyes close as if she has no control and she drops her head forward until her forehead meets my shoulder. I continue to stroke her, her panting breath, her low moans driving me on. I want to make her come. I want to *see* her come.

And then I want to send her back out to that table full of oblivious people and follow after her about five minutes later. I want to sit across from her for the rest of the night and pretend she doesn't exist, all the while knowing I just made her come all over my fingers in the bathroom.

"I've been wanting to do this to you since the last time I saw you," I whisper close to her ear just before I nibble on the lobe. My fingers never leave her pussy. I'm working her into a frenzy, my hand busy beneath her skirt, her legs still spread, her mouth falling open.

"Oh God," she chokes out, her entire body going still.

So does my hand.

Her eyes pop open and she stares at me, her expression full of agony. Full of pleasure. "Please," she whispers, and I know exactly what she wants.

But I want to hear her say it.

"Please what?" I ask innocently.

"Don't—don't stop."

Slowly, I slide my middle finger through her folds, flicking it against her clit. "Don't stop what?"

Surprisingly enough she laughs. "You know what."

"Are you saying you want to come?"

She nibbles on her lower lip again—does she know how sexy that is?—before she answers with a soft, "Yes."

I kiss her cheek. Cup her face with my other hand and turn her so I can drink from her lips. "Ask for it," I say against that tasty, plump mouth.

"What?" Her voice falters. I don't know what's possessed me, but I love talking to her like this. Treating her like this.

"I want to hear you say the words, Rose." My hand goes still once more and the whimper of frustration that falls from her lips sends a surge of satisfaction rolling through my veins.

I'm a sick fuck tonight. I don't usually do this sort of thing, but there is something very dirty about getting Rose Fowler off with my fingers in a public restroom, demanding that she tell me exactly what she wants from me.

"I want to come," she says, her voice strong, her gaze still on mine. "Please, Caden."

It's the way she says my name. It's the use of the word *please*. Would she ever beg for her pleasure? I'd love to hear her. I'd love to see her down on her knees, my cock in her mouth, her tongue teasing, her fingers stroking . . .

Fuck. I can't let myself get distracted. That'll have to happen another time.

Without a word I increase my pace, sliding my fingers inside her body, my thumb pressing against her clit. She never looks away from me, not once, as her breathing increases, her mouth works as if she wants to say something, and again her body goes rigid.

But I don't still my hand this time. I keep moving, keep fucking her with my fingers, keep teasing her clit with my thumb, and then her entire body is quaking, a gush of wetness bathes my fingers as her shaky moan lets me know without a doubt I just made her come. Her gaze is still on mine and I can't look away, I can't say a thing. I can only watch as she falls apart and then just as quickly pulls herself back together.

She licks her lips as I remove my hand from between her legs, her fingers working on the front of her dress, doing up the buttons. I step away, running my hand over my hair as she straightens her dress, then combs her fingers through her hair as she turns toward the bathroom mirror.

I just stand there like a dumbass, watching her. My cock strains against the front of my jeans and my fingers are wet. I rub them together, bring my hand up to my face, and take a sniff. They smell like her pussy and still I can't move. *Go to her, what the fuck?*

"Did you just smell your fingers?" she asks incredulously.

I don't answer her. Just continue to stare as she washes her hands and shakes them in the sink before she runs her damp fingers through her hair one more time. Then she grabs a hand towel and dries them off. A boring little ritual I'm oddly fascinated with. Finally she turns and looks at me, a pleasant smile on her face. Like we're old chums versus newfound lovers who just messed around in a bathroom like sex-crazed lunatics.

"Um, thanks. That was . . . interesting," she says as she starts to walk past me.

I'm not about to let her get away that easily. Reaching out, I grab hold of her arm, stopping her. "Interesting?"

"And satisfying," she adds, that smile still on her face.

"I'm sure," I say dryly, earning another laugh from her, surprising me. She's treating this encounter so casually. I should like it. Prefer it. Most women would freak out or expect more. Not this one.

And I'm oddly disappointed.

"I need to get back out there before Violet starts looking for me." Without another word, a glance, a thank-you, nothing from her, she walks away, head held high, a hum emanating from her as she unlocks and throws open the women's bathroom door, exiting the room.

Shit, fuck. I need to get the hell out of here before someone else finds me. I dash out of the women's bathroom and go into the men's, thankful I'm alone. The reflection in the mirror reveals the same old me, but I feel different. Stupid, I know, but I can't help it. I am not the same man I was before that encounter with Rose. I appear calm on the outside but inside, I'm rattled. Thrown. Turned on.

Jesus.

Turning on the faucet, I splash cold water on my face, hoping it'll slap me back into reality, but it doesn't. My head feels like it's in a fog.

A Rose Fowler–induced fog.

I wash my hands, fighting the bitter disappointment of replacing the scent of Rose's pussy with the sterile disinfectant smell of the liquid soap. I dry them and take a deep breath, counting to ten before I exit the bathroom, making my way back to the table. Rose is sitting there between Violet and Whitney, her cheeks still rosy, her hair tucked behind her ears, showing off that beautiful face. She doesn't so much as look at me when I sit in my chair on the other side of Whitney. I grab my beer and polish it off with one swallow.

"Want another one, mate?" asks Ryder's friend . . . Nigel. *Right.* Nigel.

"That would be great, yeah." I reach for my back pocket, ready to pull out my wallet, but Nigel waves me off.

"I'll get this round. I'm out anyway." He holds up his empty glass before he slides off the chair and heads toward the bar.

"Where were you?"

I turn to find Whitney studying me with a suspicious gleam in her eyes, her tone accusatory.

"Bathroom. Then I had a phone call I had to take."

"Who was it?"

Since when is it her business to ask me questions like that? "No one you know." I am a consummate liar. It's so easy to slip into my lies, they feel like a second skin.

"Hmm." She doesn't look like she believes me. Like I give a shit. "Rose was gone too."

Unease creeps down my spine. "So?"

"So you were *both* gone. For a long time. And her dress is buttoned up wrong. It wasn't before."

Fuck. I feel everything inside of me wilt at Whitney's words. As discreetly as possible I check out Rose, my gaze falling to her chest. Yes, the buttons are done up wrong, and I feel like a shit that I didn't catch that before she escaped the bathroom.

"Are you accusing me of something?" I ask Whitney, my voice mean. I'm irritated that she's calling me out.

"I don't know. Did you *do* something?" she returns.

"Just say what you want to say, Whit." I sound weary. I *feel* weary. "Let's get this over with."

She parts her perfectly glossed lips, swinging her hair back in a calculated move I've seen her perform before. The girl is gorgeous and she knows it, but she's also a world-class pain in the ass and has driven every guy who's been remotely interested in her far away with her needy, bitchy attitude.

I'm a shit. I put up with her, give her what she wants in bed, and then move on. What she sees in me, I have no idea. I don't deserve her kindness. I don't deserve *anyone's* kindness.

"Whitney." Violet rests her hand on Whitney's arm, startling her. "Tell my sister about the time you slapped that guy across the face at a party. I was trying to tell her about it, but I just can't do the story justice like you can."

Whitney's eyes narrow as she contemplates me, her expression tight. She doesn't have to say a word but I know she's thinking, *You just got off easy.* She turns to look at Violet, her smile back in place, her voice light and with the slightest hint of a drawl. "Violet, darling, there have been *two* face-slapping incidents. Which one are you talking about?"

Violet tilts her head, her gaze traveling to mine for the briefest moment, sending me a knowing look. "Tell us about both of them," she says encouragingly, sending me a wink before she returns her attention to Whitney.

I sit there quietly, shock washing over me as I wait for Nigel to return with my fresh beer. Contemplating what just happened because *holy hell,* that was unexpected.

As crazy as it sounds, I think I was just saved from a nasty confrontation by Violet. Meaning somehow, some way, Rose told her sister what happened between us.

Un-fucking-believable.

Chapter Seven

Rose

"YOU HAVE SOME SERIOUS EXPLAINING TO DO." VIOLET SENDS me a pointed look just before she picks up her coffee cup and sips from it.

We're at a crowded little bakery not too far from my hotel, eating decadent pastries and drinking deliciously bitter coffee while sitting at a tiny table right next to the window that faces the street. The sidewalks are crowded with Saturday shoppers, all of them bright-eyed and dressed to perfection.

All while my hair is still damp from the quick shower I took before I came here. I'm wearing skinny jeans and a boring plain blue T-shirt I threw on as I dressed in a hurry in order to meet Violet on time. I have no makeup on, a cardinal sin according to our grandma, but I don't really care.

I awoke earlier this morning from a crazy sex dream involving me, Caden, and a swimming pool to an endless stream of texts from Violet, basically demanding that I meet her here at the bakery at ten, no trying to get out of it. I replied that I would meet her only if she wouldn't badger me with questions until I'd had my first cup of coffee.

More like my first sip. The cup barely touched my lips before she said something, asking for an explanation.

But how can I explain what happened yesterday when I barely understand it myself?

"I already told you what happened." Briefly. Sort of. Last night she saw how rumpled I appeared when I returned from the bathroom, the buttons done up wrong on my dress—*God,* could I be any more foolish?—and immediately she was suspicious. I'd already told her I knew Caden, so she suspected it had something to do with him.

And she would be right.

"You told me what? That you know Whitney's boyfriend? That you disappear for a solid fifteen minutes only to return looking a little, *hmm* . . . how should I put it—disheveled? That's the polite term, at least." She takes a bite out of the gooey fruit tart she ordered, little bits of powdered sugar sticking to her lips.

I may as well tell her and get this over with. "He's the one who walked away from me," I admit, my voice low, my appetite waning despite the outrageously delicious chocolate éclair I've nibbled on. Can't remember the last time I indulged in something so sinful.

Maybe last night? When you let a handsome stranger finger you to orgasm in a bathroom?

My cheeks bloom with heat just thinking about it.

"Wait a minute." Violet licks the sugar from her lips and leans in closer. "Caden is the guy who ditched you in Cannes? When you were naked in the pool?"

Could she broadcast that any louder? "Yes. He is." Deciding to hell with it, I grab the éclair from my plate and bite into it with relish, the combination of the cream filling, the flaky pastry, and the chocolate frosting like a little explosion of heaven in my mouth.

Still not as good as that orgasm I had last night, though.

"Rose. You're messing around with a taken man."

I make a face. She makes it sound so sordid. "I am not."

"You are. He's Whitney's boyfriend," Violet stresses, looking appalled. As if she has any room to talk, torn between two men like she was not too long ago.

"No, he's not her boyfriend. At least, he *said* he's not." Doubt clouds my brain and I take another drink of coffee, feeling everything within me perking up from the jolt of caffeine. But along with the jolt comes reality.

What if Whitney really is his girlfriend? I'd feel like a home wrecker. I'd *be* a home wrecker. And that sucks.

"And when did he tell you this? When the two of you snuck off and did . . . whatever?" Violet arches a brow.

Busted. "Fine. I went to the bathroom. He followed me. End of story." I take another bite before I tell her everything. I'm so tempted to spill my guts, but some things are better left unsaid.

"He followed you into the bathroom at the White Swan." She shakes her head, a sly smile forming. "You are so bad, Rose. Whitney's my friend."

"And Caden isn't her boyfriend," I say again.

"According to Caden. Whitney might have a different perspective," Violet points out.

I say nothing. Just continue to munch on my éclair as if I don't have a care in the world.

Funny thing is, I don't feel bad about what happened. I believed Caden when he said Whitney wasn't his girlfriend. Maybe that's me being a naïve fool, but they just didn't give off that proper boyfriend/girlfriend vibe. Plus, the sparks between us were just too abundant to ignore.

I left the table on purpose. To see if he'd follow, and he did. I took that as a sign. That something was meant to happen between us. Silly, I suppose, but I was also buzzed after drinking three beers in quick succession. A girl's allowed to do stupid stuff every once in a while. That was my one stupid move.

I should probably leave it at that.

"Was he as shocked to see you as you were to see him?" Violet presses.

"I don't know. We didn't talk much." First there had been too much kissing, and then he said all of those deliciously dirty things . . . I still can't believe some of the things he said and did.

I want to experience them again.

No. No, you really don't.

"*Ha.* You didn't talk much." Violet shakes her head. "This is just so scandalous. You go from being a hermit hiding in your hotel room to getting it on in a pub bathroom. Talk about a complete turnaround."

"Violet. Please." I glance around the bakery, but no one is paying us any mind. It's a late Saturday morning and the place is busy, but everyone is too wrapped up in their own little worlds to hear my sister broadcast that I fooled around in a restaurant bathroom. "So . . . do you know anything about him?" I'm trying to play this cool, but it's probably a waste of time. Besides, I'm talking to Violet and she won't judge. Not too harshly, at least.

"About who? Caden?"

I roll my eyes. "Yes. Caden." I know nothing beyond that he's gorgeous, he has a voice that can melt me with a few whispered words, he can kiss like no other, and he knows his way around a woman's body.

Meaning, I'd love to see him again.

"Not really. I talked about him some with Whitney. You know what's weird? She's never mentioned him to me before."

"What do you mean?" I frown.

"I mean, she never even uttered his name until I met him last night," Violet explains.

"Really?" I'm eager for any bit of gossip I can discover about Caden. "If they were serious, she'd surely mention him to you, right? Aren't you two pretty good friends?"

"Yes. We've become close since Ryder and I came to London." Violet nods, takes a thoughtful sip of her coffee. "She said a few things about him right before you took off to the bathroom."

"Like what?" I finish off the éclair because *hello*, it's amazing. I'll just skip lunch. Maybe dinner, too. I don't know. This isn't a smart move, meeting my sister at a bakery full of pastries. Now I'm tempted to buy a box of those gorgeous, colorful, and delicate *macarons* that are so popular and take them back to the hotel room so I can snack on them later.

"That they're old friends, they'd known each other forever, went to school together in the States." Violet smiles. "Listen to me—I sound like I plan on living here forever."

"You'd better not," I mutter, determined to get the conversation back to Caden. "Isn't Whitney from New York?"

"Yes, and so is Caden."

"What's his last name?" A little Google could go a long way if I had more concrete facts.

"I don't know. She never mentioned it." Violet tilts her head. "Tell me what happened in that bathroom last night."

"You do *not* want to know." She doesn't. I don't want any major details about her sex life and I know she feels the same. "Let's just say it was an enlightening experience."

"And you'd like to see him again." Violet smirks.

I shrug. "Maybe. I don't know." Yes, I would. But I don't want to sound too eager.

"I'm going to call Whitney later, try and drill her for information," Violet starts, but I shake my head, cutting her off.

"Don't do that. Please. I don't want it to be too obvious. I think . . . I know she suspected something last night."

"Of course she did. That's why I interrupted her little conversation with Caden. I didn't want it to erupt into some sort of drunken argument. Because she was definitely drunk, though I don't know about Caden."

He'd seemed relatively sober, but my perception could have

been off. "Yeah, well, you probably shouldn't go digging for information and get her suspicions up."

"Do you have no faith in me? I know how to dig without being obvious." Violet laughs, but I don't.

Maybe I don't want her to find out anything else. I sort of like how mysterious Caden is. I know nothing beyond his first name, the taste of his lips, and the wonderful things he can do to me with his fingers.

And I'm thinking maybe that's plenty enough.

VIOLET AND I PART AFTER OUR LITTLE DISCUSSION AT THE BAK-ery. She has to go meet Ryder for whatever reason and I don't want to go back to my boring hotel room on such a beautiful Saturday, so I decide to wander through the shops, trying to take my mind off what happened last night.

Shopping doesn't help, though. I come upon a gorgeous little lingerie shop, and every sexy little bit of lace and silk I admire makes me wonder if Caden would like it. I don't need any new lingerie, but that doesn't stop me from buying a handful of lace thong panties, all in a variety of bright, fun colors, though I also get a basic black pair. They're thin enough that a man with strong hands could probably tear them right off my body.

Clearly my imagination is running rampant today.

Plus, every tall man with light brown hair I see I immediately think is Caden. Stupid, really, but I can't help it. He plays heavily on my mind, and I keep reliving that moment when he followed me last night. When I glanced in the mirror and saw him stand-ing there, his expression thunderous, his gaze dark and unwav-ering. How we never said much beyond a few words before he pulled me into his arms and kissed me senseless, then stroked me into oblivion.

Does he think I'm easy? Is the conquest completed and he's

ready to move on? What does he do? Who is he exactly, and why was he in Cannes? *God,* was he there with Whitney and after our weird little encounter, ran off to return to her?

No. Of course not. If Whitney had been there, Violet would have seen her and mentioned it.

But what if he has another girlfriend? Maybe he has a woman in every city. Maybe he's a world-traveling trust fund baby who has time to kill and plenty of money to spend. I could do the same if I wanted. In fact, I'm doing exactly that right now, pretending to work at Fleur while I hide out. From what, I'm not sure.

My boring life? My responsibilities? Myself?

Or all of the above?

I'm so lost in thought that I plow right into a solid someone while I'm walking down the street, offering a quick apology as I'm about to dart out of his way when I feel strong hands grip my shoulders and a sizzling awareness heats my veins.

Only one person has been able to make my body react like that.

Glancing up, I'm staring into his face. Caden's. "Are you stalking me?" I ask incredulously.

He offers me a lopsided smile and slowly shakes his head, his hair falling into his eyes. He looks young. Boyish. That doesn't distract from his sex appeal, though. "I'd hoped to run into you, but not quite so literally."

"So you *are* stalking me." I take a step back, sad yet relieved when his hands fall away from my shoulders. I can't think when he touches me. I might do something stupid.

"Sort of." He shrugs in this completely unassuming way and I'm charmed. "Nigel mentioned you were staying at a hotel not too far from the Swan."

"And you thought you'd come back out here on a Saturday afternoon and hope to find me?"

"Rather ambitious, right?" He steps out of the way of shoppers trying to pass by and I do the same, the both of us leaning against a brick building that houses a hair salon. He looks good in faded jeans and a black T-shirt, much how he looked last night, only this time there's more stubble on his face, though his hair is somewhat tamed.

I immediately imagine him rubbing those stubble-covered cheeks against my inner thighs and just like that, I'm wet.

"I've always appreciated an ambitious man," I tell him, folding my arms in front of me, trying to keep my distance.

"Whatcha got there?" He lifts his chin, indicating the tiny shopping bag dangling from my fingers.

"Oh, this?" I glance down at the bag advertising the name of the shop. "Nothing much." Quite literally.

"I'm sure," he drawls, his expression knowing. "So tell me . . . bra or panties?"

Did he see me enter the lingerie shop? How does he know about it? I've never heard of the store before and it's not a chain. Maybe he's bought Whitney stuff from there.

Ew.

"Like it's any of your business." Dropping my arms, I turn away from him, intent on returning to the hotel so I can hide out. It was a mistake, shopping. It was probably more of a mistake to fool around with Caden last night. I know nothing about him. He has a girlfriend. He's probably a loser. A sexy-as-hell, gorgeous loser, but a loser nonetheless.

"Hey, hey, why the attitude?" He grabs hold of the crook of my elbow, stopping my escape. I glare at him from over my shoulder and the confusion written all over his face doesn't offer any satisfaction. It just makes me feel bad. "What did I do?"

"You found me, that's what you did." I jerk out of his hold. "Go buy lingerie for your girlfriend." I turn and he lets me leave. I'm fighting the disappointment that's trying to take hold when

I realize he's walking right beside me. What's wrong with me? Do I want to shake him or do I want to keep this going? He confuses me completely. I don't like it.

I stop and so does he. "Go away," I murmur, keeping my head averted so I don't have to look at him.

"She's not my girlfriend," he says for what feels like the fiftieth time. "I already told you that."

Finally I look at him. "You're staying with her," I point out.

"Doesn't mean that we're together."

"Are you sleeping with her?"

"We sleep in her flat, yes."

I roll my eyes, irritated that we're talking in circles. "Are you fucking her?"

He cocks his head, contemplating me as a ghost of a smile plays at the corners of his too sexy lips. "I've fucked her before."

This time I can't fight the disappointment. It settles over me heavily, making my shoulders slump. "Then this," I wave my hand between us, "can't happen again." I start walking and damn it, so does he, keeping pace, which means he probably has to slow down because his legs are infinitely long and mine are not.

"Who says it can't happen again?" he asks.

Do I need to break into a full run to get away from this guy? "I do." I thrust my thumb at my chest. "I don't care if you say you're not with Whitney. If you're casually banging her, then I'm not going to casually bang you."

He bursts out laughing, the asshole. Sexy, insufferable asshole. "What if I told you the last time I casually banged Whitney was months ago? Maybe closer to a year ago?"

He's tempting me just by saying that. And I shouldn't be tempted. I should walk away from this man and remember my two interactions with him fondly. A girl is allowed to indulge. To make mistakes and do careless things, all in the name of stupid youth. That's all Caden is to me. A careless mistake. A naughty indulgence.

"I'd say you're probably lying, thinking you can get in my panties," I throw back at him. I'm just saying this out of spite, feeling defensive. I have no idea if he really is lying or not.

"You don't usually wear panties," he drawls, and I want to punch him.

Or kiss him. Take your pick.

Caden moves closer, the heat of his body emanating toward me, drawing me in. I take a step forward, as if I have no control over my feet, and he grabs my shopping bag, snatching it right from my fingers. He opens it, pushing aside the tissue to examine the contents nestled within. "Looks like I can get in your panties right now, hmm?" He reaches into the bag and pulls out a handful of colorful lace.

I pluck a few scraps of lace from his grip, my cheeks hot with embarrassment. "Put those back," I hiss when he lifts the bag high above my head right as I reach for it.

"Are you embarrassed, Rose? After everything we've shared?" He shakes his head, then glances down at the small pile of lace in his palm. "I thought you weren't a big believer in panties. You weren't last night."

I hate him. Making fun of me, throwing my underwear around on a public street. *God,* it's so embarrassing. "Give them back." I hold out my empty hand, clutching the rest of my new panties in my other hand behind my back.

"Say please." He smirks. I usually hate when guys smirk at me but for whatever awful reason, this guy looks particularly hot while smirking.

"No." I scowl.

"Then you won't get your new panties."

We stare at each other for a long, heat-filled moment. People are still passing us by. We're on the sidewalk, for God's sake, and fighting over my new underwear. This is the stupidest thing ever. I don't need to deal with this crap.

"Fine," I finally say. "Keep them as a memento." I turn and walk away, one last time.

And this time, he doesn't follow me.

Chapter Eight

Caden

I FOLLOWED HER, THOUGH SHE DIDN'T SEE ME. FEISTY LITTLE thing, calling me out on my shit. No one ever does that. I get away with everything. Hell, I'm a criminal. I steal jewelry for a living and I've yet to be caught. I'm either extremely lucky or extremely good.

I'm going with the former mixed with a hint of the latter.

It's easy to believe the lies I tell myself. I staked her out because I want another chance at that necklace. That's why I'm here. That's why I found her, why I'm following her.

But deep down inside, I know that's not the truth. I'm here because I wanted to see her again. Talk to her. Touch her. Kiss her . . .

It feels like a battle of wills every time I interact with Rose and I like that. She feels like a challenge. And there is nothing that I appreciate more than a challenge. No woman has ever truly interested me because they always feel so damn easy.

But not Rose. She gives off mixed signals. I know she's attracted to me. Last night I'd barely touched her, kissed her, and the minute I had my fingers between her thighs, she was drenched. That had been hot.

Everything about her is hot, even when she's mad. And I definitely make her mad. I almost enjoy it.

Fine. I do enjoy it. Around her I feel like a twelve-year-old antagonizing the girl he has a wild crush on. I've turned into a stupid twelve-year-old giving the girl he likes endless grief. I lose all my cool when I'm around her.

The moment she walked away—again—I let her go. But I never let her out of my sight. I kept my distance as I followed her, tracking her every movement, and she stopped at a lot of the shops, wandering in for a few minutes before she came back out empty-handed. She'd stashed the remaining new panties in her tiny purse, and every once in a while I'd see a flash of turquoise lace peek out of the top of the black leather. Or neon pink lace.

Looks like Rose has a fondness for bright colors.

I tell myself I'm still following her so I can get to the necklace. The fucking necklace I can't forget about, though the woman who wore it looms in my mind much more than the stupid necklace. That's what I should be focusing on. That's what I tell myself.

But I want the woman too. I want the woman *more*.

After almost an hour of aimless wandering, she finally makes her way to a hotel. She's staying at the Covent Garden Hotel, how original. If I'd had a single cell in my brain, I would have gone there first and just waited for her. Nigel had mentioned casually last night that Rose was staying at a hotel near the pub.

Increasing my pace, I catch up with her without being too obvious, not wanting her to notice me yet. She strides across the street, looking this way and that, and I follow after her once she enters the lobby, eager to reach her before she ends up in the elevator and I can't find her.

I'm intent on getting into her room. She wants me. I want her. This is an easy second chance to snag that necklace. Why are we playing these games anyway?

You're more to blame than she is.

Yeah. No shit.

I enter the lobby of the Covent Garden Hotel and see her

standing at the registration desk, talking with two male employees. They've got dopey smiles on their faces, nodding and "yes, miss-ing" her over every single thing she's saying.

Suckers. She's got them wrapped around her finger, just like that.

It almost infuriates me, because I feel just as suckered as they are.

"Thank you for your help," she murmurs just as I come up behind her. She turns, stopping short when she finds me standing in front of her, and that cute scowl is back. Her eyes narrow and her mouth forms into a little sneer. "Not you again."

"I wanted to return these to you," I say solemnly as I thrust the bag toward her, the lingerie store's name blatant on the side. The hotel employees are doing their best to act uninterested, but they're watching us. I can feel their gazes, sense their curiosity.

The scowl vanishes and is now replaced with faint embarrassment. "Um, thanks," she says, her voice soft as she takes the bag from me. Our fingers brush, and the heat that shoots through me at her touch makes my knees fucking weak. It's not just electric. It's magnetic. Like we're drawn to each other despite everything else. We can't fight it.

I don't *want* to fight it.

Rose feels it too. I can tell by the way her eyelids waver, the little shuddery breath that escapes her. She's affected by me.

Good. She affects me, too. I'm tired of wasting time.

"Hey, you want to—" Before I can come up with something to say she's cutting me off, interrupting me as if she knows what I'm asking her.

"That would be great. Just—let me drop this off in my room first." She lifts the bag and then starts walking, leaving me no choice but to follow after her.

She doesn't protest. Doesn't say a thing, doesn't send me a look as she stops at the elevator doors and hits the up button. "You really want me to come with you?" I ask, my voice low.

Rose nods, still not looking my way. "Please."

Triumph surges through me when the elevator doors slide open and I follow her inside, waiting until those doors slide shut. I turn and grab hold of her by the waist, the shopping bag falling to the floor as she wraps her arms around my neck and tilts her head back, ready for my kiss.

But I don't give it to her. Not yet.

Instead I touch her face, skim my fingers down her cheek, along her jaw. Her eyelids flutter and she exhales shakily. "You followed me," she whispers. "Again."

"I did." There's no point in denying it. "I can't stay away from you."

"My own personal stalker."

"I wouldn't call what I'm doing stalking." I touch her lips, the soft plumpness sending a surge of heat straight to my cock. I want those lips wrapped tight around my dick. Whitney offered me a blow job last night when we came home from the pub, but I turned her down. After walking away from Rose with aching blue balls, I still didn't want one. At least, I didn't want one from Whit.

The only person who could have given me satisfaction is this woman right here, in my arms.

"What would you call it, then?" she asks. I'm tracing her perfectly shaped mouth, my finger getting caught between her lips, and I can feel the damp heat of her tongue.

Fuck.

"Hot pursuit." I slide my finger deeper into her mouth and she accepts it, circling it with her tongue. "Show me what you can do." My voice drops about ten octaves with my request.

She furrows her eyebrows and pulls my finger out of her mouth. "Show you what I can do with what?"

"Pretend it's my cock in your mouth," I whisper. "Show me what you would do."

Her eyes darken, honey gold and electrifying as she grabs

hold of my wrist and draws my entire finger into her mouth, right to the base. She holds it there, her gaze never leaving mine, her tongue sliding over my skin, her entire mouth sucking and then she's withdrawing, dragging her tongue along the side of my finger before she gets to the tip and sucks just that part back into her mouth.

"Jesus," I mutter, my skin tight and hot, my cock straining. She smiles and I trace that pretty smile with my damp finger, her hand dropping away from my wrist at the exact time the elevator comes to a stop and the doors slide open.

"Come on," she says, and I grab the bag from the floor before I follow after her, my blood pumping, my head spinning. Everything inside of me is a jangling, out-of-control mess, clamoring to get at her and strip her clothes off, feast on her naked flesh, sink deep inside her hot, wet body and lose myself. Forget about the world.

At least for a little while before I get back to business and grab that damn necklace.

Rose tries to open the door with shaky fingers, shoving the key card in again and again, but the light flashes yellow every time, making her curse. I gently push her out of the way and pull the key out of the slot, then shove it back in slowly.

The light turns green.

"Slow and easy, baby." Flashing her a triumphant smile, I open the door and take her hand, pulling her inside. The bag goes flying onto a nearby table, the key card dropped onto the floor as I grab hold of Rose by her slender waist and pull her in to me, our chests meeting, legs tangling. We eye each other, breaths mingling, hearts thumping in time. Adrenaline pours through me as I cup her face with one hand and take her lips with mine.

I consume her and she consumes me right back, our mouths wide, our tongues dancing. She slides her leg up, close to my hip, and it's like she's trying to climb me. I break the kiss first and she nips at my chin, the sting of her sharp teeth making me wince.

"Careful," I murmur.

She smiles, nuzzling my cheek with hers. "I want you."

"Then get on your knees," I command, dying to see how fast she'll agree, but preparing for a fight.

Surprisingly enough, she doesn't fight. She falls to her knees without hesitation. Her hands go to the waistband of my jeans to undo the snap before she tugs down the zipper, spreading the fly open to reveal my black boxer briefs. My cock strains against the thin cotton and she smiles, drawing her index finger along the length of my dick, making it twitch.

"I owe you, don't I?" she asks as she tilts her head back, the sultry expression on her pretty face just about doing me in.

What is it about this woman? I should be casing her room for jewelry. Normally I would be. That damn Poppy Necklace is here. I can feel it. At the very least, I should be searching for it. Fuck her hard, wait till she falls asleep, and then go on the hunt.

But that's the last thing I want to do. Oh, I definitely plan on fucking her hard. Again and again, until the both of us fall asleep. I feel anything but normal in the presence of Rose Fowler.

And that should scare the ever-loving fuck out of me.

She's also talking about owing me and she's the last person to be in debt to me. No one is in debt to me. More like *I'm* in debt to everyone else.

"You owe me for what?" I hold my breath as her fingers curl around the band of my underwear, her fingertips brushing against my stomach, making the muscles there flinch.

Her lips curve. "For last night."

Not that I'm keeping count of orgasms or anything, but hey. I'm not about to refuse a blow job. "Take your clothes off first."

She releases her hold on my underwear and I feel the loss of her touch like a physical blow. "You want me naked?"

Always. Like she has to ask? I'd keep her locked up and naked in this hotel room for days if she'd let me. "Definitely."

Standing, she tugs her shirt off, then undoes the clasp on her bra before she whips that off too. One shove and her jeans and panties are sliding down her legs, until finally she's standing before me with that perfect little body, completely bare.

"Your turn," she says, her voice raspy as she carefully settles back onto her knees, resuming the position like a good little girl. Her eyes are trained on me as I pull off my shirt, then shove my underwear and jeans down my legs until I'm kicking them off along with my shoes. Until I'm just as naked as she is, on display and . . . feeling oddly vulnerable.

She stares at my cock, her eyes wide, her lips parted. Reaching out, she draws her index finger down the length, along my balls, making me shiver. I'm hard as a rock, my cock arcing toward my stomach and already leaking pre-come. I'm dying to feel her mouth on me, her hands . . .

And then she's there, her mouth on my skin. Soft and warm and damp, her lips blazing a trail from my hip to my stomach, her fingers going around the base of my erection, gripping me firmly. My breath stalls in my throat as I watch her, her long hair falling around her face, tickling my cock, hiding all the good action from view.

Since I'm only a man, I reach out and brush her hair away from her face, tucking it behind her ear so I can watch. Rose sends me a knowing smile before she darts out her tongue and traces just the head of my cock, circling it, flicking at the flared ridge.

Driving me out of my fucking mind.

She's putting on a show just for me and I'm her captive audience. I can't tear my gaze away as she strokes and licks, alternating between the two, teasing me with those glossy pink lips and that talented long tongue. Until finally, finally she purses her perfect lips at the tip, drawing my cock into her mouth deep. Deeper. She closes her eyes and relaxes her throat, taking me just about as far as I can get, and the guttural groan that rips from inside me expresses my pleasure at what she's doing more than anything else I could say or do.

Holy hell, her mouth is like magic. I brace myself, tensing my muscles so I don't collapse as I slowly start to move my hips, adjusting my grip on her hair so I'm holding it like a ponytail away from her face. She bobs on my cock, up and down, in and out of the warm cavern of her mouth, and when she lifts her honeyed gaze to mine, I'm fucking lost.

The orgasm barrels down upon me like a damn freight train. Like every cliché you've ever heard describing an orgasm, that's what I'm feeling. The wave. The warmth, the tingling at my spine, the heat in my balls, the tightening of my sac. I've got it all going on and then some and I fuck her mouth, thrusting hard and deep, the vibrations of her moan making my entire body shiver and shake.

"I'm gonna come," I tell her through gritted teeth, wanting to give her the warning in plenty of time, in case she wants to pull away. Girls don't usually want to swallow. I get it. I've never particularly gotten off on it, either. I'm more of a visual type, so I prefer . . .

I tear my cock out of her mouth, a reluctant gesture that has her pouting at me. "I wanted to swallow," she says, and a fresh wave of arousal takes over me at her words.

This girl is a constant surprise. She goes against every stereotype I've projected upon her and I love it.

"I want to see it," I tell her as I wrap my fingers around my cock and start to stroke. She watches in fascination as I increase my pace, my blood rushing, my ears roaring. "Part your lips, baby."

She does as I say and I lean toward her, my cock practically touching her mouth. That's all it takes. With an agonized groan I'm coming, spurting semen onto her lips, little drops of white even hitting her tongue.

It's the hottest thing I think I've ever witnessed.

Rose remains in place until the very last drop is squeezed out of my dick and I slump against the wall, panting for breath like I've run fifty miles, my skin covered in sweat, my eyes closing for only a brief moment because I don't want to miss a thing. Even after that major orgasm, my cock is still semi-hard and I know it won't be a problem getting it up so I can actually fuck her.

And I definitely plan on fucking her.

Opening my eyes, I watch in disbelief as Rose licks and then smacks her lips together, like she just indulged in the tastiest treat ever. She glances down, sees the splatter of come on her tits, and wipes it away with her fingertips just before she sinks them into her mouth.

"Jesus," I mutter, making her laugh.

"Are we even, then?" she asks huskily after she removes her fingers from her swollen mouth.

"I didn't realize this was a contest." I watch as she gets to her feet and walks away, heading toward the bathroom. The sway of her hips, that beautiful ass—I can't stop staring. She doesn't shut the bathroom door, just yanks a tissue out of the box near the sink and dabs at her chest, cleaning up the mess I made.

The possessive surge that moves through me is foreign. I don't think of women as mine. I definitely don't take pride in marking them with my come like some sort of rutting animal. So what the hell?

"It isn't a contest." She exits the bathroom, coming to stand before me, gorgeous in her nude state. Her breasts sway when she walks, the nipples hard and this delicious rosy pink that makes my mouth water. She's not shy, not hiding or worried about imperfections or weight or whatever else women tend to freak out over. Her confidence is sexy.

"Then why did you ask if we're even?"

"Because I never want to owe you a thing, Caden." She brings herself closer to me, my erect cock rising between us as she rests her hands on my shoulders. "We need to be equals in this . . . whatever it is we're doing." She runs her hands down my chest, her gentle touch sending a wave of gooseflesh over my skin, and the shudder that escapes me can't be contained.

I couldn't agree more with what she says. Reaching out, I thread my fingers in her hair, give it a tug, and pull her in. "You need a definition?" It's best we don't. I've never defined any of my so-called relationships. It's easier that way.

Easier for me to walk away. And I'm going to walk away from Rose. I have to.

She slowly shakes her head, my grip on her hair not lessening, the intensity of her stare not lessening, either. Our breaths are rapid; my heart beats wildly and I'm guessing hers does too. "I don't like you," she murmurs. "You drive me crazy."

The chuckle that escapes can't be helped. I've never been told by a woman that she doesn't like me while we're standing together naked, so this is a first. "You drive me crazy, too," I answer, not bothering to confirm whether I like her or not.

Does that really matter? We're naked together. She just sucked my dick into her mouth and made me come. I'm about to fuck her until she comes her brains out. Do I really care if she likes me? Or if I like her?

Heartless motherfucker, yes, you do actually like her. And you want her to like you, too.

I also want her. I'm drawn to her despite myself. Falling for a woman like Rose would be a huge mistake. I could put everything at risk.

Everything.

She's the type of woman who would want to know my secrets and will dig and dig until I finally give.

And I'm not about to give. Some things are better left undiscovered. The wall I've erected around myself can't be torn down. The thing with a secret is that it becomes a secret no longer when someone else knows. There are very few people who know what I do—and most of them are participating in illegal activity too, so I don't worry about any of them ratting me out.

"Then why are we doing this?" She sounds genuinely perplexed. Confused.

She sounds exactly how I feel.

"Maybe because we can't resist each other?" I kiss her, my lips whisper-soft, pleased at the little sigh that escapes her. She likes a gentle touch. I could be down with that. The mere idea of spreading her out on that big bed in the middle of this hotel room and touching Rose for hours tempts me beyond anything else.

Well, once I finally get inside that tight little body. After that, I'll be game for anything.

Everything.

Chapter Nine

Rose

CADEN'S RIGHT, DAMN HIM. I CAN'T RESIST HIM. I DON'T *WANT* to resist him. He drives me crazy and I don't like talking to him much because he challenges me. Makes me want to open up to him, yet he's so closed off. I don't like that. What is he hiding?

Whatever it is, his avoidance of all personal subjects isn't stopping me from engaging in any and all sexual activities with him.

I can't go wrong with that. The man is just as responsive to me as I am to him, and the flavor of him still lingers in my mouth. A delicious, tangy, slightly salty, all masculine taste that makes me want to get his cock into my mouth again.

Soon.

Which is crazy because I'm not one for blow jobs, especially with a man I don't know very well. But I feel like with this situation, I need to take advantage whenever I can. That the opportunity to be with Caden could be as fleeting as the weather here in London. One day sunny, the next day rain.

One elusive encounter with Caden in a bathroom, then *poof*. He's gone.

So I'll take what I can get. Take what I want. And right now, what I want more than anything else is Caden . . . and I still don't even know his last name.

"Get on the bed, Rose," he says, his voice this deep, slightly rough command, and I love it. So much that I don't say a word in reply. I merely do as I'm told, crawling onto the mattress on all fours, my ass in the air, right in front of him. "Yeah, stay just like that, on your hands and knees."

Pervert. I knew he'd like that. Not that I really think he's a pervert because if he is, then so am I. I'm the one who invited him back to my hotel room. I'm the one who sucked his cock into my mouth until he came all over my lips and chest. I have never, ever let a man do that to me before, but I let *him*. Practically a stranger, a man who drives me crazy, and not always in a good way.

What does that say about me? What is happening to me?

"Your ass is perfection," he says just as he places his hand on my right butt cheek. I still myself against his gentle caress, melting at the way his fingers slide lovingly over the globe of my ass. "I can smell you, Rose. I know you want me."

I remain silent. There's no reason to protest or argue, because I *do* want him. I'm drenched with wanting him and in minutes, if not seconds, I will have him. He'll drive that huge cock inside my body and take me with no shame. And I'll let him. If I don't watch it, I'll probably be begging him.

And I'm sure he'd love that.

His fingers draw closer and closer to my pussy as he strokes my ass and I wait with held breath, dying for him to touch me there. Slide one of those long, talented fingers inside of me, testing me. The sudden image that pops in my brain, of Caden behind me on his knees, powering inside my welcoming body, his hips slapping against my ass with his every thrust, sends a fresh wave of arousal coursing through me.

"Your skin is so smooth," he observes in that deep, mesmerizing voice that has me on edge. I close my eyes and focus on the way he's touching me. More fingers come into play as they curve around my ass, closer to my pussy, and then he's touching me there. Teasing my folds, tracing the top of them, a barely there caress that has me exhaling softly, lifting my hips the slightest bit to direct his fingers where I really want them.

Deeper.

"You like that?" he asks, sounding amused. Sounding aroused. He knows I like it, so I don't bother answering. At least, I don't answer with words.

A whimper escapes me when he slides his finger inside my body, holding it there before he slowly withdraws it. Then he adds another finger, pumping them inside my pussy just as I push against his hand. My head swims with incoherent thoughts. All I can focus on is his touch, his fingers, three of them now, deep inside. He drags them back and forth, sinking farther with every thrust, until I'm working against him, riding his hand.

Riding toward the orgasm that already hovers just out of my reach.

The afternoon sunlight shines bright in the room and I can hear an occasional honk coming from the street outside, the rush of the traffic, the rumbling roar of a city bus. Normal, everyday sounds that mean life carries on around us.

While a man works my body with his skilled fingers, a man I barely know. A man who's making me feel everything more intensely than I've ever experienced it before.

The mattress moves when he shifts position and then his mouth is on my backside, kissing and licking my flesh, nibbling it. All while his fingers still move inside of me, his thumb stretching up to rub my clit, his other hand holding my hip. A moan moves through me when he blazes a trail across my skin, his mouth drawing closer and closer, until he's right there . . . *oh my God, right fucking there.*

He licks me at the same time he removes his fingers from my pussy. I feel the loss keenly, a whimper escaping me, but then both of his hands are gripping my hips and he's sliding beneath me, his tongue playing with my folds, his lips wrapping around my clit.

"Ride my face," he instructs me and it sounds so dirty, *God*. But a fresh gush of wetness floods my pussy at his command and I do as he says, backing up against his face until I can feel the stubble on his chin tickling my sensitive flesh, his tongue spearing me, his fingers coming back into play as well.

It's sensory overload. I open my eyes and turn to look at the large mirror above the dresser on the opposite wall. I can see myself and oh, I look a mess. My hair everywhere, my pale skin blotchy and red, my nipples hard as my breasts sway with my movements. I sit up a little, the better to see myself, and that's when Caden's head comes into view, his mussed hair between my legs, his big hand gripping my hip so hard his fingers dent my flesh.

"Oh." The little sound falls from my lips, drawing his attention, and he stops what he's doing so I have no choice but to look down at him. He's smiling up at me, his lips wet, his chin wet too, and he looks so devious, like a wicked boy who's just been caught doing something extra naughty, that I can't help but smile at him in return.

"You're watching me do this to you in the mirror, aren't you?" he asks.

I nod and return my attention to the mirror, letting my gaze drift so I can take in his long body stretched out beyond me. His cock is full and thick—hard to believe I had that thing in my mouth only minutes ago, coming so much I'm downright thankful he didn't want me to swallow—and his erection brushes against my ass. I reach behind me and touch him, my fingers sliding down his length, making him groan against my pussy, and the vibrations his deep voice makes against my skin is unbelievably delicious.

I keep my fingers wrapped around him and stroke him slowly

just as he returns his attention to my clit. I watch in the mirror, the way I move my hips as I ride his face, the fumbling grasp I have on his thick cock, the way my breasts bounce when I toss my head back, my hair falling down my back and tickling my skin.

Again, it's sensory overload. It smells like sex in the room. Sex mixed with the scent of my body lotion and the scent of Caden, spicy male and clean with just the faintest hint of sweat. I release my hold on his cock and rest my hand between my legs, gathering the wetness there, lightly touching the side of Caden's face for a brief moment before I return my slicked fingers back to his cock and continue stroking.

"Holy shit," he mutters against my pussy and I go still, my breath catching, my chest heaving just as his tongue flicks my clit, sending me right over that hanging edge. I release my hold on him and practically collapse on his face, leaning forward so both of my hands are resting on the mattress.

My entire body shudders as I rock against his face, his fingers, his tongue. He encourages me with filthy words, things I've never had a man say to me while having sex. Urging me on to fuck his face, come on his lips, all sorts of wicked things that seem to somehow string my orgasm even further along, until I feel like I'm coming completely undone.

I finally collapse, rolling over so I don't fall upon him, lying there on the mattress as I stare up at the ceiling, my chest heaving, my heart beating so hard I swear it's going to break through bone and flesh and fly right out of me. Closing my eyes, I rest my forearm across them, wiping at the sweat that trickles on my forehead.

The mattress shifts again; I can feel Caden hovering above me, but I don't drop my arm. Not yet. I need the protection, the block to keep me separated from him for just a few moments longer. He touches me, drifting his fingers across my breasts, down my belly and back up, circling first one nipple, then the other. A shiver steals through me and I try to roll away from him, but he stops me with a firm hand on my hip.

"Watching you come is the single most fascinating thing I think I've ever witnessed," he murmurs, his gravelly, deep voice full of warm approval.

I slowly drop my arm from my face and meet his gaze, ready for the embarrassment, the shame to sweep over me and swallow me whole. I can't believe we just did that. Can't believe he just said those things to me, did those things to me, and how much I liked it.

But the embarrassment and the shame don't come. He bends over me, his hair tumbling across his forehead and brushing mine when he kisses me, his lips full and soft and so incredibly sweet. I say nothing. It's as if all cognitive thought has flown from my brain and my vocabulary is down to nothing. And when he lifts away from me, his brows are furrowed, there's a little line between them, and his beautiful mouth is turned down.

"Are you alive?" He waves his hand in front of my face and then holds it in front of my mouth. "You're breathing. I can feel it. Maybe I just put you into shock with that earth-shattering orgasm?"

God. Not only is he gorgeous and sexy and amazingly talented with his mouth and fingers, he's also funny. I try my best to withhold the smile that wants to break free, but it's no use. The minute he sees it, he grins in return and his hands go to my sides, tickling me.

My weakness. I try to roll away from him again but he's not having it. He attacks my belly and my sides with his wriggling fingers, his big body moving to sprawl across me as he puts his face against my neck.

I'm laughing so much it's hard to breathe. It doesn't help that I hadn't caught my breath from that "earth-shattering" orgasm Caden just gave me, either.

"Rose." His mouth moves against my neck and I go still. So do his hands. "You all right?"

I circle my arms around his neck and drape them across his shoulders. He moves against me, his hands sliding along my sides, and I spread my legs, allowing him to nestle his hips between them. He lifts up, bracing his hands on either side of my head, his scrutinizing gaze meeting mine, and I don't look away.

It's as if I can't look away. I'm ensnared. Caught. My breath stills in my chest when he slowly, very methodically, thrusts his hips against mine, his cock brushing against my belly. "I haven't even been inside you yet," he murmurs, his gaze filled with this strange but thrilling wonder that matches my own twisted emotions.

Plunging my hands into the thick softness of his hair, I pull him down so his mouth is just above mine. "I don't know if I can stand it, what with that earth-shattering orgasm you just gave me."

He smiles, I can feel it form against my lips, and the pure, unadulterated joy rising deep within me threatens to send me flying. "Just wait until the next one. I might need to perform CPR to revive you."

"Ew." I grimace and giggle, and I never giggle. But he doesn't seem to mind. He kisses the tip of my nose, my cheek, my chin, and then my lips.

And it is the best kiss ever. His mouth is pliant, his tongue slick and tangling with mine. I tighten my grip in his hair and he thrusts his cock against my belly again, making me moan. Making me want him inside me. He swallows the sound and pulls away, lifting up on his knees so he can grip the base of his cock and tease me with it, brushing the head against my clit, back and forth, bathing himself in the wetness that's gathered there.

"It would be so easy to sink deep inside you. You're so damn wet," he murmurs, his gaze locked on the spot where our bodies touch. His words make me tingle all over, I swear. "I need to grab a condom or I'm gonna blow all over your pretty pussy."

He talks like that and I should tell him to stop but I can't. I love it too much. He's so dirty and so incredibly comfortable with it. "You brought condoms?"

"I have a couple in my wallet." He doesn't look up from his task, his eyes still fixed on where he's teasing me with his cock.

Now all I can think about is the many other women he must have had sex with. How many of them did he talk dirty to? How many earth-shattering orgasms has he given? Not that I really want to know. I'm sure Whitney has had more than her share.

Just the thought of him being with her, touching her . . . moving inside of her . . . fills me with an ugly, unfamiliar emotion.

Jealousy.

"Go get them, then," I demand, earning a strange look from him before he crawls off the bed and goes to where he left his jeans on the floor, pulling out and digging through his wallet until he's got two condoms clutched in his hand.

"We might need more," he says as he stands over the bed, watching me. I let my gaze wander, taking inventory of every delicious inch of him.

"More?" I arch a brow, playing it cool, a little frightened at the thought of going at it with this intense man all night long. "I didn't ask you to stay the night."

"You didn't ask me to do much of anything. You just got down on your knees and started playing with my dick pretty much the minute we walked through the door." He arches a brow right back, resting his hands on his hips and managing to look indignant despite standing before me naked.

Well. He definitely doesn't back down from a fight. In fact, when it comes to this man, I'm sure I'm in way over my head.

"You're so crude," I tell him, immediately feeling silly for saying it.

His eyes darken and he deposits the condoms on the bedside table. "I thought you liked it."

I look away from him, wrapping my arms around myself, covering my breasts. "Maybe I don't." More like maybe I shouldn't. I shouldn't have fallen to my knees like that. Shouldn't have given in so easily. He probably thinks I'm a total slut. Every one of our encounters was trashy. Naked in a pool. Fingering me in a bathroom. Fucking around in a hotel room.

What in the world am I doing? And what must Caden think of me?

"Hey." His voice is soft, like his touch when he gently places his fingers on my chin and turns my head so I have no choice but to look up at him. "If you want me to go, I'll go."

I study him, see the earnest look in his eyes, the concern there, too. That glimpse of humanity reassures me and I slowly shake my head. "I don't want you to go," I admit in a voice so soft I can barely hear it.

He caresses the side of my face and my eyelids waver. I love how sweetly he touches me. It's a contradiction to his baser side, a contradiction I am desperately drawn to, despite my misgivings. "What do you want me to do?"

"Can we maybe just . . . lie together for a while? I need to, I don't know, gather myself."

His hand drops away from my face and I climb off the bed, bending over to pull the comforter and sheets back. Caden steps in close, his body heat warming me, his hand going to my butt so he can stroke me there. "You all right?"

I glance back at him. That's the second time he's asked me that and I can't help but appreciate it. "I'm okay," I tell him as I climb into bed.

Caden joins me, pulling me into his arms, and I don't protest. I don't usually like to cuddle but it feels nice, lying here in his arms, my arm slung over his flat stomach, my head pressed against his chest. I can hear the beating of his heart, feel it thump-thump-thumping against my ear, and I close my eyes. Lose myself to the sound of his breathing, the gentle rocking of his chest, the beat of his heart. He strokes my arm, up and down, his fingers as light as a butterfly's wings, and I shiver. Move my head so my mouth is pressed against his chest and I kiss him there. Once.

Twice.

Three times.

Until I'm climbing on top of him without thought, straddling his hips, my legs draped over his thighs and my still aching sex pressed up against his cock. His big hands settle on my ass and he's rubbing me there, holding me close. I prop my hands on his firm chest and our gazes clash, his full of longing and confusion.

"I thought you said . . ." he starts but I rest my fingers on his mouth, stopping him.

"No thinking allowed," I murmur, removing my hand from his lips to reach toward the bedside table and grab one of the condoms. I don't look away as I tear open the wrapper and remove the condom from within. I still don't look away as he reaches for me, his hand going for my breast, his fingers stroking my nipple.

Lifting up, I smooth the condom on his cock, his hand still working my nipple, my hand working his erection. I slide against him, not allowing him to enter me yet, enjoying the anticipation for just a little bit longer.

"Feels good, doesn't it?" he whispers, his hands going from my hips to my ass and back to my hips again. "Playing with my cock?"

Ah, there are those dirty words again. They're like an aphrodisiac. Everything within me goes molten and I lean forward, working my hips against his cock as I press my mouth to his.

The kiss is decadent. Probably bordering on obscene. Nothing but open mouths and tongue and long, tortured moans. His hand drops from my ass to grip the base of his cock and then he's entering me. Just the head at first, the perfect tease to make me tense up, hold my breath, and wait for more.

"Relax," he urges, his fingers drifting up along my spine, higher, almost to my shoulders before they fall back down. He is so attuned to my body already, knowing just how to work it, how to make me respond. I feel myself loosen up at his touch, at his words, and I close my eyes when he lifts his hips, sending his cock a fraction deeper. "Fuck, you're tight."

It's been a long time since I've had a man inside my body. That might be why I'm so tight. Or maybe I'm just naturally tight. I don't know. I'm not like Lily with her endless revolving door of men, though who really knows exactly how many of them she's had sex with.

Me? The number is embarrassingly small. Like I-can-count-them-all-on-one-hand small. I was always just so serious, so determined. Determined to get through high school, through college, through *life*. I didn't let a thing like boys get in the way.

Caden has gone still beneath me, his hands locked on my hips, his head pressing deep into the pillow. His jaw is strained, as is his neck, and I realize he's doing everything he can to take this slow, for my sake. Again, he's paying attention to me and my heart melts.

Lifting up, I send him deeper, earning a groan from him for my efforts. I grind my hips, flex them back and forth, testing his fullness, the way he stretches me so deliciously it almost hurts. It's a sweet sting, though, one that fills my blood as I begin to move, as he helps me along by lifting me, his gaze zeroed in on the spot where he can watch his cock slide in and out of my body.

I close my eyes, little white sparks lighting off behind my lids at the way he's working me on his cock, lifting me as if I weigh nothing. I lean my head back, lost in the sensation, the rhythm of our bodies working together, his fingers finding my clit and stroking the little bundle of nerves, sending more of those hot sparks through my veins, across my skin. I feel like I'm chasing after my orgasm as I begin to move faster, riding him harder, sending him deeper.

He grabs hold of me and rolls over as if he can't stand it any longer. I'm pinned to the mattress, imprisoned by his body as he powers his cock inside of me, again and again, and I can do nothing but take it. Enjoy it. Lying there helpless, I wrap my legs around his hips, anchoring myself to him as he reaches between us and strokes me, the creamy sound of my pussy making us both moan.

"I couldn't wait." He presses his face to my cheek, his mouth at my ear as he begins to fuck me hard. "I had to get you beneath me so I could fuck you properly."

Caden can fuck me any way he wants as long as I'm coming. And it's close. So close. I arch against him, closing my eyes, everything within me going perfectly still, perfectly quiet, as I reach and reach and finally claim my prize.

The orgasm steals over me, robbing me of my breath, of my thoughts, of everything and anything until he's the only thing I can focus on. I open my eyes to find him watching me, his gaze hungry as he leans in and kisses me, his mouth opening on a groan as his own orgasm takes over his body, leaving him a shuddering, gasping mass of flesh before he collapses on top of me, pressing me even deeper into the mattress.

I hold him close, clinging to him, our sweaty bodies sticking to each other. I'm thrilled at what we just shared. And horrified.

Definitely horrified.

Chapter Ten

Caden

I'M STILL ON AN ORGASMIC HIGH, JUST ABOUT TO DRIFT OFF into sleep, when I hear Rose say something. I decide to ignore her since I really didn't hear her anyway, squeezing her shoulders with my arm, pulling her closer to my chest. We're lying next to each other in postcoital bliss, the sheets kicked off and in a pile on the floor, the cool air bathing our heated skin. I feel good. I feel on top of the motherfuckin' world and nothing is going to get me down. At least not for the next few hours.

"Hey." Rose pokes my side, making me yelp. *Damn*, her finger's sharp. Pricking my good vibe like a pin pops a balloon. "Shouldn't you, um . . . be on your way?"

I crack open my eyes and stare at her in disbelief. "Are you kicking me out?"

She makes a face, one that says, *I'm so sorry, but yeah. You gotta go.*

Right. She's definitely kicking me out.

"Well, this is awkward," I say as I let go of her and slide out of bed. She scrambles into a sitting position, yanking the sheet up so it covers her breasts, and I almost want to laugh. I've seen every inch of her. Explored every inch of her, too, with my fingers and mouth and tongue. She has no reason to hide from me.

"It's just . . . it's getting late and I don't know what's going on and . . ." Her voice trails off and she shrugs those pretty, slim shoulders, her hair spilling everywhere, sliding against her skin, tempting me to touch her there.

But I resist because *what the fuck,* she's kicking me out. No woman kicks me out. They're always begging me to stay and I'm the one shoving them off, desperate to escape.

I didn't even get a chance to search her suite for the necklace. I'm failing on all sides here. I need to play this off and see if I can get back in her good graces.

Were you ever in her good graces?

That's probably a no.

"You're cute when you're flustered," I tell her, pleased when I see her cheeks turn pink. "And that you can blush after everything that's happened between us . . ."

"Yeah, that." She points her finger at me, the sheet dropping to reveal her breasts. My gaze falls there, staring at them, the rosy nipples that match her name. Everything about her is pink and rose, creamy and sweet and so fucking tempting. "Your mouth makes me crazy."

"In a good way or a bad way?" I thought she liked my mouth. She definitely didn't protest when I had it between her legs. Or pressed to her lush lips. Or wrapped around her nipples.

"In a bad way." She glances down at herself and pulls the sheet up again, ruining my view. "Besides, we've run out of condoms."

Like that would stop me. "I bet if I called the concierge he'd get us more." I stride toward the phone sitting on the bedside table, reaching for the receiver, but she slaps her hand over it first, stopping my progress.

"You will absolutely not call them," she says, her voice low, the sheet forgotten again, much to my pleasure.

"Why not?"

"Then they'll know what we're doing." Her cheeks turn even

brighter pink and I chuckle, curling my hand upward into hers so our fingers interlock.

"We're consenting adults, Ro. If we want to get naked and fuck for hours in a hotel room on a Saturday afternoon, then that's our God-given right."

"*Ro?* No one's called me that before." She disentangles her fingers from mine, scooting away from me until she's sitting in the middle of the bed, the sheet still puddled around her lap, offering me that stellar view. I could stare at her chest all day. Now I get why artists are compelled to paint nudes of beautiful women. I've never painted in my life, but I'd love to capture Rose in this exact moment on canvas. "And please don't bring God into this conversation," she says weakly.

I sit on the edge of the mattress, not about to give up. I need to get closer to her and eventually get closer to that damn necklace she wore. Dexter wants it. He's been hounding my ass for it. And I'll get it.

Eventually.

I'd rather focus on her first. Earn her trust. So I'm not casing out her hotel room. I'm not looking for any stray jewelry lying around.

Hell, I'm in too deep now.

I'm here with Rose because I want to be, not because I want to steal something from her.

Yet. Don't forget the "yet" part at the end of that last thought.

Yeah. Who wants to focus on trying to steal a necklace when I could be sliding back into bed with her? I want to feel the hot, tight clasp of her pussy milking my cock again. I want to feel her touch me, feel her lips on my skin, hear her moan when I hit a spot that feels particularly good. I want to learn all of those spots, memorize them for later. Because there will be a later for Rose and me. I plan on that. And she'd better plan on it too, no matter how much in denial she is.

"Rose." She turns to look at me, her expression wary.

Guarded. I know the feeling. More than anything, I know that look. I've been wearing the same guarded expression pretty much all my life. I trust no one. They're all out to screw me over; it doesn't matter who they are. I've become so good at playing the part, of being whoever I need to be at any given moment, I have no idea who the real me is anymore.

Being with Rose is the closest I've felt to myself since I don't know when. I want to explore this. Explore what we share, what she makes me feel, what we are when we're together.

She's ready to kick me out and I'm ready to cling. Talk about a total role reversal. I need to get my head back on straight and focus.

"Caden." She matches my tone, watching me expectantly. When I don't say anything she rolls her eyes. "Do you realize I don't even know your last name? What does that say about me, that I'd let you into my room and—fool around with you for hours and I don't know your last name? It's appalling behavior."

"Appalling behavior? You sound like a crabby old school-teacher." I want to laugh but I don't. She's dead serious. I think she's just shocked herself with what we've done.

I've shocked myself too, but in a good way. While she acts like we've committed the ultimate sin.

"You wouldn't understand." She averts her head as if it pains her to look at me and I move closer to her, reaching out to tuck a stray strand of hair behind her ear.

"It's Kingsley," I murmur, wishing I could kiss her. Comfort her. But that's not happening, not yet. I've got to take it slow.

She turns, a little gasp escaping her when she discovers how close I am. "What?"

"My last name. It's Kingsley."

"Are you serious? Of course it is." She tosses her hands up in the air, making her breasts jiggle, and I jerk my gaze away from her chest.

"What do you mean by that?"

"It's such an—arrogant name. Caden Kingsley. Please don't tell me your friends called you King or something silly like that when you were in school."

Hell, no, they didn't call me that. They teased me unmercifully when my father lost all his money in bad investments and when he became involved in a pyramid scheme. In his shame and embarrassment he did the unthinkable.

Killed himself.

And I've dealt with his choice ever since. Worn it like it was my cross to bear. I hate him for what he did. Hate him for how he destroyed my life, Mom's life, lost all our money until I turned to the one thing that was the easiest fix.

Stealing.

I guess I'm more like my old man than I thought.

"I was born with the name." I shrug, uncomfortable thinking about my past shames. "Not like I chose it."

She's studying me a little too closely and I want to squirm like a little kid. But I don't. I remain as still as I can, returning her stare, wanting her to think she doesn't scare me.

But *fuck,* she does. She scares the crap out of me. Maybe I should leave. Bail out of here like she wants me to and forget all about this woman.

You won't be able to. It has nothing to do with the necklace or anything that you can gain from her. You just want her. Pure and simple. What's the harm in that?

It's who she is. What she represents. She's exactly the type of woman I need to avoid. Not cling to.

"I should go." I start to rise but she clasps my wrist, her fingers keeping me in place.

"Wait."

I stare at her hand clasped tight around my wrist, then lift my head to meet her imploring gaze.

"Don't go," she whispers.

Go. Go. Fucking go. "What are you saying? You changed your mind?"

Her gaze never leaves my face and I know she's searching for something, some hidden secret I supposedly have. And I do have them. A ton of them. I'm not about to reveal them to her, though. She'll only use them against me. No one knows my secrets. I keep them close to my chest.

It's better that way. Easier.

"Do you want to go to dinner?" She's changing the subject and I'm okay with that. The conversation was taking an uncomfortable turn, one I didn't want to deal with.

"With you?" I ask.

She laughs and shakes her head, her grip on my wrist easing, but she doesn't let go. And I like that. "I deserve that, don't I? Yes, with me."

Her honesty is refreshing. The women I've been with always play games. Natural, I guess, considering I'm a game player too. We say one thing and mean another. Being with a woman was always about chasing the pleasure, seeking the orgasm. Whitney is the only female friend I have and I still end up seeking the orgasm with her, so much so that I have her conditioned to want it anytime she's with me.

Meaning I'll eventually ruin that friendship too.

"Yeah, that sounds good." The relief in my voice is evident and for once I don't care. I don't want to hide it. For once in my life I'm tempted to be open with a woman.

Real.

More like real *scary*. What the hell am I thinking?

"I need to take a shower first." She waves a hand at me. "So maybe you can turn around so I can go to the bathroom?"

"Are you serious?" I grab her, causing her to shriek. Clamping my hand over her mouth loosely, I roll over so she's beneath me, her breasts pressed against my chest, her sheet-covered legs squirming beneath mine. "Baby, I've seen you completely naked. You rode my face. You *came* all over my face. And now you're acting shy?"

She struggles against me, reaching out to shove me, and I grab at her wrists, lifting her arms above her head and pinning them there. "Let go of me."

"Don't be embarrassed." I dip my head, brush my nose against her cheek, along her neck. Her struggle eases, her body going limp beneath mine when I run my mouth along her skin, scenting her, tasting her. My body is spent but my cock is hard and I'm afraid I could become easily addicted to this woman.

"I'm not used to a man sticking around after sex," she admits softly.

I lift my head so I can look at her. "What do you mean?"

"I mean, they all bail right after, even the ones I'm in a committed relationship with." Her cheeks go red yet again and I kiss her there, my lips pressing into the heated skin of her left cheek, then her right.

"You've been in lots of committed relationships?" I ask, almost afraid of her answer. Because if she has I should probably go. Now.

"No." The word comes out strangled, though that could be because I slipped my hand down to cup her breast. "I've had one serious boyfriend. And he was the worst of them all. I found out later I wasn't the only woman he was seeing, though I thought I was."

Asshole. I may not commit, but at least I don't string women along and pretend I want a relationship with them.

"I shouldn't even be talking to you about this stuff. Like you care." She turns her head to the side, staring at nothing, her body tense.

I kiss her jaw, her lips, my hand still on her breast, gently stroking. Her nipple pebbles against my palm, her body growing warm and pliant beneath me, and I place my mouth at her ear. "Let's take a shower together."

"I don't know . . ." Her voice trails off when I kiss and nibble her earlobe.

"I'll wash your hair."

She smiles and lifts her shoulder, trying to shrug me away like she can get rid of me, but I don't budge. "That sounds nice," she admits.

"I'll wash your entire body." I lick her ear, making her shiver.

"Okay," she whispers.

"But no more shyness, all right? I like what I see. I don't want you to be bashful."

Her gaze meets mine, then drops to linger on my mouth before returning to my eyes. "Bashful? You make me sound like one of the Seven Dwarfs."

"You're the one who wanted me to close my eyes so you could run to the bathroom. That sounds like bashful to me." I'm still cupping her breast, and my cock is hard as steel where it rests against her belly. "We'd better go take that shower before I give up and fuck you again."

Her eyes widen the slightest bit. "We don't have any more condoms."

"I'd pull out." Just the thought of coming all over her stomach and chest has my balls aching.

"I don't have sex without a condom."

"Neither do I."

"The pull-out method is one of the least reliable."

"I've heard that." What the fuck is wrong with me, suggesting such a thing and not being the least bit concerned about it, either? I'm a fucking nut job of the highest proportions right about now.

I blame the woman squirming beneath me.

"Yet you suggested it." She's calling me out yet again.

"You think too much." I kiss her nose and climb off of her, standing by the side of the bed with my hand held out. "Come on. Let's go take that shower."

She studies my hand warily, looking as unsure as I feel. There's a heaviness in the room. A sense that the two of us are about to embark on a crazy adventure neither of us will ever fully recover from.

Will she take my hand? Or tell me to get the hell out? She should do the latter. It's the safest bet. The easiest out. And I'm always about the easiest out.

But she takes it. Curling her fingers in mine, she allows me to help her out of bed so she's standing in front of me, naked and beautiful. Without a word I lead her into the bathroom and let go of her hand, admiring her ass as she walks over to the shower and starts the water, flicking her fingers in the spray as she waits for it to warm.

"Ready?" she asks when steam starts to billow out of the shower stall.

As I'll ever be.

WE END UP AT A HOTEL IN TRAFALGAR SQUARE, TAKING A TAXI to get there, one of those little black cabs you see on TV when you're a kid. I've been to England once before, but I was too young to care and not really paying attention to my surroundings.

London is exactly what you'd expect it to be. Bustling and full of people, quick paced and crowded, its streets packed with those red double-decker buses. History is everywhere, staring down at you in the form of one statue or another. They give everyone a statue in this damn city. I bet if I paid enough money I could have my own motherfucking statue erected in some small park.

I tried to feel Rose up in the back of the cab since the driver wasn't paying us any mind but she wouldn't have it, slapping my hands away every time I tried to grab her. You'd think I wouldn't feel the need to grab her, since she gave me a soapy hand job in the shower that had me coming so hard I had to brace myself against the shower wall for fear I'd slip down the drain.

Not that I hadn't returned the favor, fingering her into another orgasm while my mouth remained tight around her nipple. She's so damn responsive, I had her coming in minutes.

"Why are you taking me to another hotel?" I ask her as we enter the building. There's a noisy bar to the right, filled with people around our age dressed to trendy perfection, standing around drinking and talking, loud music blaring over the speakers. I start to head toward the bar but she stops me, dragging me toward a short bank of elevators to the left, just beyond the registration desk.

"We're going to the restaurant up on the roof. It's supposed to be one of those hidden-gem secrets of the city. Violet told me about it. She came here with Ryder a few weeks ago and said the view and the food were excellent." Rose hits the up button and we wait for the elevator to make its way to the ground floor.

"Better than The Shard?" The newest skyscraper, close to the London Bridge, is one of the more popular spots for tourists to check out a view of the city. Not that I'd been there, but I'd heard all about it from Whitney.

"Not as crowded, at least. I don't know about better." The elevator dings and the doors slide open, revealing a crazy interior.

I start to laugh as we walk inside, earning a weird look from Rose. "What's so funny?"

"This elevator looks like a damn nightclub." It's dark inside save for the glowing purple and green lights that shine on the black floor, the little glints of silver embedded in the solid surface shining bright. The walls are mirrored and covered with a faint black brocade print, and there's even mood music.

"It does," Rose agrees with a little smile. She starts to move as if she's dancing, and I watch in fascination as she sways her hips in time to the music.

She's wearing a short pastel-colored lace dress and I'm not sure if she has panties on beneath it, but now is not the time to check. I'm hungry after expending my energy for the last five hours or so of straight fucking and eager to get to this restaurant so we can order something to eat.

"You trying to turn me on?" I ask her.

Rose flashes me a smile over her shoulder and shakes her ass. *Jesus*, the woman is hot. "Maybe."

"It's working." I grab hold of her hips and pull her to me, stifling the groan that wants to escape when her ass brushes against my cock. It stiffens, though I can almost hear it protesting in agony, *enough already. Let me rest.*

She swivels her hips, her ass pushing against my cock, and I hold her still, my mouth against her hair as I whisper, "Do you want me to fuck you in the elevator?" I bought condoms at the Boots drugstore not far from her hotel, running in to purchase them while she was getting ready, blowing her hair dry and all of those other things women do before they go out on a date.

My entire body goes still. Is that what this is? A date? I've never been on one in my life, not even when I was young. It was all about the hookup. That's all it's ever been. Why let someone get close to me when I had all of these deep, dark secrets I didn't want to share? My life turned into a tragedy, and then it turned into a joke. But the joke was on me and Mom, no one else. We became the punch line and it sucked.

I didn't want to share that with anyone else. Of course, I'd never met anyone like Rose, either.

"I'm just playing." She rests her hands on the outside of my thighs, her touch burning me even through the thick denim of my jeans.

"With fire," I murmur just as the elevator comes to a stop and the doors slide open.

Rose pulls away from me, practically running out of the elevator, and I follow after her down the narrow hallway that turns into an even narrower staircase. She glances down at me, making sure I'm right behind, and I fall into step after her, cocking my head so I can sneak glances up her skirt.

Just as I thought. The little tease isn't wearing panties. She's going to drive me straight insane before the night is done, I swear.

We reach the top of the stairs and the night air hits me, cool but with that hint of lingering heat that declares summer is coming. Rose sends me a smug look over her shoulder and I'm about to say something when the hostess approaches, a cute, petite thing dressed all in black, the skirt of her dress so short I'm afraid one wrong move and she'll be showing the world—or at least us—everything she's got.

"Two for dinner or just drinks?" the hostess asks, her accent thick, a little sneer curling her upper lip.

"Dinner, please." I wrap my arm around Rose's waist, pulling her into me. She goes willingly, her curves fitting perfectly against my side, and we follow the hostess to a high table that faces directly out over Trafalgar Square. She hands us our menus with a quick smile and then scurries away.

"If she would let me, I would so give her a makeover," Rose says as she flips open the menu. "If I suggested it, though, she'd probably be insulted."

"You think she needs a makeover?"

Rose glances at me from over the top of her menu. "Did you see all the eyeliner she had on? And mascara? Hell yes, she needs a makeover. When I was in high school I worked the Fleur counter at Bloomingdale's for one summer. I was sixteen and loved it."

"Really? One of the Fowlers working the makeup counter?" I'm surprised. Figured they would think that sort of work beneath them.

She sends me an irritated look. "My grandma made me and my sisters do it at one point or another. I'm the only one who enjoyed it, though. I loved giving makeovers."

"Why?" I forget about the menu and my hunger and wait for her answer. I like that she's opening up to me. Though of course, her opening up means she probably expects me to do the same.

And I don't know if I can.

"I don't know." She shrugs, her expression thoughtful. "It was fun, to make that transformation happen. And to see the joy on the women's faces when they saw what I did, it made me feel good. I didn't even care about selling them the product. I just wanted to make them happy."

"Isn't that the point of a makeover at a cosmetics counter? So you can sell them the product?"

"Yes, and I failed miserably at that part. I'd take over an hour on a woman's makeup and let her walk without spending a dime." Rose shakes her head. "I was awful."

"Sounds like you did it just for the fun of it."

She smiles wistfully. "I did. That was the one time when working for Fleur truly felt like fun." Her smile falls, and it's as though she just caught herself in a terrible confession. "Lately working for Fleur, sometimes it feels like so much . . ."

"Work," I finish for her.

"Right. Work." Her voice is faint and she turns to study the view, offering me a glimpse of her profile. The single candle sitting in the middle of the table casts her face in a golden glow, emphasizing the shape of her jaw, the straight angle of her nose, the plumpness of her lips. The longer I stare, the more I become entranced. She's stunning, looking a little sad, a little lost.

"Ready to order?" The waitress appears and I turn to her, my gaze dropping to the neckline of her dress, her cleavage on obvious display. She's a pretty girl but there's nothing subtle about her, from the bright blond of her hair to the short skirt and loads of makeup on her face.

"I haven't had a chance to look at the menu yet," I admit, tearing my gaze from her boobs.

"Me either," Rose says, her voice tight.

"Want something to drink then?" the waitress asks, sounding bored.

"Yeah, that sounds good." I order a beer and Rose orders some fancy little cocktail I've never heard of before and the waitress walks away, an extra swish in her step, as if she wants me to look.

And I do.

"God, you're a pig," Rose says with a little groan.

I look in her direction. "What do you mean?"

"Staring at the waitress like you want to molest her while you're sitting at the table with me," she accuses, her eyes flaring with anger.

"She wants me to stare at her like that. Look at the way she's dressed," I say in my defense. *Damn*, look at her, acting like a possessive girlfriend.

"I couldn't take my eyes off her bad makeup," Rose retorts.

"Yeah, well, I couldn't take my eyes off her short skirt."

"And her boobs."

"Fine, and her boobs." I shake my head. "Are you jealous?"

"What? No." She sounds horrified. "Why would I be jealous? You can look at whoever you want."

"Uh-huh." I let my gaze return to the menu, checking out what they have to offer, which is a lot. Just reading the descriptions of the various entrees is making me hungrier.

But I can feel Rose's anger radiating off her in palpable waves. She doesn't like that I called her out on her jealousy.

"You're an ass," she finally says, the last word ending in a hiss.

"Just speaking the truth." I don't look up from the menu and I can feel her glaring at me. That old saying "if looks could kill" would definitely apply here.

I'd be dead right about . . .

Now.

Chapter Eleven

Rose

I'M MAD BECAUSE CADEN'S RIGHT. I AM JEALOUS. HE STARED AT her chest right in front of me like he couldn't help it and fine, he probably couldn't, but *oh my God,* have some restraint, please. We're on a date.

Staring at the menu, my vision blurs so bad I can't even read it. Is that what we're doing? Are we really on a date? I went from asking him to leave my room to behaving like an embarrassed idiot to letting him take a shower with me, all in about a five-minute span.

That shower had been so worth it, though. The man fulfilled his promise, washing my hair and massaging my head until I wanted to melt into the tiles. Then he proceeded to soap up my entire body, rubbing his hands all over me, making sure to get "everything clean," as he said. He then proceeded to bring me to orgasm with just his fingers. Oh, and his mouth wrapped tightly around my nipple after he rinsed off my chest, sucking it so deep I felt the pull of his lips and tongue to the depths of my being.

Dramatic but true. I bet he could make me come with only his mouth on my breasts. I'm squirming in my seat just thinking about it. Doesn't help that I didn't wear any panties. Again. He makes me do these things, I swear. And I don't understand why.

Glancing out of the corner of my eye, I spy on him, my anger slowly dissipating. The breeze makes his hair flutter across his forehead, into his eyes, and he absently swipes at it, brushing it back. He's wearing the same clothes from earlier because of course, he didn't have anything new to change into after our shower. It doesn't matter, though. He looks good.

Too good.

"Are you plotting my death?" he asks, startling me. He still hasn't looked up from the menu but I can see the faint smile curving his mouth. I feel myself start to smile in return, and I immediately frown instead.

"What are you talking about?" I sound bitchy and I clear my throat, mentally telling myself to ease up. The man is worth keeping around for the orgasms alone.

Ack. That's the shittiest thought ever.

I like him for more than just orgasms. He's . . . challenging. Funny. Fun. I've been so serious lately. So wrapped up in my own problems, my own worries and concerns. Reading my mother's diary brought me further down and I feel terrible that I haven't even mentioned it to Violet or Lily. If I were them, I'd want to know.

But what good would it do, telling them? What would it gain? Nothing but sadness. I'm sick of feeling sad.

Caden makes me smile. He makes me moan. More than anything, he makes me feel good. I need that right now. I need to remember that I can smile and laugh and have a good time. Caden is the ideal remedy to my problem.

"I can feel you staring at me. Still pissed?" He finally looks up, those deep brown eyes meeting mine, filled with amusement, the smile stretching into a full-on grin, and I can't help but smile at him in return.

"Why can't I stay mad at you?"

"I don't know. My irresistible ways?" He raises his brows, making me laugh.

"Not so sure about that. We seem to argue a lot." The laughter fades. I don't know how I feel about that particular fact. It's disconcerting, how easily we fall into an argument and then into each other's arms. I've never experienced anything like it before.

"They call it passion," he says.

I go completely still. "What?"

"What's happening between us. It's called passion." His smile fades and he leans across the table, his voice lowering. "You get mad at me and then you want to kiss me and then you're yelling at me and then . . . we're fucking. Passion."

He makes it sound so simple. But it's not. It feels terribly complicated. "Passion," I repeat.

"Yeah." He shrugs, as if it's no big deal. Which, of course, infuriates me.

"Have you ever experienced this with someone else?" I ask. That has to be the reason for his total nonchalance over it. He talks of passion like it's nothing special, while I sit here filled with it. I feel like a bottle of Champagne that's been shaken up so much the cork is this close to popping across the room and sending half the alcohol shooting out in a white frothy mess.

That's me. I'm the white frothy mess.

His jaw works and he leans back, as if he needs the distance. "No," he says, his voice short. And he doesn't look very happy about it, either.

Pleasure fills me at his admission and I want to say more, but the waitress makes her reappearance with our drinks, setting them in front of us before she takes our dinner order.

"What are you drinking?" he asks after the waitress leaves.

"It's called a Trafalgar Tease." I swirl the thin red straw in the glass, mixing everything so I won't take a sip of straight alcohol.

"I should call *you* a Trafalgar Tease," he says, his voice deepening in that way of his that makes me think of naked skin and twisted sheets and sex.

"Why?" I pluck the cherry out of the drink and pop it into

my mouth, the tart sweetness spurting all over my tongue as I chew.

"There are a few reasons." His gaze is locked on my lips, and my breasts grow heavy the longer he stares. "First, for the way you just ate your . . . cherry." Okay, that sounded incredibly dirty. "And second, for the fact that you're not wearing panties. Again."

I swallow the cherry. "How do you know?"

"I caught a peek up your dress when you were climbing the stairs." He flashes this wicked, one-sided, closed-mouth smile that makes everything inside of me go fluttery and weak. "Like you didn't do that on purpose."

"I didn't." I had no idea that he was looking up my skirt. Though I should've known.

"And then there's the way you were grinding your ass against my cock in the elevator." He shakes his head but he doesn't look mad. No, he looks very, very pleased. "You were just daring me to lift your skirt and fuck you right there, weren't you?"

"N-no." *Oh God,* I'm stuttering. He's saying these things so casually, all while we're surrounded by plenty of people. The rooftop restaurant is crowded. I can hear the chatter, the laughter, the clinking of glasses and silverware against plates, but it all fades as we continue to stare at each other. Until I feel like Caden and I are the only two people in this restaurant, in this city, in this country.

He leans back in his chair, looking every inch the casual playboy hell-bent on seducing me. Though it wouldn't be much of a seduction. I'd give in too easily and he knows it. Whatever he wants to do to me, I'll take it. And I'll enjoy it. Because he's not a selfish lover, oh no. He makes sure I get my pleasure.

Lots and lots of pleasure.

"I think I'll make an attempt when we leave," he declares as he grabs his beer and drinks straight from the bottle despite the glass the waitress left for him.

"An attempt at what?" My mind is awhirl with all sorts of . . . things. I can't keep up with the conversation and I feel a bit of a wreck.

"Fucking you in the elevator." He takes another swig. "Don't give me that look. You know you want me to."

He's right. I do want him to. *God,* what's wrong with me?

My throat is dry. Reaching out with a shaky hand, I grab my drink and take a big sip, the sweet liqueur going straight to my head and empty stomach. I feel Caden's eyes on me and I lift my gaze, my lips still wrapped around the straw, to find him staring at me, his dark eyes filled with hunger.

Slowly I withdraw the straw from my mouth and set the glass on the table, my breath increasing, my skin growing hot. The table we're sitting at couldn't be called a table at all, more like a narrow counter attached to the low wall, a candle burning in between us, our chairs sitting next to each other but at an angle. We have the best view in the entire restaurant, straight out over Trafalgar Square, the National Gallery lit up like an elegant beacon in the night. Tons of people still fill the square, spilling all over the stairs that lead to the gallery.

I keep my gaze focused on the view, the billowing British flags snapping in the wind that top so many of the buildings spread out before us like a blanket. This city seems to go on forever, majestic and white and full of history and beauty. While I'm here, I should be out touring, wandering through museums and absorbing the history. Becoming inspired so maybe I, too, could one day have my own cosmetics collection like Violet.

Instead I'm having dinner with an impossible man who makes me feel impossible, wonderful things. It's crazy. *I'm* crazy.

His hand settles on my knee, a casual touch that looks like nothing to anyone else who would happen to see but feels like everything to me. I keep my gaze purposely averted from his, watching the people mill about below, the music some kids are playing drifting up as they put on a performance for a handful of observers standing around.

All the while, Caden's hand moves up. Skimming past my knee, along the top of my thigh, farther up, until he's sliding it down to my inner thigh and I hear him say in that sexy, gruff command of a voice that's barely above a whisper, "Open your legs."

I do so without hesitation, my breath hitching in my throat when his fingers brush against my bare pussy. I close my eyes, my legs falling open even more when he slides his finger inside my body.

"Look at me," he demands and I snap my eyes open, turning to face him. His eyes are hooded, his lips parted, the candlelight playing shadows upon his face, and I've never seen him look so sexy.

"Can I make you come right here in the middle of the restaurant?" He presses his thumb to my clit and I jolt in my chair, the little whimper sounding in my throat earning a stern look from him. "Be quiet, Rose. Don't want to draw a crowd."

No. I definitely don't want to draw a crowd. But I do want to come. I glance around the restaurant to see that no one is paying us any mind, everyone too wrapped up in their own conversations, their own personal dramas. All the while, I have a man's hand up my skirt, his finger buried in my pussy, trying his best to draw yet another orgasm from me.

He can do it, too. I have faith. My body responds to his touch, his words, as if he owns me. He steals words and thoughts from me so effortlessly it's as if I have no control. I'm his to play with as he chooses.

"Come here," he whispers and I lean closer to him, sucking in a surprised gasp when he presses his mouth to mine, kissing me right there in the middle of the restaurant, his fingers busy, his tongue tangling with mine, and I can't take it. The orgasm sweeps over me, short and hot, just enough to send a shiver through me, my belly clenching, my inner walls grasping around his finger, wanting more before he withdraws his fingers from my body and breaks the kiss.

The satisfied expression on his face cannot be denied. He enjoyed that tremendously and I can't lie, I did too.

"You're flushed," he says, his voice a lower murmur that prickles along my nerve endings.

"Do I really need to explain why?" My hands are still shaky as I grab my drink and drain it, the potent alcohol swimming in my veins.

He grins and brings his hand to his mouth—the very hand that had just been between my legs. "I already know why. What I'd like to know is did you enjoy it?"

"Yes."

"Ever done anything like that before?" I swear he's sniffing his fingers, sniffing me, and I want to melt. I want to take his hand and drag him off somewhere private so we can finish what we started.

"No." I shake my head, all the breath leaving me when he licks the tip of his index finger, his eyelids wavering the slightest bit.

"Passion." He rubs his fingers together and I see them glisten in the candlelight. "You're still on my fingers."

I don't say a word. I can't. He's stolen my ability to speak yet again.

"And you taste pretty fucking amazing, Rose. Better than any drink or dinner I can get here." He sucks his index finger into his mouth for the briefest moment before he withdraws it, reaching out to draw a line of dampness across the top of my forearm. "Marked."

I feel like everything inside of me is being strangled. I can't breathe right, I can't think, I can't hear or smell or see. The waitress is back but I have no idea what she's saying to us, and Caden is chatting her up as she places his dinner in front of him, then sets my plate in front of me. I think I murmur thank you to her but I can't be sure.

I'm not sure of anything anymore.

The moment she's gone, I focus on Caden, see that he grabs his beer bottle with the hand that had been between my legs and rubs his fingers all over the surface, gathering up the condensation so he can clean his hands of . . . me.

That's sort of hot.

He picks up his silverware wrapped in a pristine white cloth napkin and unrolls it, setting the napkin in his lap and placing the knife and fork on either side of his plate.

"Rose?"

I shake my head, my gaze refocusing on him to find Caden staring at me, concern lighting his eyes. "What?"

"Is something wrong with your dinner?" When I shake my head in reply he continues. "I gotta admit. I'm disappointed in your choice."

"Why?" I glance down at my salad and grab my silverware, placing the napkin in my lap and pulling out the fork.

"You got a salad." He says *salad* like it's a dirty word. And not a good dirty word, either.

"What's wrong with a salad?" I spear up a few pieces of lettuce and a chunk of chicken, then take a bite, my tongue doing the happy dance when the medley of flavors and the sweet and tangy dressing hit my taste buds. What the hell is Caden talking about anyway? This is a damn good salad.

"At the White Swan you had a steak. Rare. And you ate every last bit of it."

"So?" I fork up another bite and chew, thankful the food came so quickly. I think the potent drink and my empty stomach combined with the overwhelming sexiness that is Caden was doing a number on my mental state.

"It was the sexiest thing I've ever seen, you eating that steak like you couldn't give a fuck what anyone thought." He grabs the gourmet hamburger from his plate and takes a big bite, chewing it with relish before he swallows. "So a salad seems sort of a . . . weak choice."

This conversation is just beyond bizarre, but I'm starting to realize nothing is normal when it comes to me and Caden. "But the salad has chicken and bacon in it." I push the giant white bowl toward him so he can check it out. "See? You can't go wrong with bacon."

He contemplates my salad, then lifts his gaze to mine. "Can I have a bite?"

Nodding, I push the plate closer to him. "Go for it."

"You feed me," he says, his voice soft, his eyes intense.

"Okay." My voice is shaky and I clear my throat, hating the little sign of weakness. I flick the contents of my salad with the fork, looking for the extra-good stuff to feed him, like a little piece of bacon and chicken, making sure to get some Parmesan on the fork as well. I hold up the fork and he leans closer, parting his lips so I can feed him the bite, and he closes his lips around the tines of the fork. I slide it from his mouth, wondering when did feeding someone become so sexy.

"Very good," he says after he swallows, then gestures to his plate. "Do you want to try mine?"

"Only if you feed me," I say, pleased at the dark flicker I see in his gaze. He cuts his burger in half and then holds out one of the halves toward me.

"Take a bite," he urges and I lean in, sinking my teeth into the burger, lifting my chin as I pull away and chew, savoring the delicious flavor of the meat and cheese and sauce. "Good?"

"Delicious," I say before I burst out laughing. Like, uncontrollable giggles that draw the attention of more than a few diners and even our waitress. I rest my hand over my mouth, trying to contain the laughter, but it's no use.

"What's so funny?" he asks, the smile on his face so cute that

I do finally stop laughing, enraptured with his gorgeous face instead.

"I feel like we're seducing each other with food. Burgers and salads," I say, sounding ridiculous.

"We are," he agrees. "This has been one night of long, strung-out foreplay, don't you think?"

"Yes." I take a sip of my drink and realize there's not much left beyond melted ice. I rattle the ice in my glass, glancing around for the waitress, who's already disappeared. "Though so far I'm the only one who got off."

He laughs and shakes his head. "Stick with me for a while and I'll have you being brutally honest in no time."

I like the sound of that. Far more than I care to admit.

Chapter Twelve

Caden

THIS IS THE LONGEST DAY OF MY LIFE AND I'M NOT COMPLAIN-ing. It didn't start off well. I woke up to Whitney standing over my bed, demanding that I go to breakfast with her, so I did. But all I could think about was Rose. Where was she? Who was she with? The woman is distracting and my wayward thoughts are stupid. Detrimental to my original intent.

Getting that damn necklace.

When I turned down Whitney's offer of no-strings sex earlier this morning, she informed me I might need to find somewhere else to stay. Which was fine, because I figured I needed to get the hell out of London anyway. Things were getting too weird with Rose. As in, my feelings for her were getting too weird. I was thinking about her too much.

So I called my friend, the rich asshole with the jet, Mitchell. But he informed me that he's sticking around for a few more days. I could always go hang out with him at his parents' town-house in Belgrave Square, but I passed on the offer. It's just one party after another at that place.

And I craved something different. Found her, too. Luck was on my side, even though I tried to talk myself out of searching for her. It's been a strange experience with Rose. Fun and infuriating and sexy as hell and draining and exhilarating, she is all of that. All the emotions, all the effort and work and trouble.

Worth every bit of it, too. She's much like her namesake, a beautiful, tightly furled flower, and I'm slowly but surely peeling the petals back, bit by bit. Give her a little attention, some sun and water, and she begins to bloom.

That's exactly what's happening between us, to her. She's slowly but surely blooming. Coming into her own. And the more I discover, the more I like her. She doesn't take this thing between us too seriously. As in, she knows how to laugh at me, at herself, at the two of us. It's refreshing. She's adventurous, too. Never backs down from a challenge.

I like that. A lot. Too much, even.

Which means . . . I'm completely fucked.

I'm following her down the stairs toward the elevator. We finished dinner and had a couple more drinks, talking about everything and nothing as the restaurant slowly started to empty out. Until we were one of the last remaining occupied tables and the employees were starting to clean everything in preparation to close.

As I walk behind her, all I can think about is kissing her. Fucking her. I have a condom in the back pocket of my jeans and I'm definitely going to use it. She wants it. I know she does. I saw the way she looked at me over her shoulder as we walked toward the elevator. We're waiting for it to arrive now, standing side by side, not looking at each other.

But the connection is there, vibrating between us like a living, breathing thing. She takes a step forward and I move so I'm standing directly behind her, resting my hand at her waist, pressing my face into her hair and taking a deep breath, the sweet scent of her shampoo filling my senses.

She ducks her head forward and I brush the thick, soft waves away from her neck, leaning in to kiss her nape. She shivers, her breath leaving her in a shuddery rush, and I slip my arm around her front, bringing her to me so her ass makes direct contact with my hardening cock, my hand splayed across her quivering stomach.

"Caden," she starts, a warning in her tone, but the arrival of the elevator stops her.

The doors slide open, revealing the elevator is empty, and I push her inside, the doors closing behind us, sealing us into this tiny, facsimile club atmosphere.

She turns so her back is pressed against the mirrored wall, her eyes wide, her chest rising and falling rapidly. She's aroused. I bet if I reached between her legs my fingers would come away wet.

The music is low and sultry and the purple and green lights seem to flash in time to the beat. The elevator starts with a shake, making its descent slowly, and I turn to the control panel, pushing the red button that stops the elevator in its tracks.

"What are you doing?" she asks, inhaling sharply when I crowd her, bracing my hands against the wall behind her. Her pulse is hammering at the base of her throat and her pupils are dilated. She's excited.

So am I.

"Giving us enough time so I can fuck you properly," I murmur just before I kiss her. Hard. She tilts her head back, her hands settling on the waistband of my jeans, undoing them and finding my cock quickly since I'm not wearing anything underneath.

"You're just as bad," she breathes against my lips as she strokes my cock. I falter in her hands, her touch driving me closer to the edge. I've been sitting on that fucking edge since I fingered her in the restaurant. "Not wearing any underwear."

"Wanted to be ready for you," I say, kissing her again, dropping one of my hands to her thigh so I can tug up her skirt. Her thigh is soft and trembles beneath my fingertips. "We're going to have to be quick."

"Okay," she says eagerly as she pushes at my jeans, shoving them down so they're wrapped around my thighs.

I reach behind me and pluck the condom from my back pocket, tearing open the wrapper and slipping the ring over the head of my cock. She watches in fascination, reaching out to touch the tip, then running her finger along my length before she wraps her fingers around the base and guides me toward her.

"Come here." I pick her up with ease and she wraps her legs around my hips, her skirt shielding us. Without warning I thrust deep inside her, all the way to the hilt, and our mingling moans are loud, overpowering the low thrum of the music playing from the elevator speakers.

"Oh, God." She slams her head against the wall, her eyes falling shut, her teeth digging into her lower lip as I begin to thrust. I study her with fascination, loving the way her face hitches with my every push deep inside her body, a little whimper falling from her lips when I withdraw. She's so wet, it was easy to slide inside her pussy and I can feel it twitch and tremble, driving me fucking insane.

"Don't stop," she whispers, and there's no way in hell I can. This is going to be fast and it's going to be brutal. I'm ramming myself deep, as deep as I can go, my balls tightening, the familiar tingling at the base of my spine already starting. I'm gonna blow soon.

And I want to make sure she's coming along with me for the ride.

"You close?" I ask her, reaching in between us to stroke her clit. She's sopping wet and sticky and I'm smearing it everywhere, on my cock, on her clit, trying my damnedest to work her into a frenzy.

"Yes. Please, please, please." She's chanting, her mouth hanging open, her head thrown so far back her hair is like a crazed cloud against the mirror. I glance to my left, see that the wall isn't covered with the black pattern. It's nothing but plain mirrors.

Offering me a clear view of the two of us fucking.

"Look," I tell her, grasping her by her chin and forcing her to look to her right. Our gazes clash in the reflection and I reach between us, shoving up the skirt of her dress to her waist so our connected bodies are on perfect display.

"Oh, Caden." The words rush out of her breathlessly as I withdraw almost all the way out, my cock glistening with her juices before I shove myself back inside. It's hot as hell in the elevator. I'm sweating, she's sweating, the scent of sex is heavy in the air and the music keeps playing, the green and purple lights casting us in a weird glow, the sight of my cock moving inside of her body hurtling me closer and closer to the brink.

"You feel so good," I whisper, my words making her pussy clench tight around me. I grit my teeth, trying to control myself for at least a little longer. I want to ensure she's close to coming too, damn it. "I think I'm addicted to your pussy."

She laughs. I love that she finds my remark humorous but I'm not lying. "Are you serious?"

I play with her clit, her laughter dying on her lips, replaced by a moan instead. "Dead fucking serious, Ro. I love that pretty little pussy of yours. I never want to stop fucking it."

Her inner walls ripple with my words and I press my mouth close to her ear, whispering all sorts of dirty nothings, trying to get her off. Hell, getting myself off. She likes it dirty, this girl. I squeeze her ass, thrust my cock so deep inside her she screams and then she's coming, my name falling from her lips, her hands clutching me as tight as her pussy clutches around my cock and then I'm coming too . . .

Right at the moment the little hideaway phone in the control panel of the elevator starts ringing.

"What the hell is that?" she asks breathlessly.

"Shit." I withdraw from her reluctantly and pull off the condom, tying off the end before I go to the stupid phone and answer it.

"Sir, is everything all right? We received an emergency notice that the elevator you're in has come to a complete stop," the nasally disembodied voice asks.

"We're fine," I say gruffly, hitting the button again so the elevator starts once more with a violent jerk. I hang up on her before she can ask me anything else just as the elevator comes to a stop and the doors slide open.

Thank Christ no one is waiting for it. I turn to Rose to see she's set herself back to rights, though her hair is still a bit of a mess. I smooth it down for her in the back, earning a quick smile for my efforts.

The sight of that smile sends a strange little pang straight to my heart. I'd do anything to see it again.

You've turned into a complete pussy.

I ignore the shitty voice in my head and take Rose's arm, leading her out of the hotel so that we're standing on the sidewalk, the busy Saturday night traffic passing us by.

She turns to face me, her expression unreadable, and worry fills me. Is this it? Is she going to tell me thanks for the fucks but she's gotta go? I don't know if I can take it.

"Well, that was . . . interesting," she finally says, making me chuckle. That's exactly what she said to me after our incident at the White Swan, when I had her coming all over my fingers in minutes.

Our every encounter is what I would call interesting. And I'm interested in seeing her more.

I wrap my arm around her waist and pull her in close, relief flooding me. It's time for me to be honest. "I don't want this night to end," I whisper close to her ear.

She leans into me, her hair brushing against my chin. "I don't, either," she admits.

"Do you want to go somewhere else?" It's late, but the city is still busy and it's a Saturday night. There's plenty we could find to do.

But all I want is her. Naked. Beneath me in bed, her legs wrapped around me, our bodies locked together.

Rose slowly shakes her head, tilting her head back so her gaze meets mine. "Let's go back to my hotel room. That is, if you want to. Or maybe you need to get back to . . ."

I rest my finger over her lips, silencing her. "I don't need to get back to anything or anyone. Just you."

She smiles and I drop my hand, wrapping it around her nape so I can pull her in for a kiss. "Come back with me, then," she whispers just before I kiss her.

We kiss for so long out on the sidewalk a passerby tosses out a glib, "Get a room," bringing us back to reality. I hail a cab, Rose hanging on me like she's become an extension of my body, and when the little black cab pulls over, we pile into the back-seat, my hands on her ass since she crawled in first.

She rattles off her hotel name and address and then she's falling on top of me, her hands scratching down my chest, her mouth on mine. I pull her closer, my hands on her waist as I lose myself in her kiss. This all just feels so normal. So fucking regular. This is what guys do, right? Find a girl and fall hopelessly in lust with her. Think about her all the time. Flirt with her, fight with her, have awesome makeup sex with her. Eventually fall in love, move in together, get married and have kids.

I have never in my life wanted that. I saw what marriage did to people. It fucked them up. Look at my parents. I figured from a young age that I was better off alone. I protected myself. No way did I want to fall for one girl. Why would I want to do that when I could have many girls?

But I like this one girl. I like her a lot. And I don't want her to know anything about me. My truth is my shame. If she knew what I was really about, if she learned why I originally started talking to her that night in Cannes not so long ago—because I want to steal her family's necklace—she'd hate me forever.

I don't think I could deal with that.

What are my choices, though? Keep up the pretense that I'm something I'm not and eventually let her go? Eventually steal the necklace and leave in the dark of the night, never to return?

That's your only choice, asshole.

Then I guess that's what I'm going to do. Savor every sweet smile she gives me. Savor the way she touches me, kisses me, looks at me . . .

And then walk away.

"I really like kissing you," she murmurs against my lips, pulling me back into reality.

I brush her wild hair away from her face and smile up at her. "I like kissing you too."

"Even in uncomfortable taxicabs." She kisses my cheek, my jaw, my chin. "I could do this all night."

"Kiss me in the back of a cab?" I ask her.

"No." She rolls her eyes. "Just . . . forget it. I'm being silly."

"Tell me." I cup her cheek, my expression serious. I'm dying to know what she's going to say. "What is it, Rose?"

She lifts up a little, adjusting herself so she's straddling me, her breasts in my face, her slender legs wrapped around my thighs. I don't have another condom, they're all back at her hotel room sitting safely in the box I bought them in, and besides, I'm not about to fuck her in the back of a cab.

But you'll fuck her in an elevator.

Yeah. So I did.

"I'm hiding out, here in London. Things aren't good for me at my work right now. I, uh, sort of gave notice and I'm avoiding all responsibility like a complete loser," she admits. "So it feels good to just . . . have fun. With you. You're helping me forget all my troubles."

Ah. I'm a vacation fuck, then. Well, fine. That's about all I can be anyway, so I'll settle for it.

"That sounds awful, doesn't it? I don't mean to be so crass, but I never take time just for myself, you know? It's always been about work and family and Fleur and the Fowler name. My older sister told everyone to fuck off a long time ago and no one gives her grief. That used to make me angry, but now I'm . . . I'm envious of her. That she has so much freedom and can do whatever she wants. While I'm working and trying my best to get in my father's good graces and failing miserably."

Okay. I thought this conversation was going to be dirty and crude and I could practice my dry humping skills with her, but we've taken a serious turn here. And I can't help but feel for her, want to help her.

Shit.

"I don't know what to say," I start and she shakes her head, moving like she's going to climb off of me.

"Forget it," she mutters. "I'm being stupid."

"No. You're not being stupid." I stop her from leaving, one arm clamped tight around her waist, my other hand on the back of her neck, keeping her in place. "I want to help you, but I don't know how."

She smiles tremulously. I swear to God, if she starts crying I might need to go kick someone's ass, because the very last thing I want to see is Rose's tears. I don't think I could handle it. "You could just listen. That's enough."

"Then I'll listen." I pull her down so our foreheads meet and I stare into her eyes. "Whatever you want to tell me, I'm here for you." I mean every word I say, too.

She tilts her head, our lips brushing, the kiss sweet at first, then turning deeper, until my hands are buried in her hair and our tongues are tangled and the cabdriver has to yell at us to let us know we're at her hotel.

Fucking embarrassing. I've never become so wrapped up in a woman so quickly.

And I don't want to stop.

Chapter Thirteen

Rose

"ARE YOU AVOIDING ME ON PURPOSE OR WHAT?"

I clutch my cell close to my ear as I slip out of bed quietly, not wanting to disturb Caden, who's sleeping peacefully in my bed. We stayed up late into the night, doing what we do best.

Sex. And lots of it.

Sneaking into the bathroom, I close the door with a soft click and crawl into the giant sunken tub, curling up inside and leaning my head against the cool, smooth edge. "What are you talking about?" I ask Violet.

"I've been trying to call you for days, Rose. The last time we talked was Tuesday, and that was almost a week ago. I thought you were dead! The only thing that gave me reassurance was the fact that you returned Ryder's texts yesterday." Violet sounds completely put out.

Not that I can blame her. I *have* been avoiding her. And Ryder tricked me with those texts, asking innocent work-type questions he really had no business asking. I replied automatically, then wondered at my mistake because I knew my sister would be calling eventually. I avoid her like the plague, but not Ryder? I blew it there.

And here she is. Calling me just as predicted. Though I don't want to tell her anything. Caden is my secret, and I'm keeping him and what we've been doing all to myself.

"Your future husband is a dirty trickster," I tell her, skimming my fingernails down my thigh, tracing the little bruises that Caden put there a few days ago. They're small and a purplish red and they don't really hurt, but he did that with his fingers, gripping me so tight when he fucked me against the wall that he marked my skin.

He got upset when he saw the bruises, but I love them. He marked me. It felt so primitive and possessive, seeing those fingerprints on my skin. I've never been a man's possession before.

But I feel like his. And he feels like mine.

"I'm the one who texted you from Ryder's phone," Violet admits.

"So you're the dirty trickster, then." I should've known.

Violet sighs, sounding sad and irritated and frustrated. I'm sure she's feeling all three, and the expected guilt comes at me full force. "Father won't leave me alone, calling me all the time asking about you. He's worried."

"What about? If he has questions, why doesn't he call me himself?"

"Because he knows you're avoiding everyone, so he thought he could get to you through me," she explains wearily.

"Well, he shouldn't bother you." I feel bad. Violet is having to deflect him for me and I didn't mean to put her in that position. "Next time you hear from him, just tell him to call me. When I see it's him, I'll answer."

"You promise?" Violet sounds skeptical.

"Swear." Daddy's going to burst my bubble and bring me back to reality, but I guess I have to return sometime. This thing with Caden can't last forever. It's been fun, though. He's fun. Though a little closed off.

Okay, fine, a *lot* closed off. But he's so good with his hands and mouth and tongue that I let that all go.

Mostly.

"You didn't tell me you tried to give notice," she says, her voice soft. Deceptively calm. I'm sure she's furious with me.

I sigh. "I knew you'd flip, so I kept it to myself."

"But why? Why are you doing this? Why are you giving up so easily?"

"I have my reasons." Reasons I'm starting to doubt. Why did I give him my notice anyway? And why did I send my lame attempt at giving notice to Daddy via an email a few days ago that I knew would make him so mad? It was a bad move. An impulsive move. And I'm rarely impulsive.

Funny, since I met Caden, I've become even more impulsive.

"What have you been doing anyway?" Violet asks. "Now that you're no longer working for Fleur."

I wish I could tell her. But I'll probably shock the hell out of her, so I restrain myself.

Nothing much. I barely leave the hotel room. Caden is with me and we are constantly, and I mean constantly, *fucking. He's amazing. I've never had so many orgasms. We had to buy the economy-sized box of condoms and I got embarrassed when he set it on the counter at the drugstore. Oh, and he's so sweet. Attentive. Funny. Infuriating. We argue; he says something stupid and I want to hit him. And then the next minute, I'm on my knees in front of him, kissing and sucking his cock and enjoying every single second of it, too. There's nothing I like better than servicing my man.*

Does that make me sound ridiculous? Wait. Don't answer that.

Yeah. I can't tell her what I've been doing. She'll flip out.

"I've been exploring London," I say. That's code for "I've been exploring Caden's body." "I've learned a lot." Like how he loves it when I lick his inner thighs. Well, he doesn't really love it, more like he starts laughing because he's ticklish there, and it's the cutest thing I've ever seen.

"Like what?" Violet asks.

"Uh . . ." That goose bumps race over Caden's skin right before he comes. That he truly enjoys going down on a woman, specifically me. Oh, and that he dreams about me sometimes. I heard him say my name two nights ago but when I answered him he didn't reply, and I realized he was asleep.

"You're with that Caden guy, aren't you?" she spits out, shocking me silent.

Well. I was already silent because I was scrambling to come up with something to say, but now I'm *really* quiet.

"Your silence is as good as an admittance of guilt," Violet says. "I've been talking to Whitney. She says Caden went to her apartment Sunday, grabbed all of his stuff, and hasn't been back since. Hasn't called or texted her, either."

Damn right he hasn't called or been back, because he's with *me*.

Oh, dear. I sound ridiculously possessive. What has this man done to me?

"Does she think he's with me?" I ask nonchalantly.

"She has no idea where he is. I love Whit, but she's kind of clueless sometimes." Violet's voice turns brisk. "But that doesn't matter. What matters is what are you doing, hanging out with him? You know nothing about him."

"You're right. I don't." I know plenty, but none of it is for public consumption.

"You don't even know his last name," she points out.

"I do, too. It's Kingsley." I clamp my lips shut, wishing I hadn't said that. Not that she couldn't have asked Whitney for that information, but now I'm afraid Violet will run off and do a Google search on him.

I should do a Google search on him, but I'm . . . scared. Of what I might find out. What if it's bad? I'd rather exist in this blissful ignorant state. It's nice here. Full of good food and sleep and lots of naked touching time. I like it.

I don't want to end it.

You have to end it.

"Well, this Caden Kingsley person can't be good for you. He's encouraging you to ignore all of your responsibilities," Violet says. "You need to come in to the office. I want to talk to you. Leaving Fleur is not the answer to your problems."

"You're the one who told me to let go and indulge in myself for a while," I point out. "Now you're nagging at me like an old maid."

"I'm nagging you because I'm concerned," she says. "You're right. I told you to indulge in yourself and have a good time and all that nonsense, but I didn't expect you to completely fall off the grid like you have."

"It's not going to be forever," I say, my voice small, the sound echoing in the empty bathroom. "I plan on returning to New York . . . soon."

"How soon? And are you going back to Fleur? Father didn't take your notice seriously. He believes you'll come back."

That almost pisses me off, that Daddy didn't take my giving notice seriously. But then again I shouldn't be surprised. "I don't know." Plus, it all depends. How long is Caden staying in London? Is he eventually returning to New York? Would he want to—*gasp*—see me once we're both in New York?

Probably not.

"Well, you'd better figure out a firmer answer than that, because that'll be the first thing Father will ask you." Violet pauses and when she resumes speaking, her voice is softer. Lower. "He has some news for you."

Dread slithers down my spine, settling in an ice-cold pool in my stomach. "What sort of news?"

"I should let him tell you," she says vaguely.

"No. Tell me, Violet. I want to know." I think I already know, but I don't want it to be true. It can't be true . . .

"He asked her to marry him." Violet releases a shuddering sigh. "She's wearing a ring. One of Grandma's old rings, a tacky-looking diamond that's so large it doesn't look real. A castoff. At least, that's what Grandma called it. You know she hates Pilar as much as we do."

I say nothing. What *can* I say? I knew this moment was coming, no matter how much I wanted to deny it. "I'm sure she's getting the promotion then, too," I finally say, my voice raspy, my throat dry.

"That hasn't been formally announced yet, but I'm guessing the answer is yes. He's willing enough to marry her, so I'm sure he's more than willing to give her the coveted promotion," Violet says snidely.

I wanted that promotion. My current position—or the position I left, that is—isn't even a real one. It was created for me when I started working at Fleur full-time. I wanted to earn a vice-president position on my own merits. On my talents and the love and hard work I put into Fleur, not because I'm a Fowler.

And here's Pilar, getting a promotion, getting an engagement ring . . . getting everything she wants. Stomping all over me in the process, too. I know she just about had a party when Violet left to work in London. Now she can get rid of me too and take over completely, standing right by Daddy's side and waiting for the day he retires? I shouldn't give her the satisfaction.

I turn and press my forehead against the wall of the tub, closing my eyes. Violet is still talking and she sounds so furious, so frustrated. I know it's pointless to get so upset, to waste so much energy.

What's done is done.

She catches my attention when she declares that she and Ryder have no plans to return to New York anytime soon. I open my eyes and sit straight up in the tub. "What do you mean, you're not leaving London anytime soon?"

"We can't go back there, not with Pilar. Ryder refuses to. There's too much bad blood between them. Too much bad blood between us as well," she adds.

"How can Daddy do this? Is he blind to all of the awful things she does? She's tearing our family apart." I told myself it didn't matter, that I wouldn't expend so much energy being upset over this, but I can feel the tears threatening. And I refuse to let them fall. "I hate her."

"Maybe he'll see one day," Violet says softly, her voice choked with emotion too. "She makes him happy, Rose. We can't deny him happiness."

"You would say that," I mutter with a wretched laugh that turns into a sob. I slap my hand over my mouth, trying to stop it, contain it, but it's no use. The tears are flowing freely now. I wonder if I should tell her about our mother's last few entries in her diary before she died. Violet deserves to know. But how can I say anything about them after the news she just delivered? The timing is all wrong. "I have to go," I say with a loud sniff.

"Rose. Rosie. Don't cry, sweetie. She's not worth your tears, trust me." Violet pauses, and I can practically see her brain scrambling as she tries to figure out what to say next. "You want me to come over? Or how about you come over to our place? I'll take you out to dinner. You can spend the night and we can stay up late and watch movies. What do you think?"

"No. I'm fine. Really." I wipe the tears from my face, rest my hand against my mouth and nose. "I'll call you later, okay?"

"Promise?"

"I promise." I end the call and set the phone carefully on the side of the tub before I push myself out of it, going to the sink so I can splash cold water on my face.

But it doesn't help. My cheeks are tinged with pink and my eyes are rimmed with red. I look miserable. I feel miserable.

It's not even so much over the fact that our father actually wants to marry that bitch—though that sucks no matter which way you look at it—it's the idea of me not feeling welcome at my family's business. That I would rather walk away from my legacy than work with a woman I despise. Once Violet left, it's as if everyone at Fleur forgot I existed, even our father. I wasn't called into strategy meetings anymore. I attended the publicity events and that was it. I was bored. Unused. Frustrated.

I *should* go back. I can't stand by and watch my father fall deeper and deeper into Pilar's control, can I?

Leaning my hands on the edge of the sink, I peer at my reflection in the mirror, desperately looking for something. An answer, a solution, an idea . . . anything to help me figure out what I should do next.

But I see nothing. Just my pitiful face staring back at me, the remnants of my tears drying on my cheeks and the hopelessness in my eyes.

I push away from the sink with a little sound of frustration and exit the bathroom, returning to the bed to see that Caden hasn't moved at all. He's still sprawled on his stomach, his arms stretched up over his head, his left leg bent upward. The sheets lie across his lower back, revealing all that delicious muscled goodness, and the familiar tingle sweeps over my skin, setting me on fire.

When do I not want him? And there is no better time than now, when I'm feeling at my lowest point. Caden will know how to make me feel better. A teasing comment accompanied by one of his sexy smiles will help me forget. An orgasm will chase away all of my blues. I take off the tank top and boy shorts I wore to bed, leaving them in a pile on the floor. My nipples are already hard and between my thighs I'm wet. Eager.

Ready.

Sliding beneath the sheets, I lie on my side facing him, my gaze roaming over his sleeping face. His features are relaxed, his lips slightly parted, his breathing slow and even. His hair is a mess, but what else is new? The man is in desperate need of a haircut, but I refuse to suggest it because, well . . . I love his hair. It's long and soft and constantly bothers him, and I love it when he flicks his head to get the annoying strands out of his eyes.

I love it more when I feel it brush against my skin as his lips make their way down my body.

"You're staring," he murmurs, his eyes still closed, his expression not really changing beyond his moving lips.

A squeal escapes me and I press my lips together, irritated that he caught me. I shove at his shoulder but it's like pushing a wall of steel, so he doesn't so much as budge. "You scared me."

"Good. Stalkers scare me too." He cracks open one eye and smiles. But as fast as it appears, the smile fades, and he moves so fast he turns into a blur. He's sitting up, pulling me by the shoulders so I'm in his lap. "What's wrong, baby?"

Great. Not only is he knowledgeable in the orgasm department, but he's also perceptive to my moods. "I'm fine," I say with a shrug, refusing to crack.

He streaks his fingers down my cheek, his gaze never leaving mine. "You sure?"

I waver. Should I tell him? We've never discussed anything too personal. Nothing about our pasts, very little about our present, definitely no discussing the future—absolutely nothing about it is mentioned. We don't talk about my job or his. We don't talk about my family or his. Current events, movies, what's going on around London, what's happening at home . . . those are safe topics.

He mentioned a friend who's visiting in London like he is, a guy named Mitchell who's a total asshole and worth a ton of money, but other than that, there's been nothing. No major reveal, no intimate conversations beyond the *I want your pussy* or *Please let me suck your cock* variety.

Okay, we're not that crude all the time. But our moments

together are hotter more often than not and I love it. I love losing myself when I'm with him.

But maybe . . . I do want his help. His input with this problem. It could bring us closer. "I'm sure." I nod, trying to breathe past the sudden ache in my chest. I'm such a chicken. From the skeptical look he's wearing, I know Caden doesn't believe me, and that's fine. I'm not ready to share this piece of me all the way yet. "Could you just . . . hold me for a while?" I grimace the second the words are said and I shake my head, burying my face in the crook of his neck. "Never mind. That was so incredibly cheesy . . ."

"Sshh." He silences me and gathers me close in his strong embrace. I wrap my arm around his waist, splaying my hand across his back as I press my face against his chest. I hear the steady beat of his heart, and it reassures me as it always does.

He rubs my back, his touch gentle, but then . . . slowly . . . it becomes firmer. His hand sweeps across my backside as he picks me up and readjusts me so I'm straddling him, my legs wrapping around him so my ankles press against his spine.

"I know how to make you feel better," he murmurs in my ear, nuzzling my cheek with his nose as he reaches for my breast, cupping it in his big hand.

"I'm sure you do." This is what I was counting on, what I needed from Caden. He *does* know how to make me feel better. He washes away any of my doubt, my uncertainty, my insecurities with his irresistible hands, his smart mouth, his perfect cock . . .

But there's more to this man than his body. He's inherently kind. He wants to take care of me. Though he might not say those words out loud, his actions speak for themselves. It doesn't matter to him who I am or what I represent. He just . . . likes me. Rose. Not Rose Fowler, youngest daughter of Forrest Fowler and heiress to the Fleur Cosmetics line. I'm not Violet's sister or Lily's sister or Dahlia's granddaughter to Caden.

I'm just me. Rose. Or Ro, as he likes to call me sometimes. I like that too because no one else calls me that. Just Caden.

Together we're just Rose and Caden, hanging out in London. And that works. No matter how temporary or fleeting this moment is, I'm here, in it. Living it.

And I'm going to make the most of it.

Chapter Fourteen

Caden

"Violet wants us to go out with them tonight."

I'm sitting in bed—we walked around earlier, getting some fresh air and picking up coffee—watching Rose as she gets dressed for work. Yes, work. She's actually going into the Fleur offices for a mid-afternoon meeting after much wheedling and persuading on her sister's part. I don't know exactly what's going on between the sisters and Fleur and the rest of the family, but I know it's not good. It's making Rose upset.

And I don't like seeing my girl upset.

Not that she's talking to me, confessing all of her problems, which I get. I totally get it. Really, she's not my girl. I have no right to think of her that way—even though I do.

"Go out where?"

She adjusts the thin black belt that goes with the cream-colored sleeveless dress she's wearing and turns to face me. "You'll never guess."

"The White Swan," I say in perfect deadpan.

"You're so smart." She leans over me and drops a kiss on my waiting lips. "We don't have to go if you don't want to."

"Who's going to be there?" I ask warily, waiting for her answer.

"Violet, Ryder, and Nigel. Maybe another woman from work, but no Whitney," she adds hurriedly.

Thank Christ. I haven't talked to Whitney since I fled her flat and I know she's pissed at me. I need to call her soon and make up to her, but not yet. She needs more time to get over it. "I like Nigel."

She smiles. "So do I."

"I think we should go." I lean back against the padded headboard, bending my arms behind my head and interlocking my fingers against my neck. "It's time for you to get back out into the real world, sweetheart."

Rose rolls her eyes as she grabs a pair of earrings from the top of the dresser, slipping one pearl into her ear, then the other. They're gorgeous pearls. Perfect luster, perfect color, and the perfect size, they'd get a fair amount on the black market. I know this because if they weren't Rose's earrings, they'd already be in my possession. *Hell,* I probably would've already cashed them in and wired the money into Mom's bank account.

She'd notice, though. She wears them every single day and no way could I risk snagging them. The Poppy Necklace on the other hand . . . I have no idea where it is. And I'd like to find it.

But the minute I find it, I'm out. Headed back home to cash it in and then go see Mom in Miami.

Thinking of my mother reminds me that I need to call her. This afternoon would be good, since I'll be alone for the first time since Rose and I got together. Or whatever we can call this . . . thing we're doing.

"And what do you do in the real world anyway?" she asks, her voice casual though I know she's fishing.

Finally. I wondered how long it would take for her to start asking questions.

"I do exactly what you see." I grip my hands together tight, hating the lie that's about to fall from my lips. "Travel around, see the world." Well, part of that is true. I just left off the other part. I tried going to college, but it was too damn expensive and I couldn't focus. Tried going straight and finding a real job, but that was an epic fail on all accounts. Got Mom the hell out of New York and moved her to Florida, somewhere I've thought about going more than once.

But I don't. Maybe I should. It might be easier, going there. Then I'd have to explain to Mom what the hell I do for a living, but I've been lying to her for this long. I can keep it up.

I'm all she has. Stealing keeps her and me afloat. I don't know how to do anything else.

I am a world-class fuckup.

"Must be tough," she teases.

"Oh yeah." I thunk the back of my head against the headboard, wishing it weren't padded and soft. I need to knock some sense into my stupid brain. Not like I can come clean to Rose, but maybe I can turn my life around for her. I've tried before, but I could never stay clean. She could give me purpose, though. A real reason to be good—all for her. If she'd have me.

She won't have you.

I tell the voice in my head to shut the fuck up.

Rose comes to a stop at the foot of the bed, her gaze wistful as she studies me. "You really shouldn't sit like that."

"Sit like what?" The woman straight up makes no sense sometimes. Like right now. I have no idea what she's talking about.

Slowly she shakes her head as she approaches me. "With your arms behind your head. Your biceps are bulging and your shoulders and chest look exceptionally broad. Makes it hard for me to leave. I'd rather stay here with you."

Ah, poor Rose. She's scared to go back to Fleur. She mentioned that she didn't approve of the woman her father is involved with and that this woman works at Fleur, which makes her uncomfortable. But that's all I know. And they're back in New York, not here in London. "Then don't leave." I drop my arms and reach for her, but she sidesteps away from me. "Stay with me."

"You just encouraged me to go and now you're trying to tempt me to stay?" She laughs. "You're a bad influence."

She has no idea.

After ten minutes of heavy kissing, I finally shove her ass out of the suite, glancing around the room after I shut the door behind her. This is the first time I've been left alone in the suite. My first opportunity to go through her stuff, and I'm hesitating like a wimp.

I need to see if she has anything of value stashed in her suitcase. Like maybe the Poppy Necklace, because I'd really like to know where it disappeared to. Though she'd be damn crazy to keep that thing in her suitcase. The hotel provides both an in-room safe and an even harder-to-crack safe behind the front desk. The in-room safes are useless. I've cracked hundreds of them over the years.

So I decide to go ahead and crack this one. Just for curiosity's sake. No way would I take whatever I find in there.

My heart squeezes when I open the little metal door and see there's a box inside. Slowly I reach in, tentatively grabbing the box, as if it's some sort of wild animal ready to bite my fingers off at any given moment.

Withdrawing the box from the safe, I examine it. It's old, covered in faded black velvet, and I open it, not surprised at all to see the necklace nestled within. Pink and white diamonds, each cut precise and perfect, each stone chosen for its flawless clarity. The necklace is going to fetch me an absolute fortune when I turn it in to Dexter. He'll add it to his private collection, never to be seen in public again.

Collectors of rare stolen goods are weird. Me? I'd want to show that shit off, but in this kind of situation, you can't. Everything's a secret.

I'm starting to really hate secrets.

Without thought I shut the safe and take the velvet box with me, stashing it deep in the bottom of my duffel bag. Sweat dots my forehead when I zip up the bag and sit back, my heart hammering so hard it's all I can hear.

I shouldn't have taken the necklace. If Rose finds out, I'm ruined. Not only because she could rat me out to the police.

But because she'll hate me for stealing from her. And I can't blame her.

Muttering under my breath, I go to the closet and slam the door shut, banging the wall with my clenched fist. I don't know what the hell is going on between me and Rose, but she *means* something to me. She's more than a friend. More than a casual fuck. I like her. I could see myself falling for her if I don't watch it.

Which means I need to fucking watch it.

Grabbing my cell, I call Mom, waiting for her to answer. She does on the third ring, sounding breathless and harried and so fucking annoyed I almost hang up.

But she has caller ID and she will know it's me on the other end, so I don't bother. I'd rather get this conversation over with.

"Mom," I say, and she cuts me off before I can get another word out.

"Caden! Where the hell are you? You need to come home."

Shit. "What's wrong?"

"Oh, you're going to be so mad at me." She's walking through the house, I can tell by the briskness of her words, the sound of her heels clicking loudly on the tile floor. I hear the yip of one of her annoying-as-fuck dogs in the background and I settle heavily in a chair, bracing myself for the bad news.

"What did you do?" I ask wearily, ready for one of her usual excuses, wondering which one it'll be this time.

"Well, you know I've been having trouble lately with my headaches. Did I tell you about them? No? Anyway, I've been taking it easy, staying at home because I think the weather is causing them. It's so blessedly hot here. But I broke down because I needed to go to the store a few days ago so I hopped in the car, went shopping, and when I was done, I had a blinding headache. Positively blinding. It was awful. So miserable. The sun hurt my eyes and not even my sunglasses could help, and those Chanel glasses are some of the best I've ever owned. I've had them for twenty years. Did you know they were a gift from your father? Well, anyway . . ."

"Mom," I interrupt her. "Get to the part where you did something that's going to make me so mad."

"Right, right. Fine." She takes a deep breath. "I became frustrated with the headache and the fact that I couldn't get rid of it, so I finally just got back into the car and drove home. I miss not having a hired car and driver, Caden. I miss it so much."

Oh my God. The woman wants and wants. I've wondered more than once if she drove Dad to do what he did. Not fair, but . . .

Yeah. Something to consider.

"So I'm driving. The sun is so bright and traffic was so heavy. I panicked. I don't do well under pressure, you know. And then I . . ." Her voice drifts and I close my eyes, pinching the bridge of my nose.

It's going to be bad. I think I know where she's going with this, but I need to hear what she has to say. "You what?"

"I wrecked the car. Oh, Caden, I'm so, *so* sorry. I don't know what happened. One minute I'm driving along and everything is fine, though the headache is making it a bit hard for me to see, but the sunglasses helped a little. And then the next thing another car darts out in front of me and I hit it. God, the noise! The crunching and the squeal of the tires were so loud. I got so scared I swerved right and hit the curb, smashing right into a fire hydrant."

Of course she did. "You're kidding."

"I wish I were, darling. It was just a mess. Water everywhere. The horn got stuck and went on and on, bleating like a dying cow. The accident made the local news," she admits, her voice low. She sounds embarrassed. "It was awful."

Hell. It sounds like my very worst nightmare come to life. "So the car is a lost cause."

"Both cars a lost cause, and since it was my fault . . . and the lady got so mad at me she started to yell and was throwing around words like *lawsuit* and, well, I didn't know what to do. So I called Stanley."

Great. Here comes another bill. "Why did you call your lawyer?"

"I thought he could help me. Give me the proper advice I needed," she admits, her voice small.

"Mom. He just wants to keep you talking so he can then send you a ridiculous bill for three hours' worth of assistance on a phone call. And he can't help you yet. You need to talk to the insurance company first."

"That's exactly what Stanley said!" She sounds surprised, like she has zero faith in me and I don't know what the hell I'm talking about.

"Why didn't you call me?"

"Oh, you know me. I get confused about the time change with you being in London. And you're with your little friend, so I didn't want to disturb you."

"What little friend?" Unease creeps over my skin. What does she know? How could she know who I'm with? *Hell,* how could she know anything?

"That Mitchell Landers. Remember how pudgy he was when you two were in the seventh grade? That boy drove me crazy. I know he's the one who introduced you to marijuana," she says irritably.

I almost want to laugh. Almost. "Mom, I'm the one who gave Mitchell his first joint. Not the other way around."

"You're so funny, trying to make jokes during a time like this." She sighs. "When are you coming home?"

"When do you want me to come home?"

"Tonight? Get on pudgy Mitchell Landers's jet and come right home, Caden. Come to Miami. I'm tired of you living in the city. That place is awful. I need your help. I'm getting phone calls from the insurance company and I don't know what to tell them. You'd know what to say."

Hello, real life, you've just come pounding hard on my front door. "I can't come home tonight. Mitchell's not leaving London until early next week." *Thank Christ.* We've both been in agreement about extending our stay here in England. But that leaves me only a few days with Rose before I have to return.

And that's not enough time.

"Oh, poo. Come home now. Book a flight, then."

"You can wait a few more days, right?"

"I suppose," she says sullenly.

"Besides, a last minute flight costs big money and I don't want to waste a dime. Not after your car accident. God knows what else you're going to be billed for," I say, exasperated with her, with my entire life. "I bet the city is going to make you pay for that busted hydrant."

"I'll fight it. That's the most ridiculous thing ever. I can't help it if they place their hydrants in ridiculous places where any car could come along and destroy one."

I'm not even touching that statement. "Listen, I'll come home in a few days, okay? In the meanwhile, direct all calls from the insurance company or anyone else to me, got it?"

"They won't talk to you, Caden. They want to talk to me. I'm the one who caused the accident," she points out.

"I'm trying to help you, Mom. Okay? So give them my number. At the very least, stop answering the damn phone unless it's me."

"And how am I supposed to know if it's you calling?" she asks, sounding well and truly puzzled. She's older than most of my friends' moms, close to seventy, since she and my father had me late in life. I was one of those cherished babies after they tried so hard for so many years to become pregnant. The prized baby boy, the son they indulged and spoiled, turning me into an utter brat. Until I had to straighten up and become a man when I was only a teen after my father jumped off a building and ended it.

Fucker.

"You have caller ID, Mom. Remember?"

The conversation goes on like this for a few more minutes, me trying to calm her down, Mom trying to tell me story after story that I couldn't give two shits about. I let her ramble on, the familiar guilt that washes over me expected. I'm all she has. She doesn't have many friends, because all of her supposed dear friends ditched her after Dad jumped to his death and we lost most of our money. What the bank didn't take, we sold, and I managed to somehow move Mom into a small condo in Miami once I graduated high school.

I finally end the call with Mom and immediately call Cash, tapping my foot against the floor as I wait for him to pick up. Cash isn't his real name, because come on, life isn't that funny, but he's the man we all go to in order to turn our loot into cash, and so it's a nickname he picked up ages ago. Way before my time. The old geezer is close to Mom's age and as slick as anything you've ever seen. Smart, too. He's been doing this for years and took me under his wing when I first came to him.

I owe him lots of things, but mostly my sanity.

"Caden Kingsley. Where the hell are you, son?" Cash greets me in his familiar gravelly voice.

"Still in London, old chap," I say, making him laugh at my horrible attempt at an English accent. "Where are you?"

He travels around as much as we all do, though he's based out of Miami most of the time. He's checked in on Mom more than once and I appreciate that, and so does she, since she flirts with him every chance she can get. Plus, he looks like a typical lounge lizard. Slicked-back silver hair, overly tanned skin, shirt unbuttoned halfway down his chest to reveal the gold medallion as big as his fist hanging from a thick gold chain.

Yeah. Cheesy. But the man is worth a load of cash and has no problems flaunting it.

"I'm in New York, motherfucker," he says in a tough-guy New York accent before he bursts into laughter that turns into wheezing. I let him ride it out. "I've missed you."

"I saw you a month ago."

"And it's been three weeks too long. You've been coming to me so much these last few months it seems odd, not seeing your handsome mug," Cash says.

"Yeah, well, you'll see me soon. Gotta get home so I can take care of Mom. When are you headed back to Miami?" I tell him briefly what she did, which only makes him laugh harder. He's always had a thing for my mom. Sometimes I wish I could hook the two of them up so they could fall madly in love and he'll take care of her for the rest of her life, not me.

But that'll never happen. She refuses to let anyone in after what Dad did to her. Not that I can blame her.

"You know what your mom needs?" Cash asks once I finish the story.

"To be institutionalized?" *I wish.* And then I immediately don't wish, because what kind of shitty son am I? "Hell, I'm kidding. You know I am. I'm the one who should be institutionalized."

"Naw. You're fine. Though you do need to straighten up your act. But your pretty mama? She needs a good man to keep her straight. And I could be that man, you know." He's always making statements like that. Maybe I should take him up on it. But I figure that as usual, he's joking.

"Right, right, in my dreams you'll become my stepfather, Cash."

He laughs. Wheezes some more. The man needs to lay off the

cancer sticks. "It could happen. You're the one who throws the roadblocks."

"Uh-huh. Look, I'm going to grab a few things over the next few days. Nothing too big, but I'll need fast cash." I clear my throat, fighting off the guilt that threatens. Guilt that I haven't felt in a long-ass time because damn it, I do this to survive. I shouldn't care what other people think of me, especially Rose. "Will you still be in the city next week?"

"Yeah, though listen. There's a little something I want to discuss with you. Hold on." I can hear him as he exits his office and I assume he's just walked outside. "I have a proposition for you."

"What sort of proposition?" It better not be some crazy scheme. The man used to come up with some outrageous shit, especially when I was younger and more daring—or stupid, take your pick—but he's laid off that stuff, thank God.

"Nothing bad, son. I swear. This is actually legit. Like a real job—no criminal activity involved."

Now that piques my interest. If I want Rose to take me seriously—and *holy shit,* I'm pretty sure I do—I need to go straight.

I need to leave my past behind.

Chapter Fifteen

Caden

"THEY SHOULD BE HERE ANY MINUTE, MATE," NIGEL SAYS, glancing at his iPhone. He's texting some female who's clearly not interested, since he keeps muttering under his breath every time he gets a reply he's not happy with.

"No problem." Rose had called me and asked that I meet them at the White Swan since it's so close to the hotel, and I agreed. When I arrived, though, only Nigel was waiting for me, with a half-empty beer in front of him and a morose expression on his face.

Woman problems, I learned once I settled in and ordered my own beer. I let him ramble on, griping about a certain Clare who works at Fleur. A woman he's had a crush on for far too long and she knows it but doesn't seem to fancy him, and now she's just turned into this enormous tease and good God, all his chatter is exhausting.

Considering I've dealt with Mom's constant chatter and Cash all in one day, poor Nigel is not gaining my full attention. I'm like the beautiful, aloof Clare at Fleur. She's not giving him his full attention, either.

Jesus, I feel like a prick.

I rub my hands over my face and drain my beer, the alcohol flowing through my veins easily since I never really ate lunch. I still can't wrap my head around what Cash offered me. I think I'm going to take him up on it. And if I do, there won't be any need for me to cash in the Poppy Necklace to Dexter. He's going to be furious, but . . . *fuck it.*

I can make my own money—legitimately. I have no idea what that's like, but I'm willing to give it a try.

Especially if Rose is willing to give *me* a try.

But I can't talk about my potential new career with anyone. I have no friends. Mitchell knows what I'm all about, but that fucker doesn't know shit about having a career. He's never had to work a day in his life. Neither have I. Not a real job, at least.

"So what exactly do you *do* anyway?" Nigel the mind reader asks, slurring his words a bit. Sounds like someone's already had too much to drink.

"You wouldn't believe me if I told you," I say, deciding to fuck with him. The guy needs to loosen up a little. Constantly sending the noncaring Clare texts is probably annoying the shit out of her. He needs to focus on something else.

"Ah, you can't say something like that and not expect a de-mand that you tell me exactly what it is you *do.*" Nigel lifts his hand, garnering the attention of the barmaid. "Two more for us," he calls.

"Make it four," I say after him, earning a strange look from Nigel. I shrug. "May as well be prepared for the next one, right?"

"Right. Bloody good call." He nods in affirmation. "So tell me. Are you a spy?"

"Yes. I am," I answer, my tone grave. "My secret spy number is double-O-five. Or Hawaii Five-O."

Nigel laughs. "Don't you Americans have a show called that?"

"Yep." *A spy. Ha. I wish.*

"So you're definitely not a spy. How unfortunate." He shakes his head. "An actor?"

Sometimes. When need be. "Can you imagine? But no."

Nigel wags his brows like an exaggerated cartoon character. "Rose's butler?"

"Well, I *am* servicing her." We both crack up over that just as the barmaid brings us our four mugs of beer, the tiny round table we're sitting at now crowded with them, though at least she takes away the empties. Hell, by the time the working stiffs show up, I'm afraid Nigel and I will be good and drunk.

So that's what we do. We drink and I let Nigel continue guessing, which helps distract him from his texting Clare, not that I point out that little fact to him. His guesses at my profession get more and more ridiculous until . . . he finally fucking nails it. After my third beer and God knows how many he's had, he gets it right.

"You're a thief."

I go completely still and unfortunately, become completely sober just with those three words. "What makes you say that?"

"You're a sly motherfucker, that's why. Fucking wanker, distracting me from texting the most impossible girl on the planet so you can get me drunk." Nigel shakes his head and smiles. He saw right through my plan. "I bet that's how you trick all the defenseless people you steal from." He laughs hysterically and I know I should join right in with him.

But I don't. I feel like absolute shit. Nigel's right. I'm a sly motherfucker who tricks defenseless people and then I steal from them. I'm a terrible person, a terrible fucking man. I don't deserve Rose. Not at all.

It's at that particular self-loathing moment when I see her. Rose. She's just entered the pub, Violet by her side, Ryder right behind them and accompanied by another man. I don't know who the man is, but I know in a second I can't stand him. He has his hand on Rose's shoulder, his fingers pressing into the skin of her upper arm since the dress she's wearing is sleeveless and jealousy fills me, blocking everything out until all I can see is that asshole's hand on my woman's arm.

She laughs at something he says, glancing over her shoulder at him, and he gives her arm a squeeze—*fuck me*—and she's never looked more beautiful. The white dress fits her to perfection, showing off her every curve, and I can see why that dick has his hands on her because right about now I'd have my hands all over her too.

Hell. I need another beer.

"Jeeves. I do believe you've been replaced," Nigel says, his English accent becoming more pronounced. He chuckles and shakes his head.

"What the hell are you talking about?"

"Uh . . . looks like Watson has his hands all over Rose. I thought you were the one who serviced her." At my blank look, Nigel continues. "You're her butler, right? Servicing her? That's why I called you Jeeves. Get it? Huh. Well, it appears you have some competition from Hugh. He can't seem to stop touching her."

"Who the fuck is Hugh?" I can't tear my gaze off of them. They're making their way toward our table and the smile on Rose's face is aimed right at me. But is it really for me? Or was it spurred on by whatever Hugh-the-fucker-Watson said?

"He works at Fleur. Right arrogant bastard, too. The women love him," Nigel mutters. "Probably even Clare."

"If she does then she's not worthy, Nigel. Don't forget that," I say, putting on my best phony smile for the group of four that approaches our table. Rose stops right in front of me, her eyes clouded as she stares at my face. Am I scowling? Hell, I hope not.

"Are you okay?" she asks.

I up the watts on my fake smile and take her hand, pulling her close so I can kiss her cheek. "I'm great," I whisper close to her ear. I glance to my right, see that Hugh is watching our every move, and I want to kick his face in. "Who's this?" I ask casually.

"Oh, Caden, this is Hugh Watson. He works in marketing at Fleur. Hugh, this is my—friend Caden." She smiles toward Hugh, who takes a step forward so he's standing right next to her. Like he belongs at her side. I must admit they look good together. They look right. Two young professionals, dressed expensively and working their way rightfully up the career ladder.

Shit.

"Great meeting you." He reaches out a hand and I take it, the both of us in a who-can-give-the-firmest-handshake standoff.

"A friend of Rose's, eh?" He gives me a grim smile as he releases my hand. I have a feeling he believed he was going to be Rose's special friend this evening. "Nice meeting you as well."

More rounds are ordered—though Rose chooses a mixed drink because she is not much of a beer drinker after all—and chairs are taken, Hugh making sure he's sitting on the other side of Rose when she scoots her chair close to mine.

Fucking great.

"How was the meeting?" I ask her, keeping my voice low, wanting our conversation to be just between us. Having her gone even for a few hours . . . I missed her. Sappy but true.

Missed her after going through her stuff and stealing the most valuable piece of jewelry she owns? Nice, asshole. Real nice.

I ignore the mean-ass voice in my head.

"It went really well. My father was a part of it via Skype and it was . . . good to talk to him." She smiles and nods, but that pretty smile doesn't quite meet her eyes and I know she's not telling me everything.

Which is fine. Really. I'm not telling her everything, either. How can I? My life is fucking chaos at the moment. I should be home, back in the States. I should be cleaning up the mess Mom made, I should be meeting with Cash so he can give me the low-down on the interview he's setting up for me, but no. I'm in London, because I don't want to leave this beautiful woman sitting by my side.

My priorities are all fucked up. I want what I can't have, the story of my life.

"How many beers have you had anyway?" she asks when I make a quick grab for the fresh one the barmaid delivers.

"Too many." I point at Nigel, who's laughing hysterically at something Ryder is telling him. "It's all his fault."

"Nigel?" She sounds surprised. "He's harmless."

"Not really. Wait until you have to hear him drone on about a certain Clare. Then you won't think he's so harmless," I mutter against the rim of my glass before I take a swig.

"Ah, Clare. Really? He's still talking about her?" She shakes her head with a sad smile. "She likes *this* one." She points at Hugh.

Asshole. Stealing my friend's woman. *Shit.* Maybe I am drunk. "I think that one likes *you*." I tilt my head in Hugh's direction, thankful he's talking to Violet and not making eyes at my girl.

Rose blushes. She actually fucking blushes. *Christ,* she's cute. "He does not."

I crane my neck to check him out. He's still chatting with Violet, but I see the way his gaze slides to Rose every few seconds, lingering on her face, her chest, her whatever he finds particularly appealing.

Can't help but wonder if he would find my fist connecting with his nose appealing? Probably not.

"Yeah. I think he does." I can grudgingly admit he's a good-looking fucker with the dark hair styled in an expensive cut, the high-end suit he's wearing, and that gleaming smile that probably cost a fortune.

I hate him.

"Well, it doesn't matter, because I'm here with *you*." She leans into me, her mouth right at my ear, her lips moving against it when she speaks and making me shiver. "I missed you."

Her confession pleases me more than I care to admit. "Yeah?" I tuck a strand of hair behind her ear, my gaze roaming over her pretty face. "Did it really go okay? The meeting?"

She shrugs and pulls away from me, reaching out to grab her drink and take a sip. "It went as well as I expected."

"And that means?" I press. I'm not one to push. If she doesn't want to share details of her personal life, I can deal with that. I'm sharing the most intimate experience with this woman two people can have. I know her body inside and out. But we don't talk about personal things. Our private lives. She mentioned she gave notice at Fleur and that surprised me, but she never went into detail and I didn't push. We told each other that first night, lying in bed together in the hushed quiet of the hotel suite, that we wouldn't push. We wouldn't ask too many questions.

I regret making that promise. More and more as each day passes by.

It's stupid. How can we ever turn this into something more if we don't really talk? Does she want to turn this into more? Do I?

I go back and forth. Having Hugh Watson show up is not helping my case, either. He's the type of man she should be with. One who's her equal, not a criminal who's faked through most of his life and doesn't know how to let a woman get close.

"It means that my relationship with my father is what I would call strained at best." She looks sad. I hate it. I want to chase away her sadness and make her feel good. Help her forget.

"My relationship with my father sucked too," I admit, feeling the need to share something. A bit of my life I've never really talked about with anyone. Mitchell knows what happened to my dad and so does Whitney, but we've never really spoken of it. No one talks about suicide.

No one.

"Really?" She sounds curious but she says nothing more. Probably doesn't want to press for more.

I nod and draw my finger through the ring of condensation my glass left on the dark table. "I was a shit growing up."

"Nooo," she drawls with a little laugh, making me chuckle.

"It's true. I was spoiled rotten. He created the monster and then I think he regretted it." I know he did. He created a monster out of all of us, including himself. Spending money like it was nothing, buying us whatever we wanted. Eventually, all that cash he spent became money he obtained illegally. Money he stole from clients. Investors who had faith he would do them right. Instead he did them wrong.

And then he did us all wrong by ending his life like a chickenshit.

"Do you guys still talk?" she asks, her voice as gentle as the glow in her eyes.

"No." I take a deep breath. "He died a long time ago."

Her eyes go instantly dim and she settles her hand on my arm, the sympathy written all over her face so clear. "I'm so sorry," she murmurs, her fingers squeezing. "I lost my mother, too, you know."

I nod in answer. I watched the documentary on Dahlia Fowler. They mentioned the girls' mother and that she died when they were young, but they didn't offer many details.

"I don't remember her, though. I was too small." The look on Rose's face . . . I can only describe it as heartbreaking. "I wish I'd known her. I wish I had the chance like Violet did and especially Lily, since she's the oldest. There's only a couple of years between me and Violet, so she doesn't remember her much, but at least she has *something*, you know?"

That we're having this conversation in the middle of a crowded pub surrounded by people is frustrating beyond belief. I want to take her hand and drag her out of here. Go back to the hotel where we can talk some more, and then get her naked and offer her comfort in the only way I know how.

"You two look awfully serious," Nigel interrupts, trying his best to look terribly serious as well but failing miserably. His stony expression cracks in an instant when we both turn to him and he bursts out laughing, clutching his gut like it was the funniest thing ever.

Clearly he's beyond drunk.

"He's had way too much," I tell Rose.

"Nigel." She shoves at his shoulder, which makes him stop laughing. "You didn't text Clare this afternoon, did you?"

"Erm, why would you ask that?" He tugs at his collar, pulling at the already loosened tie that hangs limply around his neck. "I have no idea what you're talking about."

"Bullshit." Rose points her finger at Nigel, and he looks caught in the crosshairs and scared shitless. "Caden told me you've been texting her."

Nigel sends me a look. "Traitor," he mutters, and I consume my beer, feigning innocence.

I'm enjoying this, as weird as it is to admit. It feels good. It feels . . . nice, hanging out with friends at a pub and drinking beer and eating bad appetizers. I've got a good buzz on, but no one's buzz is as good as Nigel's. The man is clearly feeling no pain, hanging on Hugh, asking him what the secret is, which sends them into a twenty-minute deep discussion about increasing Nigel's sex appeal among the ladies at the office.

Un-fucking-believable.

But I let it slide because hey, I can get along with the best of them. I'm excellent at faking it. No matter how much it infuriates me.

No matter how much it hurts.

Chapter Sixteen

Rose

AFTER THE MEETING AT FLEUR AND DEALING WITH MY FATHER— his disappointment in me palpable even through the computer screen—I needed to escape. I needed a drink. I needed to laugh and let loose and feel free.

More than anything, I needed Caden.

I thought Daddy would be pleased, seeing me there with Violet, working at Fleur even after I gave my notice, but he actually said to Violet, "What is *she* doing here?" and that about broke my heart.

Something Daddy is becoming quite an expert at.

Hugh asked if he could accompany us to the pub and I readily agreed, though Violet shot me a look. One that said, *You should consider this man. He's perfect for you.*

Yes, I'm that good at interpreting my sister's looks. After living with her my entire life, I've become somewhat of an expert.

Talking with Hugh in the cab we took over to the White Swan, sitting snugly against him on the bench seat, Ryder on my other side while Violet sat across from us on the fold-down seat chattering away on her phone, I could sense Hugh's interest.

If Caden weren't around, I could be interested too. Hugh is almost unbearably handsome. Brilliant blue eyes, dark, almost black hair, and a finely tuned body beneath the expensive suit.

He's intelligent, good at engaging in eye contact and easy conversation, and he has a nice smile, a pleasant laugh, and a deliciously deep voice with a lovely accent.

But I don't want Hugh. I want Caden. I like Caden. The moment I saw him sitting at the table with Nigel inside the pub, the both of them apparently drunk and laughing and looking like they were having so much fun, my heart leapt. His gaze caught mine and when I saw the disappointment there for the briefest second, the guilt hit me, swift and strong, stealing my breath. Did he see something between Hugh and me? I'd laughed at something Hugh said when we first walked in, and he touched me, but I didn't feel any sort of sizzle, no connection from his fingers on my skin.

Not like when Caden touches me. He looks at me and my knees grow weak. They're weak now, while I'm sitting in the chair next to him, leaning my head on his shoulder, the alcohol buzzing through my veins. He's talking to Ryder about soccer or some such nonsense and his voice vibrates in his chest, I can practically feel it in his shoulder, and I close my eyes and smile blissfully.

"Rose, are you all right?" Hugh asks.

My eyes pop open like a doll's and I sit up, offering him an embarrassed smile. "Just a little tired," I admit.

His smile is warm. "You were magnificent in the meeting this afternoon."

Hmm. There's a word I don't think anyone's used to describe me before. They usually save that sort of praise for Violet. "Thank you," I murmur.

"No, really. Your ideas are very innovative. We need more new blood here in our office, especially American blood." His smile fades and he leans in closer. "Fowler blood is especially good, since you are the leaders of this company."

I really hope he's not trying to butter me up because he's wasting his breath. "How long have you worked at Fleur?"

"Three years. I came here from Harrods."

"The department store?"

He nods. "I was one of the perfume buyers. I started out working in the men's department when I was sixteen. I got hooked into the retail cycle but was promoted rather quickly, and was working at corporate within five years of my starting work there."

"That's amazing." I have no idea how old he is and I'm not about to ask, because that would be rude.

"You're probably wondering how old I am, aren't you?"

I feel my cheeks heat with embarrassment. "Maybe. But that would be awfully crass of me to ask, right?"

"I'm twenty-nine." His lips quirk to the side. "Older than every one of you at this table, I bet."

"I suppose." Definitely older than me and Violet and Ryder. Nigel, he can't be over twenty-five, twenty-six, and Caden . . . I have no idea how old he is. And that's just weird. Why haven't I asked him? Why hasn't he told me?

He doesn't tell you a lot of things.

Isn't that the truth?

"How old are you?" Hugh asks.

"You should never ask a lady her age," I chastise teasingly, making him grin.

"Forgive me, madam." He bows and I laugh.

"I'm twenty-two."

"Ah, so young. And so incredibly smart." I see the interest flare in his eyes again. It's hard to miss. He's not being inappropriate or anything, but he's definitely flirtatious. "Beautiful, too."

There go my cheeks again. "Thank you."

"How much longer are you in London?" he asks.

"I'm not sure." I'm hedging because I honestly don't know how much longer I can stay here and avoid my father and my job. I need to return to New York. I have things I need to take care of there. The plants in my apartment are probably dead, though Lily just texted me a few days ago, asking if I wanted her to stop by and check on things. I did and thanked her profusely.

Good thing I don't have pets. I got so wrapped up in Caden and our whirlwind holiday romance I forgot about everything but . . . him.

"I could show you around if you like," Hugh says casually, his expression neutral. "I've lived in this city my entire life. I could take you to the best restaurants—"

"The food here isn't that great, you know," I interrupt, earning a laugh from him. "Sorry, just being brutally honest."

"You're right. That's why if you stick with me, I'll steer you to the best food this city has to offer."

He's being so nice. If circumstances were different, if Caden weren't sitting next to me, if I were here on my own and this friendly, handsome, kind man was asking me out I would readily say yes.

But I feel Caden stiffen beside me. He's gone unusually quiet and I didn't even notice. He's probably heard every bit of my conversation with Hugh. I feel sick to my stomach, as if I've somehow betrayed him, and all traces of happiness evaporate from within me, just like that.

"Thanks for the offer," I say sadly, "but I'm afraid I have to decline."

Hugh's eyes dim the slightest bit, but otherwise he appears completely unruffled. "No worries. Some other time perhaps?"

"Yes. That sounds good." I nod and slide from my chair, smoothing out the wrinkles from my dress. I don't make eye contact with anyone as I say, "I'm going to the restroom. I'll be right back."

I leave the table without another word, not looking back, keeping my head held high as I make my way through the crowd. The pub is full of young professionals just off work, most of them dressed like we are. Suits and dresses, ties loosened and high heels kicked off. Lots of raucous laughter and pounding of their beer mugs on tabletops; everyone's having fun.

So why do I feel so miserable?

Shoving the women's bathroom door open, I rush to the sink and turn the faucet on so I can splash water on my face. It's total déjà vu, remembering this almost exact moment from a week ago, when I hid in the bathroom to escape Caden and he followed me in here.

The door swings open and my heart lightens in my chest, only to come crashing down with a dull thud when I see Violet standing there.

"What's wrong?" she asks.

I turn away from the sink and grab a few paper towels from the dispenser, drying my hands before I toss them into the trash can. "Hugh basically asked me out on a date."

Violet smiles. "That's wonderful."

Ugh. Of course, she would say that. "He asked me out in front of Caden."

"So?"

"Violet, *God.* You're being awful." I shake my head. "I've just spent the last week with him, pretty much the entire time naked in bed. And now you're encouraging me to agree to go on a date with another man, while sitting beside Caden? That's low."

"Rose. Listen to me." She comes to stand directly in front of me, grasping hold of my shoulders and giving me a firm shake. "Sometimes we meet people in our life and they're exciting. Different. Unlike anything or anyone we've ever experienced before."

"Like Ryder for you?" I throw at her.

Nodding, she presses her lips together. "Yes," she admits. "Like Ryder. But sometimes these people you meet, they're not meant to be in your life on a permanent basis. They come in at the right time, send you spinning, lift you up, and then they leave. A pleasant diversion to help you realize what you really should be doing with your life."

"So now you're saying Caden is nothing but a pleasant diversion while I figure out what I want next," I say dully.

Violet nods. "Exactly. Yes, Ryder has turned into a permanent part of my life, but I can't see Caden being there for you when you really need him."

"Why not? And how can you say that? You don't even know him," I accuse, my voice small, my thoughts all over the place. Would Caden be there for me during my time of need, like . . . now? If I asked for his undying support, would he give it to me? I think he would.

But I'm not sure.

"I know there are—things to him that he's not telling you. I've done a little Google research . . ." She lets her voice trail off, but I hear all the doubt and worry in her tone.

"Of course you have," I say, pushing away her hands so I can step around her.

"And Ryder has this . . . sense about him. That he's not being honest with us," Violet continues. "Says he knows the signs of a con man since he was once one himself, and Caden reminds him of . . . himself, when he was younger."

I stare at the tiled wall, blinking hard. I thought Ryder was on my side. But no, he's filling Violet's head with stories of Caden being a lying con man. *Just freaking great.* "Don't you think you two are being a little harsh?"

"No. I call it being protective of my baby sister." Violet reaches out to rest her hand on my shoulder, but I shrug out of her touch. "I don't want to see you get hurt."

I turn on her. "I'm a big girl. I can handle myself."

"Just be careful," she pleads. She looks worried and I feel bad, but her worry isn't going to stop me from continuing to see Caden. "And Hugh is like . . . the perfect guy for you. I wish you could see that. He's smart and handsome and he works for Fleur."

"What, you want me to be just like you and Ryder? Give me a break. I don't know if I want to continue working at Fleur." I throw my hands up in the air, so frustrated I could spit.

"You don't mean that," Violet whispers. "You gave your notice after you argued with Father. You know he'd take you back."

"I do mean it. Daddy is furious with me and the feeling is mutual. Pilar is getting everything she could ever want and you're the wunderkind of the family. No one gives a shit if I'm there or not. I've disappeared for the last couple of weeks and no one's missed me. Fleur goes on whether I'm there or not," I point out. "Can the same be said if you weren't there? Or Daddy? Or even . . . Pilar?" *God,* it kills me to say her name, but I'm feeling pretty low right now.

"*I've* missed you," Violet says.

"That's not good enough." I shake my head, refusing to feel guilty over disappointing Violet. "When I go back to New York, I'm not returning to Fleur."

"Why? I don't understand how you can even consider that as an option." Violet looks incredulous and I don't know what to tell her. How to explain.

Because I don't have the proper explanation myself.

"See, that's just it. You wouldn't understand." I'm tired. Tired of explaining myself, defending my actions, defending Caden. "There's nothing more to say, Violet."

She studies me, her arms curled in front of her, her expression unreadable. I've disappointed her. She's probably mad. But for once, I don't really care. "You're making a mistake," she finally says.

"I'm sure I am," I say wearily. "I think I'm allowed to make one every once in a while."

Without another word Violet turns and leaves, the door slamming hard behind her, and I slump against the edge of the countertop, throwing back my head with a sigh so I can stare at the ceiling.

That went over well.

I use the facilities and wash my hands, splashing water on my face yet again. Another woman walks in and throws down her makeup bag, opening it to pull out a Fleur lip gloss. She slicks her lips a deep red shade as she stares at her reflection before she puts the cap back on and throws the tube into the bag. She notices me watching her and gives me a puzzled smile.

"Beautiful color," I tell her. I recognize it, of course. One of the shades from our Winterberry collection, the name of the color is Blackberry Ice.

"Oh, thank you." She smiles, revealing she has a bit of gloss stuck to her front teeth. I rub at mine and she does the same with her index finger, giving me a rueful look. "Right. Appreciate that. I bet my friends wouldn't have told me and had a good laugh over it later."

"Wow, really?" Sounds like they aren't very good friends.

"It's dog-eat-dog out there, haven't you noticed? I've been flirting with the same bloke for the past half hour and then another pretty girl turns his head and the ass leaves me standing there alone." She zips her makeup bag up almost violently. "What's a girl got to do to keep a man's interest in this city? Show her tits?"

I feel like a complete shit, since only a few minutes ago I had the interest of *two* men. How selfish am I? "Do you like smart guys?"

She laughs. "I certainly don't like dumb ones."

"I know someone . . . he's sitting at my table. Really sweet, but always seems to be overshadowed by the other men he works with."

The woman raises her brows. "Is he ugly?"

"Not at all." I shake my head, enjoying her brutal honesty. "He's cute. In an understated way, you know? Fun. Earnest. I could introduce you."

The woman smiles. She's dressed nicely in a pretty green dress and with her dark auburn hair and pale complexion, I'm sure Nigel would be bowled over to talk to a woman like her. "That sounds great. But if he's so amazing, why aren't you going after him?"

"Because I already have someone amazing," I admit, thinking of Caden. I don't care what my sister said. I don't care if Ryder thinks he's a con man. Look at Violet and how she turned Ryder around. I could do the same, right?

Right?

I exit the bathroom with my new friend Louise and hopefully Nigel's future date, when we run into a glowering Caden in the hallway. I send him a pleading look, introducing him to Louise before we head out to the table.

"What are you doing?" I ask brightly, hoping he isn't as mad as he looks.

He scowls. "What does it look like I'm doing? Using the bathroom." With those famous parting words, he shoves his way into the men's restroom, the door slamming behind him.

Ignoring my worry over what he must think about me, I take Louise out to the table and introduce her to everyone, saving Nigel for last. He's a little drunk, wavering on his feet, but the spark of interest in his gaze upon first meeting Louise tells me I did the right thing.

Even better? She didn't salivate over Hugh like I thought she might.

Leaving Louise with our little group—and neglecting to acknowledge the pointed stare Violet is shooting in my direction—I go back to the restroom area, hoping to catch Caden so I can talk to him privately.

He's already there, waiting for me in the depths of the dark, short hall, leaning one shoulder against the wall, his arms folded defensively across his chest. Whereas the rest of us are in work attire, he's dressed casually in jeans that mold perfectly to his strong legs and a white polo shirt that offsets his tan skin. He stands out with his longish hair and the stubble covering his cheeks. Not that he looks unkempt. More like he looks . . . amazing.

My heart trips over itself just staring at him.

"Where's your boyfriend?" he asks snidely, sounding like a jealous idiot.

That shouldn't please me, should it? That he's jealous? Well, it does. And if that makes me petty and foolish, then so be it.

"I thought I was looking at him."

He huffs out a sarcastic laugh. "Please. You've been up-front about what we're doing from the start. Vacation sex, pure and simple."

"If this is a vacation then why did I go in to work today?" This isn't how I wanted our conversation to go. Not at all.

"Guilt? You've been fucking around with the useless guy and now you're finally realizing you need to straighten up and fly right." He pushes away from the wall and takes a few predatory steps toward me. "When are you going back to New York? Or are you sticking around here for a few more days so Hugh can show you around town?"

So he definitely heard Hugh's offer. *Great.* "I turned him down," I say softly.

"Why?"

"Because I'm with *you*." I lift my chin, hoping I don't regret that statement.

"With me? How? Don't tell me you're starting to take this— thing between us seriously?"

Yep. Guess I regret my statement. "I thought maybe we both were," I murmur.

He looks down at the floor, his hands on his hips, his hair

falling over his forehead and hiding his face from my view. "I'm not good enough for you, Rose."

His words cut like a knife but I say nothing, silently urging him to go on. I want to hear the exact reasons why he believes he's not good enough for me. I *need* to hear them.

"I can offer you nothing," he says after a few minutes of silence. "That other guy . . . Hugh. He's probably the better man for you."

He sees it. Everyone sees it. But I don't care. "I don't want him. I want you."

Caden lifts his head, his dark gaze meeting mine. "I don't get why."

I want to slap him. Really. "I don't want to fight, Caden. Please."

He stares at me for long, agonizing minutes. "Let's get out of here." His hands drop to his sides and before I can say a word, he's rushing toward me, grabbing me, pulling me into his arms, his mouth fusing with mine. I'm helpless in his arms, returning his kiss, crying out against his lips when he pushes me to the wall, pinning me there, his hips keeping me still.

I bury my hands in his hair and he tilts his head, deepening the kiss. We're right back where we started. In a hidden spot at the White Swan, losing all control, too wrapped up in each other to worry about anyone else.

The obvious throat clearing comes seconds, maybe minutes, later and Caden lifts his head away from mine, the both of us turning to see Hugh standing there watching us, appearing uncomfortable.

"We were worried when you didn't come back to the table," is his only explanation, his gaze locked on me. "I told Violet I would go look for you."

Did Violet want Hugh to discover Caden and me together like this? Doubtful, but what else could she think the two of us were doing? "I'm fine," I tell him, sounding breathless. That's because I *am* breathless. My heart is racing and my body is vibrating from Caden's all-consuming kiss.

Caden says nothing, just glares at Hugh, his hands resting possessively on my hips, his body pressed intimately to mine. He's sending a message and I can see Hugh gets it, loud and clear.

"Well, glad to hear it. I'll let everyone know the two of you are otherwise engaged." He offers a little wave and walks away.

"I hate that guy," Caden mutters under his breath.

I tug on his hair, making him yelp. "You're jealous of that guy."

He looks at me, really looks at me, and it feels as if he can see every little thing inside of me. I return his stare, leaving myself open, practically bleeding for him. Whereas he's always hiding from me, I want him to see me. See all that I have to give, that I *want* to give. "You're right," he admits. "I was jealous."

"Was? As in you're not anymore?" I relax my grip on his hair, moving my hand so I can brush those wayward strands away from his forehead. I could touch him like this for hours. I *have* touched him like this for hours.

"Not when I have you in my arms like this." He kisses my temple, his hands squeezing my hips. "I want to get you alone."

I nod and release a shaky breath. "Then let's go."

Chapter Seventeen

Caden

WE WALK BACK TO THE HOTEL AFTER SAYING GOODBYE TO EV-eryone. The only reason we went back to the table was for Rose's purse. Otherwise I would've snuck her out the back so we wouldn't have to face them.

Nigel was preoccupied with some cute redhead and Hugh looked butt hurt. Violet appeared ready to do violence if I so much as looked at her wrong and Ryder shook my hand, seemingly oblivious to what was happening around him. It all felt very . . . odd.

Tense.

Truthfully, it was a damn relief to get outside, away from the pub, away from the people who are making me feel guilty. Damn it, I like all of them, with the exception of Hugh the fucker Watson, and I bet he could be a friend now that he knows Rose is off-limits.

As in, she belongs to me.

I feel like my truth is hanging off the tip of my tongue, dangling, really. Ready to be revealed so I can get it over with and face my reality—face Rose. I'm both dying to tell her and scared out of my mind over how she might react, especially with the necklace sitting in my bag. I need to get it out of there and back into the safe, stat.

I'm more scared, though. Afraid she'll reject me. Hate me. Worse? That she'll tell the authorities and I'll end up in jail for the rest of my life.

She wouldn't do that to me . . . I don't think.

We're silent as we walk, though at least she lets me hold her hand. She looks beautiful, her head held high, that white dress hugging her breasts and waist and hips, the high black heels she has on making those sexy legs of hers look impossibly long.

I am a lucky man, walking down the street holding this woman's hand. Random guys take a second look as they walk past and I send the ones that do a murderous glare. Can't they see she belongs to me? Do I need to write a sign across her forehead that declares, *Property of Caden Kingsley—Eyes and hands the fuck off?*

Yeah. I think I do.

"You're awfully quiet," she says as we enter the hotel lobby and head toward the elevators.

I shrug, feeling morose. Like the end is coming and there's nothing I can do to stop it. "I'm moody." And now I sound like a whiny girl.

"Too many beers?"

"Unfortunately, I'm pretty sure I'm completely sober."

She flinches at my choice of words and I curse inwardly. I can't fuck this up now. My time with her is limited. She's going to leave me soon.

I have to make the most of it.

"I'm being an asshole," I tell her when we enter the elevator and the doors close us in.

"Yes, you are." She smiles.

"I'm sorry." I never apologize. There's usually no need, because usually I'm long gone by the time anyone I've wronged finds out.

For once, I want to stick. I want to live a real life, not some constant con game. I want to be real with Rose. And if that means sometimes it gets ugly, and sometimes I'm scared, mad, sad, or whatever-the-hell emotion I'm struggling with, I still want to do it.

So I've got to fight for it. Own it. Own me. Own her.

Own us.

"You're forgiven," she says, her voice soft, her gaze open, showing me all she's got. And I like what I see. "I'm sorry, too."

"For what?" I frown.

"For that whole thing with Hugh." She waves a hand. "He's nice. I like him. But not . . . not like that."

"He likes *you* like that." Just thinking about Hugh makes me want to hit something, specifically his smug face.

"I bet he doesn't anymore." Her smile grows. "You couldn't have been more possessive, what with the way you practically growled at him when he caught us kissing by the bathrooms."

"I didn't growl at him." Did I? I don't remember.

"Yes. You definitely did. You should've just hung a sign around my neck that said *Property of Caden*. That would've sent your message loud and clear."

"I considered it," I say truthfully. "But I guess my growling was good enough."

Her eyes sparkle with amusement. "I thought it was kind of sexy."

"Oh yeah? You like it when I growl?" She can't be serious. That smile on her pretty face is telling me she's making fun of me, but you never know with Rose. She's a constant surprise. A dirty, naughty, fun, extremely sexy surprise.

"I do. Maybe you can growl for me later."

"I can growl for you right now if you want me to." I go for her, my arms sliding around her waist just as the elevator comes to a stop at our floor and the doors slide open. She slips out of my embrace and practically races out of the elevator toward the room.

"You have to catch me first," she calls over her shoulder, the key card already clasped in her fingers.

I saunter after her, not bothering to run. I'll catch her; I have complete faith in that. She *wants* to be caught. Maybe she's a little buzzed from the two drinks she had. Maybe she's relieved to get out of the tense atmosphere of the pub. Maybe she's just happy to finally be alone with me.

Whatever it is, I'm letting her have her fun because I reap all the benefits.

She opens the door just as I approach her, my hands going to her waist so I can shove her into the room. Crowding her, I wrap my arms around her from behind and pull her to me, her ass pressed against my front, my hands reaching for her breasts as I kiss her neck. The door shuts behind us, closing us in so we're all alone. "Caught ya," I mutter against her skin and she giggles.

"I let you catch me," she murmurs, tilting her head to the side to give me better access.

"Where's the fun in that?" I ask, skimming my teeth along her neck, making her shudder. I slide my hands down, along her waist, her hips, gripping her there so I can pull her tight against my growing erection.

"Oh, I can guarantee you loads of fun." She reaches behind her, her hand wrapping around my cock that's straining against my jeans, and I grunt into her neck, thrusting against her ass.

"Are you saying you want to play?" I tug on the fabric of her skirt, easing it up slowly, resting my chin on her shoulder so I can watch her dress rise higher and higher on her slender thighs. "Because I'm always up for that."

"You certainly are." She laughs, then moans when I nip and suck on her neck. Her skirt is bunched around her waist, revealing the skimpy panties she's got on, and now it's my turn to moan. "What in the fuck are you wearing?"

Rose tilts her head back so her gaze meets mine. "You like them?"

"I think I need to look at them closer." I release my hold on her and turn her around, falling to my knees so I can examine the scrap of material she's calling panties. They're white. Sheer, so I can see her scant pubic hair, her plump pussy lips. Lace trims the outer edges and tiny white silk bows dot either side of her hips. "They're indecent."

"I knew you'd approve," she teases.

I glance up at her, smoothing my hands up along the sides of her thighs. "I love them." I grip her hips, turning her around, and I close my eyes for only a second, leaning my head against one exposed butt cheek for a brief moment before I drop a kiss on it. "Why did you even bother wearing panties? There's nothing to them." The back consists of a silk string around her waist and between her cheeks, another innocent bow dotting the top center of her ass.

"I wore them for you." She glances over her shoulder, smiling down at me. "They make me feel sexy. Like *you* make me feel sexy."

I palm her ass, gripping her ample flesh. She has a perfect butt. Round and full and with two little dimples at the base of her spine, I don't appreciate this particular body part of hers enough. I need to rectify that. "Well, these little panties are definitely sexy, but I think they're going to have to go."

"Really?" She sounds thrilled at the prospect.

"Definitely. But first, we need to get rid of the dress." I stand, my hands going to the zipper, and I slowly draw it down, revealing her back and the matching white lacy bra she's wearing. I swallow hard, imagining what the bra must look like in the front. Probably completely sheer and offering me a perfect view of her nipples.

With eager, shaking hands, I pull the dress up over her head before I toss it onto the floor. I turn her around, my gaze dropping to her chest, and hell, yes, just like I knew it would be, the bra is a killer. Sheer white and trimmed with lace, with more innocent white bows, one in the center, two more on the top of each breast. Skimpy as hell and probably not offering much support, the bra and panties are all about the visual.

And I fucking approve wholeheartedly.

"You've been wearing this all afternoon and I had no idea." I reach out and tease the little bow at the center of her bra.

"Isn't it a pleasant surprise?" She hitches in a breath when I trace the edge of her bra with my finger, touching her skin, seeing the goose bumps rise.

"Very pleasant." Total understatement. I'm going to drive myself out of my mind if I keep this game up, but it's worth it. I want to savor this moment. Rose in her pretty lingerie she wore just for me, standing immobile in front of me like some sort of offering, still wearing the sexy black heels, her body trembling, her nipples hard, and I can just about guarantee in between those pretty thighs she's soaked.

Bending my knees, I rain kisses across her chest, the tops of her breasts. She tilts her head back, her eyes closing as she reaches for my head, but I duck away from her hands, dropping to my knees once again where I scent her arousal, heady and sweet. She gazes down at me, the beautiful agony etched across her face making my cock jerk in my jeans, and I reach between her legs, drifting my fingers gently across her mound.

She jerks against my touch, a whimper escaping her, and I smile. Just as I predicted, the thin fabric of her panties is damp, and I sneak the tip of my finger beneath, teasing her pussy with a quick flick before I pull back out.

"You're mean," she accuses, though there's no anger in her tone.

"You fucking love it," I return, knowing I speak the truth. "You look at me and get wet."

"Arrogant much?" she asks, and I chuckle.

"Just stating the truth. Considering every time I look at you I get hard, I figure your body is having a similar reaction." I press my mouth to her pussy and kiss her there, breathing deep her scent, my hands coming up to grip the thin band that rests on her hips. Leaning back, I tug the panties down, torturing her, torturing myself as I slowly pull them down her thighs, going past her knees until she's lifting one foot, then the other before she kicks them off.

Leaving herself bare.

"Take off the shoes," I demand, and she steps out of them, pushing them away with two quick kicks. Her pussy is even closer to my face and I glance up to find her watching me, her eyes wide, her cheeks flushed, her hair falling around her face.

She looks beautiful. Aroused.

She looks like mine.

Resting my hands on her ass, I pull her in and she takes a step closer. "Spread your legs," I mutter against her thigh and she does, offering me a heart-stopping view of her glistening pink depths. I lick her there, one long swoop across her folds with my tongue flat, and she shudders, my name falling from her lips.

"You like that?" I ask, not needing to hear her answer. I know she likes it. She loves it when I go down on her and I love going down on her, so it's a win-win for us both.

Like when she sucks my cock. I know she enjoys it. Hell, one time she gave me a blow job while grinding her pussy on my upper thigh the entire time, coming all over my leg just as I was spurting inside her mouth.

Talk about hot. The woman is insatiable.

I lick and tease, flick my tongue against her clit, thrust it inside of her, my hands gripping her ass and keeping her steady. She settles her hands in my hair, her little moans and whimpers driving me on, and then she's pulling my hair, begging me to stop.

That's not a normal request. Pulling away, I gaze up at her. "You want me to stop?"

She nods furiously, her hair spilling everywhere. "I want you inside of me," she whispers.

I'm down with that. Standing to my full height, I strip off my clothes in a hurry, watching as she removes her bra and goes to the bed, pulling back the comforter so it falls on the floor. She crawls onto the mattress, her body gleaming with a light sheen of sweat, her breasts jiggling as she falls on her back in the center of the bed.

Bending at the knee, she plants her foot on the mattress, her thighs spread, the look on her face pure temptation. "Going to join me?"

I say nothing, just go to her like a man caught in her spell—and I *am* a man caught in her spell. She pulls me down on top of her, her mouth meeting mine in a hot, wet kiss that I drown in.

Her legs hook around my hips and she anchors herself to me, her pussy nestled close to my cock. She's wet and slippery and I thrust against her once. Twice. Slip just the head of my cock in, and the heat radiating from within her body feels incredible.

"Oh, God," she chokes out as I slip a little deeper inside, the breath leaving my lungs in one harsh gust when I feel the velvety hot clasp of her inner walls tighten around my cock. No barriers, just flesh on flesh, and I realize my mistake as I thrust deep, filling her completely.

"Fuck, Ro, you feel so damn good." I remain unmoving inside her body, my cock pulsing, her pussy twitching. "I forgot the condom."

She goes still, her hands resting on my chest and giving me a little shove. It changes the angle, sending me deeper, and then she's clutching my shoulders, moaning as she arches against me, and it feels like my cock is touching her womb, I'm so deep. "I . . . clean," she gasps.

Bracing my hands on either side of her head, I stare down at her, watching as she writhes against me, working herself on my cock, her eyes closed, her head thrown back. "I'm clean too," I whisper. "But are you . . . good? Like on the pill or . . . whatever?" Could I sound more like an asshole teen making sure the girl I'm fucking in the backseat of my car isn't going to get knocked up?

Rose opens her eyes, a little smile curving her lips. "I'm fine. My period should be here any day now."

Uh-huh. Isn't that what they all say? Not that I've ever had personal experience with this sort of situation, but . . .

"I'll pull out," I reassure her, loving the way she feels, my entire body tense and ready to fuck. All I want to do is take her. Ram myself inside of her body again and again and fill her with my come, which has got to be some weird, primal, instinctual thing. I don't know. I've never had these sorts of thoughts.

Then again, I've never felt like this for any woman until Rose.

Finally unable to stand it any longer, I begin to move, slowly working my cock in and out of her body. She moans with my every thrust and I bend over her, kissing and sucking her nipples, gathering her ass in my hands so I can hold her closer and control my movements within her.

Her legs are tight around my hips, her arms wrapped around my neck. Our bodies are so close, chest to chest, heart to heart, and I'm panting in her ear, whispering how good she feels, how much I want to come, how much I want her to come.

She nods furiously, her hair tickling my cheeks, strands catching in the stubble that lines my jaw. "So close," she whispers as she turns her face into my neck. I can feel her lips brand me, hot and damp, as she speaks. "Harder, Caden. Please."

Losing all control at her urging, I fuck her fiercely, my movements ragged as I grip her ass tight and pound inside of her. My mind is empty and all I can focus on is my need to come, my need to make Rose come. Like an animal intent on reaching my satisfaction no matter what it takes. Primitive. Possessive.

Lost.

Rose falls first, a long, shuddery moan sounding from deep within her as I feel her pussy clench and ripple along the length of my cock. I grit my teeth, fighting against the need to spurt deep inside her body, and then I'm pulling out of her in a rush, my hand going around the base of my cock as I come all over her quivering stomach.

"Jesus," I utter, my breathing so hard my chest aches as I stare down at her. I'm on my knees, my cock in my hand, my semen all over her stomach and her pussy. Did I come in her? *Fuck*, I hope not. And I hope she means it when she says there's no possibility she could get . . . pregnant.

Wiping a hand across my mouth, I shake my head, unable to speak.

What the fuck did I just do?

Chapter Eighteen

Rose

I can't move. I can hardly breathe. My God, I don't think I can even *see*.

I believe Caden just fucked me to death.

My bones are like jelly, my heart racing triple time, and I trail my shaky fingers through the semen that's splattered across my belly, smearing it across my skin. It's warm and sticky and thank God he pulled out in time or else I'd be worried.

It was so amazing, though, having Caden inside of me without a condom on. Risky and stupid, but he felt so good. *Too* good.

I want to do it again.

I can feel him above me, hear him breathe, hear him swallow hard. He sounds just as overwhelmed as I feel and when I finally crack my eyes open I see him reach out, his fingers light on my stomach as he, too, touches the come he left there. Marking me like some sort of primitive beast, it had been all sorts of hot.

"I, uh, got a little carried away there for a moment," he admits, his gaze lifting to meet mine. I see a hint of doubt in the depths of his gaze and I want to reassure him. I want to tell him I liked it. Loved it, even.

He can't take the entire blame for this. I was just as out of control. Out of my freaking mind with pleasure. "It's okay," I reassure him, reaching for his hand so I can clasp our fingers together.

He smiles at me, flicking his head so his sweat-dampened hair isn't hanging in his eyes. "You're fucking beautiful," he whispers.

I shake my head, embarrassed for some reason. What just happened between us . . . I can't explain it. I feel closer to him. I feel as if he's become a part of me.

Does he feel the same?

"Don't deny it." He collapses beside me, gathering me in his arms so he can hold me close, my back to his front. His cock is still hard, poking against my butt, and I'm amazed.

And aroused. Still. But I don't know if my body can take another round. Yet.

"You're gorgeous, you know. All limp and sated after I made you come." His voice is full of pride. He likes that he just did this to me. That he wrecked me for any other man. No one has ever made me feel like Caden does.

Never.

"I made you come too," I point out, smiling when he squeezes me close and drops a kiss to my shoulder.

"Yeah, you did," he murmurs against my temple. "It felt fucking amazing, being inside you bare."

It so did. I need to get on the pill stat if we're going to continue this . . . relationship. Whatever the heck we're doing. I've never had sex without a condom before and when he first slipped inside me, hot and slick and with no thin piece of rubber between us, I almost came on the spot.

His hands move up so he's touching my breasts, rubbing them, circling my nipples, and I sigh as my body melts into his, savoring his touch, the little sparks of heat that light my skin as he continues to toy with my nipples. "I love the way you touch me," I tell him in a heated whisper.

He doesn't falter, just keeps caressing my skin, driving me

crazy, ramping up the warmth within me when I came only moments ago. "I love touching you," he murmurs. "I could fuck you all night. For days. You're all I want, Ro. All I need."

I want to believe him, but I don't know if I can. He's opened up some but not enough. Our sexual connection is so incredibly strong, but what about our emotional connection? Would he want a real relationship with me? Or are we both caught up in the fantasy of being in another country, not dealing with work or friends or family—for the most part, considering I'm dealing with the life-changing choice of quitting the family business—all alone, just the two of us in this hotel suite?

His cock is rock hard, pressing between my butt cheeks, and I squirm against him, making him groan. "Tease." He grips my hips, brushing the head of his cock along my crack, and I roll away from him, onto my stomach. He follows me, tugging on my hips so I lift myself onto my knees, and another moan escapes him as he runs his hand across my backside, his fingertips playing with my pussy. I'm so wet, and it would be so easy for him to slide back inside me. I want it. I want him. I feel almost crazed with it. "You want my cock?" he asks.

"Please," I say into the pillow, my voice muffled. My legs are shaking, my entire body is trembling, and I brace myself on my elbows, wagging my ass at him to spur him on to do something about it and quick.

"Ah, baby. You drive me fucking insane with this sexy body of yours." He pulls me back, his hands firm on my hips as he guides me onto his cock. My body takes him, slowly but surely, until my ass is brushing his stomach and I can feel his heavy balls press against my pussy.

He is so thick and so long. When he pulls out, it seems to take forever, a delicious drag of flesh against flesh, and I shudder and cry out, a surprised gasp flying from my lips when he rams his cock back inside of me, hard and so fast I swear I see stars.

"I gotta be careful," Caden says, his voice tense, his fingers gripping my hips so hard I know he's going to leave bruises again.

But I don't care. I want the bruises. I love the reminder that he's taken my body so perfectly.

"Why?" I ask on another gasp. I swivel my hips, working his cock, and he smacks my ass playfully, commanding me to stop.

I don't want to stop. I want to come again. I *need* to come again. When we're naked together, it's as if I have no control. All I want are the endless orgasms he's so good at delivering. I crave his touch, his words, the comfort he gives me.

More than anything, I crave the way he looks at me. His eyes are full of untethered emotion, his touch gentle and full of reverence. He cares, more than he'll ever admit, and I love that. I need it.

"I'm gonna blow and I don't want to do it inside you," he says, sounding tortured. He holds my hips still, preventing me from moving, and I release a little moan of frustration. "*Sshh.* Let me make this good for you."

Anticipation races through my veins when he touches me, his fingers tickling my skin, drawing closer to my pussy. He touches me there, tracing my folds where they rest against his cock, a fleeting tap against my throbbing clit. He's trying to drive me out of my mind and I'm about to yell at him when he draws his finger up, up, until he's touching a forbidden spot, circling around and around my little hole.

"Ever had a man take you here?" he asks, his voice deep and dark and rumbling along my nerve endings, making me weak with desire.

I shake my head, unable to speak. I'm holding my breath, biting my lip when he presses, slowly breaching the barrier with just the tip of his finger. A moan escapes me at being filled in both holes and I hang my head, again waiting for the shame or embarrassment to come.

But it doesn't. All I can focus on is the way he moves in me, the way Caden is making me feel. His finger slips deeper as he starts to move and I give myself over to the pleasure. My head is spinning, my body feels like it's spiraling out of control, and I whimper when he pulls out of me, replacing his cock with his mouth as he licks and sucks my pussy, fucking my ass with his finger, sending me right over the edge with a scream.

I slump onto the mattress as he moves away from me, trying to catch my breath, gather my thoughts. With much effort on my part, I finally roll over to find him sitting on his knees, his cock sticking straight up, the tip covered with creamy pre-come. He looks as if he's in pain and I go to him, wrapping my fingers around the base so I can draw him into my mouth.

"Fuck yeah," he practically growls, his hand pushing away my hair before he slides his fingers into it and tugs so hard, I feel the stinging pain in my scalp. "Harder, baby. I want to come in your mouth."

I do as he commands, giving him all of me, opening my eyes so I can stare at his face. He's seemingly transfixed, his eyes flaring with unmistakable lust as I pull his cock from my mouth and lick the head, down his length, mapping every distended vein with my tongue. His entire face flinches, a shuddering sound coming from his lips, and when I draw him back into my mouth he explodes all over my tongue, the salty musk taste of his semen filling my mouth.

Withdrawing from him, I let some of it spill out of my mouth and onto the head of his cock, getting him nice and sloppy, and I swear that brings on another spurt of semen. He's groaning and shouting and saying the crudest things ever and all I want to do is make this good for him.

So good he'll never, ever want to leave me.

"You are a filthy, dirty girl," he says after long, quiet moments of our panting breaths as we both try to calm our racing hearts. He collapses onto the mattress, his head buffered by a pile of pillows. I crawl alongside him, lying on my side so I can press my body close, throwing my leg over both of his.

"You like it," I whisper as I race my fingers down his stomach, feeling the muscles shiver beneath my touch.

"The question is do you like it. What I did to you."

I gaze up at him to find him studying me, worry making his brow furrow, that wrinkly spot above the bridge of his nose a sure sign he's apprehensive. "I liked it."

"Enough to take it . . . further? Sometime?"

I skim my fingers lower, into his pubic hair, the head of his softening cock brushing against me. "Yes," I whisper as I turn my face into his shoulder. I'm a little embarrassed, but not enough that I don't want to talk about this. "As long as you're gentle. You're . . . kinda big."

He laughs a little as he slips his arm around my shoulders. "Did I hurt you?"

I shake my head. "Not really. It stung a little."

"I'll be careful. I'll always be careful with you. You know this, right, Ro?"

I don't know. Do I?

"Caden?"

"Yeah?"

I clear my throat, scared over how I'm about to change the subject big-time. "You mentioned your father earlier."

He tenses up; I can feel his muscles go completely still. "Yeah?" he says again.

"Can I ask you a question?"

He's quiet for a moment before he says, almost reluctantly, "Go ahead."

"How . . . how did he die?" I trace patterns on Caden's skin, running my finger through the little patch of hair in the center of his chest. I feel like I have every right to ask him that question. I have a dead parent too. One nobody talks about and I want to share in our past grief together. Not get weepy or anything, but I want . . . I want reassurance that it's okay to talk about our parents. It's fine to speak of the dead, you know? I'm tired of hiding my feelings.

Caden lets out a harsh breath and gives my shoulders a squeeze. "It isn't pleasant."

"Death never is," I reassure him.

"He killed himself." He stiffens against me for the tiniest moment but I continue touching him, my heart full of sadness but also . . . relief. We have something in common, however terrible it may be. "He worked for an investment firm in Manhattan and was a real hotshot. Worked up the ranks quick, made all sorts of money."

"And then?" I urge because I know there's an *and then* moment. Something awful must have happened for the man to take his own life.

"And then he got too greedy. Started using his clients' money for personal expenses, figuring he could gain it all back with his investments. But that didn't work. He got caught in a vicious cycle and once it was discovered . . . he was ruined. He lost his job. There were threats of lawsuits and criminal prosecution. My mom said she would stand by him no matter what, that we could get through this together because we were a family, but he . . . went to work to finish cleaning out his office and then threw open the window and jumped out."

"Oh, God." I sit up to look at him, our gazes meeting, his full of pain and irritation and . . . yes. Anger. "That's awful."

"Yeah. I was mad for a long time. I still am. He hurt my mom almost irrevocably. After he died, she wouldn't date, had no interest in men at all. She still won't consider letting anyone into her life for fear they'll leave her," he explains, sounding sad. He reaches out and grabs my hand, playing with my fingers.

That explains so much. So, so much. I'm having a total *aha* moment here and it's at his expense, making him have to tell this painful story. But it needs to be said. This sort of reveal will only bring us closer and I want that so badly.

"How old were you when it happened?" I squeeze his hand in mine.

"Thirteen."

My heart hurts for him. And for me, too.

Swallowing hard, I decide to share my own secret. "My mom committed suicide, too."

His eyes widen the slightest bit. "She did?"

I nod, dropping my head so I don't have to look at him. You'd think it would be easy to share this, but the topic of my mother is hardly ever discussed. I find it difficult to talk about her and I didn't even know her. "I was practically a baby. She overdosed on prescription pills. My father woke up one morning and she was lying next to him, cold and still. She took the pills during the night and he had no idea."

"Ah, Ro." He pulls my hand so I'm falling on top of him and he gathers me close, my head tucked under his and my cheek pressed against his shoulder, our arms around each other. "That's terrible."

"I know." I bite my lip, ready to reveal the secret that has been weighing on me since I read her diaries right before Cannes. "What's worse is I think I know why she did it. Why she killed herself."

"What do you think?" He runs his fingers up and down my arm lightly, making me shiver.

"I read her diaries. Our father gave us each a box of her personal items and I found her last diary inside." I take a deep breath. "She met someone else. Another man. She was having . . . an affair and when the man broke up with her, she was completely devastated. She wanted to leave my father. She'd been making plans."

Caden says nothing, just keeps stroking my arm, holding me close. I close my eyes and breathe in his scent, not sure if I should say anything else or let it go. It feels so good to confess what I found. I've kept this as my personal burden to bear and it's been so hard. No one else knows about my mother's indiscretions. At least, I don't think anyone knows.

My father might know, but I'm sure he didn't want to shatter my mother's image. And I appreciate that, but I also feel like it's such a lie. We're a family full of lies and secrets.

But maybe every family is that way.

I decide to continue on despite how hard it is to say everything. "In her diary, her last few entries were so . . . sad. They were so full of hopelessness. I can feel her pain come across the pages, in her handwriting, and it hurt me to read it, but those entries also made me mad. That she gave up so easily on her life. That she gave up on us, on my sisters. On *me*." I'm crying. The tears are flowing down my cheeks and the sob that comes from me sounds like it was wrenched from deep inside my soul.

"Baby. *Sshh*. Come here." Caden pulls me even closer and I sob all over his shoulder, his neck. My tears won't stop, my entire body is shaking, and I cling to him as if he can save me from all the horrible truths in the world. He's stroking my hair and kissing my forehead, whispering sweet words to console me, and I've never felt more cherished.

"I'm sorry," I murmur against his neck long minutes later. "I haven't told anyone about the diaries yet, not even my sisters. I've never even given myself a chance to cry over it, you know?"

"I know. I do." He squeezes me. "You okay?" Slipping his hand beneath my chin, he tilts my face up so our eyes meet. With his other hand he swipes away the tears from my cheeks. "You need a drink of water or something?"

"I'm fine," I whisper, my gaze roving over his face, taking in his handsome features. A face that has become dear to me, a man that has begun to mean something to me these last couple of weeks. "I just . . . thank you."

He frowns, his beautiful mouth curving downward. "For what?"

I touch his lips, streaking my fingertip across his full lower lip. I love his mouth. I love everything about him. Everything that I know, that is. I wish I knew more. I wish he would be honest with me. Open. Slowly but surely I can make this happen. I know it. "For being there for me. For letting me talk and for listening."

"I should say the same to you." He parts his lips, drawing my finger into his mouth, and I feel his teeth graze the tip of my finger.

"Then why don't you?" I'm teasing him, and it feels good to be light and silly after only moments ago revealing such heavy information.

He smiles and I pull my finger from his mouth. "Thank you, Rose." His smile fades, his expression going dead serious. "I mean it. It's been a long time since I've talked about my dad with anyone. Even my mom."

"I'm sure *especially* your mom. I know my father gets uncomfortable when any of us ask questions about our mother."

He strokes underneath my chin with his thumb, his gaze thoughtful. "Have I told you lately that I think you're beautiful?"

"Stop." I bat at his hand but he doesn't let go of my chin. He tells me I'm beautiful more than any other man has ever done but when he talks to me like this, I get embarrassed. "Seriously. You're going to give me a complex."

"A complex over your beauty? That doesn't sound like such a bad thing." He releases his hold on my chin so he can touch my cheek and run his finger down my nose, along my brows. "You're unnaturally pretty, I swear. Like a little angel face."

I roll my eyes and grimace. My cheeks are hot and I don't know if I can take much more of this. "That's what Violet says and it's so embarrassing. She claims I look like one of Botticelli's angels." I don't really believe it. Lily's the beautiful, outrageous one. Violet's the quiet, smart one, but truly? She's just as beautiful as Lily.

"I had thoughts of wanting to paint you a few nights ago," he admits sheepishly, flashing a lopsided smile.

My brows go up as if I have no control over them. "I didn't know you were a painter."

"I'm not." He chuckles. "But you were lying on the bed, naked and spent, your skin all rosy and your hair everywhere. You had this satisfied look on your face, and I totally understood at that moment why artists always want to paint nudes of beautiful women."

"Please." I shake my head but he leans in and drops a kiss on my mouth, his lips lingering. "You don't mean it."

"I totally mean it," he whispers, his lips moving against mine. "You make me . . . feel things I've never experienced before, Ro. You've changed me."

I'm speechless. Not that I could say anything anyway. Not with the way Caden's kissing me, his tongue sneaking into my mouth, sliding against mine. His hands start roaming my body and soon we're lost in each other.

Not that I'm protesting.

Chapter Nineteen

Caden

"When you coming back, son? I need a firm answer. They're ready to interview you. Whenever you're ready, so are they. You're spending way too much time over there and if you don't hurry home, your opportunity is going to move on without you."

I'm out in front of the hotel standing on the sidewalk, having escaped from the room and Rose so I could call Cash. He's been blowing up my phone the last two days in a variety of ways including missed calls, texts, and voicemails. I had no idea the old man was so savvy with a smart phone. He even tried to Face-Time me.

I've avoided him, which is stupid. I'd rather spend time with Rose than face my reality. I need to man the fuck up and do what's right.

Blowing out a harsh breath, I run a hand through my hair. I need to get this shit cut. It's driving me crazy, always falling in my eyes. "I'm not exactly sure."

Cash wheezes. Or maybe he's sighing. I can't tell. "I'm telling ya, you need to get your ass back here. The position needs to be filled and he's going to find someone else for the job, which would be a damn shame because you're perfect for it and you know it. You've got an eye like no one I've ever met. They would kill for your expertise."

"Put me down for Monday, okay? Let them know I'll be there first thing in the morning or whatever works best for them." If I can't go back to New York with Mitchell, then I'll have to find my own way home.

This means I have approximately forty-eight hours left with Rose.

Not enough time. I don't want to leave her. Worse, I don't know how I'm going to tell her I'm leaving her.

"Sounds good. Just know that this position can't wait for you." He keeps telling me this and I know he's right. "It's the opportunity of a lifetime. A *lifetime,* kid. It'll help you go legit. Keep you out of the shit."

"*You've* done all right for yourself," I point out.

"I don't know anything else. I got in so deep, there's no way I could get out. Next thing I knew I was forty. Then fifty, then sixty . . . hell, I can't even make myself retire. I'm addicted to this game. It's ridiculous." Cash pauses. "But *you,* you can pull yourself out of this. You're young. You're smart. You can do something with your life and actually become something."

That's why I'm going to the interview. Cash talks like the job is mine already, but we don't know that for sure. I still need to interview and prove myself. It's still hard for me to believe I've been handed this opportunity. An established and respected jeweler with a store in Brooklyn needs someone with a good eye who can evaluate and price jewelry. Considering I've been stealing copious amounts of jewelry for years and can price the shit out of it—both on the black market and legitimately—this is right up my alley.

And Cash knows it. The second he heard about the position—he's friends with the owner, talk about ironic—he knew I was the perfect candidate. I'm flattered he even thought of me.

"I'm going to call Mitchell right now and see when he's going back home," I reassure Cash. "I'll call or text you when I find out more details."

"If you gotta fly commercial, book a flight. I'll front you the money."

His offer makes me feel like shit. "I can pay for it. I have money." I don't want to be his charity case.

"The offer stands. If you need it, tell me. I want to help. You can always pay me back," he says firmly. "Keep me posted when you know more." He ends the call and I immediately look up Mitchell's number and call him.

"Tell me you're finally coming over." This is how Mitchell greets me. He's already slurring his words. It is way too early for him to be drunk. "We're having a party tonight. In your honor."

"Give me a break. And I don't want to go to your shitty party."

"You're an asshole. A stupid asshole. This shit will be amazing tonight. There will be alcohol. There will be scantily clad women with sexy British accents and cock-sucking lips. Oh, and there will be all the drugs you could ever ask for. All of it. Maybe drugs you never even knew existed." Mitchell laughs. "God save the Queen, man. I fucking love England."

Sounds like an absolute nightmare. I decide not to even acknowledge what he just said. "So when are you returning to the States?"

Mitchell makes an irritated sound. "Is that all you ever want? To know when we're leaving? Are you that anxious to get out of here?"

"I have an appointment I need to go to on Monday."

"And that's my problem how?" Mitchell laughs and I hear a female voice in the background, asking him if he wants another round. *Great.* He's entertaining.

"I'll find my own flight back home," I tell him irritably. I don't need this shit. "Talk to you later, Mitch." He hates it when

I call him that. Thinks the nickname sounds too blue collar. Such an elitist prick.

"Wait, wait, wait, Kingsley. I'll get you back home." He pauses and I hear ice clink in a glass, so I can only assume he's having a drink. He smacks his lips together before he says, "I'm flying out Sunday night."

"Sunday night?" I turn and watch the front doors of the hotel, hating the hinky feeling I have that Rose is somehow lingering nearby. But she's not. When I left her in the room she was on the phone with her sister and planning on going in to Fleur this afternoon. "Is that confirmed?"

"Yeah, yeah. Confirmed. Around seven, though I'm not exactly sure about the departure time. I don't want to leave too early or too late."

"Makes sense." I breathe a sigh of relief. "Thanks a lot for helping me."

"Not a problem. But hey."

"What?"

"I have one condition, my friend."

My sense of relief flies right out the window. I hate conditions. "What is it?" I ask warily.

"You need to come to my party tonight. You *must*. I'm insulted you haven't stopped by and visited me at Mum and Dad's." Mitchell laughs at his fake British accent and I wish like hell I could tell him to fuck off and hang up on him.

But I can't. We've been friends for a long time, and yeah, he drives me crazy with his partying ways, but I can't treat him like shit. "Can't make it. I have plans," I answer.

"Cancel them."

"No can do, bro."

"Don't 'bro' me. Since when do you decline attending a drug- and sex-filled party? You found God or something?" Mitchell asks incredulously.

He is the worst ever, I swear. But this is how our relationship has always been. We give each other constant shit. Plus, he knows most of my secrets. If he really cared, he could call the police and have me apprehended in a second.

But he never has. He's always turned a blind eye to what I do. He's always been there for me despite the constant amount of crap he dishes out to me.

"It's nothing like that." Should I tell him the truth? He won't stop badgering me until I do. Yet my confession might make it worse. "I'm . . . seeing a woman."

"Oooh." Mitchell sounds like his ten-year-old self. When we used to give each other shit over girls and other dumb crap. "Well, bring her with you. I can't wait to meet the fancy piece of ass you're fucking around with."

I'm pissed. Did he really just call Rose a fancy piece of ass? "Don't talk about her like that," I snap.

"What the hell, man. Are you seriously into this chick?" Mitchell is full-on laughing now. "Who'd have thought it? Mister Renegade Thief always on the go, falling for a *girl*? Have you lost your balls or what?"

"You're an asshole," I mutter. "And I'm not coming to your shitty party."

"Then I guess you're not coming home with me on my plane, either," he says cheerfully, clearly enjoying this conversation.

"You wouldn't."

"Don't test me. Come on, Caden. You know I get upset when you don't show up to my parties. You bring the good time."

I *used* to bring the good time. I drank plenty of booze and did all the drugs and the women, but I pulled myself off the party scene a few years ago. The more alcohol and drugs I consumed, the more reckless I became, and I didn't need the trouble.

Major mistakes could mean jail time. Something I definitely wanted to avoid. That meant the partying had to stop.

"That's not my scene anymore and you know it," I tell him. "Don't make me go."

"Just stop by. For a few minutes. I won't take up too much of your time." Mitchell is practically pleading. *Weird.*

"Fine." I blow out an irritated breath. "I'll stop by for thirty minutes. That's it. No more."

"Perfect. You won't regret it. I swear."

"What time you want me there?" I ask, suddenly feeling tired. Like old-man-with-the-world-on-his-shoulders tired. I am so through with this sort of shit.

"Anytime. The party has already started."

"It's not even eleven o'clock in the morning."

"I know. Isn't it fucking great? I love this town. You can party whenever you want and no one judges you for it." Mitchell laughs. "I'll text you my address."

"Great." I end the call and shove my phone into the front pocket of my jeans. This is all sorts of fucked. How am I going to explain to Rose where I'm going? I sure as hell can't bring her with me. I don't want her anywhere near Mitchell and his sleazy friends.

You're one of Mitchell's sleazy friends.

That thought doesn't settle well.

I go back up to the hotel suite to find Rose in the shower, the bathroom door open though the space is full of steam and billowing out into the rest of the suite. I should put the necklace back in the safe, while I have a chance. Or I should go in there and join her. Surprise her. But if I do, that'll lead to soaping up her body, which will turn into touching her body. Then kissing. Then fucking.

Yeah. I can't risk it. She probably has to go in to work and I need to go to Mitchell's.

Can't wait.

Dread consuming me, I grab my duffel bag, figuring I may as well start packing now so I don't wait and do it at the last minute like I usually do. I unzip it and start folding everything I'd shoved in there over the last few days. *Hell,* weeks. We've had to use the hotel laundry service and I paid for my clothes to be cleaned. I even went to the front desk a few days ago and tried to pay for the stay up until then, irritated when the desk clerk told me it was already taken care of. I want to take responsibility for something beyond a few dinners out.

"Shit." I see the velvet box nestled deep and I glance at the open bathroom door. The shower just shut off and I shove everything back into the bag, zipping it closed. Frustration rolls through me that I didn't just put the necklace back into the safe and I have no one to blame but myself.

I walk around the suite, picking up my clothes where I left them, which is all over the place. Rose and I have acted like horny teenagers, locking ourselves away in this suite, ordering room service or takeout, lazing around. Having sex, talking, more sex, sleep, eat, sex, sleep, talk.

Sex, sex, sex.

I wouldn't trade these days for the world, but I need to get back to reality. Rose has slowly but surely been acting like an actual grown-up already. Now it's my turn.

But that means I have to leave.

"Oh!" I turn at Rose's startled gasp to find her standing in the bathroom doorway, holding a thick white towel in front of her. "I didn't realize you came back."

"Sorry." The towel isn't actually wrapped around her, offering me a glimpse of her waist and hips and upper thighs. All those wondrous curves I've run my hands over again and again. I tear my gaze away from her and turn back to my duffel, zipping it back open so I can shove everything I grabbed back inside. "You going in to Fleur this afternoon?"

"I am." She approaches me and I step away from the bag, not wanting her near it. What if she saw the velvet box? I can smell her as she draws near, clean and fresh, and my hands literally ache to touch her. But I don't. I won't. Touching her makes me lose brain cells, I swear to God. Until all I can do is focus on her. "What are you doing?"

"Ah . . ." How can I broach this subject lightly? "Cleaning up around here, putting away my stuff. I'm sure the maids hate us."

"I'm sure," she agrees wryly, her arms sneaking around me from behind. She presses her body to mine, her hands slipping beneath my shirt to rest lightly against my stomach. I can feel every naked, damp inch of her. She must have ditched the towel. I close my eyes, inhaling deep. She's trying to kill me, I swear. "I have a little time before I have to get ready," she murmurs.

Her voice, her words, are pure temptation. Temptation I must avoid. "Yeah? Well, I, uh, gotta go in a little bit."

She releases her hold and steps away from me. The loss of her touch hits me like a punch to the gut. "Where are you going?" Her voice is wary. Unsure. I never leave. She's the one who has a life. I'm the one who's been so completely focused on her and nothing else.

Behaving like this can't be good for me. She has the upper hand and I never give anyone that power. Rose makes me vulnerable.

And I don't like it.

I turn to face her again, my expression impassive. Trying my best to throw up the wall I used to be so damn good at erecting around myself so no one can penetrate it. "Going to my friend Mitchell's. I've mentioned him before, the guy with the jet? He wanted me to come over for a bit, so I thought I'd see him while you're at work."

Rose tilts her head, contemplating me. "When is he supposed to leave for New York?"

She's not stupid; she knows why I'm talking to Mitchell. We've talked about me heading back, though I haven't mentioned to her that I don't really have a true home there. That I just stay at Cash's apartment because he lets me. She doesn't even know Cash exists. She doesn't know much about my private life at all and for once, I'm ready to tell her everything.

But she's also naked and my gaze is trying to stay firmly fixed on her face. It's so damn hard. I've had her every which way. We've had so much sex I'm surprised my dick hasn't given out on me yet, I've worked it so hard.

Yet I take one look at her, naked and still flushed from her warm shower, and I want to jump her. Push her onto the bed and slide inside of her. There is nowhere else I'd rather be than with Rose.

Everything inside of me goes cold. That is about the scariest revelation I've ever had. Because I don't do commitment, I don't do relationships, and I definitely don't do love. I don't even think I know *how* to love.

I could learn, though. For Rose.

Fuck no, you can't. You're a worthless piece of shit who doesn't deserve a woman like Rose. When she finds out the truth, she'll kick your ass to the curb.

That's an even scarier revelation.

"I'm not sure when he's leaving yet," I lie. "It'll be soon, though." *Damn it*. If I want to actually love this girl I need to tell her the truth. It's just so hard to come out and say, *I'm leaving you in two days. Sorry to take off like this, but hey. It's been real.*

I don't know how to end this. Or continue it, either. She should be going back to New York soon too, but I don't think she wants to go. Late at night, when we're both exhausted and drifting off to sleep, she talks of staying in London. Or maybe even Paris. Not that she wants to continue working at Fleur; it sounds more that she wants to explore Europe and be on her own for a while. I think she's trying to find herself.

And I can't help her do that. How can I when I don't even know who I really am?

"You could go with me," she suggested a few nights ago, and I was thankful for the dark. So she wouldn't see the mixture of hope and horror that surely crossed my face.

I never did answer her. Like a wimp, I pretended I was asleep. But there's no pretending now. Yet I still lie like the hustler I am.

"Oh. Okay." Her face falls and seeing that . . . hell, it wrecks me. I start to say something reassuring, start to reach for her, but she turns away and I drop my arm, feeling like an ass.

Feeling like I somehow just ruined everything.

"I should go back too. Eventually," she says as she slips on a pair of skimpy black lace panties. Her back is still to me and I watch in fascination as she goes about her preparations. She pulls a black lace bra from the drawer and hooks it on. I could spend a lifetime watching her get dressed and never get bored. "I have to face my father sometime."

"Are you scared to face him?" *Like I'm scared to face you? I don't want you to find out my truth. I'm afraid you'll hate me.*

Rose goes still, her hands dropping to her sides, her head bent almost as if in prayer. Slowly she turns toward me once again, vulnerability and sadness etched across her face. "Yes. He's going to give me the 'I'm so disappointed in you' speech. I've heard it before and he knows I hate it. But I have to do this. I can't work there any longer. I'm spinning my wheels at Fleur."

"Are you sure that's what you want to do?" I ask. "Quit Fleur for good?"

She lifts her chin, defiant. "I've thought long and hard about this. I'm not making this decision lightly."

"So you're really going to do it." The last few nights we've talked, tentatively revealing things. Personal details, though nothing ever too incredibly deep, especially coming from me. I've listened to her talk for hours about Fleur, her father, her father's skanky girlfriend whom he just asked to marry him. Rose has mentioned off and on that she's considering leaving Fleur but I thought it was just talk.

Guess not.

She nods, her eyes dimming. Hearing the word *quit* can't be easy. "I don't know what else I can do. I can't go back there and continue on as if nothing's wrong. I'll be too miserable."

"So you'll just give up on the family business. On everything you've worked toward since you were a kid." I can't believe it. I would never call Rose a quitter. She's so determined, so fiery when she sets her mind to something. Like I told her a couple of weeks ago, she's got passion.

She's also been handed an opportunity so many would kill for—hell, *I* would kill for it. My family has nothing. My family *is* nothing. Me and Mom. That's it. Whereas Rose has her sisters, her father, her grandmother, and who knows how many more people who love and support her.

And I've got shit.

"There's more to it than that." Her lips thin and her gaze slides away from mine. "You wouldn't understand."

"No, I guess I don't understand why you would trash your career and a job you love all over a woman you don't like. All because you feel underappreciated." I shake my head. Am I trying to goad her on purpose?

She looks at me, her eyes flaring with anger as she clenches her hands into fists. Standing like she is in just her black lacy underwear, the fury and frustration pouring off her in waves, I can't help but think how beautiful she looks.

Beautiful and super pissed.

"There's more to it than that," she says. "This isn't just about Pilar."

"Really? Could've fooled me."

Her jaw drops open for the briefest moment before she snaps it closed. "Why are you being such an ass?" She goes to the closet and yanks a black dress off the hanger almost violently, shaking it out so the fabric snaps. "You don't know what it's like to be me. What I have to deal with. It's really unfair that you sit and pass judgment on me when you have no clue what you're talking about."

A strangled sound leaves her as she tugs the dress over her head, working her arms through the sleeves, then shoving the skirt down past her hips. I don't say a word; I hardly react, and I think that only makes her angrier.

Which will only make it easier when I have to walk away from her. She won't mind as much when I go if she's mad at me.

At least, that's what I tell myself.

"They won't miss me when I go." She reaches behind her to zip the dress up and she's having a hell of a time. She isn't asking me to help her, either. "Trust me. No one cares about my pitiful contributions at Fleur. I'm more of a figurehead than anything else. Violet is the one who'll take Daddy's place when he retires. Unless Pilar pulls a fast one and somehow takes over, snagging the position from Violet. Not that I want to be there and witness that mess go down. *Ugh.*" She yanks on the zipper but it's not budging.

I go to her, batting away her hands and pulling the zipper up into place with one smooth tug. I trace my finger across her nape and she steps away from my touch, glancing over her shoulder to glare at me. "You needed help," I say with a shrug as I take a step back.

"My anger has nothing to do with you helping me with my dress and everything to do with how . . . unsympathetic you're being toward my problem," she explains.

"I don't really think you have a problem at all. That's why." I go to her, kiss her cheek and give her shoulders a squeeze. She shrugs out of my touch and I let my hands fall, irritated. "Your pity party isn't getting you anywhere, Rose. Before you make such a life-changing decision, talk to Violet. Listen to her. Listen to Ryder. Get their opinions on what you should do." *Listen to reason,* I almost add, but that would really infuriate her.

"'Pity party.' God, you're rude." She reaches for the pearl

earrings resting on the dresser and puts them in. "I'm tired of listening to them. I need to listen to my instincts, and trust me, they've been screaming at me lately."

I say nothing again and she glares as she shoves her feet into those incredibly high, sexy-as-hell black stilettos she wears. I need to watch what I say before she kicks me square in the nuts with one of those things.

"I'm going with my gut on this one," she says. "And my gut is telling me to leave. For good."

"And what are you going to do after you quit Fleur?" I ask. "What then?"

She shrugs. "I don't know. Hang out with you? We can stay here, in London. Together."

Yeah. That is the last thing she should want and I know it. But how can I convince her otherwise?

Chapter Twenty

Rose

HOURS AFTER MY *DISCUSSION* WITH CADEN I'M STILL FUMING. He was just so smug. So rude. Completely lacking any sort of understanding of my feelings, acting like a typical asshole guy.

And I didn't really think he was that way. Yes, those first few encounters with him he'd been a complete ass, driving me insane but in a frenzied, angry, almost sexual way. Yes, definitely in a sexual way because though he made me angry, he also made me yearn.

Earlier today, though? He'd been almost condescending. Awful.

Worse? He never said a word when I mentioned I wanted to hang out with him once I quit Fleur. Acted like I'd never even *said* it. All of a sudden he was all smiles and kisses on the cheek as he said he needed to go. Who does that?

Whatever. Men. At the moment, they suck. I'm also blaming my irate, irrational anger on PMS. That has to be a contributing factor.

"You look ready to tear someone apart," Violet says as she enters her office. I'm sitting across from her desk, trying to read over a report on my iPad but failing epically.

We've been sharing her office since I've been in London. Today she had a marketing meeting to attend, and I'm tempted to ask if Hugh was in the meeting with her—why I don't know—but she would jump on my question and tell me I needed to go on a date with him or something equally insane.

Though maybe I should consider going out with Hugh because clearly, Caden is leaving. And Caden is an asshole.

He is not an asshole. You're just hurt because he didn't acknowledge your girly feelings. Get over it.

I don't *want* to get over it. The anger is fueling me and I like it. It makes me feel strong.

"I'm grumpy," I warn my sister. She settles behind her desk, her expression impassive, and when her gaze meets mine I know there's something on her mind.

"Maybe that's the mood you need to be in when I tell you what I've just discovered." Violet rests her hands on top of her desk, clasping them together.

I decide to beat her to the punch with shocking news. "I have something to tell you too."

Her eyes narrow. "What is it?"

"Did you know Mom was having an affair with someone else? And that when he broke it off with her, she fell into a downward spiral and became so depressed she finally killed herself?" I throw it out there, in all its brutal, harsh glory, and Violet blinks at me a few times, her cheeks going pale.

"How . . . how did you discover this?" she asks, her voice small.

"I have her diary. The last one she wrote in. Everything's there, in her own writing." I feel bad, telling her like this, but I had to get it off my chest. It's been driving me crazy, holding in this secret.

"I already knew." She nods when I gape at her. "Father told me a while ago. He asked that I never mention anything to you, so I respected his wishes."

"*What?*" Why am I the last to know everything? Unless . . . "Does Lily know?"

"Yes."

Holy crap. I just . . . I don't understand why I'm always kept in the dark. I can't believe I let this eat me up inside when everyone already knew. *God,* I hate secrets. "So you knew she was having an affair. And Daddy knew, too."

Violet nods again. "I guess the marriage wasn't good for a long time. Ever since . . . after you were born, it went downhill fast." She acts like it's no big deal, but her words are like a fierce blow to my stomach.

"Downhill fast?" *Great.* So it was my fault? I can't take this. May as well urge her on to blurt out her bad news. "What were you going to tell me?"

"It can wait." The smile she gives me is false. Bright and cheery, though her eyes are dim and dark. "Let's talk about it another time."

Meaning she doesn't want to make this conversation worse. Everything within me goes still. Now I *must* know. "What is it?" I ask cautiously. It must be something else about Daddy. Or Pilar. Or maybe Daddy *and* Pilar. *God,* if they ran off and eloped I'm going to lose it. Completely lose it . . .

Violet interrupts my thoughts, her voice soft but the words deadly.

"Your boyfriend is a thief."

I stare at her for a moment, my brain trying to process what she just said. *Caden* and *thief.* The words together make no sense. None. I'm caught so off guard, I start to laugh, because I don't know how else to react.

"This isn't a laughing matter, Rose," Violet says sternly, but her matronly tone only makes me laugh more. She's glaring at me, her mouth working, her jaw clenching. "I'm serious!"

Okay. I need to straighten up before she smacks me. "Oh, come on. You can't be for real, Violet. A thief? Really? Where did you hear that?"

She sniffs. "I did a little investigating. So did Ryder. Talked with people who know Caden, or know of Caden. We share a lot of the same social circle. Or at least we used to, when we were younger. Turns out rumors have floated around him and his family for years."

"What sort of rumors?" I sound snippy but I don't care. I already warned her I was grumpy.

"Did you know his father committed suicide?" Violet asks abruptly.

I blink, startled at the harshness in her tone. "Yes. He told me about his dad." I send her a look. "I would think you'd be a little more sympathetic considering our mother did the same thing."

She ignores my remark. "His father was an investment banker and stole from his clients. They were going to bring criminal charges against him. A few civil suits had already been filed when he took his own life."

"I already know this. He told me everything." I turn off my iPad and leave it on the edge of her desk, frustrated.

"Did he tell you that he and his mother were left with nothing after his father's death? Not even the life insurance would pay out, because they don't on suicides."

"What does that have to do with anything?" I lean forward in my chair, imploring her with a look. "Are you purposely trying to rile me up? Disappointed that you haven't shocked me yet with all of Caden's so-called secrets?"

Violet doesn't even acknowledge my remark. "We went to the same private school, Caden and I. We were in the same *grade*. I knew he was familiar—I just couldn't place him, not that I really knew him. Lily remembered him, though."

"Lily?" *Say what?* "What does she have to do with any of this?"

"She had an interesting story to tell me. Remember when she said she lost Mom's diamond earrings? Father gave them to her for her sixteenth birthday and then they went missing. She said she lost them at some party and they got into a huge fight over it?"

I have no idea what Lily and her earrings have to do with Caden. "Sure," I say weakly. I remember an argument. Missing earrings. But that was typical Lily. She was so careless. She still is.

"She didn't lose them. They were stolen. She just didn't know how to tell Father, so she lied and said she lost them." Violet pauses and I swear she's enjoying this roundabout storytelling method of hers. "She said Caden Kingsley stole those earrings. *Mom's* earrings."

Frowning, I slowly shake my head. "And you believe her?" This makes absolutely no sense. "This is crazy. She doesn't know Caden."

"Yes. She does. She remembers him from high school because he had a crush on her and she knew it. But he was younger and she wasn't interested in anyone who couldn't get her booze or drugs back then." Violet rolls her eyes and I want to slap her, I swear to God. "They were at a party together years ago and she said they . . . hooked up. She was drunk or whatever and passed out. When she woke up, the earrings were gone."

I go cold inside. Like iceberg-freezing temperatures blowing through me, making me shiver. "They hooked up? What exactly does that mean?"

Violet shrugs. "You know Lily. The term could mean *anything*. Plus, she said she passed out, so she's not exactly sure what happened between her and Caden. She does know they kissed, though. She remembers that at least." She makes a little face, the one that says, *and you're having sex with a guy who possibly had sex with our big sister.*

I know she's thinking that because *I'm* thinking that.

Maybe he only kissed her. Funny, though, how Caden never mentioned it to me. Not that I'd expect him to say, "Yo, I kissed your sister once," but he's never said anything about knowing Lily. I would think that should come up in one of our passing conversations.

"She has no proof he stole those earrings, right? She was drunk or high and passed out. It could've been anyone who took them from her." Why would he do such a thing? And even if he did, one time doesn't make him a thief.

Or maybe he was a teenage thief. He probably grew out of it. It might've been some sort of reaction to his father dying. Kids do crazy things when they lose their parents; they react in all sorts of nonsensical ways. Violet sort of lost it when we were teens. Well, she had reason to lose it with that jerk she trusted who attacked her, but still.

"It's not just what he did to Lily, Rose. It's what he's been doing for years. He travels all over the place and steals from the wealthy. Usually jewelry."

I'm incredulous. Even if it were true, how in the world could she know this? "You're making this up."

"Ryder's asked around. You know his past is . . . shady." She makes a face, but I know how she really feels. Pretending she's disgusted by his rough past to me when secretly it's a huge turn-on for her. Ryder has an edge of danger that still clings to him, even when he's conducting meetings and representing Fleur in public appearances. The man is magnetic and people can look past the edge. Or cling to it. Whichever they prefer. "He has connections. People who've given him information about Caden."

"I don't believe it."

Violet raises a brow. "You should. Ryder wouldn't come to me with this information if he hadn't confirmed it. He cares for you and doesn't want to see you get hurt."

"So what you're saying is Caden could hurt me."

"No, what I'm saying is Caden is a known criminal and it's only a matter of time before he gets caught and is thrown in jail." She looks at me. Really looks at me, as if she can see to the very depths of my soul, which she probably can because no one knows me like Violet. She's seen it all—the good, the bad, and the really ugly. "If you care for him—and I think you do—then yes, he'll hurt you, Rose. He'll break your heart even if he doesn't mean to, because the things that he's doing will put you at risk. He steals from the rich."

"And gives to the poor? Is he a regular Robin Hood?"

"Not even close. Well, he gives to the poor only because he *is* the poor. He has nothing."

"If he's stealing expensive jewelry and using the money to live on, he has to have something," I point out.

"Maybe he uses the money to finance his lifestyle. You have to admit, he certainly knows how to look rich. And act rich."

He doesn't really dress expensively. His shoes are average; he doesn't own an expensive watch or . . . anything, really. Yes, he came to the UK on a jet, but his friend is the owner of said jet, not Caden. "He's not overly excessive."

"Right. Because he's using you right now." The look on Violet's face is nothing short of smug. I sorta want to smack it right off of her. "Who's paying for the hotel bill, *hmm*? Who's paid for meals and entertainment? You?"

There hasn't been much entertainment beyond the naked variety and that's free. When we've gone out for meals, usually Caden has paid. But we haven't gone out much. The hotel is my expense—well, Daddy's. He told me to put it on the company credit card, so I did. We've ordered plenty of room service and the bill is probably the furthest thing from cheap. I gave myself a month to stay there and my time is almost up. I either need to go back home or stay with Violet and Ryder.

I really had no plan beyond getting back to the States and trying to continue seeing Caden. I haven't been thinking about the future. It's been freeing to let go and just live in the here and now. But maybe I should have questioned him more. Then I'd know what was really going on in Caden's life rather than have Violet so gleefully tell me all the dirty details.

Everything he's told me is a lie.

But has he really told me anything? No, not beyond the story of his father's death. I really know nothing else about the man. I know he has a way with words. I know I tremble every time he touches me. I know I love the way he says my name every time he first enters me.

"I'm just . . . worried about you, Rose," Violet says, her voice soft, her gaze full of concern. I know she means well, but it doesn't stop me from being angry at her for butting in where she's not wanted. "I don't want you to get hurt. I want you to be aware of what you're dealing with. *Who* you're dealing with."

"I know who I'm dealing with," I say, fighting the unease that wants to sink its sharp grip in me. "He won't hurt me. This isn't some grand love affair. It's a little fun while I'm in London, nothing else."

The look Violet shoots me is full of skepticism. I hate that look. She knows I'm lying. I know I'm lying, too.

I just don't want to admit it.

"Have you spoken to Whitney lately?" My rapid change of subject makes Violet blink.

"We went to lunch yesterday," Violet says. I can tell she didn't want to admit that. Her friendship with Whitney almost feels like a betrayal. I know it's stupid, but I can't help it.

"Maybe she could shed some light on Caden."

"Do you really think that's a good idea, you talking to Whitney about Caden? Considering their shared history . . ." Her voice drifts off.

Yeah. I'm more determined than ever to talk to Whitney about Caden. "Could you give me her number?"

"You'll only stir up trouble," Violet says, her voice firm in that *I'm your substitute mother and what I say goes* way of hers.

"You should keep her out of this, Rose. You'll only get mad if you talk to her. She might tell you things you don't want to hear."

"That's for me to decide. Besides." I shrug, trying for non-chalance. Hoping I don't fail. "I'm not getting her involved in anything. I just want to talk to her."

Liar.

"Uh-huh." Violet grabs her iPhone and starts texting.

"What are you doing?"

"Texting Whitney." She shoots me a look. "Telling her not to talk to you."

"God, you're a witch." I won't call her the B-word. That would start a fight of epic proportions. I did it once when I was sixteen and I still regret it.

"I'm doing this for your own good."

"You're telling her to avoid me. How is that for my own good?"

"I'm trying to protect you." Violet sets her phone down on the desk. It dings and she glances at the message. "Great. Now she's curious."

"Of course she's curious. If you told me I shouldn't talk to someone, I'd want to talk to them even more."

"Kind of like how I'm telling you to stay away from Caden and you want to go run to him now?" Violet asks pointedly. "Because I know you. He's like forbidden fruit. All you want is another taste."

"You did the same exact thing with Ryder."

Her expression flickers. She can't deny it because I'm speaking the truth. "A different situation," she says hurriedly.

"How? You're being a total hypocrite right now. I didn't think you had it in you."

Her phone dings again and she glances at it. "Oh my God," she whispers.

"What?"

Violet snatches up her phone as if she doesn't want me to see it. Leaping out of my chair, I round the desk, trying to make a grab for her phone, and she clutches it close to her chest. "You do not want to see this," she says, her voice low and full of warning.

The hairs on the back of my neck stand up and I reach for it again. "I do."

"No. You don't."

"Hand it over, Violet." I hold out my hand, palm up, and she looks at it before she lifts her gaze to mine.

"No."

I drop my hand and roll my eyes. "You're being ridiculous. Just show it to me!"

Slowly she holds her phone out toward me and I squint, trying to see what it is.

A photo. Of the perfect blond-bobbed Whitney, her lips covered in gloss and puckered against a man's cheek.

But not just any man's cheek. *My* man's.

Caden.

I snatch the phone out of Violet's hand and she yells at me but I ignore her. The message below the photo says: Don't tell your sister I'm sitting on his lap.

I text Whitney a reply, pretending I'm Violet, trying my best to quell the rage rising within me.

What are you doing with him?

"You're not texting her, are you?" Violet sounds horrified.

Good.

I'm at a little get-together. You and Ryder should swing by. It's a crazy one though. I must warn you.

"She's at a party," I say, my voice hoarse. My heart is cracking in two. Caden mentioned he was going to his friend's house, but he didn't say anything about a party.

"With Caden?"

I nod, unable to speak. I'm afraid I'll start yelling or worse, crying. He's with Whitney. At a party. And she's taking pictures of the two of them together, and . . .

God, *what are they doing together?*

My imagination kicks into overdrive and I send that bitch Whitney another text.

Where are you at exactly? Maybe we will stop by.

I wait, my patience, my control, my emotions . . . all of it fraying at the seams. I feel like I'm about to break apart into a trillion tiny pieces. No way could Caden be cheating on me with Whitney. *No. Way.* He wouldn't do that. We've become too close; we've shared too much.

Well. We haven't shared much beyond our bodies. I can't even begin to deal with or process what Violet just told me, either.

I just want Caden. Is that too much to ask?

Apparently it is.

The phone dings and I check it.

Belgrave Square. Want me to text you the address?

The most hoity-toity neighborhood in all of London. Of course. Maybe Caden's not there to screw around with Whitney. Perhaps he's there to steal from his friend, or anyone else who happens to be there and dripping with fine jewels.

Oh, God. This is all just too much. I think I'm going to be sick.

Ignoring the nausea that threatens, I reply to Whitney, refraining from calling her every whorish name I can think of. Talk about a dead giveaway that she's not texting with Violet.

Send it to me. We'll come by later.

"Give me my phone back," Violet demands, holding out her hand.

I send her a withering stare. "No." Tapping my foot, I'm instantly relieved when Whitney responds quickly with the address. I copy the text and send it to my number before I hand the phone back to Violet. "Fine. Here."

She reads back over the texts I sent, my conversation with Whitney, then glances up at me. "What are you doing, Rose?"

"I'm going to that party," I say determinedly, grabbing my purse and slinging it over my shoulder. "I have to know what's going on."

"This isn't the way to go about it."

I start for the door. "Isn't this what you wanted? Me breaking up with Caden?"

"You're going to break up with him?" she asks.

The hope in her voice is clear. And that kills me. I've always wanted her approval for everything I've ever done. Violet's opinion has always mattered.

But I'm not going to end a relationship with a guy I care about because she thinks he's bad for me. Maybe he's not. Maybe he could change for me.

Classic, stupid way to think, Rose.

"No. Maybe. I don't know yet," I admit, reaching out to grasp the door handle. My hand is shaking, I'm so upset, and I grip the handle tight, trying to control my nerves. "I'm sure I'll tell you all about it. Eventually." *Maybe.*

Maybe not.

Without another word I open the door and exit her office, making my escape.

Headed straight into the unknown.

Chapter Twenty-one

Caden

THE PARTY IS INSANE AND IT'S NOT EVEN FIVE O'CLOCK. THERE have to be almost one hundred people crammed into Mitchell's parents' massive Belgrave Square townhouse. Music is pumping through the whole-house sound system and the kitchen is overtaken with every type of liquor imaginable. The place is a mess, empty glasses and beer bottles and cans everywhere, empty platters where appetizers once sat. Tiny red stirring straws and crumpled napkins and cigarette butts litter the floor.

The Landerses would absolutely shit if they witnessed the destruction happening in their London home. I kick a plastic champagne glass out of my path with a sneer. Hell, the mess disgusts me, and it's not even my place.

There are more women than men in attendance and they're all gorgeous. They all happen to be scantily clad as well. How Mitchell made that happen I'm not exactly sure, but I can assume it took a huge outlay of cash to convince the women to come here. At the very least, a most excellent array of drugs and alcohol was probably offered, and that'll draw just about anyone to a party.

I know that's why Whitney's here. She loves a party, especially one with plenty of cocaine and vodka. Those are her weaknesses. They used to be mine, too, before I stopped partying.

The minute Whitney arrived, she came running for me, a giant smile on her face. She deposited herself in my lap, holding out her cell phone in front of us and shouting, "Selfie!" before she snapped a pic, pressing her lips to my cheek at the last second.

Fucking annoying. I shoved her off my lap and told her to delete the photo but she took off running, giggling like a madwoman. I could almost feel sorry for her and her total lack of direction. Almost.

I'm skulking near the front door, lingering in the foyer and ready to make a run for it, when I hear Mitchell call my name. I turn to find him smiling at me, a girl under each beefy arm.

Mom wasn't too far off when she called him pudgy. He's still carrying extra weight around the middle, but he's somehow grown into it. He's broad like a tank and of average height and looks, but the guy is bleeding money. Since he arrived in London he's been a partying fool. I know this because he filled me in on all the dirty details when I first arrived. We chatted for a while before everyone started to show up, and I somehow got stuck here.

But I'm ready to go, ready to head back to Covent Garden and the hotel and my girl. I have only two more nights with her and I need to make the most of them.

"Where you going, Kingsley?" he asks, squeezing the girls close to him. They giggle and smile, one of them flashing me a sultry look. "I brought entertainment just for you."

"They look far more interested in you, Mitch." I smirk when he glares at hearing his hated nickname. I've told him time and again that Mitchell makes him sound like an uptight asshole, but he doesn't agree.

"Nah. This one likes you a lot. She told me." He shoves the one who made eyes at me forward, earning a grumble from her before she smiles up at me. She's cute, her tits are barely covered, and her legs are long. I don't feel a thing for her. Not even a twitch of appreciation.

Seeing this girl only makes me miss Rose.

"Sorry. Not interested." I shrug.

Her smile fades and she narrows her eyes. From pretty to mean, just like that. "Fuck you," she spits out before she turns on her heel and leaves with a flounce.

"Classy," I mutter, shaking my head. "Where do you find them, Mitch?"

"I'll catch up with you later, okay, sweetheart?" Mitchell kisses the other girl on the forehead and shoves her out of his arms. She doesn't seem to mind, though, and offers him a soft smile before she walks away. He turns to me, making a soft *tsk*-ing noise. "You broke that girl's heart, Caden. That's why she's so hostile. Have you lost all your finesse or what?"

"Whatever," I mutter. "Listen, bro, I gotta get out of here. It's been real, but I'll see you Sunday, okay? Text me the exact departure time so I know what's up."

"Where's the fire?" He comes a little closer, an easy smile on his face, but I see the look in his eyes. He doesn't want to take no for an answer. He doesn't want me to leave. I don't get it. Why torture me when I clearly don't want to be here? "Don't leave yet. The party's just getting started."

I've been here for hours. If the party is really just getting started, I'm beyond done. "This type of thing really isn't my scene anymore," I tell him. "You know this. When was the last time I partied with you like this?"

"When did you become such a drag?" Mitchell shakes his head and pulls a pack of cigarettes out of his back pocket, extracting one from the pack. "I miss the good old days, man. When we used to drink and fuck around with girls. Get high, get laid, eat, take a downer and crash out. Remember how much fun we used to have?"

I remember how empty my life felt. I remember hating the hangovers the next day. The humiliation when I couldn't quite recall what happened the night before. Finding a gold necklace in my pocket with an emerald-and-diamond pendant dangling from it one time, so freaked out and worried over who I'd stolen it from. Whether that person saw me, because I couldn't remember for the life of me what exactly happened and how I became in possession of that necklace.

That was the last night I partied. The last night I let myself get out of control. *Never again,* I told myself. It's one thing to be a sly criminal. It's another thing entirely to be a reckless thief who doesn't give a shit if he's caught or not.

That moment taught me a lesson. One I'll never forget.

"You know why I stopped," I tell him, my voice low, my gaze intense. "I have my reasons."

He stares at me and then offers a short nod. "If you've gotta go, go. But I think Whitney is looking for you, so you better tell her goodbye. This might be your last chance before we leave London."

The absolute last thing I want to do. And from the look on my face, Mitchell must have sensed it because he bursts out laughing, not giving a shit about my predicament. "Man up. She's not that bad."

"She's insane. Besides, she knows I'm with someone else and doesn't give a shit," I mutter.

"Yeah, what's up with that anyway? Who is she? The girl you're with. I'm curious."

"You don't know her," I say quickly, *too* quickly. Though he probably does know Rose. At the very least he should know Violet and Lily.

"That means I must totally know her. *Hmm.*" He takes my arm and drags me back into the living room, which is crowded with people. At least the music has lowered, so it's not so fucking loud. Probably got turned down so as not to disturb the neighbors.

I glance around the room, spotting her in an instant. Whitney is sitting on a couch crowded with other people, bent over a silver tray with white lines of powder on it, and I pull my arm out of Mitchell's grip.

I don't want to deal with Whitney now. She's going to be a nightmare. "I gotta go. Seriously."

"Whitney! I found him," Mitchell crows, pointing at me with a jerk of his thumb.

Whitney lifts her head and wipes delicately at her nose, a giant smile on her face. She springs up from the couch and runs over to me, slinging her arms around my neck and slamming her body into mine. She's wearing a little top and shorts, her ass cheeks practically hanging out, and she tries to give me a smacking kiss on the cheek but I dodge away from her.

She's high as fuck, zipping along at a million miles a minute and on the verge of being uncontrollable.

"You're such a party pooper, not letting me kiss you. Don't you miss my kisses?" She frowns, her arms still around me, her head slung back and her breasts smashed against my chest. Her pupils are huge—I can hardly see the color of her eyes—and her cheeks are flushed. "Come on, Caden. One last time together before you go back to New York. Please?"

I'm assuming Mitchell told her I'm hitching a ride back home with him. "I don't think so." I try to disentangle myself from her arms, but she firms her grip. "Come on, Whit. Let me go. Don't make a scene."

She pouts and slips one hand down to streak her fingers along my chest. I grab hold of her wrist, stopping her path, and she curls her hand into a fist, giving me a little punch. "Ever since you hooked up with Rose Fowler you've become a real dick."

"Move." I rest my other hand on her waist, ready to push her out of my way, but she doesn't so much as budge.

And her next words leave me cold.

"I think they've got you figured out, Caden. Violet's been asking me lots of nosy questions lately, all about you." She pokes her index finger into my chest, hard. "Maybe they know your secret."

"Ow." I rub my chest, unease sweeping over me. No way could they know my secret. Who could tell them? "You didn't say anything, did you?"

"No, of course not. I'm your *friend*." Her indignant tone is almost amusing. "But I can keep my mouth shut for good if you give me another chance. In bed." She bats her eyelashes at me and giggles.

Jesus. She won't let up. "It's not going to happen between us, Whit. Never again. So give it up." I shove away from her and she stumbles backward, her cheeks red, her eyes flashing. I'm walking away from her when she shouts for everyone to hear.

"You're a fucking prick, Caden Kingsley! I hope you get an STD and your dick falls off," she yells, making Mitchell laugh.

I send him a look and start for the foyer. "I'm out," I tell him, giving him the finger as I stride toward the door, stopping in my tracks when I see who's standing there as still as a statue, watching me.

Rose.

My heart thundering, I take a step toward her and then stop. She looks . . . cold. Empty. How much did she see? How much did she hear? Having her show up here is like my two worlds colliding, and I'm not sure I'm prepared for the fallout.

"Baby." I pause, shocked at how she doesn't so much as move an inch, how . . . plastic her expression is. "What are you doing here?"

Rose studies me for so long I'm afraid she's not going to answer. "I guess I should be asking you the same thing," she finally says coldly, folding her arms in front of herself. "Considering Whitney's hanging all over you."

So she saw Whitney touching me. *Great.* "She's drunk. High. She doesn't know what she's doing."

"Don't make excuses for her." Rose's eyes flash with anger.

Fuck. I start to approach her, but the look on her face tells me I need to stay back. "How did you find this place?"

"Whitney." Rose spits her name out. "She invited Violet and Ryder to come by after work. Nice, huh? Fun little party I supposedly knew nothing about?"

"I wasn't trying to hide anything from you," I explain. "I told you I was going to see my friend."

"Whatever." She waves a hand, her lip curling in disgust. "I pulled one over on Whitney anyway. She didn't know that when she was texting Violet the directions to this place, it was me that was asking for them." She comes down the short steps of the foyer, heading straight for me. Her posture is perfect, her head lifted, but I see the sadness in her gaze. And the anger. "I had an interesting conversation with Violet earlier."

"Yeah?" I scratch the back of my neck, wishing like hell I could pull her into my arms, but she looks ready to scratch my face off.

"Yes." She stops directly in front of me. So close I can smell her, feel her warmth, and I curl my hands into fists so I don't touch her. "It was about you."

I glance over my shoulder, thankful no one is paying us any attention. The music has been turned back up and Whitney is standing on the coffee table, doing a little bump and grind. I turn back to Rose to find her still glaring at me. "Can we talk about this later? When we get back to the hotel?" Avoidance is my specialty. It should be my middle name.

But of course, I should have known Rose wouldn't let me get away with it.

"No," she says firmly, shaking her head. "I need to talk

about this with you *now*, Caden. It's eating me up inside, what Violet told me."

Shit. I'm fucked. Reaching out, I take her arm, my touch gentle, my fingers itching to caress and soothe. I'd probably get a fistful of knuckles in my teeth if I tried at this moment. Rose looks ready to destroy me. "Let's go upstairs, then," I tell her softly. "We'll find a room so we can have some privacy." May as well get this over with. Find out if I'm doomed forever without Rose.

I already know the answer. I'm fucked regardless of what I tell her. Maybe it's better she found out now versus later. Then we can be good and done with it by the time I head back home.

The thought isn't as reassuring as I'd hoped.

"I don't know if I want to go anywhere alone with you." She tries to escape my grip, but I won't let her go.

I *can't* let her go. She belongs to me. Doesn't she see it? Doesn't she *feel* it?

"Hey, hey, who's the pretty lady?" It's Mitchell. Irritation rolls through me.

We both turn and Mitchell's eyes widen when he sees who's with me. "Rose Fowler?" He slides a look to me, surprise in his eyes. "For reals, Kingsley? Nice catch."

"Fuck off," I tell him, grabbing her hand and leading her up the stairs. She doesn't protest, doesn't say a word, and I'm thankful for her acquiescence. I need to be alone with her so I can possibly rectify this real-life nightmare I'm experiencing.

But I'm pretty sure it's already too far gone to fix.

"Don't you dare fuck her on my parents' bed," Mitchell calls after us, then yelps. "Ow, Whitney, fucking get your hands off me, you jealous cow!"

I feel Rose stiffen next to me but I don't acknowledge it. I don't need this drama from Whitney and Mitchell or anyone else. Not Violet, either. Walking down the hall, looking for an empty room, I feel like I'm being led to my death. To the gallows, ready to face my execution.

More than anything, I'm scared. Afraid of what Rose is going to say, how she's going to react, how I'm going to react. I've never faced my truth before. No one has ever called me out on it. I just do what I do and skate by, always getting by. Always getting away with it.

Rose is about to make me face my reality. I know it. And I'm not ready. Not by a long shot.

The bedroom at the end of the hall is huge and I can only assume it's the master. Rose and I walk inside and I close the door, turning the lock on the knob as I watch her go to a chair near the window and sit in it. She looks perfectly composed, perfectly beautiful in the black dress I zipped her up in only a few hours ago, when life was still relatively normal and I hadn't been laid out bare, confronting my fears.

May as well get right to the point. Suffering is not my favorite thing to do. "So. What did Violet say?"

She grips her knees so tightly her knuckles are white. She won't look in my direction and that kills me. "I don't know who he is."

I frown. "What?"

"The guy downstairs. The one who said my name." She shakes her head, then gazes out the window. "He's not familiar."

"That's Mitchell. Mitchell Landers. His dad is some real estate mogul and his mom is on reality TV." No joke. Mitchell's parents are the real fucking big deal. His dad is a billionaire and his mom was on some weird shopping show that put her excessive spending habits on display for the entire country to see.

She's still not looking at me, now keeping her gaze trained on her knees. "Oh."

The silence hangs between us, bloated and full of tension, like a heavy, dark cloud just about to explode with thunder and lightning. My skin feels tight, my stomach is doing flips, and I can't fucking stand it any longer.

"Rose." She hangs her head farther when I say her name. "What did Violet *say*?"

"I don't want to tell you." Her voice is so quiet I almost can't hear her. "I don't want to talk about it."

What? "You just said . . ." I blow out a harsh breath, resting my hands on my hips. Frustration runs through my veins. I don't know how to handle this. "You said you wanted to talk about it. So let's do it."

"I don't want to hear your side of it. Or hear you defend yourself and us end up getting into a fight. Not anymore. It's just . . . wasted breath, you know? I don't want any of that. Not tonight." She lifts her head, her eyes meeting mine. "Why was Whitney sitting on your lap earlier, taking pictures and kissing your cheek?"

Ah, hell. I was really hoping she wouldn't mention that. "How did you know about it?" I ask carefully, feeling as if I'm walking into a minefield and Rose has already set the trap.

Her lips thin. "She sent the photo to Violet and she showed it to me."

Fuck me. Everyone's out to screw me over, I swear. "Whit kissed my cheek and took the picture when she first showed up. I shoved her off my lap the minute I realized what she was doing."

Rose's gaze doesn't waver from mine. "Why was she hanging on you when I first walked into the house?"

"I told you. She's drunk. She's high. She'd just done a few lines. And she's pissed that I lost interest in her. She still tried to get me to have sex with her," I say with a grimace. I'm being about as honest as I can get. If she wants to ask me anything else, I'll tell her the truth. No matter what.

No matter how much she might end up hating me.

"I don't like her at all." She utters a little frustrated noise. "I don't know why my sister is friends with her."

I don't get it, either. "When it comes to Whitney, you have nothing to worry about," I reassure her.

"What about . . . anything else? Should I be worried?" Rose asks.

She's being purposely vague. And I don't want to say anything that's unexpected or that will incriminate me. "When it comes to other women, I'm not interested. There is only you." That statement I can stand by 100 percent. I don't want anyone else. I don't need anyone else.

Just Rose.

Her face almost crumples, like she wants to cry, but then her expression changes, becoming impassive in an instant. "Come here." Her breath hitches. "Please."

I go to her with apprehensive steps. What if she slaps my face? Kicks me in the balls with those killer heels she's wearing? She could spit in my eye and I would take it. It would be the least I deserve for what I've kept from her. For what I've done to so many people these last few years. I justified my actions by saying my stealing hurt no one since all my marks were loaded already. They had insurance. Coverage for their loss.

Where was the coverage for my loss? For my mother's loss? It disappeared when my dad jumped from that building. When he stole from his clients. Every inch of security we'd ever had was ripped from us with his actions. Actions he never had to truly face.

His unnecessary death is what has fueled me all this time. What helped me justify my actions. Twisted and all sorts of messed up, but it's all I've got.

And it's hard to face my wrongs in front of a woman who I never, ever want to disappoint.

Rose takes my hand when I stop in front of her, interlacing our fingers together. She tilts her head back so our gazes meet, and her golden eyes sparkle with unshed tears. The sight of those tears slays me dead and my chest cramps. With my other hand I cup her cheek, stroke her soft skin, and she leans into my touch, closing her eyes so the tears tangle in her lashes.

I hate what I've done to her. The torture I must have inflicted on her. The torture I'm about to put her through. It's not fair. If I could take her pain away and make it mine, I would. In a heartbeat.

"I know what you've done," she whispers, her eyes still closed as if she can't look at me. "You don't have to say anything else. You don't have to explain yourself. Just know that . . . I know. Violet told me."

Questions race through my mind, one after the other, coming at me rapid fire. How does Violet know anything? Who told her? And what exactly did she say to Rose?

She pulls on my hand and I step closer, shocked when she wraps her arms around my legs and rests her cheek against my thigh. "It doesn't matter what you've done. You have your reasons and I'm not going to question them. Just . . . let me have one more night with you before we leave. That's all I want."

"Rose . . ." My throat feels raw. My chest aches. Foreign emotions swirl within me and I don't know how to control them. Or what to do. "Baby. What are you—"

"Don't say anything." She interrupts me, squeezing my legs tighter. "Don't play stupid. Don't deny what you've done. Just let me have this time with you." She looks up at me. "Please."

"I leave Sunday," I tell her solemnly. It's time for me to be honest. "Mitchell flies back Sunday night and I'm going with him."

She lifts her head, keeping her gaze fixed on mine. "I fly out tomorrow."

"What?" I rasp. The words stick in my throat, and it takes a concentrated effort to force the rest of them out. "Where to?" I croak. "New York?"

"Yes." She nods. "Right before I came here, my father called me and we talked for quite a while. Your words stuck with me all day, Caden. You're so right. I can't quit. I'm not a quitter."

"No." I touch her hair, the silky, soft strands clinging to my fingers as I push it away from her face. My gaze roams her face hungrily. Are these really the last hours I get to spend with her? "You're definitely not a quitter, Ro."

"Will you come back to the hotel with me?" she asks.

"You don't want to talk about . . ." My voice drifts. I can't even say it.

She slowly shakes her head. "No. I don't think there's anything left to be said."

There's plenty to be said. But if she wants to play it this way . . .

I'm not going to stop her.

Chapter Twenty-two

Rose

WHAT I'VE DONE IS WRONG. I KNOW IT. DEEP IN MY HEART I CAN see the fault in my reasoning, but I tell myself I'm keeping my heart protected. I'm throwing up barriers and pretending that what I discovered doesn't really matter as long as I have one more night with him.

With Caden.

On the cab ride over to Mitchell Landers's house I finally broke down and did a Google search on him. Surprisingly, there wasn't much to be found. Society page photos, Caden posing with groups of people, all of them smiling, covering a wide range of years, from a late-teenage Caden to Caden today.

Some of those people he's standing with I know. Most of them I don't, but I've heard their names. All of them are wealthy and of a certain social status he lost long ago when his father killed himself rather than face his punishment.

There were mentions of that, too. Of Carl Kingsley taking his life. Of the many wrongs he did to his clients. Not one mention of what Caden might do for a living; not one mention of him stealing from anyone, either.

Thank God. I was both relieved and confused. What's the truth? What are lies? I didn't know. I needed more answers.

So I called Ryder during that cab ride too—traffic was unbearable and I couldn't stand to be alone with my thoughts.

"Tell me the truth," I'd said to Ryder when he answered. "About Caden. Tell me everything you know."

And he proceeded to do so, hiding nothing, being brutally honest. So honest I flinched a few times, I felt tears come to my eyes, and at one point, I became filled with utter despair. He warned me at the end of the conversation that not all of the information he told me was confirmed, but he and Caden had some mutual friends. Friends who knew what Caden was capable of.

What he was capable of. Those words devastated me.

What would I do? How could I stand by this man when he's done nothing but steal for a living? He's not an honest man. He can't be a good man, can he?

"People can change," Ryder said to me before I ended the call. He was quiet. Thoughtful. Choosing his words in order to make the strongest impact on me, I could tell. "I think he cares for you, Rosie. I think he cares a lot. The love of a good woman can change . . . everything. Trust me. I wasn't good for your sister at first. I didn't care. Hell, I wanted to hurt her. But she made me a better man. Her love is everything to me."

I couldn't believe what tough, dark, and dangerous Ryder McKay said to me. His words cracked my heart wide open and filled it with stupid, glorious, just-out-of-reach hope. Hope that crashed and burned to the ground the moment I walked into that townhouse and saw Whitney with her arms around Caden, her boobs pressed to his chest and his hands on her waist.

I wanted to kill her. Pluck every bleached blond hair out of her head. And I saw it then. My reality. I knew there was no way Caden could give up what he does all for me. He might not be stealing for the best reasons—he is most assuredly no Robin Hood, though he doesn't spend excessively, either—but he's been doing it for too long. How can I expect him to give it up for me? How can I expect him to change?

Do I matter enough to him?

What we share is good. So incredibly, wonderfully good . . . but I don't think it's everything to him. The way he is for me.

I sit in a cab now, once again. This time with Caden by my side, his arm slung over the backseat, his fingers dangling and brushing against my shoulder every few minutes as he shifts and squirms like a little boy. He's uncomfortable. I'm sure I shocked him when I told him I didn't want to hear what he's done. That I didn't want to talk about it.

Why put myself through that torture again? One last night is all I want. Then we can go our separate ways.

No matter how much it hurts.

Traffic again is awful, maybe even worse since everyone's off work and it's a Friday. The cabbie hits the brakes hard and smacks his horn repeatedly, cursing at the car in front of him when it comes to an abrupt stop. Caden's arm falls to my shoulders with the jolt and I bump against him, reaching out to rest my hand on his hard, warm thigh to brace myself.

"Sorry," I mutter, about to remove my hand when he places his free hand on top of mine, keeping it in place.

"I don't mind," he murmurs, his voice so deep it feels like he's touching my heart, my soul. "Keep your hand there."

Slowly I look up at him, his dark eyes filled with so much emotion, his hair falling across his forehead. He looks sweet. Lost. Nervous. Hungry.

I feel the same way.

His other hand streaks across my shoulder before lifting to toy with my hair and I scoot closer, resting my head against his chest, my hand gripping his thigh, never wanting to let him go. We sit like that for long, quiet minutes and I try to match my heartbeat to his, my breaths so that I'm inhaling and exhaling to his steady rhythm. Doing so helps me feel connected to him, like I'm a part of him. And when he leans into me, his mouth at my temple, his fingers playing with the neckline of my dress, I close my eyes.

And let myself fall under the spell he's so skilled at creating.

His fingers dip beneath the fabric of my dress, skimming along my collarbone. Darts of molten-hot pleasure shoot through me, and my breath grows shallow, my head dizzy. I swallow hard and lift my head to look up at him, only to find him already staring down at me. The hunger in his gaze is amplified and his lips part, as if he wants to say something.

But he remains silent, which is probably best. Words aren't necessary any longer. Empty promises would remain just that . . . empty. Tonight is about connecting one last time before saying goodbye. For good.

My heart seizes at the thought, so I push it away.

Dipping his head, his mouth brushes mine and I breathe into him, the relief that floods me undeniable. I took for granted how delicious his kisses are, his taste, his tongue, the hum that sounds from deep in his chest when my tongue touches his. His fingers grip my shoulder; his hand clamps down over mine, which still rests on his thigh. But this is as far as I'll take it. I don't want to get out of control.

I'm done doing that. Being out of control only hurts.

So when I break the kiss first and pull away from him slightly, he doesn't protest. He doesn't try to keep me close, either. We resume our position from only moments before, his arm around my shoulders, my head on his chest. I can feel the rapid beating of his heart beneath my ear and it makes me smile.

He's just as affected as I am. I find that reassuring.

It also makes me sad.

———

I SLIP THE KEY CARD INTO THE SLOT AND THE LIGHT BLINKS green. Pushing open the door, I enter the room, Caden right behind me. He slams the door and turns the lock, the click loud in the otherwise quiet of the room, and I go to the dresser, setting down my purse before I step out of my shoes. I wriggle my toes, sighing with relief, and I hear Caden's chuckle.

A chuckle I've heard many, many times these last couple weeks. But somehow, this one is different. Deeper. Darker. I glance up to find him watching me, his gaze locked on my feet, his mouth curved in a faint smile.

"Hurting?"

Nodding, I hold my foot out and wiggle my toes again for his benefit. "I go a few weeks hardly wearing heels and I guess my feet have to get used to them again."

"Torture devices," he murmurs as he points at the bed. "Sit down."

I frown. "Torture devices? Men never protest when they see a woman in heels."

"Oh, they're definitely sexy. I'm not denying that. But you must admit they torture your feet." He nods toward the bed. "Sit down, Rose."

"My grandma told me from a very young age that beauty is pain." I go to the edge of the bed and sit, surprised when he kneels in front of me, holding out his hand.

"Give me your foot."

I do as he commands, a gasp escaping me when he holds my foot in his hands and begins to rub. *Good lord,* that feels good. He presses hard, his fingers moving in circles across my heel, then the center of my foot. He pulls on my toes, each of them giving a little pop, and I'm surprised at how good that feels. He keeps massaging, his thumbs working my aching muscles, and I close my eyes, a low moan escaping me.

"Is this okay?" he asks hoarsely.

I nod, unable to speak. His thumb moves slowly over the top

of my foot, his gaze dark, his tongue darting out to lick his lips, and heat pools low in my belly.

"Want me to stop?" His voice deepens, sounding like pure sex. I had no idea a foot massage could be so sensual. "Rose?" he asks when I don't say anything.

My eyes pop open and I furiously shake my head, making him smile. He carefully sets down my foot and grabs the other one, giving it the same luxurious treatment for long, delicious minutes until I feel like I could melt. His hands start to wander. Fingers circling my ankles, tickling the backs of my calves, behind my knees, making me giggle.

My skin grows warm when I feel his intent shift. The air becomes thicker, heavier. His touch bolder as his breathing deepens. Mine catches in my throat and my eyes are narrowed into slits as I watch him slowly work his way up my leg. Until his hand disappears beneath my skirt and is touching my thighs. I widen them for him shamelessly, wanting him to slip those magical fingers beneath my panties so he can find out just how wet I am for him.

I'm completely soaked—my body aches for his touch. This moment is so charged, everything feels that much more intense, and I know why.

Because this is the last night we'll be together.

"Your skin is so soft," he murmurs as he trails one finger along the inside of my thigh, stopping just as he reaches the spot between my legs. My thighs are quivering; my breath leaves me in shaky exhales. I'm so aroused I can hardly take it, and it all started with him rubbing my feet.

But really it all started when he rushed to my defense at the party in Cannes. When he kissed me by the pool and then ran away. I was hooked. I wanted more. I wanted my adventure, and I got it in the form of Caden.

"Your panties are wet," he tells me, his deep voice drawing me from my thoughts as his fingers graze the front of my underwear. "You're always so damn responsive, Ro."

"It's because you know just how to touch me." I brace my hands on the edge of the mattress, my breath hitching in my throat when he slips those magical fingers beneath my panties and touches my pussy. My thighs fall open as much as they can, though they're restricted by the skirt of my dress, and when he slips his long finger deep inside my body the moan that comes from my chest seems to rattle my bones.

"Lift up," he demands tersely, his other hand shoving at my skirt. I lift my butt, reaching for the fabric so it bunches around my waist. My flimsy panties aren't much of a barrier and he tears into them—literally rips the fragile lace, and then he bends forward, his mouth on my pussy, his tongue lashing against my clit.

His gaze directed on my face as he devours me.

"Oh, fuck." The words are a whisper of sound. It almost looks vulgar, how we're positioned. My legs are spread, the panties hanging in tatters, my skirt shoved almost to my breasts. Caden's nestled between my thighs, his mouth working my pussy, his big hands gripping my knees, holding me wide for him. I lift my hips, another cry falling from my lips when he sinks his tongue inside me.

I throw my head back, my eyes sliding closed as I concentrate on the feel of his wet, wide tongue swirling around my sensitive flesh. He licks my clit, sucks it between his lips, his fingers digging into my skin as he braces my knees, and then his mouth is gone.

My eyes fly open and I stare at him. His expression is wild, his chin covered with my juices, his lips glistening as well. He's still fully clothed and I want him naked. I want to come. I want his mouth back on my pussy. I want it all.

"I want to watch you come," he tells me, his voice low and deep and making me wetter. "It's my favorite thing. Are you close, Ro?"

I nod and lift up so I'm almost but not quite sitting. "So close," I murmur.

His gaze flares with heat. "I want you to touch yourself."

I frown. "What?"

He smiles and darts out his tongue, flicking my clit with just the tip. "Rub your clit. Show me how you like it. And then I'll join in. The two of us can make you come hard. I know it."

Oh, God. He's probably right. But I've never touched myself in front of another man before. I've never felt comfortable doing that sort of thing because it feels so intimate. Private.

"Do it," he urges with a nod of his head. "Touch yourself."

My hand slides down my belly, tangles in my pubic hair, and then I'm touching my pussy. I reach with my index finger, pressing it against my clit, and I hiss in pleasure.

"That's it, baby. Keep touching your clit," he encourages just as he settles his mouth on my pussy once more. His tongue flicks against my finger and I press my lips together to keep the moan contained.

There's something to be said for containment, for prolonging the pleasure. He knows what I'm doing and he smiles against my pussy and continues to lick it. My pace increases as I circle my clit again and again, my hips working, his tongue flicking against my flexing entrance before thrusting inside. I start to rub in earnest when I feel my orgasm barrel down on me, coming at me faster and faster until it breaks me apart and I gasp out a hoarse, "I'm coming," as a warning.

The shudders wrack my body with such intensity I buck against his face, my hand falling away from my clit as I collapse backward on the bed, my eyes tightly closed as my body shakes. He lifts up and away from me, I hear him hurriedly shedding his clothes, and then he's looming over me, crawling onto the mattress, crawling onto me.

"Ro." His voice is a heated whisper caressing my flesh and I open my eyes to find him watching me with his dark gaze. Bending over, he takes my mouth, the taste of me clinging to his lips and tongue. I kiss him back without restraint, my hands sliding over his naked skin, and when he breaks the kiss I growl with frustration. "Let's get this dress off of you," he murmurs as he lifts himself off me.

Somehow, working together, we get me naked. We're both on our knees facing each other, his hard cock brushing against my belly, our hands in each other's hair as we kiss. I scoot closer to him, my hands sliding all over his smooth skin, across his chest, his pecs, down along his stomach. I curl my fingers around the base of his cock and stroke him, smiling against his lips when I feel him shudder in reaction to my touch.

"You keep doing that and I'll come all over your hand," he mutters like a threat.

It's a threat that thrills me, though. I increase my pace, making him curse, and then he's grabbing me by the shoulders and tossing me onto the bed, my head hitting the pillows just as he positions himself over me. I spread my legs to accommodate his body between them and then he's buried deep inside me, to the hilt, his balls brushing my pussy as he holds himself there for long, delicious seconds.

I wrap my arms around his neck and kiss his jaw, his chin, his lips. Slowly he begins to move, hot and heavy deep inside me, my inner walls grasping greedily around his length with every slip and slide. He's lost all finesse, all sense of control, as he increases his pace and pounds inside of me. I take it. I revel in it. The sound of our skin slapping together, the wet sounds of my pussy as he dives in again and again, the moans and the creak of the bedsprings and his harsh breath, his words sharp as he declares he's going to come.

I love that he's lost all control. I hold his head to mine and whisper in his ear, encouraging him. Before Caden I would never have said any of these words, but he's taught me well.

"You feel so fucking good," I whisper. "Fuck me harder, Caden. Make me come all over your cock. I want to feel you come inside me. Please."

"Ah, shit," he chokes out, lifting himself so he's propped on his hands, which are braced on either side of my head. His hips work, his cock slides deep inside of me, and then he stills. That telltale indication that he's about to come and there's no going back.

"*Fuuuck.*" He draws the word out and slams into me one more time, just as I feel the first spurt of semen inside of me. He grunts and thrusts, coming again and again, filling me completely before he collapses on top of my body with a shuddery sigh.

No condom again. How could we be so stupid? It's as if we come together and I can't even think. I hadn't lied when I said I was about to start my period. Any day now it would make its monthly visit, though I really should consider going on the pill . . .

Why? Not like you and Caden are a permanent thing.
Ugh.

I wrap my arms around his back, slide my hands down to his butt, and hold him there, savoring the throb of his still hard cock deep inside me. I feel full of him, full of his cock. He surrounds me, his come in my body, our skin sweaty and sticky, his mouth at my ear, our legs tangled.

"You're gonna kill me, Ro," he whispers long minutes later when he finally pulls himself from my body, the dribble of semen that coats my pussy a foreign sensation.

"You're going to kill me too," I murmur, my eyes closed, aftershocks still coursing through my body. I reach for him but he's not there, and when I crack my eyes open I see he's standing beside the bed, his expression one of horror as he stares at me.

"I didn't use a condom."

I sit up, wincing against the delicious ache between my legs. "I know."

"I came inside of you."

Nodding, I stretch my arms above my head, letting them drop when I see the freaked-out expression on his face. "Don't worry about it."

"Don't worry about it? We just took a huge-ass risk," he says, his voice rising. "What if I got you pregnant?"

I shrug. Why am I so nonchalant? I should be freaking out just like he is. "What if you did? Would that be so terrible?" I can't believe I just said that. I almost want to snatch the words back and pretend I never said them, but it's too late.

"What the fuck are you saying, Rose? We're not prepared to have a baby. You're too young. I'm too young. We're not even a . . . thing. We wouldn't work in the real world and you know it. I'm not good enough for you." He waves a finger between the two of us and I can feel my anger rise at his words, at the look on his face.

He's horrified. And I hate that.

"I'm not pregnant." I climb off the bed and pad toward the bathroom, feeling his gaze following me the entire way. "Stop worrying. I'm not trying to trap you."

"Rose, wait a minute! I never said that," he calls after me.

"You may as well have," I call back, shutting the door behind me and turning on the water. I bend over the sink and splash the cold water on my heated cheeks, pressing my eyes closed when I feel the sting of tears threaten.

I will not cry. I refuse to cry. He's not worth my tears.

But they fall anyway, sliding down my cheeks. I keep the water running so he doesn't hear my sobs and I know, without a doubt, it's over between us. Done. He's right. We're not meant for the long term. This was fun. A self-indulgent adventure I so desperately needed to have. Tomorrow I return to the real world, and someday I will look back on this moment in time with fondness.

As I stare at myself in the mirror, though, it doesn't seem possible. I'm crying. My heart hurts. I may be thinking all the right things, but I don't believe them. I think Caden could be the man for me.

Too bad he doesn't feel the same way.

Chapter Twenty-three

Caden

Dear Rose,

At first, I didn't understand why you wouldn't let me tell you the truth last night. Why you didn't want to yell and scream and cry at me for what I've done. Because I've done you wrong and you know it. Maybe not personally, though I have to admit, my lack of using a condom not just once but multiple times is incredibly stupid and you should hate me for that alone. I hate me for it.

But for whatever reason you don't and I'm not sure why. I know I don't deserve you. I'm not worthy of you. You've told me before you hate it when I say that but it's true. I'm not a good person. You make me want to be good, just for you, but I know that's not enough. I've made too many mistakes in my life and I don't think you could ever forgive me for them. Ever see me as the man I want you to see. The one who cares about you and would never hurt you.

I'm too lost to be saved for you, Ro. I hate that. But I have to be straight with you.

Whatever Violet and Ryder told you . . . it's the truth. I'm a thief. When we first met, yes, I saw you, a beautiful

*woman, but what really drew me to you was that damn
necklace. The Poppy Necklace. I had plans to steal it that
night.*

But then I met you. And you changed . . . everything.

*That's what I do, you see. I steal, mostly jewelry, though
when I first started out, I was a pickpocket. It all came
about when I was fifteen and realized that we had no more
money. My mom had zero skills and couldn't work, besides
the fact that she was a nervous wreck and on all sorts of
medication. What my father did wrecked her completely. I
hate him for that.*

I hate myself for what I've become.

*Stealing wallets soon became too risky and the payout
wasn't worth the risk, so I changed my strategy. The person
who gave me the idea? Your sister Lily.*

*I feel like shit for taking those earrings. Did she ever
mention that to you? That her earrings were stolen? I took
advantage of her when she was drunk and pulled the diamonds right out of her ears. It was so easy. Too easy. I
didn't feel an ounce of guilt for doing that. More like I got a
thrill. After that I was hooked.*

*My mother doesn't know how I get the money to take
care of her. At least, I've never told her. It's easier that way
and she can believe whatever she wants. I don't want to
break her heart. It's already destroyed enough over what
my father did to her. She needs me. Without me, she would
have nothing. I don't know what would happen to her. So I
keep it my secret. My burden to bear, that I've just shared
with you.*

*But it's not your burden and I don't want to become
your burden, either. You deserve more. You deserve happiness, and though I firmly believe that we shared something
special these last weeks and that I made you happy, it
would've been a temporary thing. You would've become*

disillusioned and eventually you'd grow to hate me. I hate me, so how can I expect you to forgive my sins?

I took the necklace, Ro. I found it in the safe in the closet and I kept it in my duffel bag for days, over a week, and you never noticed. I felt like such shit. I still do. But in the end I didn't take it. I just put it back in the safe. Keep it close. People want it. Private collectors who would love to add it to their collection. You need to keep it in a safe place, baby.

I hate that I was so weak and that I took it. That I was even tempted . . . kills me. I hope you can forgive me someday.

I'm also weak because I can't admit any of this to you to your face so I leave you a letter on shitty hotel stationery, written with the equally shitty hotel pen. You're sleeping peacefully and I didn't want to wake you. You look so beautiful lying there naked with just the sheet covering you. The hardest thing I've ever had to do is walk away from you.

I have to, though. It's for the best, revealing everything here in this letter. I probably couldn't have got the words out if we talked. And I didn't want to see the look on your pretty face. I didn't want to hear your angry, ugly words. You would've been justified in saying it all to me, but I can't stand the thought of our last moments together being so fucking awful.

That's probably why you did what you did. Why you told me you didn't want to hear my side of the story. Deep down, you know the truth. Why wreck what we shared when we can walk away and never see each other again?

It kills me, though. The thought of never seeing you. I'll miss your smile. Your laugh. The way you say my name just before you come, the way you kiss me and hold me, the scent of your skin and the taste of your tongue. I'll miss the late-night talks and the showers we took together and going out for coffee, and I'll even miss the White Swan. I'll miss your friends and your sister and Ryder, though they probably hate me now.

Because for that one fleeting moment, for every one of those moments I spent with you, I felt like I belonged. Like I had friends and a girlfriend and an honest life. I felt like people really liked me for me, and not because they thought I was rich or that I belonged to their social clique or whatever the fuck.

You taught me how to be real, Rose. And open. You taught me how to appreciate life and appreciate a woman who wants nothing more than to take care of me. Who likes me. Who might even . . . love me.

You stole my heart, Ro. I may be the professional, but with us, you're the thief. You reached right into my chest and took my heart like it fully belonged to you. And I think it does. I don't know who else deserves it, though really, you shouldn't want it. I can only bring you pain.

I hate that. But I love you. I do. I fell in love with you and I didn't even realize it until today, though really I think I secretly knew it all along. You make me feel like no one else ever has, so all I can say is thank you.

Thank you for teaching me how to love.

xoxo
Caden

Chapter Twenty-four

Rose

Two months later . . .

A ROOFTOP PARTY ON A SWELTERINGLY HOT SATURDAY AFTER-noon is the last place I want to be. There are so many people here, and their constant chatter is deafening. I'm shocked that we have such a large turnout considering most people abandon the city every weekend until Labor Day.

But the party is in full swing and there's no indication it's slowing down anytime soon. I've been at it since first thing this morning, helping with the setup, making sure everything arrived and everyone was staying on task. I didn't quit Fleur. I came back because I couldn't leave. And with this stupid party, even though I've been feeling like crap, somehow Daddy convinced me to help and I reluctantly agreed.

I hate that I caved so easily. I've straight up lost my balls—I can totally imagine Lily saying this—since I returned from London and now that I haven't felt well, these last few weeks especially, I seem to let everyone take advantage of me.

It's awful. I'm worse than I was before. It's as if I've faded into the background.

"Are you feeling all right? You look pale." I turn to find Lily standing before me, a concerned look on her face. She looks gorgeous as usual in a thin white sundress, her skin a golden tan, her long, blond hair up and showing off her gorgeous, perfectly made-up face. Grandma would be proud.

Too bad she's not here. She wouldn't show up because Pilar is the force behind this particular get-together. Grandma refuses to mix with Pilar in "polite company," as she calls it. Smart move. At least someone has the courage to tell Pilar to fuck off, albeit in the most polite way possible.

I smile wanly. "It's the heat. I hate being in the city in August. You know how I get." Total excuse. When I was ten I fainted. Once. It was hot as hell and at the tail end of summer, and I collapsed on the sidewalk right in front of the Fleur building. I milked that incident for all it was worth, too, and Daddy fell for it every single time.

Not anymore, though, I guess. When I mentioned my aversion to heat, he brushed me off, then begged me to help. *Violet's not around*, he told me. *Lily doesn't know the meaning of the words* help *and* work. *Could you put it together, Rosie girl? Please?*

He calls me "Rosie girl" only when he's trying to get something out of me. It worked this time. It works all the time. I'm a complete sucker for my daddy. I only ever want to please him, no matter how much he doesn't seem to care whether I'm really happy or not.

So here I am, representing Fleur at a so-called summer soiree originally put together by Pilar. She's here, hanging on Daddy's arm, looking smug and also constantly checking her watch. They're leaving early so they can get some time in at our family's summer-house in the Hamptons, Pilar's new favorite place to go.

A house I visited only once this summer because *hello*, Pilar is there.

God, I hate her.

"You're wearing the necklace." Lily's fingers graze the stones of the Poppy Necklace. "It looks good with your dress. Does it kill Pilar that you have this?"

I pull my head out of the clouds—a place I seem to visit a lot lately—and focus on her. I'm wearing the necklace because it makes me feel closer to Caden. As stupid as that sounds since the man almost stole the damn thing, it's the truth. "I don't care what she thinks. Not like it's really mine anyway. I'm returning it to Grandma when she comes home."

Our grandmother escapes the city entirely in the summer and spends her days sitting on her porch in the Hamptons, taking in the sun and the salty sea breeze. Says it's good for her complexion.

No one argues with her. Not even our diligent sunscreen wearer Violet.

Lily touches my arm, her delicate brows lowering. "Oh, my God. Your skin is clammy, Rosie. I swear, you look like you might faint."

That's because I feel like I just might. Glancing around, I see a few empty chairs at a nearby table and I hurry over, practically collapsing into one of them. Lily follows me, pulling the other chair close before she sits in it, staring at me as if I've grown two heads.

"Tell me what's wrong. Are you sick?" she asks.

I laugh weakly. *I wish.* No, I'm not sick, not in the way she's thinking. Not that I can tell her the truth. Not yet. This has been my secret to bear and it's a doozy. "I've been working too hard, getting this party put together. I think . . . I'm just tired."

Lily's lips firm into a straight line. "I still can't believe you helped out with this party. You hate Pilar." She looks over her shoulder, presumably making sure Pilar isn't anywhere close, before she starts talking again. "What happened to you quitting anyway?"

I keep my gaze fixed on my knees, plucking at the fabric of

my pale pink dress, the necklace weighing heavily around my neck, my legacy heavy on my heart. I told Lily all about my grand plans when I first came back from London, all fired up and ready to set out on my own. I'd been angry, so furious at Caden's abandonment and that shitty, awful letter he left me. It had given me an inkling of hope. He said he *loved* me. I truly believed he would cave and contact me. I figured he just needed some time.

But no. There were no calls, no texts, no emails, no in-person confrontations. Nothing. He disappeared as if he'd never existed and at times, late at night when I'm exhausted and can't sleep, lying in my bed and staring at the ceiling, going over every single moment I spent with Caden in London, I wonder if I did imagine our time together.

I know the truth, though. I have undeniable proof that our time together happened.

"I didn't know what else to do," I say miserably. "If I quit, where would I go? What would I do? I couldn't find a job elsewhere, like at a rival company or whatever. Daddy would've been so mad. I would've never heard the end of it."

"Oh, screw him," Lily says bitterly. "I've disappointed him time and again, yet here I am, hanging out at another Fleur party and wishing I'd never showed up. He said a few choice words to me when I first arrived and so did that bitch girlfriend of his, but I sent her a look that said I would cut her in an instant if she so much as breathed another word to me. She shut up after that. So did he." Lily sighs and shakes her head.

I smile, wishing I could laugh. I can't remember the last time I laughed. My misery has hung over me like a dark cloud and everyone can see it. Most choose to ignore it, though. "I've always been envious of the fact that you can basically do what you want."

Her smile is fleeting, her eyes full of sadness. "What makes you think I can? I'm just as controlled by him as you and Violet. He just chooses to do it in a different way. I'm the shunned one. The outcast. At least you're the favorite."

"I am not," I say indignantly. I can't believe she thinks that. "Violet is the favored one."

"And she'd tell you *I'm* the favored one. So there you have it. We're all pretty much screwed." She smiles grimly.

A wave of nausea hits me and I rest my hand on my stomach, feeling it clench. *Oh, God.* I think I'm going to be sick. I tried my best to curb it all day, drinking ginger ale whenever I got a chance and making sure saltines were always nearby. "I need to go to the bathroom," I mumble as I leap out of my chair, escaping the party as fast as possible.

"Rosie, wait!" Lily follows after me but I can't stop. My stomach is pitching and roiling like a ship in a violent storm and I push open the women's bathroom door with a loud bang, collapsing on my knees in front of the toilet in one of the stalls just in time.

"Jesus," Lily breathes, coming up behind me. "Rosie?"

I'm too busy throwing my guts up to answer her. Not that I have much coming up. I haven't really eaten much the last few days. The floor is cool on my knees and I brace my hands on the edge of the toilet, gasping and spitting and generally feeling like a total ass. The necklace dangles from my neck and I rest my hand over the front of it, not wanting to get anything on it.

So gross.

Lily rubs my back, pulling back my hair when I bend back over the toilet to retch one last time. The wave of nausea leaves as fast as it came and I fall against the cool metal wall of the toilet stall, pressing my forehead to it and closing my eyes.

"Rose." My big sister's voice is stern. She's rarely tried to pull her authority on me, even when we were young. I'm the annoying baby sister she didn't want to deal with, especially when she went through her wild years. But right now I can tell she means business. "You need to tell me what's going on. This is beyond feeling tired and overheated. Are you drunk?"

I laugh weakly, but it hurts my stomach so I stop. "I wish I were drunk," I mutter. I could drown all my sorrows in booze. But that's not happening.

Blowing out a frustrated sigh, Lily reaches over and flushes the toilet before she grabs hold of me under my arms. "Come on, let's get you over to the sink so you can wash up."

I let her lead me there and I wash my face, then rinse out my mouth as best I can. Lily presses a stick of gum into my palm and I thank her gratefully, relieved that the strong minty gum nixes all bad flavors in my mouth with a few chews.

Lily fixes my hair and whips out a lipstick from her purse, slicking it on my lips for me. I let her take care of me, thankful someone is doing it because for far too long, I've been taking care of myself. Watching out for myself. For those blissful weeks I had someone take care of me, comfort me, and I miss it.

I miss him. Caden.

Stupid, stupid, stupid.

"You want something to eat?" Lily asks once she's finished putting me back together.

I make a face and shake my head. "Absolutely not."

"Something to drink, then. Maybe a little wine to calm your nerves?"

"I can't." I press my lips together, not wanting to give my secret away. "I'm trying to stay off alcohol."

Lily's eyes narrow and she studies me for a long, nerve-wracking time. "Why?" she asks skeptically.

"Because it's bad for your skin." I shrug.

"Honey, if that's the case where you're concerned, I'd recommend you chug a bottle of the stuff because your skin looks terrible right now. You're so pale, and you have dark circles here." She runs her finger below one eye, then the other. "And here."

I bat her hand away. "I don't want to talk about it."

"Why not?" She rests her hands on her hips, her expression one of pure skepticism. She doesn't believe anything I'm saying and I can't really blame her. I'm a terrible liar.

More than anything, I don't want to lie to Lily. I want to tell her the truth. Then I won't feel so alone anymore.

Turning away from her, I start for the door. "I'd better get out there. I'm sure Daddy needs my help with . . . something."

"He'll survive." She follows after me, I can hear the click of her heels, but I don't look back. I exit the bathroom and start for the door that leads back out to the party but she grabs my arm, stopping me from leaving her.

"Tell me what's going on, Rosie. Spill." I try to pull out of her hold, but she won't let me go. "And if you don't tell me, I'm going straight to Dad and telling him something's up with you."

"You wouldn't." I glare.

She raises a brow. "Try me."

Damn it. She will. Lily plays dirty. She always has. Glancing around, I step closer to her, lowering my voice almost to a whisper. "You have to promise you won't tell anyone. Not even Violet."

Her brows go up. I've surprised her. "So Violet doesn't know your deep, dark secret?"

"This is not a laughing matter. Promise me, Lily."

"Fine. I get it. I promise."

I haven't uttered these words out loud yet and suddenly I'm scared. What if Lily breaks her promise? *God,* what if she runs off and tells our father? I will flip the fuck out. "I'm . . ." I take a deep breath and close my eyes, exhaling shakily before I open them and force the words out. "I'm pregnant."

Lily's eyes are so wide I swear they're going to bug out of her head. "Are you serious?"

"No, I made it up. April fool's." I roll my eyes. "Yes, I'm serious. I'm almost nine weeks along."

She covers her mouth with her hand, slowly shaking her head again and again. "Ah, Rosie. How did this happen? When exactly are you due? Who's the father?" Realization dawns at the exact moment she says that and I know she knows.

I start to open my mouth but clamp my lips shut. There's no use explaining or arguing. What's done is done.

Lily snaps her fingers. "This doesn't have anything to do with that guy Violet asked me about a couple months ago? The one you were messing around with in London?" I must give myself away because she starts shaking her head. "You're pregnant with Caden Kingsley's baby? Oh, my GOD!"

"Sshh." I glance around, thankful no one's near. At least we're having this conversation near the bathrooms. Why does everything seem to happen by the bathrooms? "Say it a little louder so everyone outside can hear you. *God.*"

"Rose! This is crazy. Does he know? You have to tell him. Make that scumbag pay, because he owes you."

"Stop it. He's not a scumbag and he doesn't owe me anything. I'm the one who owes him—an explanation. I haven't told him because I don't know where he is."

"He can't be that hard to find," she says drolly. "I've heard his mom is in Miami. Maybe we need to start there."

Miami? I frown. Caden never mentioned Miami to me ever.

"And no one else knows? Daddy is going to lose it when he finds out."

I really don't need the reminder. I want to enjoy this pregnancy. I do. But it's so hard when I'm feeling so awful and Caden is not around. I miss him. I want him back. He deserves to know he's going to be a father.

He will also probably freak the fuck out when he finds out he's going to be a father.

"Have you considered having a . . ." Lily flicks her chin, looking uncomfortable. "An abortion?"

"No," I say vehemently. "I'm not against them. They have their place. But . . . I can't do it. I know it'll be hard being a single mom, but I want this baby."

"You're just so young. I don't know what I would do if I found out I was having a baby. I'd be the worst mother ever." Lily laughs, but it doesn't sound sincere. More like it sounds sad.

"You don't know that, Lily. And you can test out your mothering skills on your future niece or nephew."

She slaps her hand over her mouth again, tears springing to her eyes just before she hauls me into her arms and hugs me tight. "If you need me, I'm here for you," she whispers. "Whatever you want, I'll come over whenever. You can't go through this alone. And you need to tell Violet."

Violet will kill me. She will hit me with *I told you so* and all of those other annoying statements I don't want to hear at the moment. I'm beating myself up quite well on my own, thank you very much. "Not yet," I tell Lily. "Give me time to work up to it."

"Lily Fowler, is that you?" A booming, gravelly male voice asks and my sister and I spring away from each other, Lily hurriedly wiping away the tears from her cheeks. Of course, she looks beautiful while crying, her hazel eyes this brilliant color, while I'm a red-nosed freak. Sometimes I really hate my sister.

But right now, I love her more than anyone else I know. She wants to help me. And I need her. More than I want to admit.

"Cash, is that you? Oh my God!" Lily squeals as she runs and throws herself into a man's arms and he clasps them tight around her waist, picking her up off her feet as he spins her around. He's older, much older, with very tan skin and very white hair and wearing a pair of thick-rimmed black glasses that somehow look good on him.

"Baby girl, it has been far too long since I've seen your pretty face. How have you been?" He squeezes her again and I assess his age as at least seventy. Possibly older. I really, really hope this isn't one of Lily's ex-boyfriends. I wouldn't put it past her, but if she messed around with this guy?

Ick. He's probably older than our dad.

"I'm doing well," she says as he sets her back on her feet and she releases her hold on him. "How about you? You look great, Cash."

They make small talk and I try to sneak past them, but Lily's having none of it. "Have you met my baby sister, Rose?" She snags my hand and stops me so I'm standing right next to her. "Rose, this is Cash. We've known each other, oh, what? Since forever?" She laughs, her gaze meeting mine. "An old boyfriend of mine introduced us a few years ago when we were out in Miami. We've stayed in loose contact ever since, huh, Cash?"

Miami again. Weird coincidence.

"Why, no, I haven't had the good fortune to meet your sister yet. Though I've heard plenty about her." He turns toward me, his smile wide, his teeth blindingly white. He's a good-looking man, if a bit plastic, as if he's been well preserved. But his warmth is genuine and I take his offered hand, which he shakes vigorously. "A pleasure. And aren't you a pretty little thing? All you Fowler girls are beautiful, almost as beautiful as that pretty necklace you've got around your neck, Rose."

I reach up, touching the stones absently. I regret wearing it. All I can think of is Caden.

Of course, I think of him always, necklace or not.

"Oh, stop trying to flatter us, you big flirt," Lily teases good-naturedly.

"Hey, hey, no flirting allowed. I've given it up for good. I'm here tonight with my new lady friend." His smile grows wider if that's possible. "She's a real beauty, Lil. You'd like her. A little ditzy, but I think that's my favorite quality of hers."

They both laugh and I try to do the same, but I just can't. It's as if I'm . . . broken inside. Nothing's funny, and I feel so crappy it's all I can focus on. I'm also thirsty. As in, my throat has turned into the Sahara Desert. I'm about to excuse myself to go in search of something to drink when the women's bathroom door opens and a beautiful older woman glides through it, a serene smile on her face, her eyes lighting up when she spots Cash.

"Darling." She comes toward us and stops at his side. Cash slips his arm around her waist and pulls her in close, sending her a look of pure adulation.

Seeing it makes my heart hurt. Caden used to look at me like that.

"This is my lady friend, Cora. Rose and Lily Fowler, meet Cora Kingsley." Cash sends me a knowing look that confuses me for a brief moment.

Until I get it.

My head spins and everything starts to fade. Cora smiles at me—*God*, I recognize that smile—and reaches out her hand to shake mine. But I don't grab it. I feel like I'm frozen. My ears are roaring with my thundering heartbeat and I hear Lily call my name, but she sounds so far away.

"Rose. Rosie!" I hear just before my eyes roll to the back of my head.

And I collapse on the floor.

Chapter Twenty-five

Caden

"MET SOMEONE YOU MIGHT KNOW," CASH SAYS CONVERSATIONALLY as I sit across from him. We met on my lunch break since he called me first thing this morning, saying he wanted to see me.

We're at a crowded restaurant that's close to where I work. Yes, work. I have a job. A job that I love. One that'll pay almost enough to maintain Mom's many expenses, though I'm guessing the man sitting across from me might help me with the load considering they've been dating hot and heavy since I returned from London.

Weird but true. They finally made it happen. Mom is head over heels in love and I think Cash is, too. They're already talking marriage. At the very least, they're going to move in together. Mom's already preparing to sell the condo.

"Who was it?" I ask just as the waitress sets my plate in front of me. I lift the bread off my turkey sandwich to check for pickles and yep, there they are, the offending little bastards. I pick them off, wipe my hands on my napkin, and then take a big bite. I'm starved.

Only just got my appetite back, too, since I've been a miserable little fuck the last two months.

"I went to this rooftop party. Got invited . . . not sure how, but I'm not questioning it. Big shindig. Took your mom and she was dazzled. She met your friend, too. Once we got over the initial shock of her passing out cold, Cora found her a truly lovely person."

I go still. I have no idea who he's talking about and he's being evasive. Drawing this out. I know lots of women in Manhattan and most of them I've done wrong. Hence my happiness that I'm working in Brooklyn. I know hardly anyone here and I like it that way.

"What do you mean? Are you talking about Mom?" Worry consumes me and I set down my sandwich. "Is everything okay with her?" She's getting older. Her health could be failing for all I know.

"She's fine. Stop your worrying." Cash waves a hand and grabs his sandwich, taking a bite. His expression is contemplative as he chews. "Though maybe you should start worrying once I tell you what I found out," he says after he swallows.

I push my plate away. "Quit being so mysterious and just spit it out."

"So cranky. Jesus, you haven't been the same since you returned from England—you know that, right?"

"I have my reasons," I mutter, wishing I could have a beer. Not that I've been drinking excessively or anything, but a few beers help numb the pain. Help me cope with my troubles. Help me forget I'm missing a particular woman so much my entire body aches.

"Well, maybe I can push you out of that shit mood once and for all." Cash leans over the table and lowers his voice. "I saw Lily and Rose Fowler Saturday afternoon."

What the fuck? "Are you serious?" I swallow hard, trying to get past the lump that formed in my throat. "You met Rose?"

Cash nods, looking smug. "So did your mother."

Holy shit. "Wait a minute." My mind is racing, going over everything Cash just said. "Who passed out? Was it Lily or—"

"It was Rose," Cash says, interrupting me.

My heart grows heavy and I absently rub at the center of my chest, messing up my tie. Now that I'm a working stiff, I have to dress like one. I bought a few new suits and dress shirts and a handful of ties. Though I usually come to work in trousers and a button-down shirt with the tie, nothing too formal. I like my boss, Stanton, and I like my job. I'm damn good at my job.

Considering it's pretty much all I have, I put my heart and soul into it, vowing I wouldn't fuck it up. I can't afford to fuck it up. I refuse to go back to my old lifestyle.

"You going to ask what happened or what?" Cash says, blasting me from my thoughts.

"Tell me," I say, worry clawing at my chest. I hope Rose is all right. I miss her so damn much. I've been working hard to make myself a better man. I had a loose idea of what I needed to do to make things right. Secure myself in my job, guarantee I'm not going anywhere after the ninety-day grace period, and then go to her with my heart in my hands and words of undying love falling from my lips.

Sappy and ridiculous, but that was my plan.

"She looks frail, Caden. I'm not going to lie. A little pale and tired, and when I introduced your mother to her—"

"You introduced her as my *mother*?" *Holy hell.* I'm sweating. No wonder Rose dropped to the ground.

"No, jackass, I introduced her as Cora Kingsley. But I knew she'd put it together. Or at least assume something. Or think of you. I don't know what she thought." He shrugs and takes another bite of his sandwich, chewing for what feels like forever. "All I know is once I said the name Kingsley, Rose fainted."

"She fainted?" *Aw, hell.* What did that mean? Is she okay? Cash said she looked frail. Why? What's going on? I should call her. She might hang up on me—not that I can blame her, I still regret that stupid letter—but I need to make sure she's all right.

Cash sets his sandwich down, his expression serious. Scary serious. "You need to know what's going on, son. Your mom was in the restroom and overheard a few . . . things, which was semi-confirmed after Rose fainted."

"Jesus, what is it?" Cash is talking in circles and he's losing me. I hate it. The panic has grabbed hold of me and isn't letting go. I feel its fingers sinking deeper and deeper . . .

"There's no easy way to tell you this, so I'm just going to be frank." Cash's eyes narrow. "We think she's pregnant."

Panic has its claws fully embedded in me now. I feel like I can't fucking breathe. "Are you serious?"

He says nothing, just gives me a tiny nod.

"Pregnant? With my baby?" Of course it's my baby. Why didn't she call me? *Holy shit,* this is all my fault. Those few times we had sex without protection and now she's paying the ultimate price . . .

I start to push away from the table, ready to go in search of her, but Cash reaches out, clamping his hand around my wrist and keeping me in place. "Where do you think you're going?"

"I have to find her. I have to talk to her." My mind is going a hundred miles a second and I'm desperate with the need to see Rose.

"You need a plan, son. You can't just go after her and, say, burst into her office at Fleur and offer your undying love or whatever the hell. She's probably mad at you."

"She should be," I agree wholeheartedly. "She has every right to be furious with me."

"Right. So you need to think this through. Make this right. You can't tell her you want to be with her because she's going to have your baby," Cash says.

"Why the fuck not?" That just gives me more reason to want to be with her. She needs me now more than ever and I want to be there for her.

"She'll think you're with her because of the baby and for no other reason."

"But that wouldn't be true. I love her. I want to be with her."

I blink, absorbing his words. What Cash is saying does make sense . . .

"What was your plan anyway, huh, kid? You've avoided her for the last two months. What exactly were you doing?"

"Straightening out my life. I already told you that."

"You got that job within a week of your return," Cash points out.

Less than that. I interviewed on a Monday and was working my first day that Wednesday. "Yeah, but I didn't know if it was going to stick. I still don't know if it is. I have another month before Stanton decides to make me a permanent employee," I say.

Cash makes a frustrated noise. "You're in. You don't have to worry about that."

"And I wanted to get a nice place. I can't keep staying at your place, Cash." I've been looking for something in Brooklyn, closer to my work.

"Rose has a very nice apartment downtown."

"Yeah. I know. I wanted to have things on my own merit. I wanted to prove to her that I can be the man she wants. The man she needs. I don't want to have to rely on her money or anything like that," I say bitterly.

"I don't think she'd care as long as she has you." Cash's eyes are full of sympathy. "She looked so lost, Caden. Just about as lost as you do. When Cora and I left that party, I told her who Rose was to you."

"Ah, fuck." I rub the back of my neck, hating that he said anything to Mom.

"She burst into tears, son, and told me Rose had thrown up in the bathroom when she was in there. And then she fainted . . . It was your mom who came to the conclusion that she must be pregnant. She cried because she knows that Rose is carrying her grandbaby."

The guilt is heavy, almost too much to bear. Cash is laying it on thick, the ass. He knows just how to work me. I can hardly process the thought that Rose is pregnant. With my baby. "Have you had this confirmed? That Rose is really pregnant?"

"No. But it's simple math, son. Two plus two equals baby."

"I need to go to her," I say, shaking my head when the waitress pauses by our table, a pitcher of iced tea held up high in her hand, indicating she wants to give me a refill. "But you're right. I need a plan."

"You need to tell her that you want to be with her not because she's having your baby but because you love her." Cash shakes his head. "Jackass move, leaving her that note, staying away from her so you can try and prove that you're worthy."

At the time it seemed like the right thing to do. We needed distance, because with distance comes clarity. I left her the note and went back to Mitchell's house, hiding out there until we flew out of London that Sunday night. I immediately went to my job interview with Stanton first thing Monday morning and he gave me the position right then and there.

It all fell into place, just as I hoped it would. I'd work hard, save up, live a respectable life, and give up all criminal activity once and for all. I changed my phone number, not wanting any of those old temptations to call me and try to coerce me into something I shouldn't be doing. No one could reach me, beyond Cash, Mom, and my new boss and fellow employees.

I am a new man. A working man. An honest man.

A man who's going to be a father in approximately . . .

"How far along is she?"

"You should know better than I do."

I shrug, feeling like an idiot. I'm a guy. I don't pay attention to those types of things. "Around two months I guess?" So I'll be a father in seven months. I mentally count. There will be a baby born in March. My baby.

Holy. Fucking. Shit.

"She's so young," I tell Cash, soaking up the guilt that's consuming me at the realization that I did this to her. I'm the one who got her pregnant. Does she hate me for it? Or is she happy that she's having a baby? Does she feel all right? If she looks pale and is vomiting and fainting, then no, she can't be. This pregnancy must be hard on her.

And I'm the one to blame.

"So," Cash says, peering at me, his gaze hard. "Are you sure you're ready for this type of responsibility? It's big, son. It'll change your entire life, leave you connected to this girl forever, whether you end up together or not. So know where you stand on this. Don't go running to her declaring your true love for her and then ditch her months later. She's going to need you more than ever. This is a huge commitment. So." He stares at me hard and repeats himself. "You ready for this?"

Am I ready? I think I am. I should be. I left Rose because I didn't feel worthy of her. I firmly believed she deserved a much better man and I would never measure up. I wrote that letter pouring my heart out on the pages and the minute I snuck out of her hotel room, leaving her all alone and sleeping naked in that bed, my baby already inside her and oblivious to what I'd just done, I became consumed with regret.

You don't walk out on love. You stay and fight for it. You prove to the woman who means more to you than anyone or anything else that you will do whatever it takes to make her happy.

It's been two long months now. More than enough time to fuck everything up. She might have changed her mind. She's probably over me. She *should* be over me. I'd deserve that.

I don't deserve her love.

I don't deserve her.

But I'm going to do whatever it takes to get her back and make her mine. If I have to beg, cheat, borrow, or steal, I will do it.

Whatever it takes.

Because Rose Fowler belongs to me.

Chapter Twenty-six

Rose

Seven o'clock tonight. Don't be late. And don't forget!

I stare at Lily's text and with an irritated sigh, I shove my cell back into my purse, then shut the desk drawer that I keep my purse in. Leaning my elbows on the edge of my desk, I press my fingers to my temples, rubbing gently. I have a headache and I'm not allowed to use ibuprofen, which sucks.

This baby is doing everything in its power to make me miserable, and the little booger is succeeding. I had no idea pregnancy was so damn hard, not that I've experienced it through anyone else, anyone close to me. None of my friends from school whom I'm still in contact with—and there are very few; most of us scattered in the wind the minute we graduated—have been pregnant. Most of them haven't even gotten married yet.

I'm young. Only twenty-two. I saw the way the doctor looked at me when I went in for my appointment last week. No man with me, I'm sure I looked young and scared and hopeless. I don't feel hopeless, though. Scared, yes. I heard the baby's heartbeat at that appointment and I almost wanted to cry. It was loud and so fast. I rubbed my hand over my still flat belly for the rest of the night, knowing that there's life in there. Real life, confirmed by my doctor.

"You're young and healthy and with no prior medical conditions," the doctor had told me before he exited the examination room. "This should be a very easy pregnancy."

Easy for him to say. He isn't the one living on crackers and ginger ale, hovering over a toilet in the middle of the night. I sleep with a plastic bowl on my bedside table just in case. I've been miserable.

But a twinge of happiness is starting to form, too. I'm closing in on the end of the first trimester, and supposedly that is the hardest part when it comes to morning sickness. I'd finally confessed to Violet about my pregnancy thanks to Lily's nonstop nagging, and though she was worried, I could tell she's genuinely happy for me.

I haven't told my father yet. As if he would care. He's too consumed in wedding plans with Pilar. *Gross.*

Then there's Lily. My crazy, without-a-care-in-the-world oldest sister, has stepped up to the plate and been there for me every step of the way. She was pissed when she found out I went to the doctor without her. She wanted to be there, to hear the baby's heartbeat too, and I felt bad that I left her out. Next time, I promised her, and I know she'll hold me to it.

Now she's setting up dinner get-togethers and she invited me over. I don't want to go. I'd rather stay home and read a book or watch TV and not think about what I'm going to do with my life. Eventually I have to try to find Caden and tell him what's going on. He deserves to know.

And I know exactly who to talk to when I'm ready to find him. That man named Cash. The one who's dating Caden's mother.

Holy shit, that entire meeting had been surreal. I'd fainted and scared them all. I woke up to all three of their faces hovering above mine, and when I focused on Cora Kingsley's features, I knew without a doubt she was Caden's mom. Same eyes, same crease in between their brows when they're worried, same smile.

I was staring at the face of my unborn child's grandmother and it was all just so . . . weird.

Lily convinced our father that I needed to go home and rest that night, laying on the guilt trip extra thick when she mentioned I threw up and fainted. She blamed it on a flu going around and Daddy fell for it.

Thank God.

I stop rubbing my temples and grab my phone again, cursing myself for being so weak. I don't want to work. I can't focus. Not like I have any big projects going on anyhow. I'd come up with a new plan where I was going to ask my father to let me go on sabbatical. For just enough time to have the baby, be home for a few months, and establish a routine before I go back to work.

I think he'll go for that idea a lot better than if I just upped and quit.

Pushing all thoughts of my father and my future firmly out of my mind, I send a quick text to Lily.

Who's all going to be there?

She answers immediately.

A few people you know.

Huh. Well, that couldn't be any more vague.

It's not going to be one of those long, crazy parties you like to have, is it?

She knows I've gone into low-key mode. And I can hardly keep my eyes open beyond ten o'clock lately. I feel like an old lady.

I wouldn't do that to you. I know you're not feeling well. Don't worry. Everything's going to be fine. I just need you there right at seven.

Weird. She's being elusive and I'm not sure why.

I'll be there. Do you need me to bring anything?

She'll say no, but I had to ask.

Just your pretty face. Wear something cute.

Ugh. I roll my eyes.

Don't you dare try to set me up with anyone. Besides, who would want to date me? I'm knocked up with another guy's baby.

Lily sends me a smiley face with hearts for eyes in answer and I laugh.

Some guys might think that's sexy.

Please. She's delusional.

There's only one guy I want to find me sexy and clearly he's not interested.

I don't know that for sure, but it feels that way.

You'll find out someday. We're going to track him down and tell him everything.

Nerves eat at my stomach just seeing those words.

Yeah, I type. Someday.

No reply.

LILY'S APARTMENT ISN'T TOO FAR FROM MINE AND I WALK OVER, enjoying the late-summer evening. For whatever reason the night sky feels full of potential, which in turn fills me with hope.

I can get through this. No trial is too big or too small for me to handle.

Resting my hand on my stomach, I'm thankful I actually feel like a halfway normal person this evening. I'm at the tail end of the tenth week, and though I don't want to get my hopes up for fear it'll come back at me tenfold, I think this so-called morning sickness—because really, it's been morning, noon, and night—is almost over.

I enter the building and smile and wave at the security guard behind the massive desk. He buzzes me in and I head to the elevator, trying to ignore the nerves that come over me.

It won't be so bad, this little get-together. Lily's been so sensitive to my feelings and I appreciate that. We've never been close, Lily and I. That was for me and Violet. Lily always seemed to be off in her own little world, doing her thing, driving our father crazy and enjoying every minute of it.

Violet and I were always closer, both in age and in personality. This baby I'm carrying inside of me is bringing so many blessings already, like my sister and me forging a stronger relationship. I'm thankful for that.

Thankful for so many things tonight that for the first time since I came home from London, I almost feel . . . carefree.

I knock on the door and wait for Lily to answer. I hear nothing coming from within, which is odd. Usually Lily's parties are loud. She always invites a bunch of people over and though she said this gathering would be small, I know how she is. If everyone else is quiet, then Lily at least is yelling about something.

Long minutes later, when I'm pulling out my cell phone and getting ready to send her a nasty text, I hear the locks being undone and then the door swings open.

"Good." She smiles but she quickly glances over her shoulder, worry in her gaze. "You're here."

I frown at her. She's not in her usual party dress, either. And when I say "party dress" like she's a little girl, I mean it. If there's a party to be had, Lily's usually the best-dressed attendee. She can't seem to help herself.

But tonight she's wearing little denim cutoff shorts and a tank top. Her hair is in a sloppy ponytail and there's not a lick of makeup on her face. *Odd.*

"I'm completely overdressed," I tell her, waving a hand at the comfortable long cotton strapless dress I'm wearing. It's turquoise and dotted with little white squiggles and currently the most comfortable thing I own. I don't have a full-on belly yet, but there's a slight pooch and I hate wearing anything that restricts my waist and stomach.

"I'm, um, still getting ready. Not everyone's here yet." Her gaze skitters away from mine and I have the weirdest sense that she's lying to me.

"Well, are you going to let me in or what?"

"Oh my God, of course." She sweeps the door open and I walk inside, glancing around for any glimpse of someone else being here. "Am I the first one here?"

"No." She wrings her hands together and I fall into step behind her as we head for the kitchen. "There's someone else waiting for you."

Huh? What is she talking about? And why is she being so strange?

"I really hope you didn't plan something unexpected, because I am so not in the mood." My earlier cheerfulness has evaporated and I want to go home.

"Stop worrying and come on." We walk through the kitchen, which leads to a small nook where her more informal dining table is. There's a man sitting there, but I don't know who he is and the room is dark. The curtains are drawn, not even letting in the dimming rays of sunlight, and he slowly stands to his feet.

Everything within me stops. The way he moves, the hair, the length of him . . .

His face comes into view as he takes a step toward us and I reach out, grasping the edge of the granite countertop to keep me from toppling over.

It's Caden.

"Okay, well, this is your chance for you two to make up. Ta-ta!" And with that Lily buzzes out of there, the loud slam of her front door indicating she's left us in her apartment. Completely alone.

"Hey," he says, the sound of his deep, delicious voice melting everything within me.

I stand taller, stiffening my spine. I refuse to cave first. This man needs to grovel a bit. I can only assume Lily found Caden on her own, through Cash. That she set this entire meeting up for me, so I could talk to him and tell Caden he's going to be a father.

But seeing him again after over two months, all the anger comes back to me, double force. I think of how he left me, snuck out in the middle of the night after writing me that stupid, irritating letter. I should hit him just for that letter alone.

"You look beautiful, Ro," he says after a long, charged moment of silence, and I clench one hand into a fist, my other hand still gripping the countertop tightly. "I've missed you."

I want to laugh. I also want to cry. "Really? Could've fooled me, what with the way you've reached out and tried to contact me."

The shadow that crosses his face makes me happy. *Good.* He should feel bad. He should feel incredibly guilty and shitty for what he's done. "I have my reasons," he starts, and this time I do laugh, cutting him off.

I can't stop laughing. I just keep doing it. He doesn't move, just stares at me as if I've lost my mind, and I do feel like I've lost it. I think I'm in a state of shock. I can't believe he's standing in front of me, looking so good, looking so clean and handsome and . . . respectable? He's wearing a button-down shirt and charcoal-gray trousers. His hair is cut neatly and though it's hanging loosely from his neck, he's wearing a tie. Like he just got off work or something.

Huh?

My laughter starts to die, tears streaming down my cheeks, my belly aching. I'm not laughing anymore, I'm crying, and a sob bursts free from my lips. Sniffing, I cover my face with my hands and he moves into action. I can hear him. Feel him. He hesitates for only a moment as he stands right in front of me and then he's drawing me into his arms, holding me close.

I stiffen in his embrace, telling myself I should be stronger. I shouldn't give in so easily. His hand cups the back of my head and he presses my face against his chest. I can feel his heart race, smell his familiar, perfect scent. His other arm goes around my waist, fingers resting firmly on my hip, and I've never felt so right.

I feel like I've come home.

Giving in, I melt into him, slinging my arms around his waist as I cry. My tears dampen his shirt, his fingers comb through my hair, and he whispers reassuring words to me. Words that warm my heart and send it aflutter, beating against my ribs so hard he can surely hear it.

"I've missed you so damn much," he murmurs against my hair. "I was trying to do the right thing. Get my life on track, be a better man before I come find you and make you mine."

Stupid, silly man. What in the world is he talking about? "What do you mean?" I ask, my voice muffled against his chest.

"I got a job. No more stealing, no more messing around. I'm an honest man now, doing an honest day's work." He sounds proud and I squeeze him tight before I lift my head to look up at him.

"What are you doing? For work?"

He smiles, and the sight of it takes my breath away. "You wouldn't believe it if I told you."

"Tell me," I urge.

Leaning in, he drops a sweet kiss on the tip of my nose. My body immediately reacts to his chaste kiss and I tell myself to calm down. I cannot make this easy for him. He needs to explain.

And then I have some explaining to do as well.

"I work at a jewelry store. It's in Brooklyn, a great place that's been around forever, and they take jewelry in on trade, or they bring it in to have it reset. I'm the one who assesses the stones and intricacy of the settings and declares its value," he explains.

I raise my brows. "Well, that sounds right up your alley."

"It is. Cash got me the interview." He pauses, studying me. "You met Cash, right? A couple weeks ago."

Nodding, I bite my lower lip. "I, um, met your mother, too."

"I know." He pushes a few stray hairs away from my forehead. "Cash told me."

Oh, God. This was all set up through Lily and Cash and maybe even Caden's mom. Does he know? Does he have a clue about my condition? And if he does know, is he mad at me for keeping it from him?

"Ro, I was wrong for what I did. I shouldn't have left you like that at the hotel back in London. I should've stuck it out and told you how I really felt rather than write it all in a stupid letter." His expression is pained, and a small piece of me is thankful that he regrets his actions.

Fine, a *large* piece of me is thankful.

"That letter almost killed me," I murmur softly. "It gave me hope. I thought you would come to your senses and find me when you got back here. But . . . you didn't."

"I always planned on finding you," he says, the words pouring out of him in a rush. "I only wanted to do it right. I wanted to make sure that I was established in my new job and that I was doing the right things. That I wouldn't disappoint you. That's the last thing I want to do. I never wanted to let you down."

"You never let me down until you left me like a coward." He flinches at that comment but I push on. "I would've accepted you as is. I *did* accept you. I . . . I fell for you while we were together in London. How I felt about you scared me, but I didn't care. I was going for it anyway. And then . . . you left."

"Stupidest thing I could've ever done," he mutters, shaking his head, looking completely traumatized.

I reach up and sink my hands in his thick, soft hair. "You cut it," I murmur.

He smiles. "Yeah. Need to look respectable."

"I miss it." I stroke his hair, his eyelids wavering at my touch, and all I can think about is how fast can I get him naked.

No. Don't think like that. Make him work for this.

"I miss you." He lets go of me and my hands fall away from him. But then he's touching me again, his hands cupping my face, and I grip his hips, overwhelmed at the sincerity and love I see shining in his dark eyes. "I fucked up. I know I did. I'm asking for your forgiveness. I need it. I need you. I was only trying to do the right thing and in the end I drove away the only woman I could ever love."

My heart cracks at his words and fresh tears spring to my eyes. He's trying to make me cry buckets, I swear. "Oh, Caden . . ."

He gives my head a gentle shake. "I'm serious, Ro. I'm in love with you. I love you. I've missed you so damn much. I should've come and got you sooner, but my stupid pride got in the way and I wanted to be worthy of you."

"You were always worthy of me. You just didn't see it," I whisper, making him smile.

"You've made me the luckiest man in the world. I don't deserve you." I open my mouth to protest, but he cuts me off by sealing his mouth over mine in a quick, firm kiss. "It's true. But I'm not going to deny it any longer. It doesn't matter if I deserve you or not. I love you. I want you in my life. I fucking *need* you in my life, Ro. I just need to know . . . will you have me?"

I gape at him, overwhelmed by his words, by the love shining in his eyes. His thumbs stroke across my cheeks, making my knees weak, and I reach up, curling my fingers around his wrists so I can cling to him for dear life. "I missed you. I was so mad that you left that note. That you left me. But I forgive you for it." I swallow hard, knowing that I have something far more important to tell him than just offering my forgiveness.

His expression is one of sweet relief. "Thank Christ," he mutters.

Worry consumes me. What if he becomes upset at my news? What if he rejects me and our baby? I don't know if I could ever recover from such a thing. "I love you, too," I whisper, my throat aching. "I love you so much and . . . I have something I need to tell you."

His brows lower in that way they do when he's worried or concerned. His grip loosens on my face and his touch becomes whisper soft as his eyes search mine. "What is it?"

I press my lips together, my stomach roiling with nerves. At least it's not nausea. I need to get this over with. Just . . . blurt it out. Like ripping off a Band-Aid instead of peeling it off slowly. This sort of thing is better if it's done swiftly. Taking a deep breath, I swallow hard and say, "I'm pregnant. With your baby."

And then I promptly burst into tears.

Chapter Twenty-seven

Caden

THE CONFIRMATION THAT ROSE IS CARRYING MY BABY IS ALmost sweeter than hearing my girl tell me that she loves me. Almost.

I don't like that she's crying, though. This isn't a sad moment. This is one of joy, one to be celebrated. Somehow Rose found it in her heart to forgive me and we're going to have a baby together. We're going to be a family.

Holy. Shit.

"Caden?" Her sweet, slightly worried voice knocks me from my thoughts. "Did you hear me?"

"Yeah, baby. I heard you." I catch one of her tears with my thumb, then lean in and catch another one with my lips. "Don't cry," I whisper against her cheek. "You're going to have my baby. I'm the happiest man alive right now."

Her crying kicks back into gear and I pull her into my arms, holding her close, pressing kisses against her forehead and telling her again and again how much I love her. My shirt is soaked with her tears but I don't care. She's in my arms. I got her back.

She's mine.

Once Cash told me about seeing Rose, everything slowly fell into place. I didn't rush into trying to find Rose. I made sure I knew what I wanted to tell her before I went to Cash and told him I was ready. I didn't want to blow it. If I came after her and told her I knew she was pregnant, she'd think I wanted to be with her only because of the baby, not because I'm madly in love with her.

And I *am* madly in love with her—the baby is just a bonus. Yeah, it's scary. I can't lie and I bet she's scared too, but together we can handle this. We're going to be a family and I refuse to walk out on my family like my father did. Like Rose's mother did to her family. We've got each other's backs. We'll be strong together. We belong together.

She knows it. And I know it too.

Cash spoke with Lily, who came up with the idea to have Rose over for a dinner party at which we'd be the only attendees. There wouldn't be any dinner, either, though now that I consider it, she's probably hungry. She needs to eat since she's doing it for two.

"Rose." I whisper her name against her forehead and she shudders in my arms. "Are you hungry? We need to get you something to eat."

Laughing, she tilts her head back to stare up at me. "I am a little hungry," she admits, then frowns. "I've had the worst morning sickness, Caden. You wouldn't believe how bad it's been."

"Yeah?" I smooth my hand over her hair. That about kills me, knowing she's been suffering and I haven't been with her to take care of her. "Are you okay? You're healthy? The, uh, baby is okay too?" I hesitate over my questions, which is dumb, but it's so weird, knowing she's going to have my baby.

I never once thought I would get married, have a baby, have a family, have a real, normal life. I didn't think it was in the cards for me. My parents were fucked and I learned all I knew about relationships and life from them. Meaning I learned jack shit.

I figured I would be alone. I would belong nowhere and to no one, and I believed that was the way I preferred it.

What a fool I was.

Instead I met this woman in my arms. She taught me how to be a friend and how to love. She's offering me a new life where I can stand on my own two feet, where I can work and have someone to come home to and a family to love. A child to bear my name and carry it on and give my mom a new purpose in life.

I'm truly the luckiest damn man in the world.

"I'm good. The first two months were hard." She offers me a strained smile. "But it's getting better and the baby is healthy, so no worries there."

"Do you know what it is yet?" What do I want? A boy or a girl? I have no clue. I just want the baby to be healthy and to look like its mama.

She smiles and shakes her head. "It's too early. I did hear the baby's heartbeat, though."

"Really?" I'm amazed. That must have made it seem so real, that she's carrying a fragile little life inside her body.

"Yeah, it was pretty awesome." She lifts her gaze to mine. "Let's get out of here, Caden. I want to go back to my place."

Lily left me a key to give to the security guard if I got so lucky that Rose wanted to leave with me. "How close is your apartment?"

"I walked over."

Relief floods me. If we go back to her place, I'm assuming—after I get her fed and taken care of—that I can take her to bed.

"Let's go, then," I say, trying to restrain my anxiousness. But it's damn hard. Especially when she flashes me that beautiful smile I haven't seen in far too long and hooks her hand around the back of my neck, bringing my mouth down to hers. The kiss is hot and wet and deep, and I haul her in close. I will never let her go again. That she forgave my stupid ass . . .

I don't know what I did to deserve her.

HOURS LATER WE'RE LYING NAKED IN ROSE'S BED, HER LEG slung over both of mine, and she's rubbing her foot up and down my calves, driving me insane with just her freaking foot. I squeeze her waist and roll her over, my cock already hard—again—and pressing against her belly. She smiles up at me, her cheeks rosy from hours of lovemaking. We have a lot of time to make up for.

But first, I want to make sure she's okay. That she's feeling well and isn't too tired.

"You all right? Are you tired? It's safe to have sex like this, right? What with the baby and all . . ." My voice trails off and she laughs.

"*Now* you ask. After you've had me every which way." She arches against me slightly, her breasts, her hard nipples, teasing my chest. "Yes, it's safe to have sex while I'm pregnant," she says softly. "I'm not high risk or anything."

Relief floods me. "Good." I should have asked her that sooner, I know I should have, but I was so eager to get her naked and beneath me I could hardly think. The moment we walked into her bedroom I was stripping her naked. Helped that her dress was so easy. Just one tug and it was falling down around her waist and she wasn't wearing a bra. I was downright disappointed to see her wearing panties.

Jesus, I am a complete pervert. But only for Rose.

Rose sighs and runs her hands along my shoulders, down my chest. "It feels good being back in your arms."

"Yeah." I swallow hard against the swell of emotion that threatens to take over me. I worried that I wouldn't get this second chance. That she was so willing to give it to me . . . I can't get over how much I love her. How much I need her. "You're different, you know."

"I am?" She frowns. "How?"

I move down, my face in direct line with her breasts. "They're fuller," I murmur against her abundant flesh, just before I draw a hard nipple into my mouth and suck.

Her hands dive into my hair, holding me close.

"And your stomach." I slide down lower, nuzzling my cheek against the gentle swell of her belly. "It sticks out a little bit."

"It's always stuck out a little bit." She settles her hand on her stomach, almost as if she wants to hide it, but I swat her fingers away, blazing a trail of kisses across her skin.

"No, it didn't. But now it does." I breathe deep her fragrant skin, kissing her belly some more, letting my lips linger. "I can't wait until you really start to show."

"I'll be fat," she mumbles.

"You'll be gorgeous," I correct. "All big and full of my baby."

"So possessive," she whispers, but I know she likes it. The full-body shiver at my words is a dead giveaway.

I shift lower still and brace my hands on the inside of her thighs, spreading her legs. "And here," I say, staring at her glistening pink flesh. "You taste different."

"I do not," she starts, then lets out a strangled sound when I lay my tongue flat against her folds and lick her from bottom to top.

"Yeah, you do," I whisper against her, darting out my tongue to tease and search, playing with her clit, circling it again and again before I draw it into my mouth.

"God, Caden," she moans. "I missed your mouth so much."

Her confession makes me pull away from her so I can laugh. She's glowering at me, frustration etched all over her pretty features. I lean back in, my gaze never leaving hers as I flick her clit with the tip of my tongue. "Well, I missed your sweet pussy, baby. More than you'll ever know."

"I missed those dirty words of yours, too," she whispers. Her legs tremble. Her body shakes. She tosses her head back, her eyes sliding closed as I slip a finger inside her body and work her clit with my lips and tongue. She's coming in minutes, a gush of wetness flooding her pussy, and I lick her clean, marveling at how responsive she is.

And yes, how different she tastes.

I move back up her body, trailing kisses along the way, until I'm sliding inside of her, pushing all the way in until I feel like I could touch every part of her. "Am I too deep?" I ask just before I kiss her.

She breaks the kiss first, panting against my lips. "No. You feel amazing."

I agree and I would have said something, but she does some little trick with her hips, shifting beneath me and sending my cock even deeper, and I groan, the sound feeling as if it's being ripped from my chest. She wraps her arms around me, her legs going around my hips, her mouth at my ear as she begins to chant dirty, loving things that drive me crazy.

"Don't stop," she whispers. "Deeper, Caden. Please. I need you. I love you. I love your cock. Your hands. Fuck me, Caden. Make me yours."

She doesn't let up and her words drive me on. I increase my speed, fucking her relentlessly until I feel that magical moment where her inner walls twitch and clench rhythmically around my cock and she's coming. I'm coming too, with a shout, spilling everything I've got inside of her welcoming body as I strain against her.

Fuck. We've already done this three times. It's like I can't get enough.

Pulling out of her, I collapse on my side, careful not to crush her. I pull her into me, holding her close, my hand smoothing over her belly again and again, marveling that a tiny little life is growing inside of her. That we created that life.

Together.

"Caden?"

"Yeah?" I'm drawing little circles on her skin, my eyes drifting closed.

"How do you know Cash? Through your mom?" She pauses. "They make a cute couple. He seems to really care about her."

"You think so, huh?" I haven't been around them since they started seeing each other. It's so weird, like my two worlds colliding . . . again. But this time, in a good way. "They've only been seeing each other for a couple of months. He's kept an eye on her since they both live in Miami, and Cash has said more than once that he was interested in her. He finally made his move, I guess."

"Your mom is very sweet," she says softly. "You look like her."

"It's weird that you two met the way you did." I shake my head, marveling at the chance. "Small world, right?"

"Yes. I can't wait to meet her formally." She lifts her head to stare at me. "I want her to be a part of our baby's life. She's going to be a grandma, after all."

"She'll want to be a part of the baby's life. I know she will," I say. "She'll be excited. Probably turn into the overbearing, spoil-the-child-rotten grandma."

"That sounds nice." Rose snuggles closer. "How about Cash?"

Oh yeah. She asked how I know him. "He's part of my . . . old life. He's sort of a con man."

"Really?" She doesn't sound fazed in the least, thank God. "Hmm."

"You're not going to hold it against him, are you? He's the one who helped me find my job. He's wanted me to go straight for years, but I kept blowing him off. Until I met you. Then I knew . . ."

She lifts her head to look at me again. "You knew what?"

"That I would do anything to keep you safe and keep you with me. And in order to do that, I needed to find a legitimate job."

"So you gave it up for me." Her voice is so soft I almost can't hear her. "Though I hope you also did it for yourself."

"I did, baby. I did it for us." I press my hand against her belly as I press a kiss to her lips. "All three of us," I murmur against her lips.

She smiles and I feel her tears slide down her face. I lick one, the salty taste dissolving on my tongue. "Now you're killing me with all those romantic words, Caden."

"I mean every one of them. I love you." I kiss her again, this time deeper, with plenty of tongue. "I love you so much."

"I love you too." She tilts her head back, so I kiss her neck. "You're going to make an honest woman out of me, right?"

I chuckle against her throat, then nip her skin. "Absolutely. I want everyone to know you belong to me. Because you do, you know."

"I know." She breathes deep and holds me close as I rain kisses along the tops of her breasts. "I definitely know."

Epilogue

Rose

"PUSH, BABY."

I'm panting, trying to focus and breathe.

"Baby. Push."

He makes it sound so easy. Just push and *whoops,* out comes a baby. Well, it's not that easy. It's hard. Fucking hard.

Oh, dear. Did I just say that out loud?

Cracking open my eyes, I find three faces looming above me. My doctor's, the nurse's, and my husband's. They're all watching me expectantly, the nurse looking bored, the doctor efficient, and my husband . . .

Well, he looks anxious. Excited. And nervous.

"You ready, Ro?" Caden asks me carefully as he tugs on my leg, his hand beneath my knee so that I bend both of my legs, ready to push this stubborn baby out of my body once and for all. I've been in labor all day, but hard, getting-ready-to-push labor only in the last twenty minutes. My doctor says I'm doing well, that we're close, and I'm so ready to meet this child who's about to change my life.

"I'm ready," I say with a nod, my voice weak, my entire body tired. I can't wait for it to be over so I can get some rest. Though my mother-in-law warned me there will be no such thing as rest, as I'll be doing nothing but taking care of my baby around the clock these first few months.

Then she promptly promised to babysit anytime I need her to.

I adore Caden's mother and I love Cash, too, even though he's a little cheesy sometimes. He has a kind heart and he loves Caden's mom so much. He cares for Caden too; he's like a father figure to him.

My father has come around somewhat and is excited for the baby to come, though I don't think he's necessarily thrilled that I'm already married and having a child at such a young age. I'm the youngest and I even beat Violet to the altar. We didn't have a big wedding, though. Just a quick little jaunt to the courthouse with our family and a few friends accompanying us. We'll have a party later, a few months after the baby is born.

The contraction comes out of nowhere and with a groan I bend forward, pushing with all my might, the doctor encouraging me, Caden holding my hand. I can feel the baby; I'm not surprised when I hear the doctor tell me he can see the head, and I fall back against the pillows, my chest heaving, sweat dripping down my face as I try to catch my breath.

"One more push, maybe two, and you'll have a baby," the doctor says.

"So much pressure," I murmur, making Caden laugh.

"You're doing so good, Ro," he tells me as he places a damp washcloth on my forehead. The cool fabric feels good on my heated skin and I close my eyes, concentrating on evening my breaths when another contraction comes, this one even stronger.

I press forward, pushing hard, and then it feels as if the baby just spills right out of my body and into the doctor's hands. She begins to cry, the little gasping sound the most beautiful thing I've ever heard. "It's a girl," he says with a smile.

We already knew. We have a name picked out and everything. Caden kisses my lips, whispering that he loves me as the doctor asks him to cut the umbilical cord, and he does so, tears actually streaming down his face as he cradles his baby girl close, holding her in his arms.

"She looks just like you," he says as he brings her to me.

I carefully shove the hospital gown from my arms so my breasts are exposed and I take the baby from Caden, holding her close to my chest. The baby nuzzles her cheek against my flesh, her little lips working, and I turn her to face me just as her eyes peer open.

They're dark, the color indiscernible, and we stare at each other for long, quiet moments as the world continues rushing around us. I touch her cheek, her lips, the tip of her nose. She's beautiful. Perfect. Her hair is dark, her cheeks round, and my heart fills to overflowing with love.

"Welcome to the world," I whisper as I press a kiss to her rosebud lips, Caden's hand coming down to gently caress her head. "Daisy."

Acknowledgments

A big thank-you to my family for coming with me to England and Scotland last summer. For indulging me in my lifelong dream to see London—I'm so grateful I was able to go, because it inspired the plot of Rose's and Caden's story.

I want to thank my editor, Shauna Summers, and her assistant, Sarah Murphy, for their guidance with this book. Extra thanks, Shauna, for reading it while you were on sabbatical! I really appreciate all that you do.

Thank you to everyone at Bantam/Random House, including Gina Watchel, Sue Grimshaw, and Jin Yu. I must say thanks to my agent, Kimberly Whalen, for smoothing my ruffled feathers. And Katy Evans—I need our daily conversations and the way you virtually hold my hand through the good times and the bad. Oh, and Kati Rodriguez! You keep me straight, woman! I couldn't function without you.

Finally, thank you to all the readers, bloggers, reviewers, etc. out there. I couldn't do this job without you and I appreciate your support. You're all awesome.

Playlist Note

What an eclectic mix! My musical taste is all over the place. Notice there's quite a bit of 80s music on this playlist and I blame my love for London (where much of this book is set) in the 80s, when I was a teen and madly in love with everything English (including Duran Duran).

Everybody Here Wants You by Jeff Buckley
To Look At You by INXS
Tessellate by Ellie Goulding
Burning Desire by Lana Del Rey
Pressed Against the Sky by Toadies
So In Love by OMD
The Only Star in Heaven by Frankie Goes to Hollywood
Straight Lines by Silverchair
Eyes Without a Face by Billy Idol
I'm Not in Love by 10cc
The Power of Love by Frankie Goes to Hollywood
Keep Me In the Dark by Arcadia
Cool Kids by Echosmith

Don't miss the anticipated finale in
New York Times bestselling author
Monica Murphy's sexy contemporary
Fowler Sisters series

TAMING LILY

Coming soon from Bantam Books

Read on for a special sneak peek

Chapter One

Max

I HATE BABYSITTING JOBS. I RARELY TAKE THEM ON BECAUSE they suck but the money was too good to resist. Not that I let money lead my dick around when it comes to work. I have integrity. An image to fulfill and maintain, especially when it comes to my business. If I took every fucking job that came my way because of how much they offer to pay I'd be a very rich man working the absolute bottom of the barrel shit jobs. Busting cheating spouses. Catching them in compromising positions. Hell, those jobs are a dime a dozen.

No thanks. I'm lucky enough that I can pick and choose. Though I felt like with this one, I didn't necessarily pick it. The job chose me.

It also intrigued me. *She* intrigued me. Not that I'd ever confess that to a living soul. Again, I'm not one to let my dick make business decisions for me but this girl . . . is unlike any girl I've ever seen before.

The moment I looked at her photo, I knew.

I watch her now, from my aisle seat on the plane, sitting five rows behind her. She's in the opposite aisle seat, I can get a good look at her profile if I lean forward slightly, which is exactly what I'm doing. It's wild, how she appears completely different from the photos I saw of her on the web last night while I did my research.

Whereas the endless images in my Google search featured a sexy as hell, scantily dressed woman doing whatever the fuck she wants all over Manhattan, this woman I'm watching now is quiet. Subdued. Wearing one of those matching sweat outfits in black with white trim, the word PINK scrawled across her very fine ass in glittery sequins. She blends right in on the plane, looks like every other woman her age. Not like the rich as fuck heiress she really is.

When she first boarded the plane her hood was up and she had sunglasses on, as if she were trying to conceal her identity, though really she looked obvious as hell. But considering she's dressed nothing like her usual self, I figure she became comfortable and eventually tugged the hood down, revealing her long, golden hair streaked with bright blond highlights pulled into a high ponytail.

And offering me a view of her perfect profile.

Dainty nose, plump lips. Long eyelashes, high cheekbones, slightly pointed chin. Every time someone passes her by she lifts her head, then immediately looks down. Almost as if she's afraid someone is going to approach her.

Like she's worried someone will realize who she is.

But no one would. She's unrecognizable. I'd bet top dollar the only one on this plane who knows she's Lily Fowler is . . .

Me.

The moment the plane touches down I whip out my phone and switch it out of airplane mode, watching as a text message appears.

Did you find her?

I answer my client with a quick yes.

Are you watching her now?

I answer again in the affirmative, my gaze fixed on Lily as

she too grabs her phone out of her purse and starts to scroll through it.

Try and grab her laptop now.

Frowning at my phone, I contemplate how to reply. I can't just make a grab while we're still on the freaking plane and run. I have to be subtle about this. I warned my client. I don't make rash decisions. I'm not impulsive, at least when it comes to work. There's a method to my madness and acting like a goddamn thief isn't one of them.

I finally decide to answer.

I already warned you I'm not going to move that fast.

We don't have much time.

Slowly I shake my head, glancing up to study Lily before I start typing.

We have enough. I'll get the job done. Don't worry.

The plane starts to slow as we make our way to the gate and the passengers are getting restless, including myself. My legs are cramped up. Sitting in coach sucks ass and is almost too much for my six-foot-two frame. My knees fucking ache. Even Lily shifts and moves in her seat, her head turning to glance behind her, straight at me. Our gazes meet briefly and she looks away, pretending like she never saw me.

Anger burns in my gut. Anger and lust. An interesting combo, one I've never suffered through before while working. I pride myself on keeping my distance. Work is work. My personal life is just that . . . personal. Not that I have much of one. Not that I have anyone in my fucking life, which is just the way I like it.

But this girl's rejection, as brief as it was, digs at me. Pisses me off.

My phone dings and I check it.

She's fast. Tricky. You need to take your chances when you can.

A snort escapes me. Trying to tell me how to do my job. I

wish I could reply with a big fuck you but I don't. I have more class than that.

I'm faster. Trickier. Trust me. I'll get the job done.

Slipping my phone into the back pocket of my jeans, the flight attendant starts talking over the intercom, telling us to remain seated until the seatbelt fastened lights turn off. We're at the gate, everyone is poised and ready to grab their shit and stand to disembark. I don't bother. I have a carry-on. That's all I brought with me and it's sitting in the compartment directly above me. I can tell the lady next to me is dying to leap out of her seat but I'll make her wait. Her irritation is already a palpable thing but I could give a damn.

I gotta move slow. The last thing I need is to catch my subject's attention. Not this early in the game.

Lily jumps to her feet the second the seatbelt light shuts off, popping open the overhead compartment and pulling out a bag. A laptop bag from the size of it.

With the coveted laptop most likely lying inside.

I curl my fingers into my palms, resting them on my knees. I want that bag. No. Scratch that. My client wants that bag— more like what's inside of it. So I want it too.

And I will do anything to get it.

Anything.

Chapter Two

Lily

I FELT HIM BEFORE I SAW HIM. HIS GAZE ON ME. ASSESSING. Watching. I let him get his fill, keeping my head bent, my eyes firmly locked on the magazine lying open on my propped thighs. It's ruining my chance to get an even tan so I'll need to ditch the magazine soon but for now, it's the perfect ruse.

Pretending to read while I look to my left to catch him staring. He doesn't realize I know yet. And he's good. No one would be wiser to his covert spying.

But I am. I've been spied upon my entire life. The media has trailed after my sisters and me, my father, my grandmother, since I can remember. We're public figures, given accolades when we do something good and torn to shreds when we do something awful.

Well. Most everyone in my family does good. I'm the something awful one. I do stupid things on a regular basis. I should know better by now but then again, why give up my reputation? Besides, it's the perfect front.

After all these years of being such a publicly mocked figure, I know when someone's got their eyes on me. It's like a sixth sense or something. And when I know they're watching, sometimes I put on a show. On rare occasions, I confront them and send 'em running—or snapping away with their cameras so they can capture me enraged with headlines like, "Lily Fowler's Lost It Again!"

Bastards.

Most of the time, I pretend I don't know they exist. Like I'm blissfully aware some shitty photographer is ready to snap a picture of me sunbathing topless (yep, that's happened more than once) or about to kiss and grope a guy at a nightclub (that's happened too).

This guy though . . . he's not giving me the paparazzi vibe. He's probably older than me, but not beyond thirty. His hair is dark. Cropped fairly close on the sides though a little longish on top. His jaw is firm, his expression like stone and his lips . . . they look like they might be soft but he's too far away to get a good look. Sunglasses hide his eyes but I don't need to see them.

I can still feel them on me.

He's wearing tropical print swim trunks and nothing else, sitting on a towel from the hotel on the scorching hot sand, his knees bent, his looped arms resting on them, acting like he doesn't have a care in the world. His shoulders are broad, his body trim and fit. Kids go running by him, kicking up sand as they pass and he makes a tiny grimace every time, but otherwise, no reaction. He's alone. There's no other towel beside the one he's sitting on. No woman asking him to put more sunscreen on her shoulders, no friends hanging out with him.

Weird.

Could he be a photographer? Part of the paparazzi? I recognize a lot of them by now so I doubt it. Unless he was sent as a ruse to trick me but damn it, I'm pretty untrickable by now. Besides, I look nothing like my usual self so I doubt I'm being followed. The Lily Fowler party girl persona is back in New York where I left her a few days ago. I, of course, had to book my flight under my real name but the airlines don't release that information to freaking reporters so ha-ha on them.

The minute I stepped off the plane yesterday and felt the

warm air caress my skin, I took a deep, cleansing breath and felt like I shed my armor. Here on Maui, I am nothing but a simple girl on vacation. No makeup, no flashy jewelry, no expensive clothing, no guys trying to get in my panties, no girls trying to be my friend in the hopes I'll make them popular. I left the trappings behind, like a snake shedding its skin.

Reborn. Fresh and unsoiled.

My thoughts almost make me laugh. In fact, a giggle escapes me and I press my fingers to my lips, suppressing it. Unsoiled, that's a joke. I gave up the goods long, long ago in the hopes that I'd find someone to love me. My beautiful mother loved me with all her heart, or so she claimed.

But not enough to keep herself alive. She'd rather be dead than raise her children. And that hurt. Daddy didn't love me anymore. I became a burden. All three of his daughters did. We were just reminders that he had a wife and she left him in the cruelest way possible.

Instead of seeking love and approval from my family, I sought it in other ways. Boys. Partying. Alcohol. Drugs. By the time I got my shit together and was ready to do right by the world? No one cared. They still saw me as Lily the party girl. So I decided to give them what they wanted and kept it up. Why disappoint them?

Glancing out of the corner of my eye, I see he's still watching me, though he averts his head quickly when I look his way. Hmm. Interesting. Could he be just a regular guy on vacation who thinks I'm pretty? He's alone, I'm alone, it would make sense that maybe we could get together?

Huh. No, that's just too weird. Who goes on vacation by themselves to pick up on someone? That seems like a lot of extra effort. And I'm not here on vacation. I'm on the run. In hiding. Just for a little bit. I pissed off the wrong people. Again. So rather than face them head-on, I got the hell out of Manhattan stat.

Grabbing my cell, I go online and check that stupid fashion and beauty blog that seems so fascinated with my life as well as my sisters'. I want to make sure they're not talking about me. The last mention of Lily Fowler was two days ago, a photo of me with hot pink lips, heavily mascaraed eyes and a black lace dress, supposedly representing Fleur at a stupid party for . . . something. I'd forgotten exactly what. When I'd entered my apartment late that night and found it ransacked, I freaked. Nothing was stolen. No jewelry, no money and I had both on hand, stashed away in my closet but not under lock and key.

The one thing I had hidden, though, was my laptop and I breathed a sigh of relief when I found it. Then I threw a bunch of clothes into a small suitcase, booked a flight from my phone on the cab drive to the airport and got the hell out of there.

My phone vibrates in my hands, startling me and I check my texts, see that it's a message from my little sister, Rose.

Call me right now!

Yikes. Can't do that. I trust no one at this moment. Not even Rose and I adore her but what if she can't keep her mouth shut? She could slip up and tell our father she spoke to me. The wrong person finds out where I am and it's toast time.

I can't take any chances.

So I ignore her text, shoving my phone into my beach bag before I sink back into the overstuffed lounger I'm sitting on. I rented a cabana first thing this morning and it's freaking perfect. I get endless service, someone always checking on me to make sure I have enough to drink or eat and the view is spectacular. The sun is blazing, there are white puffy clouds in the startling blue sky and a breeze brushes over me every few minutes, cooling my heated skin.

Paradise.

My gaze slides toward my watcher, who's also a part of the spectacular view. The more I stare, the sexier I find him. His shoulders and chest are so wide. There's the lightest smattering of dark hair between his pecs and while I usually go for the smooth look, there's something about the hair on his chest that appeals. Makes him look so manly. A little dangerous.

I avert my head, my thoughts filled with . . . him. I'm not usually attracted to dangerous. I like easy. Fun. Attractive and confident, even a hint of arrogance. The men I've been with are similar to me. Or the me I want everyone to see. Looking for a good time, always ready to party, to shop, wanting everyone's eyes on me.

My phone buzzes again and I check my messages, see that it's another text from Rose.

You can't avoid me forever! At least tell me where you are.

I study her message, my fingers poised above the keyboard. I want to tell her but I can't. No way. She's bound and determined to get me to respond to her and I'm just as bound and determined to ignore her.

It's not that I want to. My heart, my entire body aches to call her, hear her voice, ask if she's okay. She's pregnant. My baby sister, the one who I resented when she was born because she took up even more of our mom's attention, is now going to have a baby herself. With a guy I went to high school with. A guy I might've kissed—and doesn't that make me feel like a complete slut—but if it doesn't bother Rose then it doesn't bother me. She's so blissfully in love with Caden, it's almost disgusting.

Just about as disgusting as my sister Violet and her fiancé, Ryder are together. Those two are just . . . ugh. I blame it all on him. Ryder exudes confidence. Sex appeal. I can see why my sister was so attracted to him. It surprises me that the two of them *are* together. He seems more my speed but then she spilled a couple of secrets one night after having a few too many glasses of wine. How dominant Ryder is in the bedroom.

Yeah. That sort of thing doesn't do it for me. I like to be in charge. Everything else in my life has felt so out of control, ever since I was a little kid and I lost my mom. As I grew older, I realized the only thing I can control is myself. My body. My mind. My choices.

So I'm in control, especially sexually. Forget all that growly *I will make you mine* dom shit. That sort of thing makes me roll my eyes. I mean really, who gets off on that? Maybe I haven't met the right guy but come on.

Grabbing my boozy tropical drink, I wrap my lips around the straw and drain it, casting my gaze along the beach, watching the waves splash gently onto the shore. I want to swim. I want to feel the water swirl around my legs as I slowly walk into the ocean. I can leave my stuff here. I know it's safe. The hotel employees keep a close eye on everything but what if my watcher is fast? What if he really is part of the paparazzi and he's just waiting for the chance to go rifling through my bag? Not that there's much in there beyond my phone . . .

And my phone is everything to me. It's password protected but if someone is determined, they could probably figure it out. I can't risk it. At least my laptop is safe, stashed in my hotel suite in the deep, dark recesses of my closet, sitting on the top shelf. No one would find it there.

I set my drink on the table next to me and rest my index finger against my lips, tapping them as I contemplate my next move. I don't feel my watcher's eyes on me and when I glance in his direction, I see that he's gone. Even his towel isn't there any longer which means he's moved on.

Good. That's for the best. I don't need to worry about some weird guy staring at me. I have more important things to concentrate on.

Stretching my legs out, I swing them to the side of the chair and stand, resting my hands on my hips as I first look left, then right. No watcher to be seen. Where could he have gone in that quick amount of time? I didn't even hear him leave so what is he? Stealth?

I'm probably worrying for nothing. He's just some player who liked the way I looked or whatever. I'm too paranoid after what happened. Hacking into someone else's life and messing with their personal shit has a way of making me feel uneasy, yet that doesn't seem to stop me. I'm doing something I shouldn't so I tend to think everyone else is up to no good as well.

Shaking my head, I start for the water, the sand warm on the soles of my feet. A group of kids are to my right, splashing and playing along the shoreline, their hands full of colorful plastic buckets and shovels. A couple is standing waist deep in the water, the waves crashing against them, pushing them into each other's arms and they laugh.

My heart pangs but I ignore it. I don't believe in love or couples or dating or any of that crap. Love is for fools. Despite my sisters' blissed out lives, and their steadfast belief I can find the same, I know that's not for me.

No way would I allow anyone to get too close. Hand them the power to hurt me. And I refuse to give that up.

I walk straight into the cold water, shivering as it hits my ankles. My calves. My knees. Despite the heat of the sun and the hot sand, the water is freezing but I don't care. I'm belly button deep now and I bend my knees, dunking myself to my shoulders and giving a little yelp when the cool water wraps itself around me.

The rhythmic waves push me out a little farther and I fall backward into the water until I'm floating, the sun warming my face, the water swirling around my head. I can taste the salty tang of the ocean and I close my eyes, spread my arms out and splash my fingers in the water. It feels good. Peaceful.

Until a massive wave comes out of nowhere, sending me straight under water and slams me into the bottom. I reach out to try and brace my fall, my hands scraping along the rocky shore and feel a particularly sharp rock slice across my palm.

The pain is excruciating and I kick away from the ground, trying to push myself above water but another wave slams into me, sending me rolling.

Water shoots up my nose, into my mouth and I close my eyes, struggling against the waves. I want to call out. I want to throw my hands above the water and signal to someone, any-one, that I'm probably fucking drowning here but it's no use.

I can't do it.

Another wave hits me, though this one isn't as powerful, and it sucks me farther out to sea, making me roll and tumble like I'm a ball in the wind. I kick hard, my foot hitting the bottom of the ocean and it gives me the leverage I need, propelling me for-ward. I open my eyes, I can see the water above me, the light shining down upon it from the sun and I kick even harder, deter-mination pushing me on.

Strong arms wrap around my middle, dragging me above water and when my head pops out I take a deep breath, only to immediately start coughing. The arms are like steel bands around my stomach, firm but not too tight, as if he's aware if he squeezes me too much I'll start coughing even more. I can feel his warm, hard chest against my back as he drags me back to shore, and I drop my arm against his, clutching onto him, afraid he's going to let me go.

"You all right?" His voice rasps against my ear, deep and rumbly and with a hint of a southern accent. Despite my fear, the exhaustion, the complete pain I feel radiating from the palm of my hand, my entire body tingles at the sound of his voice.

I nod, my teeth chattering, the adrenaline and terror over what I've just experienced combining to send me possibly into shock, I'm sure. My rescuer readjusts his arm around my waist, his hand splayed across my bare stomach and I glance down to study his thick, muscular forearm. His skin is golden, covered with a smattering of dark hair and his hand . . . his hand is huge. It practically covers my entire belly and I'm no skinny little twig.

His fingers seem to caress my skin and the air whooshes out of my lungs, making me dizzy. I let go of his arm, holding my hand out, palm up and that's when I see it. The jagged cut across my palm, the blood flowing freely from it.

Oh crap. That's bad.

"You're hurt." He notices the cut too and that seems to spur him into action. He moves faster and I go limp, overwhelmed at the sight of the cut, the blood, the pain that radiates from my palm all the way up my arm. "We need to find you help."

"I-I thought you were my help." My voice comes out a breathless rasp and I swallow hard, wincing at the pain that follows. I took in too much salt water and my throat aches, my nose burns.

"Medical help," he says gruffly as we emerge from the water.

I turn my head to the side, trying to catch a glimpse of my rescuer but he's so tall and my neck hurts. He glances down, his eyes going wide when he sees that I'm looking at him. Shock courses through me and I part my lips, the words that follow scratchy, making my throat ache.

"It's you." Him. My watcher has turned into my rescuer.

"Hey!" I look away from him to see a hotel employee running toward us, his expression one of pure panic and my last thought before my body goes weak and my head blanks is that he doesn't look like much help at all.

PHOTO: COLBY RAIMER

New York Times and *USA Today* bestselling author
MONICA MURPHY is a native Californian who lives in
the foothills of Yosemite. A wife and mother of three,
she writes new adult contemporary romance and is the
author of the One Week Girlfriend series and the tie-in
novella, *Drew + Fable Forever,* as well as the Fowler
Sisters series.

monicamurphyauthor.com
missmonicamurphy@gmail.com
Facebook.com/MonicaMurphyauthor
@MsMonicaMurphy
Instagram.com/monicamurphyauthor

About the Type

This book was set in Sabon, a typeface designed by the well-known German typographer Jan Tschichold (1902–74). Sabon's design is based upon the original letter forms of sixteenth-century French type designer Claude Garamond and was created specifically to be used for three sources: foundry type for hand composition, Linotype, and Monotype. Tschichold named his typeface for the famous Frankfurt typefounder Jacques Sabon (c. 1520–80).